YON ILL WIND

TOR BOOKS BY PIERS ANTHONY

Alien Plot
Anthonology
But What of Earth?
Demons Don't Dream
Geis of the Gargoyle
Ghost
Harpy Thyme
Hasan
Isle of Woman
Letters to Jenny
Prostho Plus
Race Against Time
Roc and a Hard Place
Shade of the Tree
Shame of Man
Steppe
Triple Detente
Yon Ill Wind

WITH ROBERT E. MARGROFF:

Dragon's Gold
Serpent's Silver
Chimaera's Copper
Mouvar's Magic
Orc's Opal
The E.S.P. Worm
The Ring

WITH FRANCES HALL:

Pretender

WITH RICHARD GILLIAM:

Tales from the Great Turtle (Anthology)

PIERS ANTHONY

YON
ILL
WIND

A TOM DOHERTY ASSOCIATES BOOK

NEW YORK

This is a work of fiction. All the characters and events portrayed in this novel are either fictitious or are used fictitiously.

YON ILL WIND

This book is printed on acid-free paper.

A Tor Book
Published by Tom Doherty Associates, Inc.
175 Fifth Avenue
New York, N.Y. 10010

Tor Books on the World-Wide Web:
http://www.tor.com

Tor® is a registered trademark of Tom Doherty Associates, Inc.

Library of Congress Cataloging-in-Publication Data

Anthony, Piers.
     Yon ill wind / by Piers Anthony. —1st ed.
         p.   cm.
     "A Tom Doherty Associates book."
     ISBN 0-312-86227-X (acid-free paper)
     1. Xanth (Imaginary place)—Fiction.   I. Title.
PS3551.N73Y66   1996   96-16216
813'.54—dc20   CIP

First edition: October 1996

Printed in the United States of America

0   9   8   7   6   5   4   3   2   1

Contents

$\overline{1}$
Nimby

The Demons of the system did not gather frequently unless there were intriguing contests to be made or issues to be settled. This occasion was a bit of both.

"You must have cheated!" the Demoness V(E\N)^{us} declared. Of course the Demons did not actually communicate in words or have any emphasis, but for the sake of intelligibility their interactions could be represented as such in degraded prose. "You have been winning every contest recently."

"I simply learned how to play to win," the Demon X(A/N)th responded mildly. "My victories have been fair."

"I wonder," the Demon E(A/R)th remarked. "There is something suspicious about the way that foolish mortal boy gave up his game victory at the last moment, so that you won our wager."

"And the way that crazy lesser demoness decided the obviously innocent bird was guilty, so that you won *our* wager," V(E\N)^{us} agreed.

"I merely have compatible lesser creatures in my domain, because I allow them to pursue their own mischief without interference," X(A/N)th protested. He glanced obliquely at E(A/R)th. "In contrast to some."

"If I did that, my idiot creatures would destroy my domain," E(A/R)th retorted.

"Aren't they doing that anyway?" V(E\N)^{us} inquired snidely.

"Hardly the way your lesser creatures affected your domain," E(A/R)th shot back. "Now it's all cloud and desert, instead of milk and honey."

"We all have made our little mistakes," the Demon JU(P/I)^{ter} said soothingly. "Which is why we have failed to gain significant lasting status. But it does seem that X(A/N)th has been unusually fortunate recently."

"Yes it does," V(E\N)^{us} said emphatically.

"Agreed," E(A/R)th agreed. There was a murmur of acquiescence from the other Demons present.

"It is merely my good lesser creatures," X(A/N)th insisted. "I treat them well, and they reward me by behaving well. My fortune is in the quality of my creatures."

The other Demons exchanged a hundred and fifteen glances in half a fraction of a moment. "Suppose we put that to the test?" JU(P/I)^{ter} suggested.

X(A/N)th grew more interested. "Are you challenging me to a contest?"

"Yes, I believe I am. Suggest terms."

"If I win, I will assume your status as dominant entity in this system."

"Agreed. And if you lose, you will revert to the status of least entity in this system, and yield your land to me."

That was a formidable stricture, for it had taken X(A/N)th three thousand years to work his way up to second place, and might take longer to do it again. Still, this might be his only chance to depose JU(P/I)^{ter}, because ordinarily the Dominant Demon would never put his status on the line. "Agreed. Conditions?"

JU(P/I)^{ter} smiled. This was akin to a short-tailed comet fragmenting and plastering itself across his face in a series of violent collisions. "You must subject yourself directly to the whims of these inferior creatures you claim have such good behavior. You must assume the form of a mortal entity and go among them for the duration of the contest."

Now, this was different! "But normally we don't influence the inferiors in any way, so that the outcome is completely random, or at least not affected by the touch of a Demon." He glanced darkly at $V(E\backslash N)^{us}$, whom he suspected of violating that stricture the last time.

—$SA(T/U)^{rn}$—nodded, and his rings precessed. "This time you will have license to influence them—to the extent you are able."

$X(A/N)^{th}$ realized that he had been set up. The other Demons were conspiring to bring him down, because they were miffed by his string of victories. Still, he *did* have good lesser creatures, and perhaps they would bring him the biggest victory of all. Certainly the challenge was exciting. He had on occasion interacted with them, when they had intruded on his awareness, but never done so for a prolonged period. "So I can interact. What's the catch?"

"Your awareness can not be limited," $JU(P/I)^{ter}$ said, "for you are in essence a Demon, regardless of the form you assume. But for the purpose of the contest, your expression can be limited. You may not tell any creature of your realm your true nature, and if any learn of it, you forfeit immediately."

"Provided no other supernatural entity informs them," $X(A/N)^{th}$ said, with another glance at the Demoness.

"Agreed," $JU(P/I)^{ter}$ said. "We shall enforce that stricture. Anything else you may convey to one person, in one moment. But—" He paused meaningfully. "There will be a penalty when you do: thereafter you will lose the power of verbal communication, for the duration of the contest."

But one moment of full communication should be enough, $X(A/N)^{th}$ reflected, his albedo increasing. So there was probably another catch. "What else?"

"You will have your full powers, apart from speech, limited to yourself and one inferior creature of your choosing, to the extent that creature requests them."

"But if I am not allowed to describe my real nature, in my moment of communication—"

"Invent something," $JU(P/I)^{ter}$ suggested. "Anything but the truth. But if you come close enough to the truth so that the creature, or any other denizen of your domain, catches on, you lose."

That, too, was reasonable; he could approach the truth, but if he came too close, so that the inferior creature realized that he was in fact the Demon $X(A/N)^{th}$, he would forfeit. But the contest was still incomplete. "What is the penalty for becoming what that creature chooses?"

"The power of motion," JU(P/I)^{ter} said. "After that state ends, when the inferior creature terminates the association and separates from you for more than a moment and more than a unit of distance, you will not only be mute but completely immobile. You will lose your powers of magical action, too, other than awareness. So you had better achieve your objective before such separation occurs."

"Decision, time, geography," V(E\N)^{us} said. "That is fair, isn't it? Triple termination. No accidents." Fair, to her, meant she felt assured of his loss, which she desired more than a victory of her own.

This was getting tough, all right. He could speak only once, and then could act only as long as he kept company with the creature. Inferior creatures were notoriously fickle; at any time, for little or no reason, the one selected could decide it no longer desired his association, and tell him so, and depart. By the terms of this contest, he would not be able to demur.

But it wasn't yet done. This conspiracy of Demons meant to see that he had virtually no chance at all. He needed to know the worst of it. "What is the actual item of decision?"

"You must be the recipient of at least one tear of love or grief, from a creature who has no notion of its significance."

"The creature with whom you associate," V(E\N)^{us} amended. "No other."

And there it was. He had to evoke the severe sympathy of an inferior and ignorant creature. "And how long will I have to evoke this tear?"

"As long as your mortal body remains. If you become mute and immobile without achieving it, your body will behave in the manner of mortal entities: it will slowly starve to death. When it dies, the contest will be over, and you will have lost."

X(A/N)th considered. They expected him to balk, and to have to pay a forfeit for that. "Agreed. Let me select my mortal form for the occasion." He was thinking of becoming a beautiful woman, because mortals shed tears very readily over them. Or perhaps a winsome child: better yet.

"No. That's the last detail: I will select your mortal form."

"But you could choose something difficult!"

"Exactly. It will be a real contest. Win it, and I will concede that your creatures do have good behavior."

"You will concede more than that," X(A/N)th replied grimly. "I accept your deal, and the other Demons will watch to see that every aspect of it is honored."

The other Demons nodded. This promised to be interesting.

"Then assume your mortal coil," Demon JU(P/I)^{ter} said grandly. "A dragon ass, with the voice of an aqua duck. Your role name is Nimby."

And before X(A/N)th could protest, he was in the Region of Madness, in the form of a creature whose body was that of a dragon with diagonal stripes of pastel pink and bilious green, with the head of a Mundane donkey.

"Ouch," he muttered subvocally, but even then it was the voice of an aqua duck, a sound like a cross between a goblin holding his nose and the burble of noxious gas percolating through sewer water.

There was a stir on the surface of the cesspool that just happened to be near. An aqua duck poked its head out of the pool, evidently thinking to discover another of its kind. Finding no such thing, it ducked below again, for such ducks lived underwater, and had to hold their breaths to forage for bugs on the surface.

And his name was now Nimby, which was an apt description, a digest of Not In My Back Yard: exactly where such a creature would be welcome. Nowhere.

He was in trouble. How would he convince anyone even to approach him, let alone shed a tear for him?

Well, he could look. He extended his awareness, covering all of the Land of Xanth. He knew what every creature was doing, and where every plant was. Xanth was teeming with activity. Somewhere there should be someone who wouldn't be afraid of a dragon ass, who would listen to what he had to say, and who would shed a tear for him. Maybe not immediately, but in time, after getting to know him. Because despite his ludicrous limitations, he retained considerable power to please. If the one he approached had the wit to ask for it. If that one would take him seriously.

But instead of finding a suitable person, he found another problem.

There had been a magic flux, the moment he changed form, resulting in a temporary weakness of the Interface. The spell required to fix him in this situation had done it, for even the most trifling Demon magic was stronger than that of all the lesser creatures combined. For the next few hours, it would be possible for things to pass through, entering Xanth without being twisted to some other time. That could mean significant mischief. Ordinarily he would automatically shore up the Interface to prevent such a nuisance, but as Nimby he couldn't. It was his policy to ignore the activities of his associated region, but the Interface the local creatures had established was useful, and helped keep things quiet, so he quietly supported it. He just had to hope that nothing really obnoxious passed from Mundania into Xanth, before the Interface healed itself.

It would be nice if the person he approached was extremely co-operative, and shed a tear for him immediately, giving him the victory and freeing him. But since he couldn't even say that he needed a tear, that being too close to the truth, that seemed unlikely. However, if the person asked him for information, he could provide it, and if the person asked him to do something about the rift in the Interface, then he could. Provided he did it in such a way as to conceal his real nature. So there was a chance to fix the problem, during the course of the contest. If he found the right person.

He concentrated on that, sifting through all the creatures of the land. The great majority were plainly unsuitable. Most were hope-lessly locked into their situations, and wouldn't have anything to do with a weird monster. In fact, they would either flee it or attack it, depending on the state of their courage. He needed someone reason-ably open-minded. That cut the prospects down to few.

He headed for the nearest. This was a pretty young human woman named Miss Fortune. She was smart, decent, amiable, lovely, and caring, and did not judge others too much by appearances. She would make some young man a fine wife, but for one thing. Her talent was bad luck, and it always interfered when a really good prospect ap-proached her. Thus she was perhaps ideal for Nimby, who could, if she asked him, reverse her luck. He would catch her alone, present himself, and use his one moment of speech to acquaint her with the usefulness of Nimby. Thereafter he would be silent, per the stricture of the contest, but it should be enough. She would get to know him, realize that he was not merely a monster, ask him to reverse her luck, and when he did so, she should really appreciate him. Of course, that would not make her cry him a tear, but perhaps that would come later, if she came to care for him enough. She often did cry for her pets, and for family members when they suffered mischief—which was rather often, because of her talent. So this looked reasonably good.

Nimby trotted along toward the rendezvous. His dragon body was actually quite strong, and could move well. His hide was tough enough to ignore nettles and branches. His eyes were good enough to spy out suitable paths. His nose was good enough to sniff out all manner of creatures great and small. In fact, Nimby felt his first pang of hunger. He was mortal now, so had to eat. Hunger was a new experience. So he sniffed out a fruiting pie plant and snapped up a fresh cherry pie. He gulped it down and slurped his tongue around his donkey lips. Eating was fun!

He extended his awareness again. Fortune was starting out to gather a sprig of thyme, because her mother was getting rushed and needed a bit more. "There's no thyme like the present," she said. "Go fetch it now." So Fortune, sweet as she was, set out instantly to fetch it.

Nimby explored the immediate region with his awareness. There were, it turned out, several paths to the thyme plant, because many families made occasional use of it. In fact, they found thyme to be quite precious. It would not be long before Fortune arrived there.

He considered what he would say to her when they met. Because he would appear to her as a frightening monster, he had better speak to her first, reassuring her. Then, when she was prepared, he would show her his dragon ass form. Even so, his words would have to be effective, because he would have only a moment of speech. Moments varied in length; some were long, some short. In this case it would be the time until she made a verbal response of some kind to his speech. So he would have to forestall her cry or exclamation, lest his moment end before he conveyed to her his potential usefulness to her. Such as being able to reverse her talent for a time. He could tell her that he had reverse wood, and knew how to use it to help her. No, she would just ask for the wood. So he would instead tell her that his talent could make her what she wanted to be, as long as they were together. So she would need to keep his company for a while. Because not only would he be silent after his moment of speech, he would be immobile once they formally separated. Thus his single opening monologue would be of overwhelming importance, and he had to do it just right. He could in effect win on lose his contest in that moment.

He reached the thyme plant. It was a small one, so its effects were limited. Someone had drawn a circle in the dirt around it, showing the safe limit of approach. Folk who wanted a leaf of thyme had to use a wooden hook to get it, because the inanimate was not as greatly affected. That was what Fortune was coming here to do. Then she would maneuver the leaf into a magic pouch that stifled its ambiance, and take the pouch home to her mother. Her mother, of course, would know how to handle it safely; mothers were always in need of more thyme.

Nimby ducked down behind a pile of rocks near the plant. This form was good at ducking, because of the aqua duck component. He wouldn't be able to see the girl very well from here, but neither would she be able to see him, which was what counted. Of course, he could use his awareness to see her without eyes, but it was easier just to listen for her approach while he rehearsed his moment of speech. He wanted the fewest feasible diversions for this practice.

How could he get her to listen without speaking? Maybe if he made a straight quacking noise, she would think he was a duck, and would pause, unworried. All he needed was to get the first few words in, warning her just to listen, and then he could run off the whole spiel. Fortune, with her constant bad luck, had surely learned to react cautiously, so well might listen in silence, for a time, anyway.

His donkey ears twitched. She was here! She had approached with her soft step while he pondered. She was standing at the edge of the thyme plant's limit; his awareness saw her human feminine form. He had almost missed her. He had not an instant to waste.

"Quack! Quack!" he said in his ducky voice. "Please listen to me without speaking, for I have information of interest to you. I know of your problem with your talent, and I can help you reverse it, for my own talent is to make a person whatever she wants to be, as long as she is in my company." So far so good; she had not made a sound.

But he had to get in the rest before his moment ended. "I am a friend, but I am not human. I have an ugly form, but I have no wish at all to harm you. I need the company of a person like you, and I will do my best to make my company worthwhile. To justify your trust. But after this, I will not be able to speak again; I will be completely mute. So you will have to tell me what you desire. Stay with me, and you can be what you wish to be, as long as we are together. I wish only to win your friendship. Please do not be dismayed by my appearance, which is awful. I am completely harmless to you, for I will suffer without your company." Had he covered enough? He couldn't tell her more about himself; he had come as close to the truth as he dared. But maybe he could offer an explanation for his form, so she wouldn't scream and run away when she saw him. "I am an enchanted creature, not entirely what I seem. My fate depends on you. Now, if you care to look at me, look at the pile of rocks to your right. I will lift my head and nod, and thereafter be silent. But you can talk to me, and I will understand, and do what I can for you. Please trust me. My name is Nimby."

He had said enough. Now it was make-or-break time. Slowly he raised his head and peered over the rocks. There she was, and—

It was the wrong girl.

"Oh—a funny donkey!" the girl exclaimed.

And now Nimby was mute, per the contest rule. He had had a good long moment, longer than expected, and had spoken well. But how had he come to this mistaken connection? He extended his awareness out and back, tracing the girl's travel here, and in a moment he had it: Miss Fortune's bad luck had struck again. There was a crossing of two paths, just beyond a wide wallflower, and she had collided with another girl. The two had had their breaths knocked out, and had sat down on opposite sides, gasping. Then they had gotten up, brushed themselves off, made quick curt apologies to each other though each was sure the other had been at fault, and gone on their ways—down the wrong paths. Fortune had gone on the other girl's errand, which was to fetch a nice bow from a bow-vine so her mother wouldn't give her a punish-mint. And the other girl had gone on Fortune's errand, and had been just realizing her error when Nimby had spoken to her.

She was Chlorine, whose talent was poisoning water. She was plain, stupid, and mean-spirited, in complete contrast to Fortune. The collision had been her fault, because she had been rushing along without looking, too fast for path conditions. Thus she had given Fortune the colossal ill luck to lose her encounter with Nimby, who could have helped her so much, and had given Nimby the worse luck to have wasted his opening monologue on her. What was he going to do with this wretch of a wench? Because she was the one he was stuck with.

Chlorine approached him. "And you can't talk anymore?" She inquired. "Not even to bray?" She giggled at her own clumsy humor.

She was asking for it. Nimby stood up, showing his dragon body.

"Oh—you're a weird dragon," she said. "Ugliest creature I've ever seen! Why should I ever want to keep company with you?"

Why, indeed. Fortune would have had some sympathy, for she was a decent girl. But Chlorine had a harsh personality, such as there was of it. And now, casting his awareness back across her life, he discovered something even worse: she had once had some sensitivity, but it had been beaten out of her by her abusive family. She had long since cried herself out, and now had only one tear left, and she did not know where that one was. Even if so moved, she couldn't cry a tear for him. And she wouldn't be moved, because she had become cynical and heedless of the feelings of others. Chlorine was simply no prize.

Nimby stared defeat in the snoot. He could hardly have invoked a worse companion. All because he had not been paying attention, while a girl known for her ill luck had suffered more of it. He had come up with the perfect speech—for an undeserving girl. He had thrown away his chance for victory. He hung his head in remorse.

"Still," Chlorine said, "if what you said is true, this could be my lucky day. I'm going to give you a chance. But I warn you, if you try to eat me, I'll poison your water, and you'll have one awful bladder infection." Actually, her language was somewhat more cynically descriptive, the key phrase being "pied pee," but Nimby wasn't quite current with inferior vernacular.

So she wasn't afraid for her safety. She could indeed poison any water with a touch, which meant she could kill a creature if she had to. She couldn't do it to Nimby, because he was a Demon, but of course, he couldn't afford to let her realize that. And she was what he was stuck with, and the contest had not yet been resolved; maybe he still had an outside chance to win. So he nodded, showing that he understood her warning.

"Make me beautiful," she said.

That was easy. He focused on her, and transformed her various parts. He made her straggly greenish yellow hair into luxuriant green-tinted golden tresses that curled just enough to be interesting. He made her yellowish complexion into the fairest skin seen in Xanth. He shifted the substance of her body so that her egg-timer torso became an hourglass figure. He formed her thick clodhoppered feet into dainty digits in glassy slippers. And he adjusted her shapeless dress into an elegant robe that clung to her suddenly firm curves like an artistic lover. She was now a stunning creature of her kind.

She looked down at herself, appreciating the change. "Oooo! Is this real? I mean, not illusion? It *feels* real." She pinched her delightful derriere just hard enough to verify its mind-freaking reality.

Nimby nodded, agreeing that it was real. As long as their association continued.

"I need a mirror," she said. "I want to see my face."

Nimby made one of his scales mirror-shiny and turned it so she could look. She peered at herself, thrilled.

Then she reconsidered. "I'm not just dull-looking, I'm dull-thinking. I've been told that often enough. Can you make me smart, too?"

That was phrased as a question, but it was actually a request, just as the mirror had been. Nimby concentrated on the spongy interior of her head, increasing the efficiency of her mind.

She smiled. "I'm getting smarter! I can feel it! I'm beginning to understand things I never did before. My perspective is broadening immeasurably." She paused. "And so is my vocabulary. I never talked like that before."

Nimby nodded. He had improved not only the height of her intelligence, but also its breadth. Now she could overwhelm problems by force of intellect, and have the judgment to know when to apply it. Now she really would use the term "bladder infection."

She cocked her head, looking at him. "You know, you're quite a creature, if I'm not dreaming this. Your talent is quite strong. But now I have the wit to look a gift dragon in the tooth. Why are you doing this for me? You said you need my company, but I'm sure my company is not unique. Was it chance or design that brought you to me?"

Nimby couldn't answer that, so just gazed at her.

She was quick to understand, because of her new intellect. "Let me rephrase that: was it chance?"

He nodded yes. He had been looking for Miss Fortune, and ill chance had brought him Chlorine instead.

"Chance that you found me," she said slowly, feeling her way through the powerful mind she now possessed, becoming aware of the several informational options and their bypaths. "But you must have had a design. Did you need me specifically?"

He shook no.

"Is your ultimate intention toward me beneficial?"

He nodded yes. He had to do her enough good to make her care enough to shed a tear for him.

But she was too canny, now, to accept that uncritically. "Beneficial for me as well as you?"

She had caught a significant qualification. He really didn't care about her long-term welfare, only about his victory in the contest. But since he needed her emotion, so that she would cry for him, he intended to treat her well. He wanted her to come to like him, to care about his welfare. By her definition, as he understood it, his intention was ultimately beneficial, if not totally happy. So he nodded yes.

"So you just need a person—and not to eat or otherwise harm."

He nodded yes.

"Of course, I can't be sure I can trust you," she said sensibly, for common sense was now one of her strengths. "But with the powers you have demonstrated, I'm sure you could have rendered me unconscious and consumed me, had that been your desire. So the evidence substantiates your claim. You need company."

He made a small nod.

"But there is more," she said sagely. "Yet I could surely guess for days and never happen to discover it. I've never been good at the game of nineteen questions, or even five questions." She paused again, startled. "But I could be good at it *now*. However, I see no need. As long as I keep your company, I can be as I am now—and when I separate from you, I will revert to the way I normally am."

He nodded again.

"So let's see what else I want to be," she said, getting practical. "Beauty is only skin-deep. I want to be healthy, too."

He focused on her, making her supremely healthy. He had already accomplished some of this when he made her beautiful and smart, and now her chemistry was good as well as her bones and flesh. She would live a long time, and never suffer illness, and would heal quickly if injured. While she remained with him.

"Yes, I can feel that health coursing through me," she said. "I feel like running and jumping." She did so, and her body responded perfectly.

She returned to him. "What is the range of your ambiance with respect to these benefits?" she inquired. "Ten of my paces? A hundred? A thousand?"

He nodded yes at the third suggestion. She had to be associated with him, and while distance wasn't the key, it would do as an approximation.

But she did not think to ask a related question: could she go beyond that ambiance, formally terminating the relationship, then change her mind and return, without losing the benefits? She assumed that she could—his awareness told him that—and that was potential disaster for them both. But he couldn't tell her; she had to ask.

Another notion caught her fancy. "I am now aware that though my mind and body have become excellent, my personality has not. I am a cynical mean-spirited vixen; that's one reason people don't like me. Can you make me nice?" She hesitated, caught by an errant thought. "But not *too* nice, because I wouldn't want to be washy-wishy."

That was actually another request. Nimby focused, and adjusted her personality to make her nice. Naturally he did a good job, providing her with qualities of integrity, compassion, sympathy, empathy, and thoughtfulness. She would be about as nice a person as any could be. But he added a reasonable dollop of realism, so that she would not be, as she put it, washy-wishy.

"Oh, my," she breathed. "I appreciate what a female canine I have been, and for such inadequate reason. I have some amends to make. And I shall make them, in due course." She looked at Nimby again. "What about my talent? Can you give me a better one?"

This was dangerous. She could ask for the talent of omniscience, and if she got that, she would soon know all about him—and that would lose him the contest. Her intelligence was already dangerous enough. So he shook his head no.

"Ah, well," she said, being nice about it, but realistic. "You have already done so much for me that I would be unduly greedy to wish for more. Still, now that you have done all this for me, I'd like to do something similar for you. Can you change yourself as you have changed me?"

Nimby hadn't thought of that. Of course, he could—but should he? He concluded that there should be no harm in it. So he nodded yes.

"Then make yourself into my equivalent, in form, mind, health, and character," she said. "By that I mean a princely human man."

So Nimby became a handsome, smart, healthy, nice, but realistic princely human man. Thus efficiently had Chlorine abated his ugliness, as well as her own.

"Oh, yes," she breathed. "You are the kind of man I've always dreamed of, but who I knew would never even look at me." She glanced appraisingly at him. "Look at me."

She had the notion that he had to obey her. That was not the case, but since it hardly mattered, he was not concerned. He looked at her.

"Embrace me," she said. "Kiss me."

So he held her and kissed her. She was now mostly as he had crafted her, and his own form was hardly natural to him, but he found the experience interesting and mildly pleasurable. This was perhaps because he had crafted a complete human man form, with its inherent appreciation of any woman who looked and acted the way this one did. Her exquisitely crafted human female body elicited certain responses in his supremely healthy human male body. He realized that for the first time in his long existence he was feeling a tinge of human desire.

She ended the kiss, and sighed. "Too bad you're really a donkey-headed dragon," she said. "If you were a real man, I'd marry you."

Such illusion! But it was just as well that she thought of him as the monster, and not as the Demon X(A/N)th.

"And you're still mute?"

He nodded, appreciating a benefit of this condition: he couldn't give his identity away.

"Ah, well. I'll just have to do the talking for both of us." She paused, considering. "Obviously I can't go home in this state," she said realistically. "My family would never recognize me, and would be jealous if they did. So I think I'll just disappear for a few days. They may not even miss me."

She kissed him again, rubbing close against him, so that his body began to rev up and heat in an alarming though not unpleasant manner, then flirtatiously disengaged. "So let's take a long walk to unfamiliar places, in our present forms, and when I get bored with that I'll consider what next to do. Because if this is a temporary state, I want to make the most of it." She eyed him appraisingly. "I suspect you haven't had much experience in human romance."

Nimby nodded. In fact, he had no idea what she was talking about, and though his awareness tried to grasp her larger thoughts, there was nothing there to which he could relate. What was romance? Did it have anything to do with the revving of his body when she kissed him?

Chlorine laughed. "Never fear, Nimby. I'll teach you. I had no use for it before, but now that I'm beautiful and nice, I appreciate its value. But it must not be rushed. So let's set out on our adventure." She took his hand and led him down the path, away from the thyme plant.

Then she thought of something else. "You said you could reverse my talent! How about that?"

That much he could agree to. In the course of a brief yes-no dialogue they established that she could not just poison water, but purify it. Actually she could have used her talent this way all along, had she realized it, because her poisoning was temporary, and abolished any bad living things in the water.

Nimby was feeling more positive. Chlorine had been a mistake, but had become considerably more interesting. Perhaps it would be possible to find her lost tear. He knew where it was, of course, but couldn't tell her unless she asked the right series of yes-no questions. But she was doing exactly what he wanted: building a relationship.

Meanwhile his wider awareness was informing him that the mischief he feared from the interruption of the Interface was coming to pass: a significant storm was about to forge from Mundania into Xanth. Though he could not see the future, he knew from long-past experience what that could mean. If that storm progressed until it swept up significant amounts of magic dust, there would be trouble like none seen in millennia. And he couldn't prevent it.

In fact, he now understood how thoroughly the other Demons had fooled him. They had known that the Interface would waver when he changed form and entered Xanth as a character, and that a storm was moving toward it. They had timed it precisely, distracting him so that he would be severely limited at the worst time. And he, intent on his chance to gain significant status, had carelessly let himself be snared.

2
HAPPY BOTTOM

Karen stared avidly out the window of the motor home, catching glimpses of the roiling surface of the sea. "Is Happy Bottom here yet?" she asked. She was seven, and interested in everything but home and school.

"That's Gladys, twerp," David said. He was her big twelve-year-old half brother, and he figured he knew everything she didn't. "Hurricane Gladys."

But this rebuke brought her other half brother Sean into the fray, as was often the case. He was seventeen, so ranked David by the same amount David ranked Karen. "Hurricane Happy Bottom," he said, chuckling. "I like it. But no, she's not here yet; these are only her outskirts. Enjoy them."

Karen giggled, enjoying the halfway naughty reference. She saw Mom and Dad, up in the front of the vehicle, exchange one of their Significant Looks. That was probably because of the business about the bottom and the skirts. Adults knew what was fun, and avoided it.

"Tropical Storm Gladys," Mom said. "She's not yet a hurricane. Otherwise we couldn't risk this drive across her path."

Now the kids exchanged a significant glance. Point made about adults and fun.

"TS HB," Sean remarked innocently. Then, after a pause just long enough to make someone wonder just what naughty notions the letters stood for, he clarified it: "Tropical Storm Happy Bottom."

"TS," David agreed with a smirk. Karen kept her face straight, because she wasn't supposed to know what TS really stood for, though of course, she did know. Tough Stuff. Just as she knew that PO really stood for Put Out. But what about HB, in the naughty lexicon? Maybe Hard Bone. She was sure that would set the boys to sniggering, though she wasn't absolutely sure why.

Theirs was a modern blended family. Mom and Dad had each been married before, and it hadn't worked out. Karen knew why, of course: they had been made for each other, so their first marriages had been mistakes. Likewise their first children, though it wasn't expedient to say that, except in the heat of righteous anger when one of them teased her too hard. Sean was Dad's son, and David was Mom's son, which led to certain deviously competitive crosscurrents between them. In this respect Karen ranked them both, because she was both parents' child, and a daughter to boot. So they were all half siblings, but she was the only one related by blood to everyone else. She liked it that way. She really belonged.

But there was only so much excitement to be had from watching water, even if it was stirring nicely. So Karen went back to check on the pets. They were in crates, to keep them out of mischief while the vehicle was in motion, and not happy about it.

"Hi, Woofer," she said, reaching in to pat the big mongrel dog. Woofer was Sean's pet, but got along with everyone in the family, especially anyone who had food on his person. His fur was almost black, matching Sean's hair, and through him, Dad's. "Hi, Midrange." She stroked the nondescript tomcat. Midrange was David's pet, but could be friendly with anyone who sat in one place more than a moment. His fur was mangy light, matching David's dirty blond hair, which in turn copied Mom's full blond tresses. "Hi, Tweeter." The parakeet was Karen's own pet, and was friendly only with her, though he tolerated the others. His feathers were tinged with brown, which, of course, was to match her own red curls. That was what came of trying to emulate both Dad and Mom: in-between hair.

The pets were all glad to see her, because she usually paid them more attention than anyone else did. The truth was that they were all garden-variety creatures, rescued from pound or flea market according to the whims of the various family members; nobody else had wanted any of them. But Karen thought they were all great folk, and they evidently agreed with her.

The vehicle shuddered. "Damn!" Dad said, from way up front in the driver's seat. "Motor's skipping."

"But we can't stop here," Mom protested. "We can't pause at all, or the storm . . ." She trailed off, with most of what she had to say lost in the ellipsis, as she tended to do when there was something she didn't want the children to overhear.

That meant, of course, that Karen definitely wanted to hear it. "Sorry, gotta go now," she said to the animals, and hotfooted it back to her place at the table.

Now she could hear the skipping motor herself. It sounded like one of David's model airplane engines when it was feeling balky. The motor home was slowing.

"Passengers will buckle their seat belts," Sean announced, using his airline-captain voice. "We are encountering turbulence. There is no cause for alarm. Repeat: no cause for alarm." He spoke the last words with special emphasis, as if the captain were trying to conceal the strain he was under.

Just then a terrific gust of wind buffeted the RV, giving it a scary push and shake. David and Karen laughed at the coincidence; it really did seem as if they were in an airplane landing in a storm.

"Must be someplace to pull off the road," Dad said. "Don't want to stall out on a bridge. Where are we?"

Mom looked at the map. "We're crossing Big Pine Key. You don't think the motor will . . . ?"

"Not worth risking," Dad said. "If this one's big, we're better off here, at least until I can get into the engine."

"Emergency landing," Sean announced in an especially worried pilot tone. "Passengers will remain seated. Please review the crash procedures and verify your nearest escape hatch." And sure enough, there was another buffet of wind to add realism. "Repeat: there is cause—I mean, no cause for alarm." As if the captain had repeated without making the statement the first time, really losing it.

Karen giggled, but behind the fun she was beginning to get nervous. They were on their way home from a weekend visit to friends in Key West, and the approach of TS Gladys had hastened their departure. They had a lot of long, thin, exposed causeway and bridge to cover before they got home to Miami, and the sea was looking increasingly formidable. Suppose one of those gusts blew them into the water?

The skipping got worse. "Can't nurse it along much farther," Dad said grimly. "That an intersection ahead?"

"Yes, the other road runs the length of Big Pine," Mom said, focusing on the map. "Maybe there's shelter there."

The RV swung through the intersection, turning north. The wind pushed at it, trying to make it slew off the road, but Dad managed to keep it on. Then a blast of rain came down, making the world outside opaque. Karen couldn't see much of anything through the side window, and doubted that Dad was much better off with the windshield. This was getting bad. She had been enjoying this drive, and had been intrigued by the notion of a big storm, but that delight was turning sour. This was definitely getting scary, and it wasn't even a hurricane yet. She was beginning to think that such tempests weren't as much fun as advertised.

"Can't see anywhere to stop," Dad muttered. "What's that—another turn?"

"There's an intersection with 940," Mom said, her voice wearing that carefully controlled tone that made Karen especially nervous. Even the two boys weren't joking now. It was entirely too easy to visualize the RV as an airplane descending through bad weather, and Karen wished she could get that image out of her mind.

"Intersection? Can't make it out," Dad said. "But there's got to be a big building or something we can use as a windbreak. I don't dare stop until I have a good place, because the motor may not start again."

The RV limped on, surviving the buffeting. Then Mom made a stifled exclamation—the worst kind. She was scared now, and she didn't scare easy. "Jim—"

"How did we get back on a bridge?" Dad demanded, seeing it.

"There're two roads," Mom said. "I thought we were on the left one, but it must be the right one. It leads to No Name Key."

"Well, whatever its name or lack thereof, here we come," Dad said.

Karen was relieved to see land resume outside the window; it had been a brief bridge. She peered ahead, out the windshield, and saw a sign saying ROCKWELLS. Then one saying NO NAME. They were indeed on No Name Key.

And still no place to find shelter. Finally the motor gasped its last, and the vehicle came to a stop. They would stay here for a while, ready or not. Here on the nameless key. Mom wouldn't even let Dad get out to check the motor, because now things were flying through the air, the wind making missiles of whatever was handy. All they could do was wait it out.

"Safe belly-flop landing," Sean announced. "In remote country. Do not panic; we are certain to be rescued before the headhunters locate us." But the humor didn't get off the ground.

So they made sandwiches and sang songs, pretending it was a picnic, while the wind howled and the night closed around them like some hungry monster. The RV was shaken so constantly that they came to tune out the distraction.

There was a lull. Quickly they attended to the necessary things: Dad went to the motor, and the kids took their pets out on leashes to do their natural business. Actually Tweeter didn't need any of that, but Karen took him out of the cage and cuddled him in her two hands, reassuring him. He rubbed his beak against her nose, his way of kissing her. He wouldn't do that with anyone else, and that was the only trick she had been able to teach him, but it was enough. The truth was that Tweeter was comforting her as much as she was comforting him.

The winds picked up again, and there was a power about them that indicated that what was coming would be worse than what had been. Everyone bundled back into the RV. Dad hadn't been able to fix the motor—big surprise!—but had found rocks to block the wheels, making it a bit more stable. Mom turned on the radio, briefly, just long enough to get the weather report.

"Expected to achieve minimal hurricane status within the next twenty-four hours," Karen heard it say, and she had to stifle a hysterical laugh. If this was subliminal, she didn't want to meet a maximum one! "Twenty-four point five north latitude, eighty-one point three west longitude, proceeding west northwest at ten miles per hour.''

Mom traced the lines on the map, and stifled another shriek. ''That's *here!*'' she said. ''It's coming right here.''

''Well, at least it will be calm in the eye,'' Dad said, trying for light reassurance but not achieving it.

There was nothing to do but settle down to wait it out. They didn't think it was safe to use the beds, so they just buckled themselves into their various seats and slept as well as they could in the circumstances. There seemed to be no point in confining the pets again, so they were allowed to be where they wished. Woofer settled down at Sean's feet, and Midrange chose David's lap. Tweeter, uneasy about Midrange being loose, decided to fly back into the safety of his cage. Midrange had never actually made a pass at the bird, but Karen understood his concern.

The weather report was right, because in due course the winds died out and there was complete calm. But they knew better than to leave the vehicle, because the winds could return at any time. Karen listened to the silence for a while, then lapsed back into sleep.

Karen woke to the winds of dawn. There was no sun in the sky, just brightening turbulence. She had a mental picture of puffy clouds circling the RV, firing arrows into it, but since the arrows were made of vapor, they didn't have much effect. However, the winds were diminishing, so the worst had indeed passed. The RV had not been tipped over or blown into the sea. Now she could resume enjoying the experience as an adventure.

The others stirred in their seats as the light penetrated. They took turns using the bathroom facilities. Then Mom got to work on breakfast, while Dad went out to try fixing the motor again.

''Yo!'' he called, surprised.

Karen, free at the moment, zoomed out to join him, carrying Tweeter perched on one lifted finger. And stopped just outside the door, amazed.

The outdoors had changed. They were now near the shore of a huge island. Not far from the RV was a tree that seemed to be made of metal, and whose fruits seemed to be horseshoes. And standing not far from the tree was the weirdest horse she had ever seen. It was male, with regular hindquarters. But its front rose up into the torso, arms, and head of a man. It had an old-fashioned bow slung across its back, and a quiver of arrows.

"What is that?" she asked, too awed to be alarmed.

"That is a centaur," Dad said, his voice unnaturally level.

"A what?"

"A mythical crossbreed between a man and a horse. It must be a statue, remarkably lifelike."

The figure moved. "Ho, intruders," it said. "What are you doing on Centaur Isle?"

Karen looked at her bird. "Somehow I don't think we're in Florida anymore, Tweeter," she said.

Dad seemed too astonished to respond, so Karen did. "We're the Baldwin family," she said. "We must've gotten blown here by Hurricane Happy Bottom. Tropical Storm, I mean. But where's this? I mean, which key is Centaur Isle?"

"Key?" the centaur asked in turn. "This is a shoe tree, not a key-lime tree." He reached out and touched one of the dangling horseshoes.

The other members of the family emerged, hearing the dialogue. "Gee—a horseman," David said. "I thought they were fantasy."

"They are," Dad said. "We must have stumbled into a freak show."

"Perhaps I misunderstand," the centaur said. "Are you referring to me as a freak?" Suddenly his bow was in his hand, and an arrow was nocked and pointing right at Dad.

Karen acted before she thought, as she often did. "Don't do that!" she cried to the centaur, running out between them. "Dad doesn't believe in fantasy."

The centaur was taken aback. "He doesn't? What about magic, then?"

"That neither," she said.

"What kind of a man is he?" the centaur asked, bemused.

"Just a regular garden-variety family man," she said. "From Miami."

"From your what?"

Karen tittered. "Not your ami, silly. My ami. Miami."

The centaur scowled, confused. "What part of Xanth is that?"

"It's part of Florida, America."

The centaur tilted his head and swished his tail, surprised. "Are you by any chance from Mundania?"

"No, Florida."

"Did you come through the Gate?"

Karen looked around. "We sure must've come through somewhere, because this isn't much like home."

The centaur put away his bow. "This is near the Gate aperture. The Turn Key normally supervises it, competently enough for a human. Perhaps something went wrong, and you came through unaware."

"We must've been blown through," Karen agreed. "It sure was windy. Till we were in the eye."

"An eye gazed at you?"

She giggled. "The eye of the hurry-cane. Happy Bottom."

"Cheerful posterior?" The centaur glanced at his handsome rump.

"You're funny! The center of the storm."

"Ah, the storm. We shall have to see what we can do. Let us introduce ourselves. I am Cedric Centaur the tenth, of Centaur Isle."

"I'm Karen Baldwin," Karen said.

"I must say, you don't look bald. Is that a magic hairpiece?"

Karen felt her wild tangle of blown, slept-in hair. "I don't think so. It's just the way I grew it. It's always wild in the morning until Mom brushes it down."

Cedric smiled. "Our foals have a similar problem. We try to keep the tangle weeds clear, but more keep appearing."

"Should we shake hands?" Karen asked, uncertain of the protocol.

Cedric lifted one hand and made it shake slightly. "I do not see the point, unless you are bothered by flies."

She suppressed another titter. "No, I mean our two hands together, to show we are friendly."

"How quaint."

She raised her hand high, and the centaur reached his hand low, and they shook hands. "And that's my family," she said, nodding behind her. Dad had been joined by the others, all appearing somewhat stunned.

"Indubitably. Follow me." He turned and walked away.

Karen turned to address her family. "Well?" she inquired. "Are you coming?" She knew she had pretty well one-upped them, and it was a great feeling.

The four of them exchanged about six glances in a scant second. Then they fell in behind without comment.

The winds remained high, blowing the foliage of nearby trees to one side. Some of the foliage looked like green tentacles. It was pleasantly weird.

Cedric led them to a village made of stalls. There were other centaurs there: stallions, mares, fillies, colts, and foals. None of them wore any clothing. Only the smallest paid them any attention. They were busy repairing damaged structures. The high winds had blown some of the stall roofs off.

They came to a central pavilion where a young stallion of about Sean's age stood. "I found these Mundanes near the shore," Cedric said. "They call themselves the Baldwin family, and seem to be stranded here. There may be a rift in the Gate. Take care of the matter, Carleton." He turned and trotted back the way they had come.

Carleton stepped forward. "Welcome to Centaur Isle," he said. "Unfortunately you can't remain here, unless you care to become servants. As Mundanes, you have no magic, which is good; nevertheless I suspect you will be better off on mainland Xanth, among your own kind."

Dad finally got hold of himself. "Just exactly what kind of a place is this?"

Carleton paused, briefly considering. "You have no prior knowledge of Xanth?"

"Unless you are referring to a yellow nitrogenous compound, xanthine—" Dad paused at the centaur's blank look. "Evidently not. Then we know nothing of this."

"Then perhaps we should exchange information," Carleton said. "Would you like a meal while we converse?"

"Yes!" Karen said, as usual, before she thought. They hadn't had breakfast yet, and she was hungry.

Carleton lifted one hand, and in a moment a filly centaur trotted over, her large full firm bare breasts quivering in a way that made

Sean and David stare. Karen felt a tinge of resentment, because she
knew that never in her fullest future adult maturity would she ever
develop a bosom like that. "Yes, Carleton?" she inquired.

"Sheila, these Mundanes are in need of fodder."

"Coming right up," Sheila agreed, trotting bouncily off.

"Fodder?" David asked.

But soon the filly returned with big bowls of odd fresh fruit and
other items. She set them on a table under the pavilion. "Yellows,
greens, reds, and oranges," she said, indicating the fruits. "Pink,
purple, black, and blue berries. A loaf of breadfruit and a butterfly.
And milkweed pods." She glanced at Karen. "Including chocolate."

Mom lifted the breadfruit. It fell into several slices. She picked up
the butterfly. Its wings detached and flew away, leaving the butter to
be used. "These will do nicely," she said, terrifically poised. "Thank
you, Sheila."

The filly made a partial bow with her foresection that almost made
Sean's eyeballs pop out of his head. In fact, Karen's own almost
popped, and she was a girl. She had once sneaked a peek at an X-
rated video, but these were more than those, and better formed. Then
Sheila trotted off, evidently to Mom's relief.

Karen picked up the chocolate milkweed pod and sniffed it. Then
she bit off the end. Sure enough, chocolate milk, and very good.
Meanwhile the boys piled into the various-colored fruits and berries.
Mom passed a slice of buttered bread to Dad, and started another for
herself.

"The Land of Xanth is magical," Carleton said. "There are many
magical artifacts, and most human beings possess magic talents, one
to each person. Centaurs don't, of course; we regard magic in our own
kind as obscene. But sometimes it happens. My sister Chena—" He
winced. "But that is irrelevant. We centaurs use magic tools on occasion, however. Beyond Xanth is Mundania, a rather dreary region because of its lack of magic. The normal route to Mundania is to the
north and west, via the isthmus. That may be your route of choice, to
return to your homeland. Now, if I may inquire, what are the details of
your arrival here?"

Dad filled him in on the drive and the storm, and how they's stalled out on No Name Key. "You mentioned a gate," he concluded. "That must be a connection between our two realms. The eye of the storm passed over us, and perhaps swept us into this, um, dimension. Unless this is after all some experimental project on No Name Key."

"Centaur Isle is no experiment," Carleton said firmly. "We constructed it centuries ago, from the scattered islets of the region. It is low on magic by our preference. But on the mainland you will see a great deal of magic, if you wish. However, I must advise you that much of it is dangerous to the uninitiated. Have you had experience with dragons?"

"Dragons!" David exclaimed. "Really? Can I see one?"

Carleton glanced coolly at him. "I doubt that would be wise. Dragons are best avoided, unless one is proficient with archery or has protective enchantment."

Mom spoke up. "Are you saying that the whole of Florida—of Xanth—is magical? That fantastic creatures abound there?"

"Exactly. We can arrange to notify the human authorities at Castle Roogna of your presence. They may send a detachment to assist you, because you surely do not wish to travel Xanth alone."

"A castle?" Karen asked, excited anew. She loved anything fantastic.

"Castle Roogna is the capital of the human beings," the centaur explained. "Their King Dor should be interested."

"A King!" Karen exclaimed, really truly delighted. "This land's got everything."

"But we can't leave our RV," Mom said, ruining things with her practicality. "We have to fix it and drive home."

"Not to mention the pets," Dad added.

That really got Karen. "Woofer! Midrange! Tweeter! They're alone!"

"They've been alone before, twerp," David reminded her.

"There are others in your party?" Carleton asked.

"Our pet animals," Sean explained. "We encountered you folk so suddenly that we never thought to fetch them out of the RV."

"What manner of creatures are these?"

"Woofer's a dog, Midrange's a cat, and Tweeter's a bird," Karen said quickly. "They're part of the family. We've got to get them."

"Of course you must, before you depart the Isle."

"First we have to get our RV running," Dad said. "And—where's the nearest gas station?"

Carleton's brow furrowed. "I do not believe I know of that creature."

"For gasoline. The fuel. You don't use gasoline here? Maybe you call it petrol?"

"We do have pet-rel seabirds. However—"

"Petroleum. Refined from oil."

The centaur shook his head. "I suspect we are on different subjects. Our pet-rels merely fly and seek fish. They do make good pets, of course, but they have no known connection with oil, apart from that with which they preen their feathers."

Dad shook his head. "I think we're in trouble. But first things first. Maybe I can get the motor running. Then maybe we'll have enough gas left to get us home, if we can find the way."

"This creature is ailing? You did say that it was limping."

"It's not a creature," Dad said. "It's a motor home. A recreational vehicle, RV. The motor was skipping, and finally quit. Maybe salt water blew into it."

"Would healing elixir cure it?"

Dad paused. "Maybe you should take a look at it, and form your own conclusion."

"Certainly. I will bring a vial of elixir."

They finished their meal, and started back. Karen was openly admiring Carleton's handsome equine body. She liked all animals, but especially horses.

The centaur caught her gaze. "You are small, Karen Human," he said. "Would you prefer me to carry you?"

She was immediately abashed. "Gee, no—I don't know how to—someday maybe I'll get riding lessons—I'd just fall off." But how she longed to try it.

"You will not fall," he said.

Karen looked pleadingly at Mom, who was sure to say no, but

maybe possibly just this once might not. Mom sighed and looked away: her way of not quite opposing it.

So Dad picked her up by the armpits and set her on the centaur's sturdy back. She grabbed on to the fur in front of her, hoping she would be able to hold her position.

Carleton took a step—and Karen didn't lose her balance despite the lack of a saddle. Somehow the way he moved supported her, giving her confidence. It was as though he were balancing her, compensating for the motions he made. She was, indeed, in no danger of falling. It was glorious.

They walked back to the RV. Now it was time to dismount, but Karen wasn't sure how. Then the centaur put back one hand, and she grabbed his hand and steadied herself as she slid down. "Thank you! Thank you," she babbled. "That was the greatest ride ever!"

He smiled faintly. "You remind me of my little sister."

"Gee, where is she?"

"She was exiled." His mouth closed so firmly that she knew he would say no more on that subject.

They entered the RV, where the pets were glad to see them. Sean put Woofer on a leash, and David did the same for Midrange. Some folk thought that cats couldn't be leash-trained, but so many cats had been killed in the neighborhood, mostly getting hit by cars, that they had done it with this one, and Midrange was used to it.

Tweeter was another matter. He always stayed close to Karen when they went out, and would come to her when she lifted a finger for him to perch on, so he had more freedom. She brought him out, proudly perched.

All three animals were obviously surprised by the centaur. They stood and stared, evidently not sure whether to be friendly or hostile.

"There is one on the mainland who has a cat-pet," Carleton said. "Her name is Jenny Elf." Then he turned to the vehicle. "This is a house?"

"A combination house and motor vehicle," Dad said. "You might call it a house that moves."

"A magic house," the centaur agreed. "How does it move?"

"The motor is connected to the wheels, making them turn and

move it forward." Dad opened the motor compartment. "Here is the motor. I couldn't find any loose wires, so it's something more subtle. I'm not an auto mechanic, so my expertise is limited."

"Mine is surely less, in this connection," Carleton said. "I make no sense of this at all. Can you make it operate now?"

"I'll try, just in case." Dad got in and cranked the starter. The motor coughed once, but wouldn't catch.

"Amazing," the centaur said. "It does seem to be alive, but in very bad health. I will try the elixir." He brought out a vial and sprinkled a few drops of liquid on the motor. Karen stifled a smile; she didn't know beans about motors, but even she was sure that wouldn't do a thing for it. She saw the boys reacting similarly.

Dad tried the starter again—and the motor caught. Suddenly it was not only running, it was purring.

Several jaws dropped. "That's either one bleep of a coincidence," Sean muttered. "Or—"

Dad got out, leaving the motor running. "What did you do?" he asked. "Suddenly it's perfect."

"I simply sprinkled some healing elixir on it," Carleton said. "Normally it has little effect on anything inanimate, but your motor creature seems to be animate, and I had nothing better to try. I'm glad it helped. Your house should be all right now, because it is completely healed." He frowned. "Though I still do not see how it can move."

"Watch," Dad said, and got back in. In a moment the RV nudged forward. It drove in a circle, and stopped where it had been. Then the engine died. "No sense wasting gas until we actually go," Dad said, emerging.

"This is phenomenal," the centaur said, obviously impressed. "A rolling house. I have not seen such a thing before."

"But there seem to be no paved roads here," Mom said worriedly. "And no bridges. We have nowhere to drive."

"I believe there is a high-way on the mainland," Carleton said. "Unfortunately, it is a troll pike. You have to pay the trolls at every turn."

"We're used to that," Dad said. "How do we get across to the mainland?"

"We shall be glad to ferry you across. We can have a craft ready by noon."

"But the winds remain so high," Mom said, worried again. "It wouldn't be safe."

"We can handle it," Carleton said in the same tone he had used when assuring Karen about riding.

Mom looked dubious, but didn't argue. So the centaur trotted off, leaving them to make ready for the trip.

Dad shook his head. "I find today hard to believe," he said. "But I'll feel better when we get on that highway."

The others agreed. The centaurs seemed nice, but this whole business was pretty weird. Karen was looking forward to getting home and telling all her skeptical friends about where they'd been. Nobody would ever believe her; that was the fun of it.

Promptly at noon, a big raft poled into view, with four muscular centaurs at its corners. At the same time, Carleton and Sheila Centaur galloped up from the village. Again the boys' eyes threatened to pop at the sight of the filly's front, and even Dad's eyes might have strained a little. Mom's mouth tightened ever so slightly: not the best sign. Karen was good at reading small signals; it kept her from getting into as much trouble as she deserved. So she didn't giggle, quite.

"I thought you would appreciate something to eat on the way," Sheila said, presenting them with a big bag marked GOODIES. "More milk pods, honey buns, nuts and bolts—"

"Bolts?" David asked.

She brought out what did indeed look like a bolt and gave it to him. He sniffed it, then bit off the end. It seemed to be similar to a nut. "Chocolate flavored!" he said.

"I could get to like this filly," Sean murmured, though his eyes weren't on the bolt. Sheila tossed back her lovely brown tress/mane and smiled at him, not at all self-conscious.

The raft nudged in to the shore. "Now, if you will have your house creature get on, we shall take it across to the mainland," Carleton said. "I have communicated with the Good Magician, who says he will send you a guide. She will arrive in late afternoon with her companion; Sheila will introduce you before she returns here."

"Sheila's crossing with us?" Sean asked, his eyeballs threatening to go into orbit.

"We would not want it claimed that we of the Isle were inhospitable to those who found themselves here through no fault of their own," Carleton said. "Normally we discourage unauthorized visits, but we do allow for special circumstances. We are doing what we can to see you safely on your way. The Good Magician is competent, and you should be able to progress with the help of his guide."

"Uh, thank you," Dad said. "We appreciate your hospitality and assistance. Perhaps we shall meet again."

"This is doubtful." Carleton nodded, then turned tail and trotted off. Dad went to the RV.

"He is a bit saddened by the loss of his little sister," Sheila confided. "If you should happen to encounter her, I'm sure he would appreciate news of her current state."

"Why was she exiled?" Karen asked.

Sheila's mouth tightened. "She was found to have a magic talent. She was a good person, but that is simply not allowed among centaurs of the Isle. We consider it obscene."

"I guess you don't want to know what *we* consider obscene," David said brightly.

"If you are typical of your species, you consider your natural body and its natural functions, other than eating, to be obscene," she replied evenly. "Therefore you cover your body with clothing, evidently ashamed of it, and pretend that you *have* no natural functions, especially not defecation or reproductive capacity."

Karen looked at David. "Well, I guess she flushed your toilet," she said, drawing on an old saying she had researched from a book of dated vernacular.

"I guess she did," David agreed, bemused. "I think I like the centaur way better."

"Me too," Karen agreed.

Mom and Sean exchanged a Significant Glance. Karen made a mental note: Sean was getting to be too much like an adult.

The RV started up and moved slowly toward the raft. It nudged onto the planking, fitting comfortably. Then David and Karen ran to put the blocks at the wheels so it couldn't roll off even if the brakes didn't hold.

When they were all safely aboard, the centaurs shoved off. Then they unfurled a sail and tied it firmly in place. The winds remained quite stiff, so this gave the raft plenty of push. It moved obliquely against the wind, tacking. The muscular centaurs clearly knew what they were doing. Each had his station, whether at sail, tiller, pole, or guard, and was intent on his business.

"This is a good time to eat," Sheila said. "It will take a while to cross the channel, and thereafter you may be distracted by the things of the mainland."

Mom recovered some of her normal aplomb. "Will you join us in the meal, Sheila?"

"Of course," the centaur said. "Let me set up toad stools for you." She went to a box at one side and brought forth stools that were indeed shaped like toads, and when they sat on them, the stools made "Ribbit!" croaking sounds.

"Now, that's interesting," Dad remarked. "Where we come from, toads are silent; only frogs croak."

"Mundania is surely a curious place," Sheila said politely. "Our toads accept no such constraints."

They ate their interesting meal as the raft forged across the channel to the mainland. The shoreline seemed to be solid jungle with strange-looking trees, but there was a golden beach. "The Gold Coast," Sheila explained. In due course they came aground, and Dad drove the RV onto land.

"I will show you to the landing site," Sheila said. "It should not be long now before your guide arrives. Can your moving house travel at trotting velocity?"

"If it has firm, level terrain," Dad said. "This beach seems suitable."

"It is at the edge of the Gold Coast," the centaur said. "Thereafter you will use the trollway, which is certainly firm. I shall run ahead, and you may follow at such speed as your house can manage."

They piled into the RV, and Dad started the engine. He turned west to follow Sheila. The kids all looked out the windshield to see how it went.

At first the centaur walked. As they caught up to her, she trotted. Then, as the RV caught up again, she broke into a gallop, her hair/mane flying back. "I wish I could see her from the front," Sean murmured.

"You have seen more than enough of her already," Mom replied primly.

They got going at about twenty-five miles an hour, which seemed to be the centaur's cruising speed. Soon they came to what looked like nothing so much as a giant pillow sitting on the sand. Here Sheila stopped, so they did too.

"My, your house does move well," the centaur said. She was breathing hard, which surely provided Sean with all the view he could have desired. "I am beginning to suspect that Mundania is not as dreary a region as reputed."

"It does have its points," Dad said.

Sheila looked at her wrist watch, which turned out to be two eyes painted on her wrist. They winked at her in what must have been a meaningful pattern. "Your guide should arrive soon," she said.

They settled down to wait for the arrival of the guide.

3
CHLORINE

C hlorine was enjoying herself. It was fun being beautiful and smart, in the company of a handsome and smart (but mute) man. But her enjoyment was fading. There was no one to see her in her lovely brilliance, and Nimby was more apparent than real. That was to say, he had the appearance but not the reality of a princely man. And he was the cause of her good fortune. So he didn't really count. She needed to be among real people, whose admiration and envy meant something. But she couldn't go to her home village, where someone might possibly recognize her and know her present beauty for a fraud, and she didn't know enough about any other village to go there. So how was she to find a suitable place to show off to real people? She put her fine new mind to work on the problem.

Then a bright bulb flashed above her head. She would go to the Good Magician with a Question! That was a legitimate activity, and of course, she would have to do a year's Service for him, and in all that time she would be able to show off legitimately. She might even accomplish something useful, assuming the Service was of a useful kind, and the new niceness in her appreciated that.

But she needed a Question. What would be legitimate? What did she really want to know?

After a moment the bulb flashed again. How she loved this good mind, which performed so much better than her old one had; when

she posed a question for it, it took hold with the power of twenty
centaurs. She would ask where her lost final tear was. She had wondered about that for years, and now she could finally find out.

"Nimby," she announced, "we are going to the Good Magician's
castle to ask him a Question."

Nimby looked at her doubtfully. He seemed a bit alarmed. Maybe
he thought the Good Magician Humfrey wouldn't like him.

"Not to worry," she said reassuringly. "I'll tell him how nice you
have been to me, though you're really just a donkey-headed dragon.
I'm sure he'll understand."

Nimby did not seem entirely reassured, but she was sure he would
relax when he saw that it was all right. The Good Magician knew
everything, so he would know that Nimby was nice, and if he had
any doubt, he could simply look him up in his Big Book of Answers
and immediately learn everything about the mute dragon. So there
was no call to be concerned on that score.

But there was one small immediate problem: she didn't know the
way to the Good Magician's castle. She lived in the northeast section
of Xanth, and the Good Magician was somewhere in the center of
Xanth. It was surely a long and difficult route there.

But maybe Nimby could help. "Nimby, I want to reach the Good
Magician's castle swiftly and safely and comfortably. Do you know
a way?"

Nimby nodded yes.

"Then show me that way."

Nimby set off at a swift walk toward a neighboring village. He
soon found a clear path, and in three moments and an instant or two
they were at the village limit. She knew because there was a sign
saying JACKS ON VILLE. Oh, yes, she remembered now; every person
in this village was named Jack or Jackie, and they all worked to
harvest assorted jacks. Little jacks were six-pointed twists of wire that
children could play with, while big jacks were solid metal twists used
to lift heavy things. So it was a thriving community.

Nimby led her to a metal box beside the sign. This was labeled
PHONE JACK, and there was a little plug dangling on a wire by it. So
she lifted the wire and plugged its end into a hole in the box. A slot
opened, and a voice brayed: "Whatcha want, Jackass?"

"I'm not the jackass," Chlorine said, realizing that it had mistaken her for her companion. "I'm just looking for a quick way to the Good Magician's Castle."

"Well, pony up some jack, then," the voice said.

Chlorine looked around. There was a pile of lettuce leaves nearby. Her bright mind realized that a pony should like that, so she picked up a leaf and wedged it into the slot.

"Not enough," the voice said. "We're jacking up the price."

So she jammed in more lettuce. "This guy's a knave," she muttered to Nimby."

"Right—the Jack of diamonds," the voice retorted. "Now I'll run up the Union Jack to signal a crackerjack cab. You have some applejack while you wait."

So they sat at the nearby table, where there was a jug of cider, and drank cups of it while waiting. It had a tangy taste, and was very good. Soon Chlorine's head was spinning pleasantly.

A burly man appeared on the path. He had a big double-bitted axe slung over his shoulder.

"Are you the cab?" Chlorine inquired, admiring his muscles.

"I'm no cad," the man protested. "I'm just a passing lumberjack." He glanced at the jug. "But you'd be best off, miss, to ease off on that applejack before your head spins off."

Chlorine put her hands up to stop her head from completing another revolution. It did make her feel less dizzy. "Thank you."

"You're welcome, lovely lass." The man ambled on.

Chlorine flushed with pleasure at his compliment. Then she remembered that she really was lovely, now, so the compliment was well deserved. Still, it was a pleasure she was not well accustomed to, so she knew she would continue to enjoy it.

In due course a cloud of dust zoomed up and abruptly stopped. On its side was printed SPEED DEMON CAB. A door opened in its side.

Chlorine didn't quite trust this. She looked at Nimby. Nimby got up and climbed into the cab. So she followed. It had a plush seat in the back, wide enough for the two of them.

The door slammed closed. The cab leaped into motion with a loud squeal. Suddenly they were zooming at frightening speed along the path; the tree trunks were passing at a blurring rate. "Are you sure—?" Chlorine asked Nimby.

Nimby nodded yes. So she relaxed. There was another seat ahead of them, and beyond that a transparent pane, and beyond that the onrushing forest. They were going somewhere very fast.

She saw a sign in the front. It said "YOUR DRIVER: Demon Strator. Unsafe, unreliable, discourteous."

For some reason, that caused her to be worried again. "Nimby, that sign—"

Then a creature appeared on the front seat. It had horns, so did seem to be a demon. "That's just to scare away low tippers," Strator said. "You paid plenty of jack in advance, so you have nothing much to fear. Unless I lose control." The cab swerved perilously close to a tree.

"Oh." Chlorine pondered. "What is a tip?"

"From you, I will accept a kiss, you luscious creature."

She glanced again at Nimby, who nodded, so she leaned forward and kissed the demon on his right ear.

The cab zoomed into the air, looped, and landed again at speed. "Hoo!" Strator said. "That's one potent kiss!"

"Thank you," she said, blushing. It was fun, because she had seldom had cause to blush before.

The cab zoomed on until it came to a squealing halt at the very brink of an awesomely deep crevasse. "Transfer," Strator announced. "The Gap Chasm is beyond my range."

"Thank you," Chlorine said, climbing out of the cab. "I think you're a nice speed demon."

This time it was the demon who blushed. He turned a rich royal purple, and steam rose from him. "Gotta go now," he muttered, and the cab spun about and zoomed back northeast.

It was now dusk, so the speedy ride had taken at least some time. A large dark shape swooped out of the deep shadow of the Gap and landed before them. It seemed to be a bird almost as big as a roc, completely black. It clutched a small basket in its talons, and on the basket was a tag: FLY BY NIGHT.

Chlorine nodded. That surely meant that this bird flew only by night, so their timing was right.

Nimby climbed into the basket, which turned out to be much larger than it had first appeared; the bird's size had dwarfed it. Chlorine joined him. Then the bird spread its wings and hopped over the brink, into the chasm.

Chlorine's gizzard surged up to her throat as the basket dropped, not realizing that the rest of her was falling. Then the wings caught the dark air, and things settled into place.

They sailed not across, but along inside the chasm, remaining in its pooled darkness while the last of daylight touched its rims and the clouds floating above it. Chlorine peered down, hoping to catch a glimpse of the notorious Gap Dragon, but all she saw was palpable blackness. Since she didn't feel like palpating it, she tried to ignore it. Then, as the darkness rose beyond the gap and spread across the terrain of Xanth proper, the bird lifted out and flew low over the jungle. Chlorine saw the lights of little fires below, where the folk of Xanth had their hearths, or maybe those were dragons pumping up their bellies for nocturnal hunting. It was all rather pretty.

The lights of a castle came into sight, showing its walls and turrets. That wasn't pretty, it was perfectly beautiful! Chlorine stared in rapt wonder, wishing she could visit a castle like that. It must be so great to live in such an edifice, to be a Princess, or even a serving maid. She just felt such longing for the kind of life she would never have. She might be beautiful now, but when she stopped keeping company with Nimby she would revert to her normal, dreary self, and her dream of the moment would be over. She would have shed a tear for her lost dream, if she only knew where her last tear was.

But of course, that was why she was going to see the Good Magician. So she laughed, instead, but there was a deep tinge of regret in it.

Then the bird flew right up to that beautiful castle, and landed outside its moat. This was her destination!

Nimby climbed out of the basket, and she followed. Then the fly-by-night bird departed, swiftly and silently. They were alone in the night beside the glorious lighted castle.

Chlorine was sure she knew better than to try to pass the challenges and enter the castle at night. She would wait until morning. That would give her the chance to get some sleep, too.

Then her bright though sleepy mind thought of something. "Nimby—do you need to sleep?"

The handsome man-form shook his head no.

"So it won't be an imposition for you to stay awake and guard me from possible harm? I mean, I think you're a great creature, but I don't want to wear you out before your time." She laughed ruefully. "In my natural self I wouldn't have thought to ask that, because I wouldn't have cared. But I'm nice now, so I do care. And it's practical too, because you're all that makes me so wonderful. So it's okay?"

Nimby nodded yes.

"Okay. You keep watch, and wake me one instant before dawn, so I can see the sunrise. I'm sure I'll appreciate its beauty much more than I used to." She started to gather some leaves to make a bed, then had another thought. "Would it bother you to revert to your natural form, so I could use you as a pillow? Don't hesitate to say no, because—"

Nimby's donkey-headed dragon form was back. He lay on the ground, and she lay down and put her head against his side. It had scales, but now the scales were soft.

"You know, you do look funny," she remarked. "But the more things you do for me, the more I like you, even as you are now. I hope that doesn't embarrass you."

Nimby wiggled an ear, seeming pleased rather than embarrassed. Chlorine stretched, snuggled down, and faded quickly into sleep.

She woke as something tickled her nose. "Who? What?" she asked, surprised. Then she realized that it was one of Nimby's ears touching her. She had told him to wake her an instant before dawn, and he had done it. "Thanks," she said.

An instant passed, and dawn appeared. Colored rays of light speared up into the sky, brightening it. Nearby clouds glowed. Then, when it was safely light, the sun poked its face up from behind the trees. The sun never came out at night, because it was afraid of the dark.

"Oh, it's beautiful, just as I knew it would be!" Chlorine exclaimed. "Thank you, Nimby, for waking me in time." She rubbed his donkey ears affectionately.

She got up and considered. "You fetch us something good to eat, while I attend to my morning ablutions," she said.

Nimby trundled off, and she found a bush for some business, then brought out her brush and went over her hair. It was now gloriously luxuriant, glistening in the brightening light of day. It was still green-ish yellow, but now the green was the luster of healthy plants, and the yellow was the burnish of gold. She gazed into a puddle, and saw her reflection: she resembled a princess just awakening from beau-teous slumber. It was really too bad this adventure would have to end sometime.

She returned to where they had slept, and saw Nimby approaching with a mouthful of fresh chocolate and vanilla pies. He must have found a good pie tree. His mouth in this form was quite large, so there was a good collection of large pies, and none of them was damaged.

Then she had a second thought. "Will I get fat, eating such stuff?"

Nimby shook his head no. He ought to know, as he was the one who had transformed her. So Chlorine dived in with gusto. The dragon watched, seeming pleased.

Until her third thought. "Aren't you hungry, Nimby? You should have some pie too."

Nimby hesitated, then nodded yes. But still he looked at the pies somewhat doubtfully.

"Oh, in your natural form you could gobble them all up, and leave no more for me? Then change into your handsome man-form, and you won't need as much."

The dragon disappeared, and the handsome man appeared. Nimby man took a pie and began to eat. He seemed to like it well enough.

Chlorine's fourth thought caught up with her. "Biting bugs! They must be all over, in the night—but I wasn't bitten. Were you pro-tecting me from that harm too?"

Nimby nodded.

"I don't know what I'll do without you, when this ends," she said. "I'm really getting to like this adventure, and we haven't even done anything significant or naughty yet." She eyed the man, but decided that naughtiness could wait; she had three challenges to pass to get into the castle.

In due course, not one moment overdue, they went to stand at the bank of the moat. The castle was lovely in the early morning, too. The moat was calm, and seemed to be without a moat monster. There was a drawbridge, but it was raised; no way to cross by foot. However, there was a boat tied to a stake in the bank.

She saw something lying in the grass at her feet, and stooped to pick it up. It was a marking pen, the kind that she had used in the past to mark children's names on clothing. There was no sense wasting it, so she put it in her purse.

"Well, let's get to it, Nimby," she said briskly. "It's my challenge, so you just follow along as I work things out. I'm sure you know how to handle each challenge, but I think it wouldn't count if you gave me any hints. Besides, I should enjoy the thrill of it. I want to put this good mind of mine to the test."

She stepped toward the boat—and a large ferocious bat appeared from nowhere. It flew straight at her, then banked and veered away at the last half instant. She saw the word COM on its underside as it did.

Chlorine was taken aback. In fact, she almost sat down as she was taken back too far and lost her footing. Fortunately she recovered her feet before going down. When she had been a plain nothing girl it wouldn't have mattered if she'd sprawled turvy-topsy and showed her panties to the sky, but now she was a luscious creature, and the humiliation would have been awful.

"That's no ordinary bat," she said. "That's a com-bat! I'll never be able to pass it."

Nimby, behind her, shrugged, neither agreeing nor disagreeing. He was being neutral. That made her suspicious, not of his motive, which was surely amicable, but that there was a way, and he was trying not to give it away. And of course, there was a way, because otherwise it wouldn't be a legitimate Good Magician challenge.

She pondered a moment, and cogitated an instant, and thought a while, knowing that this would not be easy unless she found the right approach. It wouldn't do to try to get around the bat, or to fight it. She had to outsmart it, or at least figure out the proper way to denature it. There had to be something obscure that would be obvious the moment she thought of it. Because that was the way everyone knew the Good Magician's challenges were. He didn't want just anybody barging in to pester him with Questions, so he made it difficult to reach him, but he did play fair, by his definition. By anyone else's definition he was a grouchy gnome, of course, but nobody else's definition counted for much here. So what was there? Her fine new mind focused, exploring possibilities and bypaths at a rapid rate. What was obscure but obvious? There wasn't anything special in the landscape; no evidence of doors to underground bypasses or such. In fact, the only thing even a quarter way remarkable was the marking pen she had found.

Ha! That was surely it! Things did not just lie around the Good Magician's premises; everything was here for a reason. So this had to be the key.

She brought out the pen. It was just a garden-variety marker, somewhat used but still serviceable. How could this ever help her?

Her good mind focused on the problem. Assuming that this was the key, how would it operate? It was a pen, a marker, a—a Magic Marker? To mark the com-bat? That seemed unlikely, because the bat would destroy her lovely, beautiful but not phenomenally muscular or armored body before she got close enough to do that. A pen was made mainly for writing—

For writing. Suppose she wrote something with it—something that would help her? Like GO AWAY COM-BAT?

She fished in her purse and found a little notepad. She took the cap off the marker pen and wrote GO AWAY COM-BAT.

Nothing happened. But of course, she hadn't tested it yet. She took half a step toward the moat—and the bat zoomed up before her, threateningly. She hastily canceled the rest of her step and retreated, and the bat zoomed away.

Obviously that wasn't it. But maybe she just hadn't found the right way to use it. How else would a magic marker work? She couldn't think of anything much, despite her superior mind.

She glanced at Nimby, but he remained carefully neutral. And she wasn't about to ask for his help anyway. "Um, if you want to take a nap or something—" No, he didn't sleep, he claimed. "Maybe play a mental game that entertains you? I hate to bore you with my indecisions."

Nimby nodded, and went into a state of repose. She wondered what a donkey-headed dragon had to think about. At some point she would ask him. But now she had other business.

She crossed out her message—and there was a tiny shimmer around her. She looked around, afraid that a quake monster might be approaching to shake her up, but all was normal. So it must have been an indication of magic. Crossing out the message had canceled it, and that had had magical effect. If only she knew what it was.

She focused her mind once more. Why was she having so much trouble with what should be a simple matter? Somehow it seemed that even her old, dull self would have figured it out by now.

Then a dim bulb flashed over her head. Maybe this challenge was geared to her regular self. Maybe the Good Magician didn't realize that she was now much smarter. Or maybe he realized, but didn't care. So he had set her a simple challenge, and she was being too intellectual about it.

"So let's try it the dull old-fashioned way," she said.

She turned a page on the pad and wrote COM-BAT. Then she crossed out the C and wrote W. And felt the trace tingle of magic. Had it worked?

She stepped forward—and there was a small furry creature standing barely knee-high to her. It was a wombat. It tried to bar her way, but she simply stepped around it and proceeded. She had done it! She had used the magic marker to change the name, converting the deadly creature to a harmless one. The key had been in naming it, and changing the name. Obvious—to a nonintellectual person.

She came to the bank of the moat. Now, where was that dock and boat she had seen? She saw the boat, but now it was perched on muck, and between her and it was the biggest, hugest, hairiest, awfulest spider she could remember encountering. It wasn't big enough to gobble her down in a single bite, but three or four bites would do it. Actually spiders, as she remembered, didn't gobble prey down whole; they trussed them up in spiderwebs and sucked the juice out. But she didn't want to be juiced, either, no matter how juicy her current luscious body was.

Chlorine was retreating as she pondered; it seemed to be the expedient thing to do. The spider did not follow. In fact, it had disappeared—and there was the dock she had seen before. So she reversed course, trying to reach the dock before the spider returned—and the spider reappeared. And the dock was gone.

Something was definitely odd. The spider wasn't blocking her view of the dock; she could see handily around it. There simply was no dock. Was she up against illusion? In which case, which was the illusion: the spider or the dock? It made a difference.

She retreated a step, this time watching the spider. And the spider disappeared—and the dock reappeared. They were changing into each other! This was a dock spider.

Her fine mind began to take hold. This was definitely a challenge, and she surely wouldn't be able to handle it by writing the word SPIDER on her pad and changing the SP to C. Even if that worked, what good would it do her, since she didn't want cider, she wanted that dock so she could get in the boat without muddying her pretty little feet. She needed to get to that dock without it changing into the spider. How could she do that?

What was the stupidly simple answer? Immediately it came to her: bribe the spider. But what would it want, aside from a long session sucking her succulence? What else did she have that might appeal to it?

The magic marker! She no longer needed it, but maybe the spider would like it. If she made a good enough case for it, in spider terms.

She stepped toward the spider, though she was prepared to back-pedal at a furious rate if she had to. "Hey, handsome creature!" she called. "How would you like something nice?"

The spider wiggled its mandibles, and a drop of slaver fell to the ground, where it smoked quietly as it digested an unfortunate little poul-tree that hadn't even yet grown its first chick, let alone the roc bird it might have made at maturity. Chlorine felt sorry for it, but knew she couldn't help the tree.

"No, you can't have me," she said quickly. "Under this pretty exterior I'm just a plain and rather tasteless person anyway. But I have something that may appeal to you more: a magic marker." She held it up. "This marker can change things. For example, you could use it to change a lug to a bug. Here, I'll demonstrate." She looked around and spied a lug, which was a kind of nut from a nuts and bolts tree. She picked it up and set it in front of her. Then she wrote

LUG on her notepad, and crossed out the letter L and replaced it with the letter B. And the lug became a bug.

"See—just the kind of magic you have always wanted," she said enthusiastically. "Think what you could do with a *big* lug! You could turn it into Xanth's biggest juiciest bug. And feast on it, snug as a lug in a rug."

The spider slavered some more. It liked the notion.

"And I will trade you this fine magic implement for one favor," she continued persuasively. "All you have to do is become the dock and let me get on board that boat. Then you can have the magic marker and my pad of paper, so that you can—" She hesitated, paused by an awkward thought. "You do know how to write?"

But the spider shook its head no.

This was a problem. But her fine mind rose to meet it. "Well, can you draw? Let me see if this works with pictures." She found another lug and set it before her. She quickly sketched a crude picture of it, then crossed it out and drew an even cruder bug.

And the lug became a bug. It did work pictographically. Maybe the Good Magician had figured she was too stupid to read and write. Which was actually a pretty accurate assessment; she had never gotten beyond the first year of Centaur School, so could handle words of only one or two syllables. If she had had to write "quintessential," she would have expired.

"So if you can draw, you can use this marker," she concluded. "I confess I don't know exactly how versatile it is, but since there are a number of lugs around here, at least you'll have all the bugs you want. Is it a deal?"

The spider nodded yes.

But now she had just the slightest, wee-est little tinge of apprehension. Was this spider honorable? Suppose it grabbed her and the marker? But then she concluded that it must be honorable, because otherwise the Good Magician wouldn't use it in a challenge. So she girded her loin—no, that would be unmaidenly. She lifted her chin and walked into the spider's range. If she had misjudged the situation, and the spider grabbed her and tried to suck her juice, she would turn *its* juices to poison and make it sorry. But she hoped for the best.

The spider became the dock. Chlorine set dainty foot on it and went to the boat. She climbed in. Then she set the magic marker on the dock, untied the boat's tether, picked up its paddle, and shoved off. "Nice doing business with you," she called cheerily.

The spider reappeared, holding the marker in its mandibles. It waved at her with a long forelimb. She had passed the second challenge.

Oops—she had forgotten Nimby. "Hey, Nimby!" she called. "Can you join me?"

Nimby walked down to the dock as Chlorine returned. The spider obligingly changed form, allowing Nimby to tread its planks and get into the boat. Maybe it realized that Nimby was actually a dragon with impenetrable scales, so wasn't anyone to fool with. Then they pushed off again.

She paddled across the moat without incident. But she knew there would be a third challenge. What would it be? They were never the same, she understood. Just so long as it wasn't a fierce moat monster, because she didn't know what she would do in that case.

She came to land at a garden within the moat outside the Good Magician's castle. They climbed out of the boat. The moment they did, the boat wended its own way back across, stranding them. It was now too late to change her mind.

She gazed at the garden. It was lovely and loathsome. The left side was overgrown with foul-looking and -smelling weeds and had statuary that was downright disgusting. The right side had a multitude of pretty flowers, with attractive scents. Naturally that was the side she wanted to step into.

But the path led into the foul side, so that was where she went. It would have been impossible to go into the nice side without treading on flowers and ripping out beautiful vines, and she couldn't bear to do that. But the path was overgrown with burrs, thorns, nettles, stinging vines, scratchpads, and even a stink horn she just missed stepping on. That would have wiped out all her appeal in one swell foop, for nothing and nobody could stand the sound or stench of stink horn.

The farther she went, the worse it got, until it was plain that she could not get through this way. This was one mean garden half. And obviously a challenge.

She backed out and rejoined Nimby, who was innocently waiting.

Her nice dress was smirched with refuse-colored yuck, and her arms and ankles were scratched. What an awful section!

She considered the nice side again. If only the path were there! But it wasn't, and though the garden was beautiful, it was just as thickly woven as the ugly side was. Not only would she do a horrible amount of damage if she tried to forge through there, she probably wouldn't make it to the far side anyway.

There had to be a way through. But where was it, if not the path? Chlorine looked back and forth between the two garden halves, sure that she was missing something.

Now that she took the time to wake up and smell the flowers, as it were, she saw that the path was lined with purslane, which made sense for a lane, and trailing arbutus, which made sense for a trail. There were also primroses, making it a primrose path, and at the very beginning, a trail blazer jacket. So no one could be confused about where the path was.

A dim bulb flashed. That trail blazer—suppose she moved that to the other side? Would it then blaze a new path there, where she wanted it? That might be the answer.

She reached for the jacket, but it was just out of reach. She stretched her arm out—and got scratched again. Apparently that piece of apparel wasn't supposed to be taken. So much for blazing a new trail.

So she couldn't move the path. What else was there? Move the gardens?

A dim bulb appeared over her head, but didn't flash. It simply hung there expectantly. She hadn't quite gotten her bright notion yet.

Was there a way to change the positions of the gardens, so that the same path led through the nice part? Now she thought there could be. It was exactly the kind of inverted thinking that the Good Magician was noted for.

Chlorine reconsidered the gardens and the path. Now she saw that the path wound past a nasty-looking well. She made her way to it, stepping carefully to avoid the nettles and thorns, and peered in. Smoky fumes smudged her face and jammed up her nose. Phew! That wasn't water in there, that was firewater. Not exactly poisonous; she knew poisoned water when she encountered it, that being her talent. But not exactly healthy, either. Mean spirits. This was one mean well.

Across the path from it was a dingy thyme plant. She turned to consider it. Thyme was tricky stuff, she knew; it could speed things up or slow them down, or even just change the time of day. Normally she stayed well clear of it. But could there be a reason it was growing here, so close to the path and the well? Her bulb brightened slightly.

Mean well, mean thyme. In the mean section of the garden. It figured. But there were other meanings of mean. Such as when a person meant well. Then the intention was good, even if the result wasn't. Could this be that kind of well? And the thyme plant—it affected time, and sometimes time was sort of average, and they might call that mean time. It wasn't necessarily nasty, merely rounded off. Suppose some of that well-meaning water were poured by the thyme plant—would that round off the time in a good way? Her bulb brightened. It well might!

She took the grubby bucket and dipped some of the smoking water out. Of course, it looked awful, because its true nature wasn't supposed to be obvious. But if she was right—

She poured the water at the base of the thyme plant. It turned greener and healthier almost immediately. Then night fell.

What? Chlorine looked around, startled. It hadn't been close to nighttime! Oh—the thyme plant, feeling its oats, as it were, had accelerated time, bringing the garden rapidly to night. Maybe she should have anticipated that.

But what good did it do her? It wouldn't be any easier to forge through this tangle by night than by day. Unless—

Now her dim bulb flashed so brightly that the entire garden lit up. Sure enough: this was now the kinder section of the garden. It was a kinder/meaner garden, and one section was as different from the other as day from night. So it was night, and suddenly this half was the nice one—with the path wending pleasantly through it. She had found the way at last.

"Come, Nimby," she said, as if this were routine. "We shall pay a call on the Good Magician." And she marched down the path, her way lit by pretty glowworms set along the edges.

The path led right to the castle entrance. Chlorine knocked on the door, and it opened immediately. A pretty young woman stood there.

"Welcome to the Good Magician's Castle, Chlorine and Nimby," she said. "I am Wira, his daughter-in-law. Please come this way."

So she had, indeed, been expected. She was glad she had played it straight, and found her own way through the challenges.

They followed her inside. The interior was surprisingly light, because rays shone in through the high windows. Chlorine realized that it wasn't really night; that had just been a local effect in the garden, which passed when they left the vicinity of the thyme plant.

"How did you know our names?" Chlorine inquired. "If my memory is correct, you—can't even see us."

"It is true I am blind," Wira said. "But I know this castle well, and can't get lost. And I overheard Magician Humfrey grumbling about the situation. It seems he had no trouble identifying you, Chlorine, but your friend Nimby baffled him. He had to look him up in the Big Book of Answers, sure that there was no such person. But the Book had an entry the Magician must have forgotten, and it said Nimby was a dragon ass with the magic talent of enabling himself and his companion to be whatever the companion wished them to be. That his full name was Not In My Back Yard, because most people didn't like him. The Magician shook his head, not wanting to admit that he had been ignorant of such a creature. I fear he is beginning to feel his age."

Chlorine smiled. "The Book of Answers spoke truly. Nimby is not the man he appears to be, but he is much nicer than he looks in his natural form. He is welcome in my back yard, for I have come to know him by his actions, not his appearance. His only liability is that he can't speak. He is enabling me to have a really nice time, for now."

"For now?"

"I know it has to end all too soon, and I will return to my wretched home life. But I will always have this wonderful adventure to remember, my single shining moment, thanks to Nimby. I intend to make the most of it."

"I fear the Good Magician means to make more of it than you expect."

"Oh, no, my year's Service is part of it," Chlorine said cheerfully. "I am resigned to that. It will extend my adventure."

Wira brought them to a rather dull-looking woman in a sewing room who was mending a pile of socks. "Mother Sofia, here are our visitors," Wira said.

Sofia looked up. "Are you sure you want to broach Himself with your Question? He will require you to perform a most arduous Service in return."

"Yes, of course," Chlorine agreed. "I look forward to it. The more adventurous the better."

"As you wish. Wira will take you to him now."

The blind young woman led them up a dark winding stone stairway to a squeezed crowded chamber. There in the shadows sat the Good Magician Humfrey Himself. He looked grumpily up from his monstrous tome. "Yes?"

"Where is my last tear?" Chlorine asked.

"It is in your eyes, spread across them to keep them moist. Half of it keeps your right eye well, and the other half keeps your left eye well. Without that final tear, you would immediately go blind."

Chlorine was amazed. "I never thought of that! Of course, it must be true."

"It *is* true," Humfrey said grumpily. "Now report to the cat-a-pult for your Service."

But Chlorine, being nice but not *too* nice, balked. "I know I have to serve a year's Service, but for that little bit of obvious-in-retrospect information? That doesn't seem fair."

"Please, don't argue," Wira said worriedly. "That only makes him grumpier."

"Nevertheless, I will answer," Humfrey said, more grumpily. "You knew the conditions before you came to me, so if you wasted the chance to ask a significant Question and receive a significant Answer, the fault is yours."

"Um, that's right," Chlorine said. "I did know the terms. I apologize for my intemperate remark."

Humfrey looked up from his tome again and glanced at her. His eyeballs were yellowed and streaked with purple veins, but as they focused on her they brightened and the dingy colors faded out. "My, you are a pretty one," he said, surprised. "A sight for sore eyes."

"Thanks to Nimby," she agreed, nevertheless pleased to have made a good impression to erase some of the bad impression she had made before. "In real life I'm plain and mean-spirited."

"Yes, of course. Since you have done me the slight favor of resting my eyes, I will return it by amending my answer: it is not quite as insignificant as it might seem. You do have the capacity to shed that final tear, if you ever choose to. But considering the consequence, I suggest that you never allow yourself to become that unhappy."

"You may be sure of that!" she agreed, laughing.

"Actually, I am not sure of that, which is why I have cautioned you. There may come a time. Do not react thoughtlessly."

Nimby, standing beside her, seemed uneasy.

Chlorine nodded. "Thank you for that amendment, Good Magician. I will remember it." Then she smiled. This time the gloomy study brightened, and Humfrey seemed to lose five years in age.

"Oh, I wish I could see that!" Wira murmured, aware that something good had happened. Maybe she had felt the heat of the light that had brightened the study.

"You shall," Humfrey said, almost with the illusion of fleeting mellowness. "Imbri?"

Then Chlorine saw a replay of the incident, as if she were another person watching herself, Wira, Nimby, and the Good Magician in the study. She smiled, and the study lighted, and Humfrey youthened from about a hundred to about ninety-five.

"Oh, thank you, Day Mare Imbri!" Wira exclaimed. "I saw it!"

Chlorine was amazed. The Good Magician had actually summoned a night mare, or rather a day mare, to give them all a day dream, so that the blind girl could see the event in the only way she could: as a dream. This was surely something very special. And he must like his daughter-in-law a lot, because it was clearly for her he had done it.

But now the study faded to its natural dinginess, and the Good Magician's slightly less tired eyes reverted to his monstrous dull tome. The interview was over.

Chlorine turned and followed Wira out, and down the steps. The girl was smiling with the memory. Something briefly nice had certainly happened.

4

TROLLWAY

J im Baldwin looked around, bemused. This land looked
a lot like Florida, at a casual glance, but any more careful look rapidly dispelled the similarity. It wasn't just a
matter of the presence of the fantastic female creature, Sheila Centaur.
Her phenomenal bare bosom was something he could appreciate regardless of the circumstance, though, of course, he would not admit
that in the presence of his family. Mary was a reasonably liberal
woman, socially, but it was plain that she was not at all easy about
the filly centaur, for reasons that went beyond the fantasy element.
Correction: they surely related to her concern about the male fantasy
element. Especially that of Sean and David. And Jim himself, perhaps.
With reason.

They were waiting on the beach beside what resembled nothing so
much as a giant pillow. This was where the guide was supposed to
arrive. The guide that the Good Magician was sending. After what
else he had seen in this weird land, Jim was prepared to accept the
notion of good and bad magicians. He hoped the guide was competent. He hoped to get out of this situation soon; he didn't like the way
the wind was building up, however intriguingly it played with Sheila's
hair. The storm seemed to have been subsiding, but now it was building again. That was bad news, regardless, whether in Florida or this
land they called Xanth.

The children were in animated dialogue with the centaur filly, purportedly eager to learn more about Xanth. Jim caught Mary's eye, and she joined him. "I don't want to be an alarmist, but have you noticed the wind?" he asked her quietly.

She brushed her hair out of her face. "Yes." Her tone was grim.

"So maybe the distraction of the centaur is just as well, until we are able to get moving again."

Her answering smile was genuine but somewhat strained. "Thank you for clarifying that, Jim."

Then something came flying through the air from the north. They all half ducked, not sure where it was going to land. It appeared to be a big rag doll, one of the modern type, with excellent legs.

It landed plump! in the middle of the giant cushion. It bounced, and got its skirt smoothed down. It was a lovely young woman, seemingly no worse for the experience. The boys immediately discovered a new creature to gawk at.

"Hello, folks," she said brightly, brushing back her golden-green-tinted tresses. "I am Chlorine, your guide, sent by the Good Magician Humfrey. In a moment my companion will be along; then we must talk."

Before they could do more than get their collective mouths closed, another rag-doll figure came flying across and down. It, too, bounced, but had no skirt to get in order. It wore slacks, and was a handsome young man.

"This is Nimby," Chlorine said. "He is mute, but nice. He will help me to help you. But first I must warn you that a bad storm is coming."

"We had noticed," Jim said, stepping forward. "Hello. I am Jim Baldwin, and this is my wife, Mary, and our children, Sean, David, and Karen. We're from—I believe you call it Mundania."

"We do," Chlorine agreed with a smile. She glanced at Sheila. "Thank you for guiding the lost folk this far; I'm sure you are eager to return to Centaur Isle."

"Yes I am, before the wind further intensifies," the centaur agreed. She turned to the family. "I wish you the very best. It has been pleasant meeting with you. And if you should encounter Carleton's sister Chena, do give her his good wishes too."

"We shall certainly do that," Jim agreed. "Thank you—and Carleton—for your kindness in helping us this far."

"Welcome." She turned tail and cantered back along the beach. The boys watched her until she was out of sight; then their eyes reverted to Chlorine, who was far more decorously dressed, but so beautiful in every respect that she was fully as distracting as the bare centaur filly.

Chlorine turned back to Jim. "I don't want to be impolite, but what I have to say is of some urgency. There is danger for you here. The Good Magician's wife, Sofia, was most specific about that. She's Mundane herself, so appreciates how difficult Xanth must be for you. I understand you have a moving house."

The children laughed. "Motor home," Mary said. "But yes, it is a moving house."

"Could you get it moving? There is very little time to escape before the storm intensifies. It is my service to guide you safely where you wish to go, but it won't be safe here very much longer."

"We can drive it," Jim said. "And there is room for you and Nimby." He wondered at the name, but this didn't seem to be the time to inquire about that. "But we are going to need gas soon, or we'll stall."

"Gas?" the woman asked blankly.

"Gasoline. Petrol. Fuel. It—our vehicle eats it. Drinks it."

"Oh." Chlorine turned to her companion. "Nimby, do you know where there is—gas—for this creature?" Nimby nodded. "Then show us, because we mustn't delay long."

"Come on in," Jim said. "If Nimby knows where it is, he can sit up front with me and point the way."

So they got into the van, with the silent young man taking the passenger seat in front. Chlorine joined the family in back, which Jim knew thrilled the boys. Ordinarily he would not pick up hitchhikers, but when in Rome—or Xanth—it was time to do as the natives did. Chlorine was certainly right about the dangerous storm; apparently Hurricane Gladys was reintensifying, or turning back, to catch them again. The last thing he wanted was to get caught in a hurricane, in the RV.

He started the motor. There was an exclamation of surprise from Chlorine, but the odd Nimby took it calmly in stride. He pointed to the trollway, which was exactly where Jim wanted to go. It looked like a good solid highway where he could make excellent time, storm and gas permitting.

At the entrance to the trollway stood a horrendous creature. "Don't tell me; let me guess," Jim muttered. "A troll."

Nimby smiled. Evidently he understood speech well enough; he just couldn't speak himself. Curious fellow, but seemingly amicable.

He drew the RV to a stop before the troll. Sure enough, there was a sign: STOP: PAY TROLL. But there wasn't any indication what the fee was.

Well, he would start small. "Here's two cents," he said, offering two pennies to the troll. And the creature smiled—a horrendous effect—took the pennies, and waved him on.

Maybe it was the thought that counted. Jim pulled the vehicle onto the pavement and gathered speed. He was almost beginning to feel at home here!

Now a sign said HIGHWAY AHEAD. And of course, the road rose up until it was at treetop level: a literal high way. Things tended to be extremely literal here. Unfortunately this elevation exposed them to the higher winds of the heights. "Are we going to be up here long?" he asked Nimby.

The man shook his head, but gave no other information. Certainly he was a strange one.

Jim listened to the dialogue of the others. The children were eagerly questioning the girl Chlorine—odd name!—and she was answering to the best of her ability. It was interesting.

"Yes, candy really does grow in Xanth, and cookies of all kinds along the With-a-Cookee River," Chlorine said. "Doesn't food grow on trees in Mundania?"

"Oh, sure, in a way," David agreed. "Fruits grow on trees, and vegetables grow in gardens, and grain grows in fields. But candy and cookies have to be made. And paid for. That's what allowances are for."

"Allowances?"

"Do you have a concept of money in Xanth?" Mary asked.

"Certainly. It is filthy green stuff that no clean person cares to touch."

The others laughed. "That's the stuff we have," Sean said.

A heavy gust of wind buffeted the RV. "Oh, that reminds me," Chlorine said. "I must tell you of the great danger you face. The Good Magician told me to be sure to make you understand. You see, there has been a weakening in the Interface—"

"Whose face?" Karen asked.

"The Xanth Interface. It keeps the Mundanes out. No offense. Something went wrong, and a Mundane storm came through—and you folk too. The storm is headed for the center of Xanth. That means it will sweep up a lot of magic dust, and—"

"Magic dust?" Sean asked.

"That's the dust that wells up in the center of Xanth, bringing the magic," she explained. "Without it, we wouldn't have magic, and it would be horrible. But where the dust is too thick, the magic is too strong, and so there is madness. If Happy Bottom spreads that dust across Xanth—"

"Gotcha," Sean said. "Everybody goes mad."

"Well, not exactly. But things could get very strange. However, you don't need to worry about that. I'm supposed to help you get through Xanth and out of danger before the storm gets too bad. So we must hurry. There won't be much time to stop and sleep."

"No problem," Sean said. "We'll sleep in the RV while Dad drives."

Which meant no sleep for Dad, Jim reflected. Well, it had happened before. He didn't like the way the wind was building, and would far rather stay ahead of the worst of it if he could, sleep no object.

Nimby pointed to the side. There was an exit ramp. Jim steered the vehicle to it. The thing spiraled around and around, corkscrewing down to the ground. He had had no idea they had gotten so high! The treetops had vanished without his noticing.

As they neared the ground, Nimby pointed again. There beside the road was a big ugly purple tree, and under the tree stood a big uglier purple monster with greenish gills. It looked most uncomfortable. Jim hoped the discomfort wasn't hunger, because the thing was big enough to gobble down a man and a child. He hoped Nimby knew what he was doing.

"Oh, there's a gas guzzler," Chlorine said, putting her pretty head close to his so she could peer out. She smelled faintly of delight.

A gas guzzler. It figured. "We can get gas from it?"

"Yes. Just make a deal."

A deal. He would have to feel his way through this one, as he had with the troll.

He drew to a stop beside the monster and rolled down the window, partway. "You have gas?"

The monster faced him. It belched. The putrid odor of spoiling gasoline wafted by in a noxious little cloud.

"You guzzled too much gas?" Jim asked. The monster nodded miserably. "Then maybe we can make a deal." But at this point Jim's imagination failed him. What would an overindulgent gas guzzler want to trade for?

"I think he needs one of Mom's ant-acid pills," David said brightly.

"Then hand one over," Jim said.

Mary fished in her purse and came up with an antacid pill. Jim offered it to the monster. "This ant-acid pill for one tank of gas," he said. Could this possibly work?

The guzzler took the pill and gulped it down. He belched again, this time not quite so awfully. Then he lifted his tail. Jim saw that the end of it looked somewhat like the nozzle of a gas pump. "Right here," he said quickly, turning off the motor, piling out of the vehicle, and going to the gas tank. He removed the cap and pointed.

The guzzler put the tip of his tail into the aperture. There was a liquid flow sound. The fumes smelled like gasoline.

When the tank was full, the creature removed his tail and Jim put the cap back on. "Thank you," he said.

The monster nodded. His gills were no longer green. Evidently the pill had alleviated his condition. So it was a fair bargain.

Jim climbed back in and started the motor. Then he had another thought. "We have taken the high road," he said to Nimby. "But it's pretty windy up there. Is there a low road?"

Nimby pointed ahead. Sure enough, there was a road following the ground. Jim went for it. "Thanks."

For a time the road seemed routine. Jim had a dark suspicion that it wouldn't last, but he enjoyed it while it did. The motor was running well; the gasoline seemed to be good. Which was a considerable relief. So again he listened to the dialogue behind.

"How did you get here?" Karen asked Chlorine. "I mean, you just came flying through the air, like a parachute."

"With your skirt flying," Sean added appreciatively.

"Oh, no!" Chlorine exclaimed, sounding appalled. "Did my panties show?"

"No," Jim called back, realizing by her reaction that this was a social nuance of some consequence. Just as the centaurs were evidently quite open about their apparel, or lack of it, others might be quite uptight. The children might not realize, and make a social blunder. "Just your legs." And what legs they were!

"Oh, that's a relief!" she said. "I would fade away from mortification if—but never mind. The Good Magician had us use the cat-a-pult."

"Now, why do I think that's not what we mean by the term catapult?" Sean asked musingly.

"I confess to being curious," Chlorine said. "Why do you think that?"

There was half a pause. She had, innocently enough, set the brash teenager back. "I, uh, mean that everything else is different. With us a catapult is a big engine that hurls things far away."

"Yes, that's it. It's a giant cat whose tail springs up and hurls things where they need to go. The Good Magician must have told the cat where to aim. I'm glad there was a pillow to land on."

"This Good Magician," Mary said. "He must be quite knowledgeable."

"Oh, yes! He knows everything. I came to him to ask where my last tear was, and he told me, but then, of course, I had to perform a year's Service, or the equivalent. So he assigned me to guide you folk safely out of Xanth."

"You have certainly been a help," Mary said. "As was Sheila

Centaur. But did I hear you correctly? You have to do a year's service, for the answer to a single question?''

"Oh, yes. I was foolish, wasting my Question on something I could have figured out for myself. But I really did it for adventure, and I'm getting that. You folk—this traveling house—this is fantastic.''

David laughed. "You think the RV is fantastic? After getting hurled through the air by a giant cat?''

"Of course. Lots of people use the cat-a-pult. But I don't think there's ever been a wheeled house like this in Xanth before. There aren't even many houses with chicken legs. I couldn't ask for a better adventure.''

There was a full pause. She had set them back again. So Jim filled in with a question of his own. "I do not wish to be impolite, or to seek after anything private. But since Nimby can't speak for himself, may I inquire about his background and mission?''

"Oh, there's no problem about that,'' Chlorine said brightly. "Nimby's a donkey-headed dragon in man-form. I could ask him to revert to his natural shape, to show you, but he'd be too big for this little house.''

"Then we had better take your word for it,'' Jim said carefully. This young woman, like this strange land, kept surprising him anew.

"He's doing me a really big favor,'' Chlorine continued. "You see, in real life, I'm, well, plain. And not all that smart or nice. But Nimby's talent is to make himself and his companion whatever she wishes them to be. So naturally I wished to be really pretty, smart, healthy, and nice.''

"Yeah,'' Sean said appreciatively, doubtless glancing at her legs or more. She was about as healthy a young woman as Jim had seen, and strong on the other qualities.

"I think maybe you don't believe me,'' Chlorine said. "But that much I can show you, because I'm the same size in real life.'' She lifted her voice. "Nimby, show me as I really am—for one moment.''

The young man sitting beside Jim nodded. And there was a gasp of surprise behind. Jim turned his head for a quick look.

The lovely young woman had indeed changed. She was now a plain-bordering-on-ugly girl, in unattractive clothing, with an irritable expression. Her hair was a listless, stringy, unappealing shade of green.

Then the moment was over, and she was lovely again. Her legs and bosom filled out, and her dank hair became lustrous. She smiled, and the interior of the RV seemed to brighten. "See? I owe Nimby a lot."

"You sure do," Sean breathed, as Jim turned back to watch the road.

"But why is Nimby doing this for you?" Karen asked. "I mean if he's really a dragon, wouldn't he rather eat you?"

"Karen!" Mary said severely.

"Ah, come on, Mom," David said. "She does look good enough to eat."

Chlorine laughed. "Thank you. I was afraid of something like that, at first, because that's what dragons do. But he turned out to be a nice dragon. A very nice dragon."

"Yeah," David agreed. "I wish I had one like him. I'd have him make me a star football player or something."

"Actually, he did tell me why, when we first met." She evidently held up a hand, as someone started to protest; Jim had to keep his eyes on the road, so couldn't look. "Yes, Nimby is mute now, but at first he could speak. He told me that he needed my company, and would do anything he could to make it worthwhile for me. But he warned me that that was his only chance to speak, and he has been mute since. But he understands me, and he can answer me by gestures."

"But suppose he had something important and complicated to tell you?" Sean asked, perhaps becoming intrigued by something other than her appearance. "Such as some terrible danger you didn't know was coming, so you didn't think to ask him a yes-or-no question about it?"

"Why, I don't know. Nimby, is there anything like that?"

Nimby turned to face the rear, and nodded.

"Something important? That's too complicated for me to just guess readily?"

Nimby nodded again.

Now Chlorine seemed out of sorts. "But how can I ask you, if I don't know what to ask?" she asked plaintively.

"Maybe he can write it," David said.

"But I can't read," Chlorine said. "More than big obvious signs and short words, I mean. The signs have spells to make them legible to anyone, even animals. I can't read anything significant on my own. I flunked Centaur School."

So she was functionally illiterate, Jim realized.

Sean laughed. "So have him make you able to read."

There was a flash of light, followed by a gasp of awe. "A lightbulb just appeared over your head!" Karen cried. "It glowed!"

"Yes, of course," Chlorine agreed. "I realized Sean was right. That's a brilliant idea. Nimby, make me literate, so I can read what you write, no matter how complicated it is. And write me what I need to know."

Immediately the young man brought out a pad and stylus and began writing. Jim nodded; there were definite advantages to magic. In Mundania there were no such shortcuts.

"That reminds me of something else," Jim said. "This is obviously not our homeland. The rules are mostly different. How is it that you and the centaurs speak exactly our own language?"

"Oh, that's part of the magic of Xanth," Chlorine said. "Everyone speaks the same language here. All people, I mean. Animals speak their own languages, which are different from ours, so we usually can't understand them. But often they can understand us."

"We have animals," Sean said. "But they don't speak."

"Oh, they surely do speak, at least here in Xanth. You just need someone like Grundy Golem to translate what they say."

"Who?"

"He's an obnoxious little creature who speaks all languages."

Meanwhile Nimby had completed his writing. Soon he passed the note back.

Chlorine took it and looked at the fine script. "I can read it!" she exclaimed. "I really can! I'm literate! I'm utterly thrilled!"

"What does it say?" David asked.

"Oh. Yes." She focused, and read the note aloud. " 'There are goblins along Lizard Lane who have set a trap for unwary travelers. It is an illusion barricade and detour that will lead folk into a trap, so the goblins can swarm in and capture them for stew.' ''

"Does that mean what I think it does?" Mary asked, horrified.

"Yes, if you think it means that goblins boil people alive," Chlorine said. "Goblins are mean creatures." She returned to her reading. " 'Because I must protect you from harm, and you will come to harm if the Mundanes fall into this trap, I must tell you how to avoid it. Do not honor the illusion; drive right through it without slowing. The goblins will not be able to attack this vehicle at speed.' ''

"Why couldn't they just throw some logs on the road?" Sean asked.

"Because this is an enchanted path," Chlorine explained. "The trolls guarantee that there are no dangers along it. Otherwise no one would use it. As it is, there is very little traffic, because the trollway is new and many folk are wary of trolls. Also, the trolls used to build only bridges. But they do know how to make good roads. So the goblins can't put up any real barricades. But if they trick us into leaving the protected path, then they can get us." She lifted her voice again. "Oh, thank you for warning us, Nimby!" she said. "I'm sorry I never thought to ask. After this, write me a note any time I need to know something."

The young man nodded. That was an interesting situation, Jim reflected, where Nimby seemed to know everything, but couldn't volunteer information; he had to be asked or instructed to.

Meanwhile, this was indeed a good route. "So this is Lizard Lane," Jim said. "What does that remind me of?"

"Alligator Alley," Sean said.

Jim nodded. "A parody of the world we know. So if I see a barricade and detour, I'm to ignore it, because it's illusion."

Nimby, beside him, nodded.

Jim shut up, but privately he doubted that they would encounter any such illusion.

The scenery was becoming more interesting or alarming, depending on one's view. Florida in the Everglades region was flat, but it was evident that Xanth had mountains; already Lizard Lane was wriggling between them like its namesake. There even seemed to be a volcano in the distance. In fact, the road seemed to be headed in that direction. Jim hoped it didn't erupt while they were in its vicinity.

There was also a bank of clouds looming to the northeast. That would be the vanguard of Happy Bottom, as they called Gladys here. Could there be anything to the conjecture about it sweeping up magic dust and becoming a dangerous magical storm? After what he had already seen, he was not prepared to deny it. So they were doing exactly what they needed to: driving full speed away from it, or at least around it.

Suddenly a barricade loomed up. How had he overlooked it before? The thing was huge, and extended right across the road. There was a big sign with an arrow pointing right: ROAD CLOSED—DETOUR. The detour road was clear, winding away toward a rest station. He barely had time to make it.

Jim trod on the brakes. The tires squealed as he swerved.

"No!" Chlorine cried. "It's illusion! Go through it!"

Jim had virtually no time to make his decision. She had warned him about this. A mistake could be fatal. He might regret this in an instant, but he trusted her. He straightened the wheel and stepped on the gas, heading for the collision. He barely missed the exit lane. He winced as the barrier loomed high and thick and devastating. They were going to crash!

Then they were through it, without contact. The road continued ahead, uninterrupted. Jim's pulse started its long trek back down toward the vicinity of normal. Chlorine—and Nimby—had been right.

"Gee," David said, awed. "Just like killer video."

That about covered it. Jim glanced at Nimby, who shrugged. Obviously his information had been good. He had been right about the illusion barrier, so probably was also right about the goblins.

In fact, there they were now: a horde of small, lumpy manlike figures just off the right of way, shaking their little fists. Some carried clubs, and some spears. Obviously they had intended no good. That had been one close escape—thanks to the timely warning.

"Nimby, if I may ask—how did you know about this ambush?" Jim asked. He wasn't sure the man would answer him, but Chlorine must have nodded, because Nimby began to write again. Soon he passed Jim a note.

Jim held it up by the steering wheel and read it. *I have knowledge of events around me that may affect the welfare of my companion. But I may not act on them myself; I can act only at her behest. The goblins were setting up the illusion barricade.*

Evidently so. And if Chlorine hadn't thought to ask, they would have fallen into the trap. What would Nimby have done then? Maybe he would have reverted to his dragon form and carried her away to safety—if Chlorine asked him. But the rest of them would probably have been out of luck.

Chlorine must have had a similar chain of thought. "Nimby—I have undertaken to guide these folk safely out of Xanth. If anything happens to them, I will have failed. I wouldn't like that at all. So please warn me if anything threatens them, as well as me. I mean, if it threatens them without threatening me, warn me, because that's part of me too—the decent part. If they are hurt, I will hurt too."

Nimby nodded.

"Thank you," Jim said.

Now they were approaching the volcano. Smoke was issuing from its aperture. "Is that thing active?" Jim asked.

"Yes, that's Mount Pinatuba," Chlorine said, peering ahead. "The last time it got angry, it blew out so much dust that it cooled all Xanth by a degree. But it doesn't blow its top if you don't insult it."

"Volcanoes care?" Sean asked. "How can they, when they aren't alive?"

"Don't speak loudly," Chlorine cautioned him. "It might hear you."

Indeed, that seemed to be the case, because the mountain shuddered and blew out a plume of gas.

"Oh, I didn't mean to disparage it," Sean said quickly. "I think it's a pretty impressive volcano."

The mountain subsided, and the plume drifted away in the wind.

"Everything cares," Chlorine said. "The inanimate can be very sensitive to slights. King Dor can talk to it, and it answers him. Most things aren't too smart, but they do have opinions. So we have to be careful not to insult them, unless we have reason."

"I guess so," he agreed, clearly impressed.

"Mom, can I use the privy?" Karen asked.

"It's full," Mary replied. "We need to stop where we can empty it."

She was right. The storm had confined them pretty much to the RV, and they hadn't been able to attend to certain details. "Chlorine, is there a rest stop along this road, nearby? One that isn't goblin-infested?"

Chlorine consulted with Nimby, who nodded. Soon he pointed to the side, and Jim swung onto an exit road. Sure enough, it led to a pleasant glade with a house in the center. He pulled up beside the house, and paused. "This *is* safe?" he asked Nimby.

The young man hesitated, then nodded.

The others opened the side door and piled out. But Jim delayed. He hadn't liked that hesitation. "Is there something you're not telling us, Nimby?"

Chlorine had gotten out with the others, so they were now alone in the vehicle. Nimby hesitated again, then began to write a note.

Jim waited, and in due course read the note: *Danger is looming close. Your family will learn it at this site, and be alarmed. This will make your journey more difficult.*

"What danger?"

The storm is stirring up bad creatures. They will frighten your children.

"But we will escape unharmed—if we follow your advice?"

Nimby nodded yes.

"Thank you." Jim hesitated, then spoke again. "I wish I could know more about you, Nimby, but I hesitate to inquire. Maybe some other time." Then he, too, got out of the vehicle.

The region was very nice. Karen had found a tree, and was picking a pie from it.

Jim stopped, doing a double take. A pie tree? Yes, so it seemed to be. So it really was true: pies grew on trees, here in the magic land of Xanth.

He went to the facilities, which were somewhat primitive but usable; what more was to be expected of trolls? The wind whistled through the cracks; there was no doubt the storm remained near.

Then he thought of the pets, and returned to the RV to see to them. He found Nimby communing with them; though they were normally somewhat shy with strangers, they seemed completely at ease with the odd young man.

As Jim approached, Nimby turned to face him. He wrote another note: *These creatures should not be caged. You must let them go.*

"We, do, at home," Jim said. "But we can't risk it in a strange place. Woofer would range the neighborhood, getting his nose into everything; Midrange would be chasing wild birds up trees; and Tweeter would fly into a bush and get hopelessly lost. We have been the route."

Nimby wrote another note. *They will not do any of these things. The magic is enhancing them; they understand that you mean well by them, and they will neither misbehave nor flee you.*

"How can you know this?" Jim asked skeptically. "This isn't a physical barricade, it's the nature of animals."

Another note. *I know thoughts too. It is part of my talent. I must know what is, so I can enable Chlorine safely to be what she wishes to be.*

That seemed to be true. "Look, Nimby, I don't want to get in trouble with my children. I'll ask them, and if they agree to let the pets go, we'll do it."

The children were already approaching, eating pies they had picked. Karen's hair was blowing across her face and into her pie, but she didn't seem to mind. Jim explained the situation.

"Try Woofer first," Sean suggested. "If he behaves, try Midrange."

So they freed the big dog. Woofer bounded out of the RV, went to a nearby tree, watered it, sniffed the air, and returned to the group, tail wagging. He was remarkably well behaved.

"You're not going to chase all over the region?" Jim asked the dog, surprised.

"Woof!" It was a plain negation.

David went to his pet. "Okay, Midrange. Your turn." He freed the cat.

Midrange went to a sandy spot and did his business. Then he, too, sniffed the air, and returned to the group.

So Karen freed Tweeter. The parakeet flew up to the nearest branch of a tree, dropped a dropping, and flew back to Karen's shoulder. The increasing wind made the bird's flight somewhat erratic, but he adjusted rapidly.

Jim shook his head, bemused. "Very well, pets. You have five minutes to do whatever you want to. Then return here, because we'll be on our way again."

Now the three creatures scattered. Woofer zoomed through the bushes, avidly exploring. Tweeter circled into the sky and disappeared. Midrange climbed a nut and bolt tree and was soon lost in the foliage. The three children followed them, as well as they were able.

"That's more like normal," Jim said. But he was impressed by the way the animals had waited for his word before acting on their impulses. If they actually returned on the schedule he had set, he would know that Nimby's judgment in such respects could be trusted.

Mary emerged, carrying a basket of comestibles. The wind did its best to blow her dress around, but she remained in control. She stacked the bag in the RV, then looked around. "Where are the pets?"

"Nimby said they would behave if we let them go, so we did."

She turned a quizzical glance on him, but did not comment.

Tweeter reappeared. He landed on Nimby's shoulder, tweeting at a great rate. Nimby wrote another note and gave it to Jim. *The storm has stirred up enormous birds who may be hostile. They are coming this way.*

Jim shrugged. "How big can a bird get?"

A huge shadow crossed the glade. They looked up to spot its source. It looked like an airplane, but it was silent. A big glider perhaps.

Then it screeched. It was a bird—as big as an airliner. Such a creature could probably pick up the whole RV in its talons, if it tried.

"Jim—" Mary said urgently.

"Right." He raised his voice. "Kids! Pets! Time's up!"

The summoned ones forged in from all directions. Chlorine, too reappeared, looking devastatingly lovely in her windblown state. But the boys for once weren't looking at her. "Get a load of that big bird!" David cried, pausing to stare.

"Get *in*," Mary said tightly.

They piled in. So did Jim, after checking to make sure all was in order. Nimby had told him that bad creatures would frighten the children; instead it seemed to be Mary who was frightened, perhaps with good reason.

He started the motor and moved onto the access road. There was no troll booth here, fortunately. They were able to proceed without delay.

The children peered out the windows at the monstrous bird. "That's a roc," Sean said, awed. "Fantasy's biggest bird. I never thought I'd see one."

Tweeter chirped. Jim glanced at Nimby, who wrote a note. *He says that isn't all.*

"What's *that?*" Karen cried.

"A dragon," Sean said. He wasn't joking; his tone was serious.

Now a huge and grotesque shape loomed in the sky before the vehicle. It was, indeed, a dragon. Karen screamed.

Jim looked at Nimby. "This road is protected?"

Nimby hesitated, and nodded.

"But there's a 'but,' " Jim said. "Let's have the qualifier."

The note came. *The winged monsters can not attack anything on the enchanted path directly. But they can pretend to. Do not be swayed.*

"And children can be frightened," Jim said. Nimby nodded.

"Yuck!" David cried. Karen screamed again. And this time Mary made a stifled exclamation of alarm.

Jim looked from one window to the next, all around, craning his neck, but didn't see anything. "This is an enchanted road," he reminded them. "Nothing can hurt us while we're on it."

"Physically," Mary responded tightly.

"What did you see?"

"It was a harpy," Chlorine said. "They are very ugly and nasty."

"A human-headed bird?" Jim asked. "What's so bad about one more fantastic—"

Then a filthy thing appeared before the windshield. It looked like a thoroughly soiled vulture, with the head and breasts of an old woman. "Ghaaa!" the dirty bird screeched before veering up over the vehicle. Her legs had glistening discolored talons. Jim, fearing a collision, and revolted by the sight, almost veered onto the shoulder of the road. Now he understood what had been bothering the others.

"Can this house move faster?" Chlorine asked.

"Yes. But with these crosswinds I haven't wanted to push it."

"I think you had better," the woman said, concerned. "The harpies may not be able to touch us directly, but if they think to lay any eggs on us—"

"Messy," Sean remarked.

"Not exactly. Their eggs explode. They might do damage."

Explosive eggs? Jim decided to accelerate, regardless of the wind.

There was an angry screech outside, as the harpies realized that their target was escaping. "They're coming after us, Dad!" David exclaimed. "And the dragons too."

Jim goosed the gas. As if to join in the fray, the wind increased, becoming more gusty. The vehicle swerved slightly, as Jim fought to keep it steady. He didn't like this kind of driving. Neither did the others; the kids were now uncomfortably silent.

But now they slowly forged ahead of the winged monsters. Jim was even able to ease up on the gas a bit. He appreciated Nimby's warning about the children being frightened. If they hadn't paused at the rest stop, they might have stayed safely ahead of the dirty birds. But that stop had been necessary. All the same, he hoped not to stop again if he could avoid it.

Nimby wrote another note. Jim took it and propped it before him so he could read it without taking his eyes off the road. *Soon you will come to the Gap Chasm, where you will have to stop for the ferry. It is protected, but perhaps not comfortable for you.*

"What's this gap chasm?" Jim asked between his clenched teeth.

"Oh, that's a big chasm that crosses Xanth," Chlorine answered. "It once had a forget spell on it, so no one ever remembered it was there, but that started disintegrating during the Time of No Magic, and now most folk do remember it. It's said to be very impressive."

"You haven't seen it?" Jim asked. He was learning not to take the features of Xanth terrain lightly.

"Not exactly," she said. "I never traveled far from my home village. Until this adventure, which is proving to be a great one. I did cross it, but by night; I really didn't get a good look into it. But of course, I had heard about the Gap Chasm. There's a big green dragon in the bottom who steams and eats any creatures it catches there.''

"Nimby says we'll take the ferry."

"Then maybe we won't have to get past the Gap Dragon," Chlorine said, relieved. "I don't know about the ferry, but if Nimby says it, it must be so."

But not comfortable for them, Jim remembered. He had better prepare the children. "Kids, we may have another difficult passage ahead. So brace yourselves." There was a moderate groan from behind. Obviously this magic land was losing some of its appeal.

Nimby pointed ahead. Jim didn't see anything, but wasn't about to ignore the signal. He slowed the RV. It was just as well, for in a moment he saw that the road ended abruptly at the brink of an awesome cleft in the ground. It seemed impossibly wide and deep. The last thing he would have wanted to do was zoom at speed off the lip into the depths.

$$\overline{5}$$

IMP ERIAL

Mary watched the dreadful chasm approach. Aspects of this strange realm had first been unbelievable, then disturbing; now they were becoming downright alarming. But she didn't want to express her burgeoning concern, lest it upset the children. They had already been frightened enough by the terrible flying creatures. Oh, how she hoped it didn't get any worse!

There was a small house at the brink. Another troll stood there. Jim fished in his pocket for more change. "We're taking the ferry," he told the troll, as if this were routine. She had to give him due credit: he had excellent poise in this most trying situation. And it was working; the creature accepted the coins and nodded.

But there was no boat, just the yawning deeps of the chasm. "Is it safe to get out here?" he asked Nimby. The odd man nodded. Mary knew that Nimby's help was invaluable, but she was privately afraid of him; there was something so utterly different about him as to be unclassifiable. She far preferred Chlorine, who, though not in her ordinary form, which was downright plain, was at least completely human.

But perhaps Jim and the children had some caution, for they elected to remain inside the RV, just in case the monsters should return. They watched as a cloud detached itself from a cloud bank above the chasm and drifted in their direction. It seemed to have a kind of foggy keel below.

Oh, no! Could this actually be their ferry? Mary kept her dark suspicion to herself, hoping it wasn't true.

But it was true. The cloud came to dock at the brink of the cliff, so that the road now led onto it. It looked solid—but how could that possibly be?

Jim looked at Nimby. She wished he wouldn't look to the strange man for guidance so much. "Onto that?"

Nimby nodded.

"Yes, this must be the ferry," Chlorine said. "When I crossed, I was carried by a fly-by-night."

Jim started the motor. "Jim!" Mary cried, truly alarmed.

He looked back. "Their advice has been good so far. Do we stop trusting them now?"

Mary swallowed, feeling—and surely looking—rather pale. "Drive very slowly."

He inched forward. The front wheels nudged onto the cloud surface, and held; it was as solid as it looked.

"Gee," David said, staring out and down.

"Do you believe in group nightmares?" Sean asked rhetorically.

Definitely! But Mary stifled her retort.

"Of course there are night mares," Chlorine said. "They bring the bad dreams to the people who deserve them. Don't they go to Mundania too?"

"Oh, sure," Karen said. "I get them all the time."

"Something tells me we're not speaking quite the same language," Sean said. "Are you talking about just dreams, Chlorine?" And that was another thing: Mary was quite uneasy about the lovely young woman's effect on the impressionable seventeen-year-old boy. Sean's eyes were attracted to her as if compelled by magnets; he tried to conceal his fascination, but Mary saw it. Chlorine was not trying to be flirtatious, but she didn't have to be. Her mere presence was more than sufficient. It was clear that she had not had a lot of experience being beautiful; she tended to show too much flesh, and it really was by accident. The girl was fairly innocent, which actually made it more awkward.

"The dreams and the mares," Chlorine replied. "And the Night Stallion, who governs them. They gallop out each night to carry their carefully crafted creations."

"Horses!" David cried. He, too, was all too much intrigued by the unconscious wiles of the woman. "They're real horses!"

"Of course," Chlorine said. "Except that you can't usually see them. You can't see Mare Imbri, either, though she comes by day with nice day dreams." Her eyes misted for a moment, perhaps seeing such a dream.

Well, at least their dialogue, and Chlorine's appearance, were distracting the children from the unbelievable thing that was happening.

The RV now had all four tires on the cloud. Jim set the brake and turned off the motor. "We are safely aboard the ferry," he announced.

"Aboard, anyway," Mary murmured tightly.

The cloud began to move. It carried them out over the depths of the chasm. Those depths were now darkening, for it was late in the day. The slanting sunlight illuminated the steep side, but then cut off before the bottom. The shadow was not impenetrable; there were trees and rocks in the lowest part.

"Oh, there's the Gap Dragon!" Chlorine cried, pointing.

They all peered down. There in the deep distance was a tiny worm-like thing wriggling along. But Mary was sure that it would be considerably more formidable up close. She was glad it *wasn't* close.

Karen came to climb into her father's lap. "Daddy, is this real?" she asked.

"I'm not sure," he admitted. "But I think we had better assume it is, until we get out of it." With that, Mary could agree emphatically. She no longer doubted the reality of this realm, and she most certainly wished to be out of it.

Then the wind rose again. "Oops—that looks like Fracto," Chlorine said.

"Who?"

"Fracto, the worst of clouds. He always comes to rain on picnics. Now he must be coming to mess up our crossing. I don't like this."

"A malign storm?" Mary asked, an ugly shiver running through her. She did see the cloud developing, and it looked just exactly like a thunderstorm. There were even jags of lightning projecting from it.

"Oooh, it's got a face!" Karen said.

The weird thing was that the child was right: there was a kind of pattern forming that did look like a vaguely human face. It had small foggy eyes and a big cruel mouth, with hugely expanding cheeks, as if it were taking in a breath so as to blow a blast of air at them.

"Oh, I hope the ferry is enchanted, so Fracto can't blow us away," Chlorine said.

"Ask Nimby," David suggested.

Chlorine smiled at the boy. "Of course. Why didn't I think of that?"

Nimby was already writing a note. He passed it back to her. " 'The ferry is enchanted,' " she read. "What a relief!"

She was no more relieved than Mary herself was. Presumably that meant that the storm could huff and puff and threaten, but couldn't actually "blow them away."

The storm was evidently going to give it a try, however. The face loomed up hugely, and the mouth exhaled. A stream of mist shot out, right toward the ferry cloud. But it turned aside, as if encountering a shield, and passed above them.

Fracto looked angry. Mary chided herself for personifying the cloud, but the expression was unmistakable.

"Boy, he's mad now," David said with a certain sinister relish. "He's going to get us if he can." He stuck his tongue out at the thing.

"Please don't do that," Mary said, experiencing a thrill of fear. "It's not polite."

"Awww." But this was routine. Thus Mary didn't have to admit that her main motivation was concern about making the storm furious. What were the limits of protective enchantment? She did not want to find out. And of course, she didn't want David getting into bad habits, anyway.

The cloud certainly tried. But all his huffing and puffing couldn't blow their house down. They continued their sanguine float across the chasm, and in due course came to the far brink. Karen returned to the back so her father could drive. "I could get to like trolls," Jim remarked as he started the motor and nudged the RV onto solid land.

Mary felt her tightness dissipating. They had made a safe crossing.

She had always been a bit nervous about air travel, and this had been a most precarious flight. "The trollway is the way to go," she agreed.

"Gee, that was great," David said.

Even Chlorine glanced at him, obviously not as pleased with the experience as he had been.

The RV got up speed. But now the day was dimming, and it was clear that they would be another day on the road before escaping Xanth. They could, of course, continue driving, except—

"Do we have enough gas?" Mary asked.

"No," Jim replied. "Less than half a tank left. We'll need another gas guzzler soon."

"Nimby—" Chlorine said.

The man wrote another note and passed it to Jim. "There is one ahead, but there's a problem," Jim said. "It's off the enchanted path, and there may be danger."

"That's all we need," Mary muttered. But they would have to have more gasoline. "What kind of danger?"

Nimby wrote another note. "A blobstacle course," Jim announced.

"A what?" Karen asked alertly. Jim seldom punned.

"That's how it's spelled: BLOB-stacle. I hesitate to inquire further."

"Oh, sure; there's one of those in a computer game I play," David said. "You just have to be ready to dodge fast."

"Dodge City," Sean said. He, in contrast, often punned.

Jim looked at Nimby. "Just *how* dangerous is a blobstacle course!"

The man made another note. Jim read it aloud: " 'In this moving house, not very dangerous if you avoid the blobs. But it can be disgusting.' " Jim glanced back. "Disgusting, I can handle. How about the rest of you?"

"Yeah!" David exclaimed.

Mary wasn't sure, but the thought of getting stranded without gas bothered her more. "We had better try it, dear," she said.

"You call him a deer?" Chlorine asked, surprised.

Mary smiled tiredly. "In a fashion."

Nimby signaled the turnoff, and Jim drove down the side road. Almost immediately the blobstacle course manifested: a series of huge discolored blobs sitting on and about the road. They looked like giant poisonous fungi, which might be what they actually were.

Jim slowed so as to steer around the first without going off the road, because the terrain on either side was rough. It seemed to vary from steep hill to bog: not something to stick a tire into. He got around the first, then made an S-turn to get around the second on the other side. So far so good. This at least was manageable, Mary thought.

"Bogy at three o'clock, high," Sean announced, peering up out a window.

Something was definitely looming there, rapidly approaching. "Oh, no," Chlorine said, peering with him. At any other time Mary would have objected to the way her bosom was nudging his shoulder. "That looks like a meatier shower."

"A meteor shower!" Jim said without taking his eyes from the road. "That sounds like a mundane phenomenon."

"No, it's another language problem," Chlorine said. "I have trouble hearing what you say, and you have trouble hearing what I say. Maybe it's because you didn't pass through the regular Interface when you came to Xanth. You can talk our language, but the nuances don't come through. That's MEAT as in flesh. Meatier shower. Those aren't completely dangerous, but they aren't much fun either."

"So it's going to rain hamburgers and hot dogs?" Sean asked.

"No, it will shower meat. Or am I missing another nuance?"

"Never mind." Sean continued to look out. Then something solid struck the roof of the RV. "Hey, just how big are the pieces?"

"All sizes," Chlorine said. "From gnat legs to boiled rocs. And they can be rotten, depending how long they have been traveling."

"Dad," Sean said. "Let's get the bleep out of here!" Then he looked surprised. "Bleep? That isn't what I said."

"How old are you?" Chlorine asked.

"Seventeen. Why?"

"That means you're still subject to the Adult Conspiracy. You can't say bad words until you pass eighteen."

Sean was astonished. "I can't?"

"Not in Xanth," she said firmly.

Mary suppressed her smile. This land of Xanth wasn't *all* bad!

"I can live with it," Karen said, not managing to damp down her own smile.

"Let me try," David said. "Bleep!" He looked surprised. "Hey, it's true! Bleep! Bleep!"

"Stop it," Mary said.

"But how could you tell what words I was trying to say?" he asked plaintively.

"I can read your lips—and your mind."

"Oh. Yeah." He was deflated.

There was a heavy dull thud on the roof of the RV. "Damn!" Jim muttered, and it almost seemed to Mary that the air in his vicinity turned slightly smoky. He goosed the engine, trying to get through the blobstacle course faster.

Something reddish brown splatted against a window. Dark juice oozed from it. "Ugh!" Karen cried. "What's that?"

"Part of a bleeping raw liver, I think," Sean answered.

"I'm going to be a vegetarian," she declared.

The vehicle slewed around another blob, an outer wheel riding up a bank, then squished through some stuff that surely wasn't ice slush. "There's a guzzler, Dad!" David called, pointing.

"Got it," Jim said. He slid to a halt by the creature, who looked exactly like the other one. "Got another pill, Mary?"

Mary dived into her purse. "Yes. Here." She fished out the bottle and opened it, spilling several pills. She picked one up and passed it to her husband.

He gave it to the guzzler. The creature swallowed the pill, then looked for the gas tank. But of course, it was capped. Jim started to open the door.

"No!" Mary cried. "You'll get hit by meat."

Jim hesitated, closing the door. "Somebody's got to take off the gas cap," he pointed out. "And not you or a child."

Chlorine perked up. "Nimby?"

Without a word, the young man opened his door and got out. A huge mass of something bounced in front of him. "He'll be hit!" Mary cried.

Chlorine pondered for half a moment. "Nimby, assume your natural form—with tough scales," she called.

Then the young man disappeared, to be replaced by the ugliest creature Mary could have imagined. It looked like a mule from the front, being mule-headed, and some kind of ancient dinosaur from behind, with huge overlapping scales. Furthermore, it was striped pink and green. The pink was halfway pretty, but the green was wretched. So this was the real nature of the creature! No wonder she had been uneasy about him.

But she reminded herself that he was doing them a favor. She watched as he made his four-footed way around the front of the RV. Chunks of meat struck his body, but did no apparent harm. His scales were indeed tough, as Chlorine had suggested. But rapidly getting badly soiled.

He came around to the gas tank and used his equine teeth to twist off the cap. The guzzler stuck in its tail, and the gas flowed. When the tank was evidently full, Nimby used his teeth again to put the cap back on and screw it tight. Then he trundled back around the RV. When he reached his door, he reverted to man-form. Just in time to get hit by a big blood blister from the sky. It didn't seem to hurt him, but he was completely soaked.

"Get in before you get killed!" Mary screamed, appalled.

The man opened the door and climbed in. "Oooo, ugh!" Karen said with a certain relish. "What a stink!"

She was right. Nimby now smelled of rotten guts.

"Can't be helped," Jim said, starting the motor.

"Come back here," Mary told Nimby. "I'll see if I can clean you up." She felt somewhat guilty, because he had gotten splatted while doing them a favor.

Nimby came back. The children drew away from him, turned off by the sight and smell of him, but Mary had cleaned up messes before. "We'll have to wash you off and give you some clean clothes," she said in motherly fashion. "Do you know how to use our facilities?"

He nodded.

"Then do so. Pass your clothing out, and I'll pass fresh things in."

He did so. Relieved, Mary set about a search for clothing. "He'll have to use some of yours," she told Sean. "He's about your size. It's in a good cause."

"For sure," he agreed wryly.

She dug out a shirt, jeans, underwear, and an old pair of sneakers. Then when the lavatory door opened, she exchanged them for the sodden things Nimby had been wearing. It was hard to breathe with the stench of them. She bundled them up and dumped them in a basin for laundering.

Meanwhile Jim was navigating the blobstacle course back to the main road. It seemed easier now; the meatier shower was abating, and the blobs seemed to be shrinking. Apparently even bad things didn't last long, in Xanth. Soon the road cleared, and they were back on the main haul. That was another considerable relief.

Nimby emerged, garbed correctly. Now he looked exactly like a barely-beyond-teenager. Sean's clothing fit him well enough.

"Let me fix your hair," Mary said. She fetched a brush, and trained his wet hair back in a conventional part.

"Gee, he could pass for one of us," David said. "I mean, like one of the family."

"Say, do you want to be my brother?" Karen asked him.

Nimby looked blank. "They're teasing you," Mary said. "You don't have to be part of anyone's family." She realized as she spoke that her attitude toward the young man had changed. She had been wary of him because she didn't understand him; now she had seen his natural form, she understood him better. He was surely somewhat uncomfortable among human beings, and she wanted to alleviate that. Because he was helping them significantly. Of course, she knew it was because he was Chlorine's companion, doing what Chlorine wanted, and Chlorine had been assigned to get the family safely through Xanth. Still, she appreciated what he was doing.

She put away the brush and adjusted his collar. She realized that he was looking at her. "I'm sorry," she said, embarrassed. "I'm so used to taking care of my family, I just automatically do these things. I know you're not a child."

Nimby smiled. Then he found his pad—actually it just seemed to appear in his hand, along with the pencil—and wrote a note. She noticed with surprise that he actually held the pencil still and moved the notepad against it to do the writing. He tore off the sheet and gave it to her.

Thank you for your attitude. No one has treated me like a person

*before, except Chlorine. I am glad to be thought of as part of your
family.*

"Why, thank you, Nimby," Mary said, pleased. She gave his hand
a little squeeze. Then she returned to her seat.

"If you want to be family, you have to help entertain the kid,"
Karen said. "Come here to the table, Nimby, and play solitaire."

"No, you don't have to do that," Sean said. "Don't let her push
you around."

"What is solitaire?" Chlorine asked.

"It's a card game," Karen said. "Actually there are many kinds,
and some can be played by two or three people at once. I'll show
you."

Sean and David moved out, and Chlorine and Nimby joined Karen
at the table for instruction in solitaire. Soon they were deep into it.
Chlorine had the usual miscues of a beginner, but Nimby seemed to
be a natural player. Either he was extremely smart, or his general
awareness of things acquainted him with the identities of the hidden
cards. Or maybe both.

How could a donkey-headed dragon be so talented? Mary wasn't
sure, but suspected that the relationship of animals to humans was
different in Xanth. Animals were smarter here. That business with
their own pets was eerie; it was just as if they had developed almost
human intelligence and restraint. And Tweeter had warned them about
the approach of the flying monsters, back at the rest stop. Or had he?
Nimby had claimed to listen to the bird, and written a note. It could
have been Nimby doing it.

It became important for Mary to know. The drive was quiet now,
as Sean accompanied Jim up front, and both Nimby and Chlorine
were involved in Karen's game. David was watching the game, about
to get involved himself. So she should be able to do a little experi-
mentation without attracting attention.

She went back to where the pets were. "Woofer," she said, and
the dog perked up. She unsnapped his leash, freeing him. "How smart
are you, now?" she asked quietly.

Woofer wagged his tail.

"Suppose I tell you to look out the left window?"

The dog looked out the left window.

Mary controlled her reaction. "Suppose I ask you to open Twee-ter's cage?"

Woofer turned to the bird cage, set teeth and paw to the catch, and worked it open.

"Tweeter, suppose I tell you to go perch on Karen's head?"

The bird flew out and landed on the girl's head. Karen was so preoccupied she didn't notice.

"Midrange."

The cat sat up and gazed at her.

"Suppose I ask you to roll over?" This was not a trick the cat had been taught.

Midrange rolled over.

"You animals do understand me, don't you?"

The cat nodded.

"If we treat you three with the respect due intelligent and disci-plined entities, will you behave accordingly?"

Midrange nodded.

"Then we shall do so. Do you know why you are now so smart?"

The cat shook his head.

"I think it is because of the magic of this land. It seems that magic dust is getting stirred up, and causing numerous disruptions, including enhancement of the intelligence of animals." She was speaking in a deliberately advanced manner, testing the limits. "Does that make sense to you?"

Midrange considered, then slowly nodded.

"But as you know, there are also some formidable dangers here," Mary said, surprised by how readily she was accepting this new re-lationship with their pets. "So I hope you will remain close by, when we go out of the RV, and will also warn us, as Tweeter did, when the situation warrants."

Midrange agreed again, then wandered off to find a suitable place to catnap.

Mary returned to her seat. She had satisfied herself that Nimby had not been faking it; he had understood bird talk, and the bird *had* talked.

Now Mary realized that night had fallen. She had been distracted by her investigation and not realized it. They had spoken of driving through the night, but now she was not at all certain this was wise. She didn't want Jim suffering deadly fatigue, when any accident could strand them in a really strange situation. "Dear, maybe we should look for a place to stay the night," she called.

"Is it safe to stop that long?" he asked.

Chlorine looked up from the card game. "Is it safe, Nimby?"

Nimby wrote a note: *This vehicle has outdistanced the storm. It is safe to pause until dawn.*

"Good," Mary said. She was catching on to the way of these things. "Where is a good place to stay? A camping park with some facilities would suffice, but I think I'd rather find a hotel where we can really unwind for a few hours."

There is an imp settlement near. The imps are courteous to visitors from afar, if the right village is chosen.

"Then that is where we should stop," Mary decided.

Soon Nimby indicated a side road, and Jim took it. It led to a sign saying IMP OSSIBLE, with an arrow to the right, but Nimby indicated that this wasn't the right one. A little farther was a sign saying IMP RISON, with an arrow to the left, but it seemed this wasn't right either. Mary was inclined to agree; she wouldn't want to stay at either Impossible or Imprison, considering the literal tendencies of this land. Finally a sign said IMP ERIAL, and this one was good. Mary was glad; Imperial had a quality ring to it.

The village was small but elegant. The jungle had been cleared back somewhat, and there were neat little gardens and nice little houses. In fact, everything about this community seemed small-scale.

Following Nimby's indications, they drew up to the largest building in the village. Its structure suggested that it was an enormous hotel, but it was only about two human stories tall.

Though it was night, tiny figures were scurrying about carrying torches. Each was under one foot tall—the females significantly under. But apart from that they appeared to be fully human. They were carrying things from their little houses into the forest.

"What are they doing?" Chlorine asked.

Nimby wrote a note. *They are carrying their gems to the safety of a deep cave.*

"Oh, because of the approaching storm," Chlorine said. "That makes sense."

They got out of the RV, stretching their legs after the long confinement. Woofer, Tweeter, and Midrange joined them, perfectly behaved. The hotel door opened and a man and a woman emerged. He looked to be in his seventies, by the human scale, and she in her fifties. "Hello, huge folk," the woman said, her voice clear despite her tiny size. "I am Quieta Imp, and this is my father, Imp Ortant. We are the leaders of this community, so we run the hospitality domicile. Do you wish to accept our hospitality?"

There was a pause. Then Mary stepped in. "Yes we do, please. But we—we're not sure your building is big enough for us." She glanced meaningfully at the foot-high main door.

"Oh, it has an accommodation spell," Quieta said. "It will do. Come in."

Somewhat dubiously, Mary stepped forward. As she approached the building, it seemed to shimmer, and suddenly it was human size. Quieta and Ortant Imp were human size too.

"What happened?" Mary asked, startled.

"You have been accommodated," Quieta said. "See, the others in your party haven't, yet."

Mary turned. There behind her stood several giants, thirty to forty feet tall. Even their animals were terrifyingly large. "Oh!" she said, feeling faint.

Quieta stepped up to take her arm. "I'm sorry; I didn't realize how new this must be to you. Are you by any chance Mundane?"

"Yes," Mary said faintly.

"The spell is harmless. It merely makes the various parties seem to be the same size. So we are about two and a half times as big, and you are about one two and a halfth as big, or small, as the case may be. But those outside the spell region don't see that, and to them we all look impishly small, while to us they look humanly big."

"To be sure," Mary agreed, not able to argue whatever point there might be.

Now Chlorine stepped forward. She shimmered, and became Mary's size. "Aren't accommodation spells wonderful?" she asked rhetorically. "I've never been in one before, but I love it. I thought

they were only for when folk of quite different sizes wished to summon the stork.''

"To what?'' Mary exclaimed, shocked. But she realized that in this
land of magic, storks might be literal, and that interbreeding of humans and imps might indeed be possible. "I mean, I'm surprised,
that's all.''

Chlorine beckoned the others, and one by one they stepped in,
including the animals, who seemed almost as surprised as the humans.
"Gee,'' Karen said, summing it all up.

"Come in,'' Quieta said. "I will show you to your rooms while
my father prepares the evening meal.''

They followed her to an ornate staircase that wound up to a sump-
tuous second story. Quieta opened the door on a truly splendid suite.
"Will this do?'' she asked somewhat timidly. "It has four bedrooms
and lavatories, with facilities for your animal companions.''

"But we can't afford anything like this!'' Mary protested.

"Afford?''

"What does this princely suite cost?''

"Cost?''

"Imps don't charge for their hospitality,'' Chlorine murmured.

"But we can't accept this!'' Mary said.

Quieta looked embarrassed. "I'm sorry; I thought it would be ad-
equate. I will try to find better rooms for you.''

"No, no!'' Mary said. "It's not that. It's that this suite is so fancy,
we don't have any right to take it, especially not without paying.''

"But you are guests,'' Quieta said.

Mary looked at Chlorine. "This is the way of it? All this—with
no charge? Just because we stopped here?''

"Yes. I thought you knew. Of course, if we had stopped at Rison,
it would have been much less comfortable.''

"Imp-rison,'' Sean murmured appreciatively.

"Then it's all right?'' Quieta asked hopefully.

"Oh my dear, it's wonderful,'' Mary said. "I simply had no idea
it would be so fancy. We—we are used to much simpler accommo-
dations.''

"We imps take pride in our hospitality,'' Quieta said, evidently
relieved. "Will an hour be enough time before supper?''

"Yes, of course," Mary said. "And thank you, Quieta. Thank you so much. This is really nice."

"You are welcome," the imp lady said, and departed.

They explored the suite. There was a huge master bedroom, and three smaller ones, and a sitting room with several couches, and an alcove with what looked like dog food, cat food, and birdseed, as well as the two bathrooms. The master bathroom had a tub the size of a small swimming pool, while the other had a shower. "This is just so amazing," Mary breathed. "Just to be hospitable."

The three pets were waiting expectantly. Mary realized why. "Certainly—indulge yourselves," she said. They immediately went to the pet nook and started eating.

"How about us?" David asked. "You adults have the master bedroom with the great bath, and Chlorine and Nimby have the first regular bedroom, but how do us kids split the other two?"

Mary considered. "If one of you wants to sleep on a couch in the sitting room, you can all have rooms to yourselves. But one of you will have to share a bathroom with the one on the couch. Can you work that out between you?"

All three nodded enthusiastically.

"Then let's try to be ready for supper within the hour." She glanced at Chlorine. "I didn't think—you do wish to share a room with Nimby? If not—"

"That's fine," Chlorine said. "Come on, Nimby—you still have some of that meatier shower stink. I'm going to scrub you clean." She led the young man to their bedroom.

Sean looked after them. "I wish *I* could get scrubbed clean by a creature like—" Then he realized that his mother was looking at him, and cut off, somewhat (but perhaps not sufficiently) embarrassed.

Jim and Mary entered the master bedroom and closed its door. "Who first?" she asked, glancing at the enormous tub.

"What, not together?" he asked.

"You think this is our honeymoon?" she inquired archly.

"In this suite, it feels like it."

He was right. "Together," she agreed. "But don't get fresh." She went to run the water.

This turned out to be interesting. There was only one tap, but when she turned it on, the water came out exactly the right degree of hot. The two towels were small, but when she touched one with her wet hand, it dried the hand immediately. There was one tiny bar of soap, shaped like a stone—obviously a soapstone—but when she dipped it in the water it made a big fluff of scented bubbles. There just might be some magic here. Well, she was getting used to that, in this magic land, and this was one of the first really pleasant surprises it had had for her.

Soon they were both in the tub, scrubbing each other, and it was wonderful. Jim did get fresh, and she allowed it, because it did indeed feel like their honeymoon. "If every day were only like this," she murmured.

"I think we have been selling Xanth short," he agreed. "It's like a powerful new computer program: at first you run afoul of all its traps, and they mess you up and drive you crazy, but then you start getting really into it, and you find out how nice it can be."

"Mmmm," she agreed luxuriously.

After that, things got somewhat out of hand, but it was worth it. Just so long as none of the children barged in on them.

They were ready by the time the hour was up, bright and clean and in fresh clothing. So were the children, amazingly. And the pets, who evidently intended to join them downstairs.

"But—" Mary started. Then she remembered how advanced the animals had become. "Of course." The others glanced at her in surprise, but didn't comment.

Quieta appeared promptly. "Right this way," she said.

They found themselves in a very nice dining chamber sized just about right for their party. Quieta went into the adjacent kitchen and emerged pushing a cart with a number of platters and pitchers. These turned out to have an assortment of meats, vegetables, pastries, breads, and beverages. "I would serve you, but I am not sure of Mundane tastes, so I brought a selection that you could choose from yourselves," she explained. "I shall be happy to answer questions about what may be unfamiliar to you."

Sean reached for a pitcher. "This looks familiar. What is it?"

"Boot rear."

He smiled. "Sure." He poured himself a cupful. He took a good gulp—and jumped halfway out of his chair. "Hey!"

Karen tittered. "Boot rear! I get it. Serves you right."

Mary eyed what looked like something scavenged from the meatier shower. "What is this, please?"

"That is steak, from a steak-out tree."

Mary decided to risk it, and was rewarded with an excellent entrée. The others followed suit, and did seem to enjoy the strange meal. They finished with eye scream, which turned out to resemble screaming eyeballs but tasted much like the confection they knew in Mundania.

As they finished, Imp Ortant returned. "I shall try to entertain you, while Quieta does the dishes," he said.

"Maybe we should help with the dishes," Mary said, feeling guilty again because they weren't paying for this.

"No, the spells wouldn't work for you. How may I best help you to enjoy yourselves?"

"I for one would like to know a bit more about your village, your society," Jim said. "I haven't encountered imps before." David and Karen looked as if they would rather watch TV, but Mary stifled them with a warning glance.

Ortant, however, saw and understood the glance. "Perhaps the children would prefer to remain and watch the magic mirror," he suggested. "While I give the adults a tour of our village."

"Magic mirror?" Karen asked, her interest suddenly revving up.

The imp went to a large mirror at the end of the chamber. "Mirror, would you like to entertain two Mundane children?" he asked.

A mouth appeared on the glass. It seemed to be a reflection, but there was nothing it could be reflecting from. "Why not? I'll show them the Magic Tapestry of Castle Roogna."

"A tapestry?" David asked, disappointed.

"The Tapestry shows any scene of Xanth you wish to see," Ortant explained. "Most children find it quite interesting. Of course, it won't violate the Adult Conspiracy."

"Awwww," they said together.

"But it does show historical battles where dragons chomp people, men throw women into pits, and blood flows in rivers."

"Gee," they said together again, their interest restored. Mary winced; apparently Xanth had the same standards as Mundania in this respect.

David and Karen set chairs before the mirror. "Let's see that river of blood," David said.

The mirror showed a country scene with a bright red river flowing in the manner of a normal brook.

"Aw, that's just colored water," Karen said.

The mirror's reflect-mouth appeared, superimposed on the scene. "Why don't you ask me to have the Tapestry trace up to the source of that river, where the blood is spurting from a wounded giant?"

"Yeah!" they said together.

Quieta arrived with a plate of pastries shaped like little vanilla wheels with chocolate spokes. "Here are punwheel cookies for you to eat while you watch," she said.

Mary masked her sigh. It seemed the children would be quite satisfied.

"Right this way," Ortant said, walking to the door. Jim, Mary, Sean, Chlorine, and Nimby followed him. Mary hoped the tour wouldn't be as boring as the children had feared. But they had to take it, as a matter of courtesy, to reward the imps for their hospitality. With luck it wouldn't be long; then they could settle down for a night of blissful rest.

The three pets came too. That made Mary think of something. "Woofer—maybe stay with the children?" she asked.

The dog cocked his head at her, then nodded and turned back. He was Sean's pet, but he would guard the children.

"Thank you," Mary murmured, relieved. She had no reason to be suspicious, but she did not feel easy about leaving the children entirely alone among strangers. They would come to physical harm, literally, over the dog's dead body. And Woofer would probably enjoy the exploration of the river of blood too.

6

DECISION

M eow!'' Midrange said imperatively.
Sean smiled and bent to pick up the cat. Naturally Midrange didn't want to walk when he could ride. Since Sean's dog was staying with David, David's cat would take over Sean.

Then Tweeter flew up to perch on Sean's hair. That surprised him. Karen had managed to impress on Midrange that any bite out of the bird would swiftly lead to a worse bite out of the cat, so Tweeter was tolerated unmolested. But the two had not been exactly bosom buddies. Now, with the magic, they seemed to be getting along better. And all three animals had become eerily smart. So maybe Tweeter figured the cat would understand his concerns better than human beings would.

They stepped outside the dining room, and outside the hotel. The wind was rising; it buffeted them. Imp Ortant lifted a lantern from a hook beside the door and strode out into the street.

"Uh, what about the accommodation spell?" Sean asked the imp, who now looked exactly like an old human man. "I mean, if we leave the hotel, won't we revert?"

Ortant lifted the lamp, which cast its glow more widely. "There is a duplicate accommodation spell built into this magic lamp," he explained. "As long as you remain in its light, the spell will hold. This is best, because we shall be going into some places way too small for normal human folk."

So they had it figured. Sean returned to his normal interest, which for the past day or so had been Chlorine. She was the sexiest woman he had encountered. Oh, sure, he had caught that glimpse of her when she reverted to her normal state, but that wasn't the way she looked *now*, so who cared? Consider Nimby, who had turned out to be a mule-headed dragon. Talk of damsels and dragons! Nobody seemed to be having any problem accepting Nimby as a man—in Sean's clothes, yet!—so why should he, Sean, have any with Chlorine? Nobody was very pretty on the inside, anyway; it was all blood and guts and brain tissue. By the time Chlorine reverted to her regular dull appearance, he'd be back in Mundania anyway. So he might as well enjoy it while he could.

Sean slowed his pace a trifle, so that he fell back in the group, and Nimby and Chlorine caught up to him. Now if she would just walk in front of him—but maybe that would come. He had caught enough glimpses of her bosom and thighs to keep him floating for some time; she evidently wasn't used to the fancy clothing she wore now, and didn't realize quite how much it tended to show. He sure wasn't going to tell her!

Tweeter cheeped faintly in his ear. "Eyes left." At least that was what it almost sounded like. Startled, he looked left—and Chlorine was moving close to him.

"Those are nice pets," she said, her voice dulcet. "Was Tweeter speaking to you?"

"Yeah. He told me something lovely was coming up on my left."

She smiled. "Thank you, Tweeter. I think you're lovely too."

The bird did a little dance of ecstasy, fluffing his feathers.

"Sean, you're the first young man I've met, since Nimby made me beautiful," she said. "I think I am practicing on you, to see how loveliness works. I hope you don't mind."

"I—you—you practice all you want," Sean said, startled by her candor. How he wished he could get her alone and do some real practicing!

"You see, all my life men have scorned me, because I was plain," she continued. "So I really don't know how to act around them. I can't practice on Nimby, because he's not really a man. Please let me know if I bother you."

"I don't think you could bother me if you tried," he said, feeling light-headed.

She laughed. "I could in my normal state. But I had Nimby make me nice as well as beautiful, and smart. But intelligence doesn't substitute for experience."

"That's for sure." The possibilities were setting his pulses pounding. She *wanted* romantic experience.

But now they had arrived somewhere. Just when it had been getting really interesting. Too bad.

They entered what seemed like an ordinary building. "This is where we prepare the raw stones," Ortant said. "Atient here is a very fast worker." Sure enough, the imp man was working with blinding speed, doing things to a collection of pebbles on his table. The gems were of several colors, and seemed to glow, or actually to be burning. "These are safe fire stones, used for making fires that will not get out of control."

"Sapphires," Mom murmured. She had a good eye for gems.

"What are these?" Chlorine asked, indicating several red gems that looked like little letter *L*'s and were rapidly spinning.

"Spinels," Ortant said. "They are valued for their flashing color."

They left the building and passed a mound covered with gravestones. An imp was using a scoop to pull shining bits of stone from it. "This is a die mound," Ortant said. "It is not safe to walk on it unless you wish to die. Then you never leave it."

"Diamonds are forever," Dad remarked.

"Fortunately Robable is able to harvest stones from it without getting caught," Ortant said.

"Improbable," Sean muttered, catching on.

They passed a garden with yellowish rods growing from the ground. An imp was rubbing them, collecting something in a bag. "Goldenrods," Ortant explained. "Ractical is harvesting their pollen, which we use to powder other jewelry with golden glitter."

They passed a glade where many bees were buzzing. Several of them buzzed the party threateningly, but didn't actually sting. Midrange batted at those that approached Sean, and Tweeter flapped his wings with annoyance. "What's the matter with them?" Mom asked, irritated. "Why are they so pointlessly hostile?"

"They are rude bees," Ortant explained. "Ede will stop them." And an imp walked out toward the bees, his very presence seeming to hold them back.

"Imp Ede rude bees—impede rubies," Sean murmured.

"You're so clever," Chlorine said, batting an eyelash. She was improving with practice; he felt foolishly flattered.

They came to a pool where another imp was working with a bucket shaped like an *O*. "Rovise is using the O-pail to try to dip out the matriarch of pearls."

"Opal—mother-of-pearl," Sean said. Chlorine batted another lash. He felt twice as clever as he was.

Then they came to a pen in the water where several fish-tailed equines were confined. One neighed. "Oh—sea horses!" Chlorine exclaimed, thrilled.

"In a corral—coral," Sean said, working it out.

"Ose is doing his best to tame the horses in time," Ortant said.

"In time for what?" Dad asked.

"In time to save them from the magic storm that is approaching. Our wares are very sensitive to changes in ambient magic; something we might not notice could cause them to go wrong. We need to clear the entire village by tomorrow night. That is why we are working so hard tonight; we need to complete our work and get our things to safety." He frowned. "Unfortunately these horses are ill at ease now, and not cooperating well."

Chlorine touched the water with one finger. "No wonder—this water is germy."

"Yes, the storm is polluting it with weird forms of life. But there's nothing we can do."

"I can fix it," she said. She touched the water again.

"But aren't you poisoning it?" Sean asked anxiously.

"Yes. But not so much it will hurt the horses. It will just wipe out the germs. Then my poison will fade, and leave it pure for a while."

Sean did a double take. "Of course—chlorine—the chemical—we use that in Mundania! To clear our water."

Ortant was surprised. "You poison your water to clear it? I thought there was no magic in Mundania."

Sean laughed. "It does seem crazy, but it works."

The horses already seemed to be doing better. "We thank you," Ortant said to Chlorine. "We never thought of purifying the water by poisoning it."

They moved on, and Ortant showed them other aspects of the imp operation.

"But—" Mom said, troubled. "But shouldn't you and your daughter be helping in this effort, instead of—of tending to us?"

"But you are guests," Ortant said. "We must see to your comfort."

Mom did not seem quite satisfied, but she said no more.

Ortant brought them to a burning portal. "This is the gate of fire through which we must take our wares to safety," he said. "Ressed will show us the vaults."

"Fire agate," Sean murmured. "Impressed."

"I'm impressed," Chlorine murmured. "You are just so, so clever!" She was beautiful anyway, but by this time she would have looked lovely regardless of her appearance.

"So are you," he replied.

"Oh!" she said, caught by surprise by his return compliment. Then she smiled. "It works both ways, doesn't it?"

"Yes. That's what courtship is all about," he said, feeling very wise.

"Jim . . ." Mom said with quiet urgency.

"Perhaps we have seen enough," Dad said, picking up on Mom's mood. "We should get a good night's sleep."

"Certainly, if you wish," Ortant said. "I shall lead you back forthwith."

Sean knew that they didn't want to take more of the imp's time, when it was clear that the village had such a lot to do. He understood the sentiment. He also knew that the notion of children growing up and finding love made Mom nervous. She thought no one ever crossed the line to adulthood, after her own generation.

As they traced their route back to the hotel, Chlorine expressed her curiosity. "I hadn't realized that imps made so many gems. I thought that Jewel the Nymph handled that."

"Imps make all the gems," Ortant said proudly. "From the sparkles of light in morning dew to the most enduring treasure. Where do you think the nymph obtains her supply?"

"I had thought it was from a barrel that never emptied."

"Because we imps are constantly working to replenish it. We fashion the gems; the jewel nymphs place them for others to find. So it has ever been."

"Oh, I'm so impressed!" she exclaimed. "I mean, not the imp, but the surprise, the awe of your accomplishment—"

"I understand," Ortant said, looking pleased. It was clear that her art was working on him, too.

They arrived at the hotel. David, Karen, and Woofer remained engrossed by the magic mirror. Mom rousted them out and packed everyone upstairs.

After a flurry of preparations for the night, the others were in their bedrooms and Sean was in the suite's living room with the animals. He stretched out on the largest couch, discovering how tired he was. He would lull himself to sleep with mental pictures of Chlorine innocently undressing. He knew their relationship wasn't real, but it was one hell, or rather, heaven, of an illusion, and he wanted to savor it while he could.

All three pets approached him. "Oh, you want to share my bed?" he asked. "Well, okay, but don't bleep on it." He noted with bemusement that he still wasn't able to say "poop," that evidently being on the proscribed list for his age.

"Seean," Tweeter chirped.

Sean glanced at the bird. "I swear, it sounded as if you said my name."

Tweeter nodded. "Taalk," he chirped.

"You want to talk to me? This is getting hard to believe."

"Taaalk," Midrange meowed.

"Rrryess," Woofer agreed.

"But I'm making the effort to believe," Sean said. "What is it so important that you guys have to tell me?"

The three seemed at a loss. "Aaaask," Woofer said.

"Oh, you mean it's hard for you to talk human, so I'd better play twenty questions?"

All three nodded.

"Okay. Can I take it for granted that you three remain friendly to our family, despite your new intelligence, and wish us no harm?"

They nodded. "Um, maybe we can simplify this. How about a single woof, meow, or tweet for yes, two for no, and three for I'd better do some more asking about that one?"

There was a small chorus of single sounds.

"Maybe we'd better have a single spokespet," Sean said, smiling. "I think Tweeter makes a single sound most readily, so I'll address him, but if anyone else has something to say, cut in." He pondered a moment. "Is there some danger to us?"

"Tweet."

"Does it relate to the storm we're trying to outdistance—Happy Bottom?"

"Tweet."

"Well, we're going to get moving on north in the morning. Isn't that good enough?"

"Tweet tweet."

"How about the crack of dawn, and gobble breakfast while driving?"

"Tweet."

"Okay, I'll go tell Dad now. He won't be asleep yet." Sean started to get up.

"Tweet tweet tweet."

"Um." Sean considered again. "Something more I should know about this?"

"Tweet."

"Now, let me figure. You guys must've learned something we humans didn't. But you were with us all the time—two of you with me, one with the kids. So it can't be—say! Was it from before? Did you talk with other animals somewhere along the way?"

"Tweet."

"And they know something the humans don't."

"Tweet tweet tweet."

"Okay, that *we* don't. How about the imps? They know?"

"Tweet."

"Which is why they're getting the bleep out of here. The storm. But we already knew about that."

"Tweet tweet tweet."

"Something more about the storm. Apart from stirring up things and maybe blowing us away. But I can't figure what."

"Woimps," Woofer said.

"Sure, I'm a wimp. But I still can't figure this out."

"Woof woof."

"Oh, I'm not a wimp? Then what were you saying?"

"Meoimp," Midrange said.

"Oh, the imps! They're friendly, aren't they?"

"Tweet."

"And the storm means trouble for them too. Because of the magic dust it's stirring up, which can bring madness when there's too much. So they are clearing up and out."

"Tweet tweet tweet."

"More on that." Sean pondered again. "They know what they're doing, don't they? They're on schedule?"

"Tweet tweet."

"Oho! They're not going to make it in time?"

"Tweet."

"Because we delayed them by taking up their time and effort?"

The three pets exchanged glances. "Tweet tweet," Tweeter said doubtfully.

"But we *might* have? At least we made it rougher for them by making a distraction when they're desperately busy?"

"Tweet."

"Now I got it. So is there any way we can help?"

"Tweet."

"By like maybe carrying things—say! If we stepped out of accommodation, we'd be huge compared to them, and could carry a whole lot for them. Then they'd get done in time."

"Tweet."

"I'll ask Dad." This time there was no protest as he got up. He went to the master bedroom and knocked on the door. In a moment Dad opened it. "What is it, Sean?"

"The pets told me: the imps aren't going to get their stuff all moved in time, maybe because we delayed them. We could maybe help them—"

"We'll inquire," Dad said. He stepped out, and they walked out of the suite and downstairs. The pets came along.

There was no one there. "They must be out working," Sean said. "And they never said a word to us."

"We'll find them." They went out the main door, and Dad took the magic lantern. "We need to stay accommodated for this, I think."

They had hardly started down the path before Quieta appeared. Her apron was mussed and her hair coming loose, as if she had been hectically busy. "Oh, I'm sorry! I must have neglected you," she cried. "What do you need?"

"We are concerned that we have delayed you at a critical time," Dad said. "Can we help you to do what you have to do, before we move on?"

She shook her head. "That is a very courteous thought. But though we could use your assistance, it would be at too great a cost. You have just time to get clear of Xanth before the dust intensifies, if you start at dawn and do not stop. I used the mirror to talk with the Good Magician, who is always correct. You must not delay at all. If you remained to help us, you would be caught, and then you would not be able to escape Xanth. You might be trapped here a very long and bad time. We would be terrible hosts if we let that happen."

"Maybe we could help now, at night, before dawn," Sean suggested.

"No, I do not mean to disparage your effort, but you are Mundanes. You would blunder in the dark, and be of no use. Only by daylight could you help, and that is when you must be gone."

Dad looked at Sean. "I don't like this, but I think we had better depart on schedule."

"I guess so," Sean agreed reluctantly. "The best thing we can do for these good folk is to get the bleep out of their way."

Dad turned back to Quieta. "We apologize for delaying you. We shall depart at the crack of dawn. Don't take any trouble for our breakfast or anything; we'll move out on our own."

"Thank you," she said. "But there is food you can take. Woofer knows where it is. I wish you well on your journey." She turned and went back down the path.

"I feel like a heel," Sean muttered.

"So do I," Dad agreed. "But it's the best we can do." They returned to the hotel.

Sean settled down on the couch again, and the pets settled on or around him. He closed his eyes, and saw a mental picture of Chlorine wearing a filmy nightdress. Now, if he could just get to sleep with her beside him . . .

Before dawn the parents were up and knocking on doors. Sean never knew how they did it, but they were always alert when they needed to be. Chlorine looked sleepy but still lovely, while Nimby looked the same as ever: neutral. While the others were blearily getting washed and dressed, Dad started loading things into the RV and Mom went to the kitchen with Woofer to fetch the food left there for them. Sean went from room to room and collected the used sheets for the laundry, trying to save Quieta that much effort. He still felt guilty.

He took the pets out for a quick walk so they could do their business. It was weird stepping out of the accommodation spell; suddenly they were all giants, beside the dollhouse hotel. He took the pets on to the RV, knowing how important it was to have no delay for any reason.

Just before dawn they were all bundled into the vehicle, and Dad was starting the motor. The imps were still hurrying around, doing their work. Sean thought he saw Quieta, and waved to her, but wasn't sure she saw him. She looked tired.

They drove back along the access road to the trollway. Suddenly there was a loud ripping noise, and a jagged crack appeared in the dark sky, and the whole landscape lightened. "What happened?" David cried, startled.

"Oh, that was the crack of dawn," Chlorine said. "To let in the light. Sometimes it gets stuck on night, and the sun won't come up because it's afraid of the dark, so the shroud of night has to be cracked open.''

Even Karen evidently found that somewhat far-fetched, but it did seem to be the way it was in Xanth.

They broke out the food the imps had left them, which had made the accommodation change with them. There was something for everyone, ranging from miraculously still-cold eye scream to dog biscuits. Even in their absence, the imps were excellent hosts.

The drive quickly got tedious, so Sean took a hand and taught the others how to play poker for matchsticks. Chlorine tended to let her cards show, as she did other things, which was part of her appeal; but mute Nimby turned out to be an unbluffable player. He obviously knew which cards everyone else held. Soon he had all the matchsticks, and the game lapsed.

"Did you notice that there were no women or children, other than Quieta?" Mom remarked from the front seat.

"I think they were already in the safe cave," Chlorine said. "All that was left were the men, finishing all they could."

"Which isn't enough," Sean said. "They aren't going to make it on time before the dust of madness comes and spoils their remaining stones."

"They aren't?" Chlorine asked, concerned. "How do you know?"

"The animals told me," Sean said, petting Woofer. "They talked to other animals."

Chlorine looked at Nimby, who nodded.

"Couldn't we help?" David asked, evincing a rare sign of social conscience.

"Not without being caught by it ourselves," Sean said grimly.

"You mustn't do that," Chlorine said quickly. "I have to get you safely out of Xanth."

"But the imps were real nice," Karen said. "We should have helped them."

"But if it just got you caught for the madness, that would be as much harm as good," Chlorine said.

"Yeah, I guess," Karen agreed reluctantly. Sean understood her feeling, because he shared it.

Time passed. Sean got tired of looking out the window, and it was hard to look too much at Chlorine without being obvious, so he wound up snoozing as the others got into more solitaire, a game Nimby couldn't dominate as completely.

He woke when the RV turned off the main road. He glanced at his watch. Hours had passed, and it was now near the middle of the day. "Are we leaving Xanth?" he asked, actually somewhat disappointed.

"Dad needs more gas," Karen informed him. "Sleepyhead."

Sean looked out. "Where are we?"

"Tall Hassle," David said.

"Tallahassee? That sounds familiar."

"It isn't. This is Xanth, remember? Those are tall hassle trees out there."

There were indeed some very tall trees. "Tall Hassle," Sean agreed, not wanting to get into a hassle, tall or short, while Chlorine was watching.

"We are looking for a car pool, where there should be a cargo of gas at a carport," Karen said, relishing the puns. " 'Cause there's no gas guzzler here."

"Oh? Who says."

"Nimby says."

That did seem to settle it. Sean looked out to see if he could spot the car pool.

"There it is!" Karen cried, pointing. She had the sharp blue eyes of innocent youth.

Sean looked. There, indeed, it was: a body of water in the shape of a huge car, rolling across the land on watery wheels. "I should have known," he muttered.

Dad honked the horn. The car pool seemed to hear, because it rolled to a stop by the side of the road. "Don't get out," Dad warned. "There may be danger."

Nimby nodded.

Sure enough: a giant tigerlike creature made of water came bounding toward them: a car-nivore. It loomed over the RV and tried to bite it, but its water teeth couldn't dent the metal. It made a wet roar and bounded away again.

An old woman walked out of the water. She was made of water

too, but she had a certain car-isma, perhaps because of the water car-nation in her hair. "I wouldn't give two cents for a tankful of gas," Dad called, "but I would give one."

"That's car-ma," Karen said.

"I will take it," the water woman said. "My son will give it to you." She turned and called "Toon!"

A garish water man waded out of the pool, followed by a shaggy little car-pet. "Coming, Ma!" he burbled. He brought out a big bottle of wine-colored liquid.

"And that must be the car-port," Sean said.

Dad got out and unscrewed the gas cap, and Car-toon poured the liquid in. Sean hoped this was really what they needed. Suppose it wasn't gasoline, but wine? Because port was a kind of wine.

It seemed to be okay, because the motor started up well enough. But of course, there would still be some of the old gas-guzzler juice in the tank, so it was too soon to be sure.

"Thank you," Dad called as he put the vehicle in motion. Car-ma waved affably.

Then a huge shadow crossed their path. Sean looked up—and saw a giant bird. "A roc!" he cried. "The monsters've caught up again."

But Nimby wrote a note. *No. That is a roc-ette. They congregate in the tall hassle grove to practice their dancing.*

"That explains everything," Sean said sourly.

The big bird circled, peering down. "I think she thinks we're going to molest her nest or something," David said. "She's eyeing us."

Dad was concerned too. "That bird is big enough to pick us up and dump us in the sea," he said. "How can we get away from her?"

Nimby wrote another note. *There is a B-have near. The B's will dissuade her.*

"Just show the way," Dad said gamely.

Nimby went up front, exchanging places with Mom, so he could indicate the direction. "I shall be quite glad to get out of this weird world," Mom said. "In Mundania all we have to worry about are thieves and muggers." She smiled, to show this was in jest, to a degree.

"But what about the imps?" Karen asked.

Mom sighed. "I confess, I do wish we had found some way to

YON ILL WIND   *111*

help them. They were so kind to us, despite the extremity of their situation.''

They were approaching what looked like the world's biggest, fiercest hornet nest. That would be the beehive. Or B-have, as Nimby called it.

"Just what kind of creatures are these?" Dad asked warily.

"Oh, B's are all right, if you don't rile them," Chlorine said. "Their stings are mainly emotional."

"I sure get emotional when I get stung," Karen said.

Dad, evidently acting on Nimby's written advice, rolled down his window and addressed the big insects buzzing there. "I B-held your nice hive, er, have, and B-lieve you can do something on my B-half, if you care to B-friend me. Can I B-guile you to make the roc B-gone?" And he held out an old nylon comb.

The B's clustered about the comb. This was evidently something new and exciting to them. In a moment they picked it up and carried it into their have/hive. They had accepted the offering. Then another swarm formed into an arrow and shot up to intercept the roc wheeling above. In a moment there was a loud squawk, and the bird zoomed away so swiftly as to leave a sonic boom behind.

Karen giggled. "I guess that salted her tail."

"B-nighted mission accomplished," Sean said. "That B-lies our concern about B's." He glanced at Mom, who was known to be nervous about insects of most types.

Dad looped around and made his way back to the trollway. "I am really getting to appreciate the protection of the beneficial spell on this road," he remarked. "Whenever we leave it, we get into trouble."

"Except for the imps," David reminded him.

"Except for the imps," Dad agreed as they resumed speed. "You know, we are now close to the boundary of Xanth; in a couple of hours we'll be clear of it, and back in the normal realm. Yet I almost wonder—"

"We'll have to say good-bye to Chlorine," Sean said, stricken by the realization. "And Nimby," he added, not wanting to be too obvious.

"Who have helped us as much as the imps did," Mom added.

"Is anybody else thinking what I am?" Dad asked.

Sean was suddenly excited. "Like—like maybe not leaving Xanth right now?"

"But we have to get home," Mom protested. "We're late already."

"To school," Karen said, making a wry face.

"To chores," David said.

"To work," Dad said.

"To research," Mom said. "It occurs to me that though I love my work, researching archaic languages, there may be a unique chance for similar research here. It may have escaped the notice of the rest of you, but we are no longer speaking English; we are speaking the universal magic language of Human Xanth, just as the pets are speaking the universal animal magic language of Animal Xanth. Such an opportunity should perhaps not be passed by."

Sean grinned. "Mom always did have a problem communicating. What she's trying to say is she'd just as soon stick around here awhile longer."

"Yea!" Karen cried, clapping her little hands.

Dad glanced at Mom. "When you give a scholarly rationale, you always have an underlying gut motive. What is it? Surely you aren't thrilled with meatier showers or harpy bombs."

"It's the imps," she confessed. "They were so nice to us, and we may have imposed at the worst time. I wish we could help them."

"But we would get caught by the madness," Sean reminded her, though he was as eager as any to remain in Xanth. Mom required careful managing, as Dad knew; it wasn't safe to agree with her too quickly, lest she argue the opposite case in an attempt to be Quite Fair.

"Yes. Yet it seems that all of Xanth faces that same threat. Is it right for us to escape what they can't?"

She was begging to be persuaded. What would clinch it? Sean had an inspiration. "Let's ask the pets." Before anyone else could speak, he addressed the animals. "What do you guys have to say? Do you want to stay here in Xanth longer?"

All three nodded. But that wasn't necessarily enough. He needed a good, solid argument for turning back. "What do you know that we don't?"

"Woof," Woofer said. He tried again. "Woimp."

"Something about the imps," Sean said. "The ones running the hotel? Quieta? Ortant?"

"Woof."

"Ortant. He's not what he seems?"

"Woof."

"Something bad?"

"Woof. Woof."

They were zeroing in on it. "Something good?"

"Woof woof woof."

"He's more than the innkeeper?" Chlorine asked, catching on to the mechanism.

"Woof."

A lightbulb flashed above Chlorine's head. "I remember now. He's the mayor of the village."

"Woof!"

"The mayor!" Mom exclaimed. "I had forgotten."

"The most important imp is always the host for guests," Chlorine said. "Because they feel that hospitality is the most important function of a village. I had forgotten too; I didn't pay proper attention in Centaur School, or I would have realized right away."

"But surely the mayor should have been supervising the business of clearing out the village," Dad said.

"Meow."

David looked at Midrange. "I guess so—after taking care of the visitors."

"Yes," Sean said. "Ortant and Quieta were off in the village when Dad and I went down at night. They thought we were safe asleep, so they were getting back to their business. Without bothering us about it."

"Such courtesy is rare in Mundania," Dad said. "Yet it begs to be returned in kind."

That did it. "We must go back," Mom said decisively.

"Can we get there in time?" Dad asked. "It will be evening, and that's when they have to be done."

"Nimby?" Chlorine asked.

Nimby nodded.

"And you," Mom said to Chlorine. "This will be extending your job. We don't have the right to—"

"I'm happy to," Chlorine said. "This has been more fun for me than anything. And I like the imps too."

Sean was very glad to hear that. Now he would get more time with Chlorine—maybe a lot more time. So she could practice whatever she wanted on him. Like maybe progressing beyond the verbal interplay.

Dad slowed the RV, getting ready to turn it around. "I hope we don't regret this," he said. But he didn't look regretful.

7

MADNESS

D avid was glad they were going back. This magic world of Xanth took some getting used to, but he was getting there, and it certainly was more interesting than Mundania. He knew that eventually he'd be back in dreary school, but at least he'd have a good subject for the How I Spent My Summer report.

Now they were heading into Xanth instead of out of it, and the winds were stiffening. It was bound to be a long, hard drive. That made him thirsty, as long drives always did.

He saw a sign. APPLE COLA RIVER. "Hey, Dad—how about stopping to get some of that apple cola?"

To his surprise, Dad listened. Maybe Dad was thirsty too. He pulled to the side. "Everybody get out and get anything done you want, because we won't be stopping again soon," he said.

Oh. That was fair warning. They piled out and found assorted bushes. Then David got a jug and went to dip out all the apple cola he could. That was one of the good things about Xanth: the way things were literal. If the sign said apple cola, the river was made of it. Just as that river of blood in the mirror/Tapestry had been genuine hot red giant blood, so copious it flowed for miles in a river down to the sea. This river sparkled with its effervescence, and sure enough, it was apple-flavored cola. He drank several cups of it before he left, so as to keep the jug full.

He turned to return to the RV, and saw a fire. A series of small flames was traveling along the ground between him and the others. He wasn't worried, because they were little enough to step right over, but he wondered how they had come about. So he paused to look.

They were ants. Little red ants. "Fire ants!" he exclaimed, catching on.

"Wouldn't you know it," Sean said. "I found some block parents." He gestured, and David saw several stone blocks in the shape of people. That figured.

"Hey, look what I found," Karen called from the other side. "Laughing flowers."

They looked, but didn't hear any laughing, though she stood in a patch of pretty flowers. "Where?" David asked.

"Here." She picked a funny red one and brought it to him. "Smell it."

He smelled it—and burst out laughing. The curious thing was that he hadn't intended to; it just happened.

"What's so funny?" Sean asked suspiciously.

"Smell," Karen said, handing him a funny blue flower.

Sean sniffed it—and guffawed. Then looked as surprised as David felt. Then he smiled. "I get it: these are scents of humor."

"Yeah," Karen said, satisfied.

Woofer came running up. "Woof!" he said urgently, pointing his nose toward the vehicle.

"Time's up," Sean said. "We have to get back in before Dad takes off without us."

They hurried back to the RV, because Dad didn't bluff when he was in a hurry. The RV was already starting to move, slowly. Of course, Mom wouldn't let him actually leave them behind, but they got the message and ran the last fifty feet.

"Did you see what I saw?" Dad asked as they pulled back onto the trollway. "The fly-fishing?"

"What is noteworthy about that?" Mom asked. She was sitting up front now, her normal place when they didn't need special instructions.

"They were frogs with fishing poles—casting for flies."

Mom laughed musically. "And you mean that literally, of course."

"Of course."

"And do you know what I saw?" Mom asked in turn.

"What did you see?" Dad dutifully inquired.

"A thim bull."

"A thimble?"

"A thim bull."

"A thin bull?"

"A male bovine in the shape of a thimble."

Dad laughed. "Grazing on pins and needles?"

"Of course."

David decided not to try to tell what the kids had seen, because it simply wasn't remarkable, in this magic land.

"It's good to see them enjoying it," Sean murmured. David realized that he was right. The parents had been somewhat tight and terse recently, but now they were getting into the spirit of Xanth. That was an excellent sign.

David looked around. The animals were snoozing. Karen was fiddling with the deck of cards. Sean was sneaking peeks at Chlorine's legs, where her skirt rode up carelessly high. Chlorine herself was looking out the window. But then he saw her eyes flick back, and he realized that she knew Sean was looking at her. She was showing her legs on purpose! Now, that was really interesting.

But all this left nothing much for David to do. He could play solitaire, but he was tired of that. So he considered Nimby. Nimby was one pleasantly weird character. Really a donkey-headed dragon in the shape of a young man who never spoke. So would he—

Nimby turned to face him.

Could Nimby read his mind? Suddenly David wasn't bored at all. This could get really truly superinteresting.

Can you? he thought.

Nimby nodded.

Gee. But he'd better test it. *What am I thinking of now?* He imagined a really ugly cartoon face.

Nimby brought out his pad and pencil—they just appeared from nowhere—and drew the ugly face.

Gee, again. So they didn't have to speak to Nimby; they could just think their questions to him. But maybe it wouldn't be smart to announce that.

Nimby looked questioningly at him.

Because people like to keep secrets, David thought loudly. *Like Sean's looking up under Chorine's skirt, getting a real charge from her legs, but he doesn't want anyone else to know. And she's letting him do it, and SHE doesn't want him to know. So I guess you can pick up on that* . . . He paused, and Nimby nodded. *But you better not let them know, because they'd both be embarrassed to death. Because they're both adults, or close to it. I guess it's like that Adult Conspiracy that stops us kids from saying words like "bleep." Nobody's supposed to know anything. I guess if you peek into their minds, you'll see I'm right.*

Nimby paused, then nodded, looking surprised. David was pleased; he had taught the man who knew everything something.

And Nimby nodded again.

David realized that he didn't have to work to project his thoughts; Nimby could pick them up at conversational level. But if he could read everybody's mind so well, why did he seem so, well, innocent?

Nimby wrote a note and handed it to him.

David read it. *I am aware of what is happening around me, but there is so much that I don't think to do it unless guided. There are so many thoughts that I usually pay no attention. I also have trouble comprehending human motivations and emotions.*

David couldn't resist giving some more advice. If Nimby wanted to seek mature human perspectives and motives, he should peek into Dad's and Mom's minds. If he wanted hot adolescent thoughts, Sean was the one. For naive childish attitudes, Karen would do. But for a central, sensible viewpoint, David himself was the best source.

Nimby nodded, accepting it.

But David was really curious about one thing, and maybe Nimby would give him the answer. He could appreciate why Sean wanted to see under Chorine's skirt, as David himself found that intriguing. He really did want to see someone's panties. But why was Chorine letting him see?

Nimby wrote a note. *She has not been beautiful long, and wishes to ascertain exactly how beauty works and what its limits are. So she is practicing on Sean, who is the closest approach to an ordinary man to which she has current access. She believes that what works on him should work somewhat similarly on other men.*

Yes, it should. So it was really a scientific experiment on her part; she didn't really care for Sean.

Nimby wrote a note. *Scientific?*

He didn't know about science? Okay, David would tell Nimby all about Mundane science, if Nimby would tell David exactly what he and Chlorine did overnight in their room at the imp hotel.

She slept. I sat up and watched Xanth.

What, no mush? No Adult Conspiracy stuff? David wasn't sure he believed that.

Chlorine has little romantic interest in a dragon ass.

A what?

My natural form. She seeks human interaction.

Nimby didn't have to sleep?

My type doesn't sleep.

But Nimby was in human form now. Wasn't he as least a little interested in what Chlorine looked like with her clothing off? David was only twelve years old, but he'd just love to see Chlorine bare naked nude.

I fashioned her present form, and mine. I can in any event see her natural body at all times, as I can those of everyone else. This has no novelty for me.

Evidently not. But with such powers, why did Nimby hang around a dull family like them, and never speak?

There is a geis on me to be silent until I have accomplished my mission.

Oh, like a knightly oath. David could see that. Still, keeping constant company with a beautiful creature like Chlorine, didn't Nimby get even a little curious about what human love and bleep was all about?

I would like to learn about human emotion, yes. It does intrigue me. So far it does not seem very logical.

Well, that was because he was analyzing it instead of feeling it. He was being like a teacher in school, who could make anything deadly dull in an instant. Kids fell asleep in Sex Ed class, after all. In real life people had emotions. They cared. They got all heated up about some stupid ball game, and they really got excited about boy-girl business. Maybe Nimby should try that, sort of really get into the feel of it.

I lack the emotion of the human kind. How can I experience the feelings humans do?

Well, he might try tracking David's own emotion for a while. David would do his best to feel things strongly, so Nimby could get the idea.

Thank you. I shall do that.

Now I'll think through science, David thought. The way I see it, it's the Mundane way of doing what you folk in Xanth do by magic. Maybe they're the same, in the end, just different ways. Do you know what a lever is?

And so they communed, as the RV zoomed on, and Karen played her cards, and Sean and Chlorine played their little games of show and look.

Somewhere along there it began to rain. At first David thought he was imagining it, but then he was sure: the rain was colored. Red, green, blue, and yellow drops struck the windows. Was this normal?

Yes, for Xanth. This storm is raining heavily ahead, so that by the time we reach the next river, it will be flooded. The Trolls are about to shut down the trollway as unsafe.

But we have to get to Imp Erial today, to help them move their stuff.

I will be able to guide you safely there, if you ask me.

"We'll sure do that," David said aloud, forgetting himself.

Karen looked up from her cards. "Do what?"

"Nimby says we're headed into a bad storm, and the river will flood, and the trolls will shut down the highway."

"We can't afford to get detoured now," Dad said. "We have to go on through."

"Nimby can show us how," David said.

"If this is a magic storm, he may have to," David replied grimly.

The rain intensified, exactly as Nimby had written. Dad slowed; he had to.

Nimby wrote a note. *Stop here.*

The road was not flooded, but Dad obeyed. Nimby got out, assumed his dragon form, and trundled into the rain.

"He will return, I'm sure," Chlorine said.

And in a moment Nimby did. Clenched in his donkey jaws was a branch with leaves and several fat bright cherries.

"Cherries!" Karen exclaimed happily, reaching for them. But Nimby held them away, shaking his head.

"Those look like cherry bombs," Chlorine said. "Only they're bigger and fresher and clearer than any I've seen before. I'd better hold them." She took the branch and held it carefully, while Nimby reverted to his human form and got back into the RV. He was, of course, soaking wet, so Mom came back and bustled him into the lavatory for another change of clothing. Mom just couldn't help mothering folk.

"Cherry bombs grow on trees?" David asked, as the vehicle started moving again.

"Everything grows on trees," Chlorine said. "Except people, and sometimes they do too." She sat down, and her extreme care with the cherries caused her to forget how her clothing was positioned. Twigs of the branch snagged on both blouse and skirt. David saw Sean swallow. "But these must be a special variety."

"Why can't I eat a cherry?" Karen asked rebelliously. She got that way when balked.

"Because they're cherry *bombs,* stupid," David informed her. "They go boom." He felt enormously superior.

"Boom?"

"Yes, they explode when dropped or thrown," Chlorine said. She managed to unsnag her skirt and then her blouse; the material fell back into place, covering what it was supposed to. David heard Sean resume breathing. That exposure had really been by accident.

Actually, it had been a pretty good view. David had begun to get interested in such things only in the last few months, and suspected he would be more interested in the next few months. Chlorine's body was fascinating. But so was the notion of cherry bombs growing on trees. "Does anything else do that?" he asked. "I mean, explode?"

"Certainly. Pineapples, for instance. They're more dangerous than cherries, because they're larger."

Nimby emerged, dressed in more of Sean's clothes. But it seemed Sean didn't care; he was too busy watching to see if any more twigs snagged anything.

"Exactly what variety of cherry bombs are these?" Chlorine asked him.

Nimby wrote a note. No one else seemed to notice how his pad and pencil appeared from nothing when he needed them, and disappeared similarly when he didn't. He handed the note to David.

" 'These are new, clear cherry bombs,' " he read aloud. " 'Much more powerful than the regular kind. We will need them for the river.' "

"Nuclear cherry bombs!" Sean exclaimed. "I'll *bet* they're powerful!"

Then David noticed a PS to the note: *When you saw inside Chlorine's blouse—was that emotion?*

David smiled. Yes it was, of a sort. But to fathom the full effect of it, Nimby should have peeked into Sean's mind. Because if David got slightly warm, Sean would be a furnace. And considering Nimby's apparent age, he should be reacting like Sean.

Nimby sat in a vacant seat. David was pleased to see that he was now looking at Chlorine in much the way Sean was: surreptitiously but persistently. He was learning.

"Uh-oh," Dad muttered in an ominous tone.

David peered ahead. There was a barricade with a sign DETOUR. A troll stood by it, wearing a glowing helmet.

Dad drew up to the troll. "Where does the detour go?" he asked.

"Back to the tall hassle grove, which is safer during the storm."

"But we have to get to Imp Erial before nightfall," Dad protested.

"The trollway may be impassable. There is flooding, making it unsafe."

"Suppose we are willing to risk it?"

The troll stared dourly at him. "You may proceed at your own risk. We will not be responsible for your safety."

"But the road remains enchanted? We can't be attacked on it?"

"The path remains enchanted. But water goes where it will. The flood could cause you mischief regardless of the enchantment."

"Understood. We'll proceed."

"Fool," the troll muttered, and stood aside.

"You're probably right," Dad agreed, driving forward.

David looked out. "What's that building, shaped like a huge bottle?"

Chlorine looked. "Oh, that's a whinery."

Sean laughed. "A winery shaped like a bottle! It figures."

Meanwhile the RV was forging through increasingly tempestuous rain. Colored fluid streamed across the windows and splashed up in fleeting rainbow patterns. Mist from it drifted in the open slits of the almost-closed windows.

Then some of that water seemed to get into David's eyes, for they were flowing. He was crying—and he didn't know why. He looked blearily around, and saw tears in the eyes of all of them except Nimby. Even Dad was blowing his nose. What was going on?

"Did we just drive through an onion field?" Karen asked tearfully.

"I see a sign," Mom said. "It says we are coming to the Crimea River."

"Cry me a river," Chlorine repeated. "That explains it. The whinery must use that water for its whine. But we must have crossed it on the way up. Why didn't we cry then?"

"It wasn't flooding then," Dad replied. "I saw the water passing low under the bridge. We were past it before we got a whiff of it."

The vehicle slowed again. David saw why: they had reached the flood. Tear-colored water surged across the road. It looked too deep and swift to drive through.

"I don't understand how this flooded so deeply, so quickly," Dad said. "There was ample clearance below the bridge. It has been raining, but there has not been time to raise the water level twenty feet."

Nimby wrote a note. He gave it to David, who read it to the others. "Nimby says the goblins have dammed the river just off the enchanted right-of-way. That's why it backed up so fast."

"Goblins! I should have known. Do we have any way to handle this?"

Nimby wrote another note. " 'This's why I fetched the new, clear cherry bombs,' " David read. " 'They will destroy the dam, so the water will newly clear the road.' "

"But won't the goblins attack us when we go there?" Mom asked worriedly.

" 'Not if we remain within the enchanted path, and float the cherries down to the dam,' " David read.

"But the cherries might go right over the dam before they explode," Sean said. "We'll have to use a rope to put them in place."

"Let's get to it," Dad said. At that point the rain eased, becoming only a light, windy drizzle. Dad, Mom, Nimby, Chlorine, and Sean got out. "You kids stay put," Sean called back insultingly.

They sat in the open doorway in the side of the RV and watched the adults depart. Colored mists were rising from the landscape, making a pretty vertical pattern.

There was the cheerful clangor of a bell. "Hey, I want to see that," Karen exclaimed, jumping out of the RV. "It sounds like a cowbell."

"Hey, we're not supposed to go anywhere," David reminded her. "It's dangerous."

"On the enchanted path? Pooh." She ran on back along the road, following the music of the bell. She liked bells, and just had to see any that she heard. Tweeter was perched on her hair, chirping warningly, but she ignored him.

David was torn between running after her and staying put. He compromised. "Go after her, Woofer, and make sure she's safe."

"Woof!" the dog agreed, and bounded out.

Then David heard the beat of a drum. It was a powerful, throbbing sound that seemed to penetrate to the very center of his head. What kind of drum was making it? David liked drums, because they made a lot of noise with little effort.

Before he knew it, David was walking toward the sound. But Midrange ran after him. "Meow!" the cat screeched warningly.

That jolted David back into responsibility. He was doing the same thing Karen was, running after the first intriguing sound. That was dangerous, because it was coming from the side, off the enchanted path. So he stopped. But he did pause long enough to peer in the direction of the sound, hoping to see the drum from here.

He was successful: it was in the shape of a huge ear. It was an ear drum! No wonder it had such power over his own ears.

He picked Midrange up and walked slowly back to the RV. He hoped Karen wouldn't go off the enchanted path. But she was a child; her judgment wasn't good.

The bell rang again. Surely she had seen it by now, and should have returned. Where was she?

Finally he could stand it no longer. "I gotta find her," he said. "Midrange, you stay here and tell the folks where I am, if they come back before we do." The cat nodded and stretched out on the floor by the door.

David ran in the direction of the bell. Soon he found it: a cow with a clapper, ringing as it walked. A cow bell. What else? But Karen wasn't there. She must have gone on beyond. Foolish girl!

He spied a big orange apelike creature wearing a placard saying UTAN. Was it dangerous? This thing looked so comical that maybe it was harmless. "Hey, Utan—have you seen my stupid little sister?" he asked it.

The thing paused, then pointed the way David was going. So David ran on. Only after he was well beyond the creature did he realize what it must be: an orange utan.

He saw a cat. "Hey, I told you to stay in the RV!" he cried, advancing on it. The cat turned its face toward him. Then David realized that it wasn't Midrange. It was a strange cat—very strange. It wore a flat-brimmed hat and a vest with the word ION on front. "Oh—sorry," David said, embarrassed. "I thought you were my cat."

The cat stared witheringly at him and stalked off. Then David realized its nature: it was a cat-ion, probably headed for a catamount or catboat. "He must be going to get positively charged, before he lynx up with friends," David muttered as he went on. This business of punning was infectious.

There was still no sign of Karen. He was very much afraid she had wandered off the enchanted path. Should he go and tell Mom? That would surely get him in trouble for ever letting Karen get in trouble, though.

Something came flying though the air. David ducked, afraid it was going to hit him, but it sailed on by. He got a good glimpse of it as it passed. It looked like a painting. Then another flew by, and a third. What was going on?

But a moment's thought brought the answer: "Art-illery," he said. "Someone's hurling art at me."

"Kaa-ren!" he called. "KAA-RENN!" There was no answer. Not even a woof. This was not a good sign.

He continued searching, but Karen was nowhere he could see. That meant she must have gone off the enchanted path. Which meant in turn that he couldn't wait any longer; he had to get help in a hurry.

He turned and ran back to the RV, half-afraid he would discover it gone. But it remained, as solid and reassuring as ever. Midrange remained on guard. "Anyone come back?" he asked the cat, and received a shake of the head. Well, at least that meant he would be able to report his disaster himself, instead of seeming to be caught like a fleeing rat. For whatever slight good that might do him.

"Where are the others?" he asked.

Midrange got up and came to him. David picked him up and set him on his shoulder, his normal riding position. "Meove llefft."

David bore left, following the course of the flooded river. Now that he was closer to it, his eyes were tearing. He couldn't stop them, so he just kept blinking to clear his vision. Soon he came to Mom, who was watching Sean tie a framework fashioned of driftwood together. Mom was holding the cherry branch somewhat nervously, and tears were streaming down her face. His own eyes had been flowing, but he had ignored it after the first few minutes. Beyond them the rushing river had pooled into a small lake, with what looked like a dam fashioned from brush and junk.

David hesitated to give her his news; she might drop the branch. So he sort of slid by it. "Mom, there's a problem. Where's Dad?"

It didn't work. "*What* problem?" she demanded sharply, turning her swollen eyes on him.

David wiped his eyes on his sleeve. "I, ah, Karen went out, and—"

"Out alone?" Her voice was getting shrill. That was not a good sign.

"Woofer and Tweeter went with her."

"Jim!" she called imperatively.

There was no answer. But then Chlorine and Nimby appeared. "He's spying on the goblins," Chlorine reported through her bleary visage. Her eyes looked as if they were trying to cry, but not succeeding, so they were turning red instead. It probably felt like dry heaves. "If he calls, they'll know he's there. Can we take a message?"

Mom considered. "No. Maybe you can help another way. Karen is lost. Could you find her?"

"Oh, sure. Nimby will know where she is." She turned to Nimby, who alone had no trouble with his eyes. "She's all right?"

Nimby nodded.

"Then let's get there in a hurry. You turn dragon, and I'll run along behind you. She knows what we look like, so she won't be frightened."

Nimby became the weird dragon, and they ran off in Karen's direction.

Mom turned to David. "You let her go?" There was ice in her tone despite the tears in her eyes. He wondered whether her tears were freezing into sleet as they fell.

"She wouldn't stop for me, Mom," he pleaded tearfully. "She heard this cow bell, and she just went."

Mom nodded. "That is the way she is," she agreed, sniffing. Then she smiled, tightly. So she wasn't blaming him. Nevertheless, David felt guilty.

"David, I don't want to go anywhere while I'm guarding the cherries," Mom said in a moment. "Would you go carefully and see if you can see what your father is doing?"

"Sure." He walked in the direction Chlorine and Nimby had come from. Soon he saw Dad—surrounded by ugly little manlike creatures with big heads and big feet: goblins. They had spied him, and he was probably off the enchanted path, because they were closing in purposefully.

"Dad!" David cried. "Watch out!" But it was too late. The goblins burst across the last little distance, and swarmed all over Dad. He tried to fight them off, but he was a physics prof, not a warrior, and they were many. In a moment they had him helpless.

David knew he had to do something, but he didn't know what. The goblins were carrying Dad away. There were too many of them for anyone to fight. Dad should never have gone beyond the limit of the enchanted path. Just as Karen shouldn't have. Did the goblins have her too? Nimby could have warned him—but Nimby was off fetching Karen. Because David hadn't stopped her from leaving the RV.

"Mom! Sean!" he cried, running back. "They've got Dad!"

"Oh!" Mom exclaimed, looking faint.

"One chance," Sean said grimly as he blinked away his tears. "This flotation's too slow. Give me the bombs."

Mom handed the branch of cherries to him. Her eyes were staring as well as tearing; David had never seen her so distraught.

"See if you can distract the goblins from me," Sean said. He walked purposefully toward the dam.

"From you? Not from Dad?"

"Right. Do it."

Sean seemed to know what he was doing, so David did his best. He started running and screaming and waving his arms. "Hey, goblins!" he cried. "You can't catch meeee!"

"David!" Dad called, spying him dispite his own distress. Parents were like that. "Get back on the enchanted path!"

But David didn't. He was terrified, but he had to distract the goblins, and this was the only way he knew how. So he made an Adult Conspiracy gesture at them and ran on. It probably looked like a mere bleep to them, but it did stir them up. They charged after him.

Unfortunately, goblins turned out to be swifter runners than he had figured. They could run faster than he could! He dodged and ducked, but soon they caught up and laid their grubby hands on him. Instead of rescuing Dad, he had gotten himself caught. Some help he had been.

"What possessed you to do that?" Dad demanded as the goblins hauled them together.

"Silence, morsels!" the goblin chief cried, wiping his eyes. "Or we'll cook you slow instead of fast."

Cook them? Suddenly David realized just how awful a fate they faced. All because he had let Karen get loose, then had taken Nimby away from helping Dad, so that Dad got caught by the goblins. David deserved to be cooked!

There was a deafening BOOM behind them, followed by a great rushing sound.

"The dam!" a goblin screamed. "The dam went!"

Sean had blown the dam! He must have gotten close while the goblins were distracted, and thrown the cherry branch on it. Now the water was bursting out and down—and the goblins were below it. The great frothing surge of it was already bearing down on them. They let man and boy go, and fled.

"Run for the road, son!" Dad cried.

For sure! They ran together through the flying froth, while the goblins ran the opposite way, fleeing the water. The goblins weren't being smart; they had panicked. Or maybe the water represented more of a danger to them, because they were so much shorter than human beings. That was fine with David.

They made it to the enchanted section. The water level was dropping; the river seemed to be chasing after the goblins. Maybe it was getting back at them for damming it. David hoped they all drowned.

Mom was waiting where she had been, only now the water had receded, and her tears were slowing. Dad ran up to her and embraced her. It had been one close call!

Then Mom thought of something else. "Where's Sean?"

"He must've been caught by the water, when the dam blew," David said, horrified. "He just wanted to get that dam, so as to save you, Dad."

"Oh, no." Dad looked down to where the scattered remnants of the dam lay. There was no sign of Sean.

"Jim—" Mom said in That Tone.

"I'll find him," Dad said. He ran back toward the dam.

Then David saw Chlorine. "Karen won't come with us," she said, her eyes still red but dry. "She—what happened here?" She stared at the diminished water, astonished.

"Sean blew the dam," David said. "But now we don't know where he is."

"Oh, he's all right," Chlorine said. "Nimby gave me a message to say to you. That Sean is on his way. I didn't know what it meant."

"He must have been washed away by the water," David said. "So now he has to make his way back from wherever he got washed to. But he's okay."

"That must be it," Mom agreed, evidently relieved. "Now, what's this business with Karen?"

"She's been deceived by wraiths," Chlorine explained. "Now she thinks we're wraiths, and she won't come with us. Nimby doesn't know what to do, because he doesn't really understand minds, just things."

"We must go to her immediately," Mom said, freshly alarmed.

"I think I'd better wait here for Sean," Dad said. "He may be physically sound, but he'll need a familiar face to orient on."

"But I'm not sure *you're* physically sound," Mom protested. "Those goblins—"

"Didn't hurt me," Dad said.

Mom turned to Nimby. "True?"

Nimby shook his head.

"That's what I thought," Mom said severely. "You must be bruised and bitten all over. Let me see."

Dad hesitated, and David realized that Dad probably was battered, but didn't want the children to know. "I'll go fetch Karen," he said. "She knows me too. It's my fault she got lost."

"It wasn't your fault," Mom said, and he was glad to be officially exonerated again. "But thank you for helping."

"Let's go," David said. Indeed, Nimby, knowing his mind, was already starting to move, and Chlorine with him.

The landscape became weird, even compared to what it had been. The trees seemed to be growing sideways or even upside down, and there were blobs of water floating haphazardly. But in a moment he realized that they were moving toward the three people. "What are those puddles doing out of their beds?" David asked, ducking to avoid one that came too close.

Nimby's pad and pencil appeared. He wrote a note. Chlorine took it and read it. " 'Ponds come.' "

"Pond scum?" David asked, making a face. Unfortunately, the face detached from his head and floated away, distorting grotesquely. He clapped his hands to the front of his head and found that his regular face was still there; it was only a copy that was drifting away.

"Ponds come to us," she said carefully. "I think they're getting confused as the magic dust increases. We may all suffer from its madness as we get farther into the storm."

"I think I'm suffering from it now," David said, as the face copy collided with a pond and made a splash.

They encountered a man whose face was odd in another way: the lower part of it was transparent. David could see his tongue and teeth inside, and they were also transparent. The man never paused to greet them; he hurried on to wherever he was going.

"That man had a glass jaw," Chlorine said, surprised. "I never saw one before."

Neither had David. But there were stranger things ahead. One of the floating ponds had settled into a glade, and there were creatures in and by it, facing away from him. One had the head and arms of a human being, the forelegs and torso of a horse, and the tail of a fish. Another had the head of a person, the wings of a vulture, and the body of a serpent.

David knew he shouldn't pause, but his curiosity overcame him. "Say, if it's okay to ask—what are you?" he called to the two creatures.

Both turned to face him, presenting full pairs of breasts. "We are double-crossbreeds," the one with the fishtail said. "I am a cenmaid, centaur/mermaid for long; my friend's a harga, or harpy/naga."

"But—but—I'm a child!" David said stupidly, staring at their fronts. "I'm not supposed to see stuff like that." Which was just exactly what he hadn't wanted to say; the madness had fouled him up.

The two lovely faces smiled. "Don't be concerned," the harga said. "We are merely dreams brought to you by our friend the cenmare, a centaur/night mare crossbreed. 'Bye." Both waved, and vanished.

David stared at the space they had vacated. "Did—did you see that?" he asked Chlorine.

"See what?" she asked.

So it was true: he had dreamed of those strange crossbreeds. Well, at least it meant he would not be in trouble for violating that Adult Conspiracy. But he wished he could have seen more of those creatures before they vanished.

They reappeared. "You do?" the cenmaid inquired, inhaling.

"Gee," David said. "Can you be my dreams any time I want?"

"Certainly, while the madness lasts," the harga replied, brushing out her hair and feathers. "Just desire to see us."

"I will!" he promised. "But right now I have to go rescue my little sister."

"You had better hurry," the cenmaid said. "She's about to get in trouble." The creatures faded.

David wasn't sure how much he should trust dreams, but he took the advice to heart. "Can we hurry?" he asked, breaking into a run.

"Certainly," Chlorine agreed, pacing him. "Say, it's nice being healthy; I couldn't keep this up in my natural state."

David glanced at her. "You would drive Sean crazy, if he saw you running."

"Really? I must be sure to run for him."

They found Karen perched in a fork of an enormous tree. The tree's leaves looked like swatches of cloth, and its twigs looked like pins and needles. Its trunk seemed to be made of overlaying patches.

"She must be all right," Chlorine said. "That's a tree-mend-ous."

"I can see it's very big," David said. "But she could still be in trouble.

"No, a tree-men-dous mends anyone who climbs into it," Chlorine explained. "There's one not far from my home village. She chose the right tree to get into."

"But she won't be safe much longer," he said, remembering the dream-creatures' warning.

"How can you know that?" Chlorine asked. But then she saw Nimby's nod. "I guess you do know, though. But she wouldn't come for us. She thought we were wraiths."

"What's a wraith?" David asked.

"An apparition, usually of a living person. But wraiths aren't real; they may just lead someone into mischief. Because the victim thinks the person is real, and means well, while the wraith doesn't mean well. Usually we don't see many wraiths, but the madness must be giving them more power.''

David had learned enough about Xanth to be cautious. Things weren't always what they appeared to be. Suppose this wasn't Karen, but a wraith trying to fool him into thinking he was saving her? He had seen a scary movie once about a child who got stolen by a vampire or something, who had left an animated doll in her place, and the parents never knew she was gone. The only way to tell the difference was that the doll had perfect manners.

"Try calling her," he said.

Chlorine did. "Karen! Karen, it's Chlorine. Please come with us."

"Get away from me!" Karen screamed, climbing higher in the tree. "You're just another fake!"

"At least she had the wits to realize she was being fooled," Chlorine murmured. "But now she can't tell when she's not being fooled."

"I can fix that," David said. He approached the tree. "Karen! Get down from there before Mom catches you and grounds you for a week, you stupid little snot!"

"David!" she cried gladly. She came down so fast she almost tumbled. She leaped for him and plastered a sloppy kiss on his cheek.

"Stop slobbering on me, you brat," he said. "We've got to get back to Mom in a hurry."

"Yes, brother dear," she said. Then she aimed a kick at his shin, but he got his leg out of the way in time. He knew her ways, as she knew his.

"Sean blew the dam and got washed away," he said. "But Nimby says he's okay. But there's danger coming here, so we've got to move."

"Are these really Chlorine and Nimby?" she asked. "Chlorine was trying to make me go into a dark cave. I heard something big breathing in there. I grabbed her hand, and there wasn't any. That's when I freaked out."

"Well, grab her hand now," he said.

She hesitated, but Chlorine extended her hand, so Karen took it. Her face lighted when she found that the hand was solid. "I'm sorry I doubted you—if it was you, last time," she said.

"It was me last time," Chlorine agreed. "But you did the right thing, waiting until you were sure. But how *were* you sure it was David, and not another wraith?''

''The wraiths seemed nice,'' she said. ''David's never nice unless he has to be.''

Suddenly David stopped. ''The pets!'' he exclaimed. '';Woofer and Tweeter were with you. Where are they?''

''I sent them to fetch you,'' Karen said. ''Isn't that how you found me?''

''No. They never reached us.''

They stared at each other, horrified.

8
CATATONIC

Midrange stretched and stood as he saw David return. Karen was with him, so that had worked out. But where were Woofer and Tweeter?

David rushed up to him. "Midrange, we've got a problem. Nimby says Sean will be back here in twenty minutes, and they'll have to take off then, or the madness will make it impossible to reach Imp Erial tonight. So we'll have to go. But Nimby can't tell where the other pets are, because something is hiding them. There are phantoms of hundreds of dogs and birds looking just like them, and Nimby can see them all, but he can't tell which ones are the right ones. Not without going to them, and that would take too long, because the chances of finding the right ones in time are too small. But he says he can rescue them if he knows which ones they are. He found two pieces of reverse wood—do you know what that is? Well, neither do I. But he thinks it will help. If we can find them in time. Do you think you could find them?"

Midrange was insulted. *Of course* he could find them, if he chose to. It was just a matter of sniffing them out.

"But I gotta tell you," David rushed on. "If you look for them, and get lost yourself, then we'll have to go without you too. And Nimby thinks there's danger, because whatever is making all those phantom dogs and birds must be trying to hide them from us, and it will try to stop you from reaching them—or it will try to capture you too. So if you don't want to do it—''

Midrange knew that if he didn't do it, David would think it was because he lacked courage. He didn't care for that indignity. So he would rescue the mutt and bird. He had known them for some time, after all. He got ready to sniff them out.

"But Nimby does have a way to help you—by doing the same thing back to it that it's doing to us. Making copies. He found some catatonic you can take that'll make you spin off hundreds of copies of yourself. You'll be a real copycat! Then the thing won't know which one is the real you, and you should be able to get through without getting caught yourself. We think Woofer and Tweeter are caught in a cave, because the wraiths were trying to get Karen to go into a cave, and if she had, she'd probably also be caught now. So maybe look for a cave—and watch out. If you can find them within fifteen minutes, even if you do get caught yourself, Nimby can come and rescue you in his dragon form. He thinks there's nothing around here that can handle a dragon that size. Then he'll bring you back and we'll catch the RV and get on our way. Okay?''

Midrange nodded. This was a challenge worthy of his feline mettle.

"Okay, here's the tonic,'' David said, giving him a capsule with awful-colored ick sloshing inside it. "Each time you make a sudden move, another copy will spin off and look and act just like you, but it's really illusion. It'll go seek one of the dog or bird illusions, and when they meet, the two will go poof, canceling each other out. Understand?''

Midrange nodded. He took the ugly capsule in his mouth and swallowed it. The thing was weird, but not incapacitating. Then he bounded off, sniffing the air for Woofer's canine doggy scent. He couldn't sniff out a trail as well as Woofer could, but he could do well enough. There was also Tweeter's smell, good enough to eat; that would help. It might take him a few minutes to orient, but he would get them.

He bounded in the direction he had last seen Woofer. That trail was still fresh, as it had been only an hour or so. He could see the dog's claw marks in the ground, and smell the canine odor. Not only was it doggy, it was specifically Woofer. No problem there.

But what about Tweeter? The bird had been riding on Karen's head, so the scent was very faint, and overridden by Karen's much stronger human traces. But that should improve when Tweeter left his associate and went with Woofer. Each of them had a pet human child; they had settled on that long ago, to make sure no child felt neglected. Because children were generally more fun than adult humans; they were more active, got into more mischief, and spent more time in the dirt. So Tweeter's pet was Karen, the smallest going to the smallest. Midrange had David in the middle, and Woofer tried to keep Sean out of trouble. If Woofer had been with Sean, Sean probably wouldn't have gotten swept away by the dam burst. Then he had muffed the rescue of Karen. Woofer just wasn't the most competent dog extant. But of course, no dog was really smart. That was why cats existed: there needed to be a gifted animal in every family, to keep it functional. But when a family scattered to different locales, it was hard to keep up with all its parts. That was why there was so much trouble now. Humans were incredibly dense about the need to remain close enough together for proper supervision.

It was time to test the phantom cat phenomenon. Midrange jerked to the side—and an image of himself fissioned off and bounded straight ahead. It made no sound and had no odor, but it did look solid, and it ran well. It even maneuvered around a tree. It would do to fool the dull senses of a human observer. Maybe even an animal observer, from a distance.

He jerked again, and another nondescript cat peeled off, running in the direction he had been going. So he could steer them in any direction. Good enough.

Suddenly he saw a dog. Woofer! He bounded toward the canine—then realized there was no smell. This was a clone, one of the phantom dogs put out to confuse the issue.

So Midrange jerked aside, sending a clone cat ahead to intercept the thing. He hid behind a rock, to watch the encounter. This just might be interesting.

The clone cat leaped right into the phantom dog—and both vanished in a puff of nothing. The two illusions had destroyed each other. Exactly as they were supposed to.

Very well. He would send more cats after more dogs. The more phantom dogs he eliminated, the easier it would be to locate the real one. He jerked and dodged frantically, sending clones bounding off in all directions, a veritable horde. Then he resumed the sniffing of Woofer's trail.

He saw a bird. Tweeter! But even as he spied it, so did a clone. The phantom cat leaped, catching the bird in his mouth—and disappeared. Two more images had canceled each other out.

It served the cat clone right, Midrange thought. The point was to rescue Tweeter, not to consume him. Birds were fair prey, but Tweeter was a friend. Friends did not eat friends.

He came to a large tree with funny leaves. The smells of animal, bird, and child were strong here. So this was where Karen had fled the phantoms. So it should be possible to follow her trail back to the cave she had not entered. But would that be the one where Woofer was? Surely the dog couldn't be *that* stupid, to enter the same cave they had avoided before. So that was probably not the one. There just wasn't time to check every prospect; five minutes were already gone.

So Midrange sniffed out Woofer's fresher scent, going in another direction. Now Tweeter's smell joined it, still faint, but clearer than before, because he had been flying beside the dog, low to the ground. Every so often he perched on a stalk or twig, and the scent became complete at those places. This was a much easier trail to follow.

But Midrange did not forget caution. The hound and bird had walked blithely into some kind of trap, and the cat was not eager to walk into the same trap. So once he was sure of the trail, he left it, looping around, slinking behind rocks and brush and trees as if stalking prey. Every so often he let fly another clone, to further confuse any possible watcher. Then he would sneak up on the trail and verify it in passing, as if not noticing it. It would be hard for any observer to tell exactly what he was up to.

He came to a deep crevice. The trail came to the brink and followed along it. Presumably the dog had found a place to cross it. The thing was too wide to jump. So how was Midrange to cross it, without slavishly following the exact route of the hound? Which he didn't want to do, because that might be right where the trap had sprung.

He sniffed around, and found some flowers. What good were flowers? So he went on. Then something snarled at him from the brush. Midrange leaped onto the nearest tree trunk.

He looked down, and saw that it was only a little doglike creature. "What are you?" he demanded, annoyed because he had been affrighted while off-guard.

"I'm a snarl," the little canine growled. "Can't you tell, pussy?"

This creature was not endearing himself. For reasons he didn't care to go into, Midrange did not like to be called pussy, especially in that tone. "No, I can't tell; you look more like a yelp to me," he retorted. "Where did you come from—a sick tangle tree?"

"Not quite. I was brushed out of a girl's hair. But she dropped me and left before I could adopt her as a pet. I'm not pleased. That's why I remain in a snarl." He glanced at Midrange. "I don't suppose you're looking for a proprietor?"

Midrange opened his mouth to say something truly catty, but caught himself. This creature just might be useful. It obviously wasn't a phantom. "I may be looking for a companion," he said carefully. "If he's useful."

"Useful?"

"I'm looking for a big dog and a small bird. Have you seen any such?"

"Actually I did, about two barks ago. They were following a wraith bleep."

"A wraith what?"

"The humans have this stupid Adult Conspiracy that forbids them to say the name of a female dog in the presence of a child. Since I derive from the snarled hair of a child, I, too, am bound by it. Idiotic, I know, but there it is."

Oh. "You did see them? Which way did they go?"

"That way." The snarl pointed his pug nose. "The wraith was one extremely fetching bleep, I must say; if she'd been of my species, I would have followed her too. She even smelled right. The bird protested, but couldn't stop him."

Which seemed to be one difference between a wraith and a phantom. The wraiths could emulate creatures completely, except for their solidity. So Woofer, the big male idiot, had followed her, and Tweeter had had to go along lest they be separated.

Midrange decided to trust Snarl a bit, mainly because it might help him get on with his mission. "I need to cross this cleft, but I can't see a way. Do you know a way?"

"Certainly. Just use one of those daisies there." The nose pointed at the flowers.

"What good are they?"

"They're upsy-daisies. They grow into ladders to help you up, if you pick them and invoke them by saying their name."

Well, now. Midrange went to the flowers and picked one. He carried it to the edge of the crack and set it down. "Upsy-daisy," he said.

The flower expanded. Its petals became spokes. They formed into a growing ladder. It was just long enough to bridge the chasm.

"Help me put this across," Midrange said.

"I shall." Snarl took part of the ladder in his teeth, and Midrange pawed at the end, and they managed to swing it awkwardly around until it fell across the gap. Then they walked somewhat gingerly across the rungs. Midrange, of course, had excellent feline balance, but Snarl didn't. He almost fell, but fortunately his legs poked through inside the ladder, and he was able to scramble back up.

They started walking along the far side, in the direction Woofer had gone. "Let me know if you pick up the trail," Midrange said. He could pick it up himself, but wanted to see whether the animal was playing straight with him. One of the smarter qualities of cats, of the multitude of good ones, was not to trust anyone too readily.

Every so often Midrange flung off another clone cat, though nobody seemed to be spying on them. "That's a nice magic talent you have," Snarl said admiringly. Midrange didn't bother to clarify how he had come by it; the little canine had no need to know.

Soon they came to a narrowing of the chasm, and sure enough, the trail resumed there. "Got it!" Snarl said.

Good enough; the canine was playing it straight. "Let's loop around and intercept it farther along," Midrange said, not explaining why. Snarl agreed; he seemed to be quite companionable, now that he had a companion. He probably would have made that little girl a good associate.

Then Midrange thought of something. "I'm new to Xanth," he

confessed. "From Mundania, actually. How is it that we animals learned to talk?"

"Everyone talks, in Xanth," Snarl explained. "Because of the magic. And the magic's getting much stronger now, for some reason."

"Because of the storm blowing magic dust in," Midrange said. "But soon it will be too strong, and there will be madness."

"You have learned a lot," Snarl said admiringly.

"Not enough. We animals always could understand most of what the human beings were saying, and we understood each other, in a general way. But since coming into Xanth, we have all grown much smarter, and now we can talk fluently with each other and with other creatures. We couldn't do that before."

"It's because of the Xanth common languages," Snarl said. "I have heard, though it surely isn't true, that in Mundania humans speak all different languages, and can't understand each other at all. The same must be true for animals and plants. In Xanth, all humans speak the human language, and all animals of a certain type speak their own language. That is, all mammals have one language, and all reptiles have one, and all insects have one, and so on. There are dialects, so that the way I speak isn't quite the same as you, and we'd both have trouble with a unicorn, and centaurs don't even bother with mammalian; they prefer to speak human. It has nuances that others don't, because humans are always talking. You surely had trouble understanding the bird."

"I did," Midrange agreed. "If I hadn't known him well, he would have been unintelligible. So it was because he spoke avian."

"Yes. Insects are harder yet, and plants—it's not worth bothering. Dragons aren't too bad, though they have a barbarous accent. But it's not safe to get close to a dragon anyway."

This was very interesting; it clarified what had been happening to them. But this business about dragons—"Are there many dragons around?"

"They're all over. Fire-breathers, smokers, and steamers; winged, land, and water; big, larger, and huge. They're always hungry. They're sort of the top of the food chain. Best thing is to stay away from them."

So Midrange had already gathered. But now they had to stop talk-
ing, because they were coming to a cave. The trail entered it. He even
caught the faint perfume of the bleep who had lured Woofer in.
Thanks to Snarl's help, it had taken him only another five minutes.
Now he had five more minutes to assess the situation and summon
Nimby.

"Is there another way into this cave?" he asked the dog.

"Probably. I'll sniff out one." The little canine circled to the right,
sniffing.

So Midrange circled to the left. Soon he found a winding aperture
just about right for slinking through. So he slunk through it. It was
dark inside, but he was comfortable with that. It was another of the
myriad ways in which cats were superior to other creatures.

He sniffed, and smelled Woofer. That helped him navigate the various side crevices, coming ever closer without going directly there.
Because there still could be more trouble than he wanted, if he got
discovered.

Then he heard a yip. That was Snarl! The dog must have entered
by another passage. Why had he given himself away?

Midrange slunk closer, until he could see into the central chamber.
There were Woofer and Tweeter, just lying and perching there. They
weren't even trying to escape, though nothing held them.

Snarl slunk in to join them, his tail between his legs. He was definitely unhappy, but he was obeying someone. Yet there was no one
there. Just a pile of metallic junk in the center of the cave, faintly
glowing.

Then Snarl spoke. "I did not come alone. There is a cat who is
coming to rescue the other dog and bird."

Why, the little traitor! He was blabbing the mission! Had Midrange
trusted a spy?

"The cat is coming in another way," Snarl said. "In fact, he is
crouching behind you."

That did it. Midrange leaped up, tiger fashion. "Woofer! Tweeter!
Get out of here!" he cried. "I'll pounce on it."

Something swiveled around to face him. It was a TV screen, with
icons on it. One picture expanded: a cat going splat against an invisible wall in midair.

SPLAT! Midrange suited action to picture, and fell to the floor in a heap.

Outraged, he gathered himself together for another pounce. But a picture appeared on the screen, showing a cat wading through super-sticky dense glue, and he found he could move only excruciatingly slowly.

A picture of a dog talking appeared. With that, Woofer began to speak. ''This is a machine called Sending, who was originally a pro-gram animating Magician Grey Murphy's Mundane computer. He helped Grey and Princess Ivy go to Xanth, provided they took him along. Now he is scheming to conquer Xanth. This will take time—a few thousand years—but he is patient. He is in the process of assembling a group of creatures and things to do his bidding. The recent influx of magic dust has enabled him to act more strongly. Thus he was able to lure me into his cave, though he failed with Karen. That's all right; he'll get her and the other humans when the magic intensifies enough.''

''But how does he do it?'' Midrange asked.

''Sending has the power to change reality in his immediate vicin-ity,'' Woofer said. ''Just as his sire, Com Pewter, does. Pewter prints whatever he wishes reality to be, and it is then true, near him. Only Sending works better with icons, which he expands into pictures when he wants to invoke them. So he has made us captive by luring us into his ambiance, then invoking magic icons to control us. It is not pos-sible to oppose his will, because he defines will here.''

''That's why I had to blab about your mission,'' Snarl said. ''The icon made me. I'm sorry.''

Now that Midrange had been snared by Sending, he understood how it was. ''You had no choice,'' he said. But he realized that he, Midrange, had better exert some choice, because otherwise the wicked machine could force him to blab about Nimby coming to the rescue. He had to distract Sending a few more minutes. Maybe the machine was subject to flattery. ''I thought I would find Woofer and Tweeter and rescue them. I guess I was pretty foolish.''

An icon expanded into a picture of a clown laughing. Sending thought it was very funny. ''But instead I just got caught myself,'' he continued. ''But I'm curious about one thing: how did you get those wraiths to help you, by luring folk into your cave? They were running far beyond your ambiance.'' Midrange was sure of that, because otherwise Sending would simply have changed reality for miles around, and made all creatures and people serve him.

The talking dog picture appeared again. ''He explained that to us while we waited for others to try to rescue you, and thus to fall into his power,'' Woofer said. ''He made a deal with the wraiths, that if they helped him achieve power, he would enable them to achieve solid form again. They are eager to gain some substance, so they cooperate.''

''Substance?'' Midrange asked. ''How is that possible?''

''It is our substance they will be given,'' Woofer said sadly. ''The wraiths will inhabit us and take over our bodies and minds.''

''But this is barbaric!'' Midrange protested.

The laughing clown appeared on the screen.

Then there was a sound outside. A wraith hurried in. ''A damsel and a dragon!'' it cried silently. ''She's lovely, but it has a donkey head. It forged right to this cave. They're coming in!''

The screen faced Midrange. A picture of a cat talking appeared.

Suddenly Midrange was compelled to tell all he knew. ''It is Chlorine and the dragon ass called Nimby,'' he blabbed. ''They are coming to nullify you and rescue us. I have been stalling, to give them time to get here unobserved. They have two pieces of reverse wood.''

The screen flickered violently. Evidently the mention of reverse wood bothered the machine. Then the image of a door slamming closed appeared.

Too late. A wooden ball rolled into the cave and came to rest before the screen.

A picture showed dogs, cat, and bird hastily shoving the ball out of the cave. But before they could act, the ball fell into two parts. And Sending's screen went dim.

''Let's get out of here before he recovers,'' Midrange said. The four of them, freed from the machine's power, charged out of the cave.

There was the striped dragon, with the lovely young woman. She was still leaning forward, evidently just having rolled the ball into the cave. ''Hi, fellows,'' she said brightly. ''The two pieces of reverse wood nullified each other. But when they fell apart, they nullified Sending. He'll be helpless until that wood gets moved out of his cave—which will be hard to do. Now we must hurry, because the moving house is about to start moving.''

They hurried. All of them ran, following the dragon, who knew where they were going. Snarl came along too.

They made it to the road, panting. There was the RV, just starting to move. The water had all drained away, leaving the surface drivable. ''They don't see us!'' Chlorine gasped.

Nimby snapped up a piece of wood, held it between his donkey teeth, lifted his head, and gave what sounded like a whistle in duck-talk. It was an awful noise. But it worked; the vehicle slowed.

''Nimby—you can talk!'' Chlorine cried as they raced up to it. But the dragon shook his head, and Midrange knew why: he had made a sound, but it wasn't talking. The whistle had been artificial, because of air blown past the piece of wood, and meaningless, except in the sense that it signaled the whistler's presence. It was just noise, not talk.

Chlorine realized that after two thirds of a moment. ''You made it, but it wasn't you. I should have realized.'' She smiled. ''So I'm not a whistler's mother. I'll survive.''

They got there, and Nimby changed back to his man-form. Woofer and Tweeter scrambled into the RV, and Chlorine followed. But Midrange paused. ''What about you, Snarl?'' he asked the dog.

Snarl hesitated. ''Nobody here needs a companion?'' he asked plaintively.

The dog had helped Midrange accomplish his mission in time. Generosity was not really Midrange's forte, but there was an implied deal: companionship for help. ''Get on in,'' he told the dog. ''We'll figure something out.''

Nimby had paused. Now he picked up Snarl, whose legs were too short to navigate the steep step up, and set him on the floor inside. Then Midrange bounded in, and Nimby came last.

''You did it!'' David cried, picking Midrange up and hugging him. ''You rescued them. I knew you could! 'Cause you're my cat.''

Disgusting display of sentiment, but somehow Midrange wasn't entirely displeased. He extricated himself after a moment. He had indeed done the job, though perhaps some small credit should be given to the catatonic medicine, and to Snarl, and to Nimby also.

The RV was moving, gathering speed. Snarl was in Chlorine's lap, peering out a window, fascinated by this magic vehicle. Suddenly he barked. "It's her!"

What now? Midrange looked out. There was a disconsolate dark-haired girl walking by the edge of the road. She seemed to be looking for something. "Who is 'her'?" Midrange asked the dog.

"My ideal companion! The girl whose hair formed me. Maybe she's looking for me."

Midrange wasn't sure about that, but it was worth a try. He ran up to the front, where Jim-Dad was driving. "Meop!" he said, in as plain human as he could muster.

Jim-Dad looked at him. "You want me to pick up that girl? We don't have room for—"

"Mneo," Midrange said. "Meust meop." He wished his cat tongue could form the clumsy human words better. He was trying to say, "No—just stop."

Jim-Dad sighed and braked the vehicle. He came to a stop by the girl, who paused to stare at the RV in astonishment. Obviously she had never seen a monster like this before. But at least she wasn't running away from it.

Snarl leaped to the floor and charged for the front, his stubby legs slipping on the unfamiliar surface. He arrived just as the girl was answering Jim-Dad's question. "I'm Ursa. I'm just looking for my dog. I was distracted and lost him, and I can't find him anywhere. I'm afraid he'll be hurt by the madness if I don't find him and take him home quickly. Have you seen—?"

Then Snarl launched himself out the door. Ursa saw him and plucked him out of midair. "Snarl! You're here! You're safe!" She hugged him joyfully, and his stubby little tail wagged ferociously.

So Snarl would not be traveling farther with them; he had found his ideal companion. Midrange looked out the window as the RV resumed motion. The girl waved, and Snarl barked. Then they were gone. Karen wiped away a tear, and Midrange's own eyes were wet, but of course, that was because of the lingering effect of the Crimea River.

After that, the drive became boring. Jim-Dad was driving fast, try-ing to get where he was going before the madness made it impossible. There was no other traffic on the road, which helped, but still it wasn't the safest mode of travel. The children were settling down to normal fidgeting, while Sean was oddly subdued, as if he had suffered some great forgotten adventure of his own. Midrange tuned all of it out and catnapped.

He woke when the RV swerved. No wonder: the flying dragons were back. They were swooping down to strafe the vehicle, and Jim-Dad was trying to dodge their reaching flames. But a flame caught it anyway—and did no harm.

"Illusions!" Jim-Dad said, disgusted. "Trying to trick me into swerving off the road. Because it's still enchanted, and they can't really attack us here." After that he drove straight ahead, even when a dragon came right down to smash into the windshield, and there was nothing.

Midrange sat up and watched, because this was getting interesting. Suppose one of those dragons turned out to be real, and Jim-Dad didn't dodge it? If maybe there were a flaw in the enchantment, letting one monster through. But soon the phantom dragons gave up, prob-ably because it was no fun when the vehicle wouldn't be bluffed.

Then there was a sign: JUNK SHUN. "What do you suppose that means?" Jim-Dad asked rhetorically. "I don't remember it from be-fore."

It soon turned out to be a crossroads where there was a huge pile of garbage, refuse, and junk. Was it real—or more illusion? A lot of that junk was in the middle of the road; the vehicle could suffer damage if it plowed into it at speed.

"Delay is disaster," Jim-Dad muttered, and maintained speed. He won: they passed through the junk without contact.

After that there were various weird images in the sky and on the ground. At times it looked as if the sky was solid, with mountains growing on it, while the land was gaseous, with birds flying through it. The road was a ribbon of asphalt winding between them, now tunneling through the hills and then floating on water. At one point it headed straight out into space, with the ground showing far below. But Jim-Dad just forged on, ignoring all the effects, and in the end prevailed. His natural Mundane disbelief in magic was helping him reject the illusions. As dusk threatened, they reached the turnoff to Imp Erial.

As they pulled carefully into the village, they saw that the imps were desperate. They were still working, but they looked haggard. Piles of boxes and bags of gems sat on the walks, not yet carried to safety. Obviously they were not going to make it.

The RV drew to a stop. Quieta appeared, her nice dress sweat-sodden, her nice hair in disarray. "But we thought you were safely out of Xanth by this time," she cried.

"We came to help you complete your job," Jim-Dad said. "Tell us how to do that."

Quieta wasted no time on amazement. "You can carry those piles of gems to the cave. Ersonal will show you the way."

They trooped out, not bothering with the accommodation spell this time. Each of the humans, including Nimby, picked up a pile and carried it carefully. Each load was perhaps ten times what an imp might have carried. They followed Imp Ersonal along a path that was really too small for full humans, but it had to do, because if they reduced to imp size, they wouldn't be able to carry their burdens.

They came to the cave. It looked like a rathole, so small that even the imps had to crawl into it. They set down their burdens and returned to the village.

Midrange watched, as did Woofer and Tweeter. They weren't fit for carrying, but they could still help. When the humans returned, each animal showed some of them to a new pile. That way the imps didn't have to carry the piles to the staging region; they could be picked up directly from the buildings. When the imps saw that, they increased their efforts to get their wares out on the steps. There were barrels of beryls, each gem of which was a miniature barrel that would cause anyone who invoked it to bare all. Men liked to give these to innocent women, the imps explained. There were lapfuls of lapis, which would cause people to wee-wee unexpectedly; Midrange presumed those were for unfriends or those with certain bodily complications. There were pails of fire opals, which were little O-shaped pails that would safely carry fire. There were chairs loaded with citrines, which were gems that caused folk to sit, and if they then took up a la-trine, they would sing, and more. There were collections of topaz, which were toe-shaped candies, yellow, peach, white, and blue. There were tiger eyes, through which one could catch a view of a tiger. In fact, there were so many kinds of gems that Midrange lost interest long before assimilating them all.

"What kind of goofy creature are you?" an imp demanded.

Midrange stared at the imp, who was no larger than Midrange himself. "You must be Olite," he remarked in animal language, not expecting to be understood.

"How did you guess, caterwaul?" the imp asked rudely. "Now, get your carcass out of my way so I can set these O-nix stones down where your fat rump is."

Onyx. To be sure. Midrange got out of the way. It was good to know that not all the imps were sickly sweet in the manner of Quieta.

As David came to pick up the collection here, two more imps passed by. "You know, End, those huge humans have really helped us," one said. "Too bad this is only the beginning of Xanth's mischief."

"You're right, Asse," the other replied. "They have enabled us to save our wares in time, for which we are deeply grateful, but the fate of the rest of Xanth seems worse."

"I hope that when we emerge from our safe cave, enough of Xanth remains to make existence worthwhile," End said, his tone suggesting that he doubted that would be the case.

The two walked on, checking the various houses to make sure all the goods had been taken. But Midrange was bothered by their implication. This wasn't the whole job? Then what was the point? He didn't like thinking that they had taken all this trouble to accomplish nothing really significant.

So he ran after David, with whom he could communicate most readily. The boy was just setting down his last load, as dusk became darkness. "Meavid!" he said.

David saw him and picked him up. "What's with you, hero?" he asked, stroking his fur in the way he tolerated.

"Merouble." Confound this clumsy human speech!

''Trouble?'' David asked. ''I thought we just took care of it. Now we're going to use the accommodation spell and join the imps in their safe cave and wait for the madness to pass.''

Midrange wasn't sure of that. But he couldn't get through to the boy fast enough, even if he knew exactly what the problem was. ''Meimby.''

''Ask Nimby? Okay.''

At that point Nimby approached. He always seemed to know when someone wanted to talk to him. *The imps say there is danger for all Xanth,* he thought to Nimby, who could read minds. *What is it? Can we help? Tell David.*

Nimby wrote a note and gave it to David. ''There *is* danger!'' David cried. ''And we *can* help.''

Chlorine approached. ''There is more danger?'' she asked.

David gave her the note. She read it and sighed. ''Then I suppose we'll have to tell the others, though I fear this will lead to complications.''

David nodded. ''I guess this isn't great for you, huh? It's more work with the duffers.''

Chlorine tousled his hair. Midrange saw the effect it had on the boy; if Sean was three-quarters-smitten by her beauty, David was half-smitten. ''Really, I don't mind. But how did you know to ask Nimby about it?''

''Midrange told me.''

Chlorine looked at Midrange with mock severity. ''So you're the one!'' She tousled his fur too. And he, too, loved it. There was just something about a stunningly beautiful woman with a nice personality, even if he knew it was all an enchantment made by a donkey-headed dragon.

And the truth was that this was the best adventure Midrange himself had ever had. It had everything: a dragon, a damsel, peril, magic, mystery, and madness. What more could a bored tomcat desire?

20 Questions

C hlorine went to find the adult members of the family. Jim Baldwin was just returning from his final load of gems. She intercepted him. "Excuse me, please—" She realized that she didn't know how he preferred to be addressed. "Mundane Father—"

He smiled. "Call me Jim."

That made it easier. "Jim, I have learned that there is more danger. Not just for the imps, but for all Xanth. David asked Nimby. Nimby didn't volunteer it, because it wasn't to us personally. But—"

"We were able to help the imps, but helping all Xanth is surely beyond our power," he said. "We need to use the accommodation spell now and join the imps in their safe cave until the storm passes."

"The imps are afraid that there will not be much left, after it passes," she said.

"I'd better talk with Nimby. The way the wind is rising, we can't delay about a decision."

"I know where he is." She led him back to David, Midrange, and Nimby.

"Nimby, what's this about danger for all Xanth, and how does it concern us?" Jim asked.

Nimby had already written a note. He gave it to Jim.

" 'The storm is unique because it is foreign,' " Jim read. " 'It will continue to grow in strength, and the magic dust it spreads will devastate all of Xanth if not stopped. Those who live underground, or take cover there, will survive, but those who remain on the ground, in the water, or in the air will suffer grievously. Most of the vegetation will be blown away. What remains will be a paltry remnant. But it is possible for this party to ameliorate it, if we take immediate and effective action, at some risk to ourselves.' ''

"Some risk?'' Chlorine said. "But I'm supposed to get you safely out of Xanth.''

"We negated that when we turned back from the border,'' Jim remarked wryly.

The other members of the family had assembled during the reading. "Dad, we have to take that action,'' Sean said.

"Yeah,'' Karen agreed.

He looked at Mary. "Yes,'' she said grimly.

"But that probably means danger,'' he said. "Nimby surely isn't fooling about 'some risk.' And we're already tired.''

"And all the other folk of Xanth face possible extinction,'' Mary said.

He faced Nimby. "What can we do?''

Nimby was already writing another note. Jim read it. He looked at Chlorine. "It seems we shall have to split up,'' he said.

"But I must see you safely out of Xanth!'' Chlorine repeated. "That's my mission. I can't leave you until then.''

"Nimby believes that you will not be able to accomplish that mission until Xanth itself is secured,'' Jim said. "So it seems we shall have to take the risk. You must go with Nimby to fetch the windbreaker; we must go to Castle Roogna to get help in enlisting Fracto Cumulo Nimbus in the cause of saving Xanth.''

"Wow!'' David exclaimed.

Chlorine was amazed. She looked at Nimby. He nodded. "Well, it will be your fault if I fail to complete the Good Magician's service,'' she said. "I certainly hope you know as much as you think you do.''

Nimby nodded again. He was so sure he knew, when obviously he couldn't know everything. That was about the only aggravating thing about him.

Then he wrote another note. It said: *I know what is going on in*

Xanth, not what will happen. I know that Fracto and the windbreaker can save Xanth, but not whether they will. I know the best way to achieve these things, but not whether they will be achieved. I do not mean to be aggravating.

And how could she be mad at him? He was making her beautiful, smart, and healthy, and helping her have the greatest adventure of her life. "I'm sorry for what I thought," she said, for of course, he had made her nice, too. She knew she wouldn't much care about his feelings in her natural state, but she was glad to be the way he had made her. She felt so much better about herself this way, and not just because of the way others saw her. She owed Nimby everything.

"Then so let it be," Jim said. Chlorine suspected that he, too, was beginning to enjoy this adventure, which was surely quite different from his ordinary life in drear Mundania. "We shall drive to—" He glanced at the note Nimby had given him. "Castle Roogna. We should be able to make it by morning."

Mary took his arm. "You have driven enough, dear," she said. "I will drive there, while you get some necessary rest."

Karen stared at her. "Mom! You can drive the RV?"

"Stop teasing me, you little bleep," Mary said with a third of a smile. Unlike the others, she actually said the word "bleep"; it wasn't a Conspiracy expurgation.

"But how will we find our way there, without Chlorine and Nimby to tell us?" David asked.

"Good point," Jim said.

Quieta had joined the group. "We really appreciate the way you helped us complete our task in time, at the expense of your own freedom to leave Xanth," she said. "We have not known how to repay you, but now perhaps we can. We shall provide a guide."

"But then that person won't be safe in the sanctuary cave," Mary protested.

"She will be safe at Castle Roogna, perhaps, especially if you succeed in saving Xanth. Here is my daughter Trenita." A younger imp woman stepped forward. She looked to be in her mid-thirties.

"Then we are constrained to accept your kind offer," Jim said. "Now I think the madness is closing in; you must close your cave, and we must be on our way."

So they bid a second parting to the imps, who Chlorine suspected were just as glad not to have to entertain the family in the sanctuary cave, and went their ways. The Baldwin family piled into their traveling house and moved off, Mary at the wheel, with Trenita Imp lifted into the seat next to Karen. Chlorine and Nimby saw them off. It looked as if the vehicle were stretching and twisting like a giant caterpillar, but she knew that was just the effect of the madness.

Then she turned to her companion. "So how do we find this windbreaker?" she asked.

He wrote a note: *It is one of the possessions of Sending. We must obtain it from the ambitious program.*

"Sending! The one we just messed up to rescue the Mundane pets? We're doomed."

Not if we approach him properly. Sending is rational.

"So how do we approach him?"

We must bring him a suitable gift, and answer his twenty questions.

"Twenty questions? I may be smart, now, thanks to you, but I'm not sure I could answer that many without a stumble. What happens if we miss one?"

We become two of Sending's artifacts.

"Nuh-uh, Nimby! I already have an assignment, and after that I'll have to go home and become dull again. I can't get locked into slavery for some cold machine."

But I can answer the questions.

"Oh. If you're sure. How do we get there? It was a long fast ride in the Mundane moving house, and I don't think we could walk that far tonight, even without the interference of the madness, not to mention the wind." For the wind was rising again, blowing her skirt up and about, and trying to tangle her hair enough to form a pack of snarls. Now that Sean wasn't here to goggle at her legs, she found this inconvenient.

Nimby led the way to the side of the road. "But if we go beyond the enchanted limit, monsters can get us," she said. But she knew Nimby was aware of that, and wouldn't lead her into danger.

There was a big puff of cotton caught in a tree. No, it was cloudstuff, she realized. Maybe some of the cloud that made the Gap Chasm ferry had detached and drifted here. Naturally Nimby knew where it was. So she helped him wrestle it out of the snags of the branches and twigs.

But the small cloud wanted to float; they couldn't get it down to the ground. Then Nimby boosted her up onto it. She fell into its bowl-like surface, her legs in the air, her skirt halfway to her head.

Nimby climbed up on the other side, and rolled into the cloud bowl. He, too, landed mostly upside down, but his trousers left him decorous.

"No fair," she said. "When I climbed in, I showed my panties to the sky. You didn't show anything. And you probably saw my panties, too."

Nimby nodded.

"And you're not even embarrassed," she said severely.

He nodded again.

"Or freaked out." Now she was annoyed. But then she realized that he was, after all, only a dragon, who didn't see human beings as prospects for anything social. Why should he care about panties?

She got herself in order and poked her head over the edge of the cloud. It was still floating, and the wind was blowing it north along the highway at increasing velocity. So they were being carried in the direction they wanted to go. Obviously Nimby had known that this would be the case. The trollway was bare, and the trees along the sides of it seemed to be shifting colors, textures, and natures, because of the distortion by the intensifying madness. But they also channeled this gust of wind, so that the cloud was floating straight along the channel, and still gaining speed.

"Well, if we're going to float there, let's get some shielding from the wind," she said. She took handfuls of the cloudstuff at the rim and shaped it up into higher walls, and then all the way into a dome over them. The material gleamed faintly, lighting the interior with a gentle yellow glow. It was fun to work with cloud, because it was so soft and pliable. "Just the way a woman is supposed to be," she said as she finished the job. She didn't have quite enough material to make the dome complete, so she fashioned a round window in the top, through which they could view the stars. Now they shared a spherical chamber, and apart from a certain bounciness, it was hard to tell that it was moving.

''Now let's get comfortable,'' she said, and shaped two pillows for them. ''We can just lie here until we get there. I'm sure you'll know when that is.''

Nimby nodded.

They floated comfortably along. But the novelty soon wore off. Chlorine would have slept, but it was early in the evening, and anyway, she had snoozed while riding in the traveling house. So she was wide-awake, and becoming bored.

''Nimby, exactly what are you?'' she asked. ''I mean, I know you're a donkey-headed dragon who knows what's going on, and you can make me beautiful and yourself handsome. But I never heard of any creature like you before. Where did you come from? What did you do all day?''

Nimby's pad and pencil appeared. He wrote a note, and gave it to her. She read it aloud.

'' 'I am a special variety of monster. I contest endlessly with others of my kind for status. We live only for games, whose rules are somewhat arbitrary and stringent. If we violate them, we lose the game. Some games are brief, while some take centuries.' ''

She looked up. ''Centuries! Your kind must live a long time!'' Nimby nodded apologetically.

She resumed reading. '' 'Status is indicated by the delimiters. Ordinary status is parentheses, and the next stage is brackets, and braces, and angles, though for convenience we usually just use parentheses.' ''

She broke off again. ''You must lead the dullest life imaginable, Nimby! No wonder you came to share an adventure with me. It's bad enough being a donkey-headed dragon, but to be limited, I mean delimited in braces—you poor thing!'' She tossed aside the note, which dissolved into a wisp of smoke and disappeared.

Nimby nodded. Oddly, he looked more relieved than limited. But Chlorine remained bored, and it was obvious that Nimby's background was even more boring.

So she made a decision. ''Nimby, back when we first got together, I said I would teach you romance, when the right time came. I think that time is now. We have a lot of adventure behind us, and probably a lot more ahead of us, but right now we have none. Since we can't be sure that everything will work out for the best, we might as well make the most of what offers right now.'' She glanced at him. ''Do you have any idea what I'm talking about?''

Nimby shook his head.

She laughed. ''You can read my mind, but you can't understand what I'm thinking, because you're really a striped dragon with a donkey head and you don't understand human emotion. Well, because I know what you are, there can't be anything serious between us, no lasting relationship, just as there couldn't be with young Sean Mundane, though it was fun having him watch me, though the past few hours he ignored me, even when I came perilously close to exposing my—'' She severed that unpleasant thought. ''And you will surely never break my heart and make me cry.'' Though, oddly, Nimby did seem to look sad at that point. ''But I do appreciate what you are doing for me, Nimby, and I think it only fair to repay you in my fashion. So I'll show you how to act, as if you were really a handsome human man and not a laughably weird exotic creature. Who knows, the information might come in handy sometime. And maybe it'll be fun.'' She glanced at him again. ''Do you understand anything yet?''

He shook his head.

''Well, you will find out. I am going to show you how to summon the stork. Too bad it's not for real. But we'll pretend it is. Now I think I have practiced enough with Sean to know what turns a man on. If I can turn you on, I'll know I'm getting there. Are you ready?''

Nimby looked doubtful.

Chlorine smiled. ''So we're starting from neutral. Good. Now, since you can't speak, I shall have to speak both our parts. But you can perform the actions for yourself. It's all like a play put on by the Curse Fiends, and we know we don't mean any of it, but it may be interesting anyway. Whatever I say I'll do, I'll do, and whatever I say you'll do, you'll do. Understand?''

Nimby nodded, still dubiously.

''You say with masculine boldness, 'What is your name, pretty girl?' And I flutter my eyelashes demurely and reply, 'Chlorine, handsome man, and what is yours?' And you say, 'I am Nimby. I'm a dashing dragon of a man. I have come to take you away from all this.' And I say, 'Oh, sir, how romantic! I think I will kiss you.' And

I do.'' She turned to face him, as they lay side by side within the bowl, and kissed him firmly on the mouth. Despite her artificial dialogue, she was getting into it, and the kiss felt real. For one thing, Nimby was kissing her back, so he did understand that much.

"And then you, being a man, have mainly one thing on your mind," she continued. "And that is summoning the stork. So you say, 'Chlorine, you are very pretty, but I think you would look downright lovely with less on.' And you put your hand on my knee and squeeze, gently.'' She took his hand and set it there when he hesitated. "And I say, innocently, 'Oh, do you really think so? Would you like me to show you my panties?' And you are so excited at the prospect that you can't even speak at the moment, so you just nod and smile. And then—''

She broke off, for there was a face at the window, with two big eyes. "What is this!" she cried, annoyed. She threw a cloud-fluff pillow at it. The pillow struck the head and fragmented into smithereens. Then she saw that it wasn't a head, it was a rotating set of blades. As they turned, they formed the face. It was a window fan. Such creatures loved to peer into windows. That really turned them on, so that they spun faster.

Fortunately her thrown pillow had gummed up its works and blinded it. It would peer in her window no more.

"Now, where exactly were we?" she inquired, recovering her bearings, as she unbound her green-gold hair to float in a luxuriant mass around her shoulders. "Oh, yes, the high point of any man's life: to see the color of her panties. (No, we won't mention that you made nice ones for me; that isn't part of this script. You are now in innocent horny male mode.) I have just made the supreme offer, and you are gaga at the very notion. So you nod yes, you are hot to see them, for they are surely Xanth's most delightfully naughty sight. And by this time I am hot to show you, knowing that it will probably freak you out, not to mention inflame your passion beyond endurance, requiring me to kiss you and stroke you back to some semblance of sanity. So—''

She loosened her dress and drew it up and over her head. "Of course, you can't see them yet, because I'm wearing a slip under my dress. I am such an awful tease, as is required by the Big Book of Rules for Adult Conspiracy Indiscretions. However—''

There was a shuddering in the cloud, and the sound of heavy tromping. ''What now?'' Chlorine demanded, her patience showing a sign of wanting to wander, if not to get lost.

Nimby's pad and pencil appeared. But before he completed his note, the cloud cover shook violently, sending Chlorine tumbling slip over flying hair. Then another face appeared in the window.

''I thought I got rid of you,'' she said. But then she realized that this was a different face, huge and fat and vaguely masculine.

''Any ogres here?'' the face inquired, licking its thick lips.

Her patience slipped another notch. ''Do I look like an ogre?'' she demanded, swinging her legs in his direction.

He blinked, but evidently was not sufficiently human to freak out at the sight. ''No, you look like a luscious morsel of a damsel girl with pretty good legs.''

He had been doing okay until the last three words. Her last nerve frayed, on the verge of snapping. ''Pretty good?'' she demanded. ''And just what do you consider to be *good* legs?''

''Why, ogre legs, of course.''

''Ogre legs! *Ogre legs!?*'' she screeched in what might have passed for harpy fashion, if one had that low a mind. ''What kind of creature are you?''

''I'm an ogre eater, of course,'' he explained.

''An ogre eater! You mean you eat ogres? I never heard of that before.''

''Well, there aren't many of us, because ogres don't taste very good.'' He glanced again at her legs. ''But I suppose if there aren't any ogres, you might do; your legs have a fair amount of healthy meat on them.''

''Oh no you don't!'' she snapped, clapping her legs together. ''I need these legs myself. Go find a real ogre.''

''Okay,'' the ogre eater said. The face disappeared, and the tromping and ground shaking resumed, in a diminishing cadence.

Chlorine returned once more to the business at hand. She saw Nimby holding his note. ''Never mind that,'' she told him. ''I found out for myself. Now let's resume our activity before something else interrupts. I wish this cloud floated just a bit higher, so sundry folk couldn't just peek in.''

Nimby started to get up.

"No, don't see about doing something about it," she said quickly. "That'll just distract us. I want to get the bleep on with this, before we arrive where we're going and it's too late. Can you appreciate that?''

Nimby looked appreciative. In fact, she had the impression that he was definitely getting intrigued by her ongoing lesson of love. Good. It was nice being so beautiful as to inflame men's minds, and so sexy as to force them to think of only one thing: summoning the stork. She had verified that it worked on Sean Mundane, but he was young. Nimby was mature.

She lifted her slip to knee height, tantalizingly. Nimby looked really interested. She was ready to lift it all the way clear, but didn't. Her hands just wouldn't do it.

What was the matter with her? Here was her chance to do what no man had been interested in doing with her before, yet she was stalling. Why?

Nimby wrote another note. *Because you know I am only a donkey-headed dragon, and you want a real man.*

She realized it was true. She could playact all she wanted, and craft any script she wanted, but down underneath she knew it wasn't real, because he wasn't real. In fact, she wasn't real either; she was just a plain and somewhat ornery girl making a pretense. What was the use of that?

Yet if she didn't take advantage of her opportunity now, her adventure might be over before she had another chance. So maybe pretense was better than nothing at all. "Darn it, Nimby, let's do it anyway! I want to show my panties to *someone,* and you may never get to see another girl's panties, I mean, not when she's not thinking of you as some stupid beast who doesn't count. Would you like to go ahead?''

Nimby nodded.

Chlorine took hold of her slip again. "Then watch this, and be amazed.'' She took a two-handed grip and hauled it right up and over

her head. She flung it away and stood proudly in her pale green/
yellow bra and panties.

But Nimby didn't freak out. Because not only was he a dragon, it
was his magic that had made this limited clothing, as well as her
present body. None of it was new or novel to him. "Oh, this isn't
working!" she cried, frustrated anew. "I'm just going through meaningless motions, and boring you to oblivion. I'm sorry, Nimby."

Nimby wrote a note and handed it to her. *I am not bored.*

But she knew better. "How can you be interested in what you
yourself made? I might as well revert to my natural state, where my
panties don't even pretend to be interesting, let alone man-freaking."
She fetched back her slip and put it back on. "I apologize for drag-
ging you through this embarrassing charade, Nimby. I won't do it
again. I could just cry with frustration—but I can't risk even that."

Nimby, looking alarmed, started to write another note.

"No, don't do it," she told him firmly. "Don't try to tell me something you think will make me feel good. Let's leave the illusions for
those who don't know better."

Nimby looked sad, but his notepad disappeared.

Chlorine fetched her dress and donned it. "But I want you to know
that I do like you, Nimby, and respect you, and if you were a real
man, I would have done it with you. Even if you were a near-man,
like a Curse Fiend or maybe a Demon. Demons know how to appreciate mortal women, physically at least. But a dragon? All this must
be utterly laughable to you. So I won't bore you anymore; I owe you
at least that much. You have been a really good sport."

Her dress was done. She started on her hair. Then, on sudden im-
pulse, she went to Nimby and embraced him. "Thanks for being my
friend," she said, and kissed him. The two half tears in her eyes
brimmed, but fortunately didn't lose their positions.

Nimby froze. His eyes glazed. Had she freaked him out after all?
But in half a moment he recovered, and wrote a note. *You are more
than welcome, Chlorine.*

She smiled. "At least we understand each other. Maybe that's better than the other."

He nodded, though he looked as if he had come close to some
phenomenal achievement, and lost it. Maybe she *should* have done

the stork routine with him, after tempting him so. But no; she had done her best to do the right thing, and that was to save the stork summoning for a man she really loved, rather than wasting it on a game.

The cloud floated on, sublimely unconcerned with their troubled thoughts.

Soon Nimby wrote another note. *We are there.*

"Already?" she asked, surprised. But she realized that the cloud had been moving along with deceptive velocity, so it could be. So her opportunity to do something naughty was indeed gone. She regretted and resented that, even though she had made the decision herself.

Nimby scrambled up and out the top window, and held down a hand for her. He pulled her right up; she was surprised by his easy strength, until she remembered yet again that he was really a dragon. They perched on top, and she saw that the cloud was indeed moving along at a good clip. The wind was higher; the sound had been muffled by the cloud wall so that she had forgotten it. The ill wind was still intensifying.

Nimby reached out and caught an overhanging branch. He kept his feet hooked into the top of the cloud so that it couldn't go anywhere. But neither did it sink to the ground. It was still about twice a man's height up. That ogre eater must have been huge! "How do we get down?" she asked.

Nimby nodded toward his legs. This required some interpretation. He was going to climb down? He shook his head, and she remembered—again—that he could read her mind. So all she had to do was think the right thought.

She put her bright mind to work. She must have something to do with his feet. Take them out of the cloud? But then it would float away with her. Unless she hung on to them. Aha! She could swing down on his legs; that would get her low enough so she could drop the rest of the way without harm. She saw that the ground was soft there, piled with pine needles, surely by no coincidence; Nimby always knew what he was doing. But how would he get down? He must be strong enough to handle the drop. And he nodded.

"Okay, Nimby," she said. "I'm trusting you with my safety. I guess I might as well, having already shown you my panties, for all that they bombed out.''

She leaned into him and grabbed him around the thighs. "I hope I don't pull your pants off," she said. But she knew that wouldn't happen. Nothing ever went wrong with Nimby. That thought made her regret for one or two instants that she hadn't continued her script in the cloud, at least up to the point of getting his pants off. She was curious about—but that was an unmaidenly thought—and what was he thinking of it now?

She refocused and scrambled off the cloud. She dropped down, seeing his legs release the cloud, which quickly floated on downwind, in a hurry to get where it was going. She swung back and forth like a pendulum, her body sliding down past his knees and feet, until she was just about all the way beneath him. Then she dropped, landing neatly on the needles, which were rusted and crumbly, not still sharp, fortunately. She was surprised by how readily she had done it, then realized that it was her good health that accounted for it. The health Nimby had given her. However, she still lost her balance and sat down; health did not give her perfect judgment on a landing.

Someone laughed. It sounded like the voice of an ass, but it wasn't Nimby, who was still hanging above, waiting for her to clear the landing site. She looked around.

There was a man emerging from the forest beside the road. He wore dirty clothes and had a large rusted metal can for a hat. "Do it again, sister!" he brayed. "Maybe this time I'll see something interesting.''

Chlorine knew his type. He was a junk male—who traveled around to take up the attention of people who didn't want him, and acted like trash. There were way too many of his kind cluttering up the space of decent folk. She knew exactly how to handle him.

"Is this interesting enough?" she called sweetly as she got to her feet. When she was sure he was watching, she turned around and flipped up her skirt and slip.

There was silence. She let her clothing fall back into place and turned around. The junk male was lying on his back, staring at the sky, not moving a muscle. He was absolutely stiff. He would remain that way for some time. Because he had Freaked Out.

Chlorine smiled. She had now proved the potency of her panties.

Then she remembered Nimby, who was still hanging by the branch. She hastily got out from under. "You may drop down now," she called sweetly. "I have disposed of the trash."

He dropped, smiling. He understood. That was one of the things she liked about him. He was strong, silent, helpful, and understanding.

They walked past the freaked-out male and into the forest toward Sending's lair. Nimby knew the way without hesitation, of course, despite the darkness. When she stumbled, he took her hand and led her securely along firm-footed paths. They didn't need to worry about dangers, because Nimby avoided them automatically, and knew how to deal with them anyway. Chlorine realized that she felt safe with him, and she liked that, too.

Soon they came to the dastardly device's cave. Nimby walked right in without fear, so she did too. But it was even darker here, until Nimby found a glow fungus that served as a lamp. He just always could put his hands on the right thing.

In the central chamber the two halves of the reverse wood ball still lay on the floor, nullifying Sending. Nimby picked them up and put them together again. He handed her the ball.

"But—" she said, almost dropping it in her nervousness. Then she realized that it was safe, as long as she kept it together. So she held it excruciatingly carefully. It wouldn't do her harm anyway, because if it reversed her magic, she would be able to sweeten water instead of poisoning it. But she wondered how Nimby himself was able to handle reverse wood without getting reversed.

The glassy screen lighted. A picture of a man appeared, with a big question mark over his head. Evidently the malignant machine was confused after being knocked out by the reverse wood.

Nimby glanced at her. Oh—she had to do the talking.

"Sending," she said firmly, "We have come to make a deal with you. You can't change our reality because I have this ball of reverse wood, and if anything happens to me, I'll drop it and the two pieces will fall apart and stop reversing each other and resume reversing you, as they did before. You will become an unmagical collection of junk. Do you understand?"

The screen blinked. The question mark faded out.

"We want to obtain the windbreaker," she continued. "I understand you have it, and we can get it from you if we answer your twenty questions. Is that correct?"

The screen brightened. The man figure smiled. Then the screen split, with the upper section showing an icon of a pretty young woman holding a jacket, and the lower section showing the young woman and a young man in chains.

"If we answer all the questions correctly, we get the windbreaker," she said, interpreting. "If we don't, we both become your slaves for life." She paused, glancing a bit apprehensively at Nimby. Was he *sure*—?

But Nimby nodded. So she took her courage in one trembling hand and proceeded. "That seems fair. We agree. The two of us will consult on each question, and decide on the answer; only when I address you directly, Sending, will it count. Agreed?"

A smiley face appeared on the screen.

"Very well," she said briskly, just as if her heart weren't palpating her gizzard. "Proceed."

Now print appeared on the screen. So Sending could print, when he chose to; he wasn't limited to icons and pictures. FIRST A SAMPLE QUESTION, TO BE SURE WE AGREE ON THE MANNER OF THE QUESTIONS AND ANSWERS. THIS IS FOR DEMONSTRATION PURPOSE ONLY.

"Agreed." Chlorine suspected that there were rules about such things, and Sending didn't want his prospective victory to be nullified by a technicality.

QUESTION SAMPLE #1, REFERRING TO THE THIRD OF THE MUSE'S HISTORICAL TEXTS OF XANTH: WHEN MAGICIAN DOR, THEN AGE TWELVE, TRIED TO STOP THE FORGET SPELL'S COUNTDOWN IN THE YEAR 236, IT DID NOT RESPOND. SINCE IT WAS ABLE TO SPEAK ONLY BY HIS MAGIC, WHICH ENABLED HIM TO SPEAK TO THE INANIMATE AND HAVE IT ANSWER, WHY DID HE NOT SIMPLY WITHDRAW HIS MAGIC SO THAT IT COULD NO LONGER SPEAK?

Chlorine read the question, and quailed. She remembered from her centaur history classes (before she flunked out) that Prince Dor had traveled eight hundred years into Xanth's past and detonated the Forget Spell, making the Gap Chasm be forgotten for eight hundred years until the Time of No Magic broke up the enchantment, but the logic of this was beyond even her enhanced intelligence. If this was typical of the questions to come, she would be doomed before she started.

But Nimby was writing a note. He gave it to her, and suddenly the answer was clear. " 'He did not do that because it would not have been effective,' " she read. " 'The Forget Spell would merely have counted silently, and detonated anyway. The countdown could not be stopped, once started.' "

The screen went blank for a moment. Sending had evidently expected her to get it wrong, and was disconcerted. But in another moment it recovered. CORRECT. THAT WAS AN EASY ONE, OF COURSE. THE REAL QUESTIONS WILL BE MORE DIFFICULT. ARE YOU PREPARED TO ADDRESS THEM?

Chlorine bit her tongue to get some saliva in her dry mouth, and responded with fake confidence. "Of course. Let's see a nice challenging one."

But the machine wouldn't be bluffed. QUESTION #1: WHEN MAGICIAN TRENT FIRST ATTEMPTED TO CONQUER XANTH IN THE YEAR 1021, IT WAS SAID THAT HE CHANGED MEN INTO FISH AND LET THEM EXPIRE ON DRY LAND. HE DENIES IT. WHAT IS THE TRUTH?

She quailed again, worse. How could anyone ever know what had happened seventy-five years ago?

But Nimby was writing a note. She took it and read it aloud, knowing that if it wasn't the correct answer, she would not be able to do any better on her own. " 'Magician Trent did transform men into fish, but he did it by a river, where they fell in and swam. Then he walked away. But some of the fish, thinking that they were still men, scrambled back onto land and perished. Magician Trent never saw those ones, so did not know.' "

If Sending was impressed or disconcerted, he did not show it. His screen flashed the next one. QUESTION #2: MAGICIAN BINK'S TALENT IS THAT HE CAN NOT BE HARMED BY MAGIC. THUS THE GAP DRAGON, BEING A MAGICAL CREATURE, COULD NOT HARM HIM DESPITE MAKING THE EFFORT. YET HE WAS CHOKED BY CHESTER CENTAUR AND ALMOST SUFFOCATED BY A TANGLE TREE, BOTH OF WHICH ARE MAGICAL CREATURES. HOW CAN THIS BE SO?

Chlorine was amazed. "That's Bink's talent? I always thought he had no magic!"

SO YOU WILL THINK AGAIN, FOR OTHERS ARE NOT ALLOWED TO KNOW. YOU WILL FORGET THIS QUESTION AND ITS ANSWER AFTER THIS SESSION IS OVER.

Meanwhile Nimby was writing again. She took the paper and read it: " 'This is a deceptive question. You implied a connection that does not necessarily exist. Bink can not be harmed by magic, but can be harmed by magic creatures if they do not employ magical means. That is, a dragon could chomp him mechanically, but could not enchant him magically. His talent does not regard threats or even bruising to be harm, only permanent physical damage. So there is no conflict.' "

The screen faded for a long instant or short moment; she had set the disreputable device back again. Rather, Nimby had; her respect for his intellect was verging on awe. How could a funny dragon know so much? Sure, it was his talent, but so was the way he changed the two of them into a lovely human couple. How could he have two magic talents?

Nimby passed her another note. *Only the form changing is magic; the knowledge is inherent in my nature.*

Oh. Of course. But he was still one supremely remarkable creature!

The next question was on the screen. QUESTION #3: THE FORGET SPELL CONTROLLED THE GAP CHASM UNTIL THE TIME OF NO MAGIC IN THE YEAR 1043, SO THAT ONLY THOSE ACTUALLY WITHIN IT COULD REMEMBER IT. YET WHEN MAGICIAN TRENT RETURNED FROM MUNDANIA IN 1042 HE REMEMBERED IT. HOW CAN THIS BE?

Chlorine whistled inwardly. These weren't mere questions of who did what when; they were crafted to require extraordinary comprehension of all Xanth history. Only the Good Magician Humfrey could possibly know all the answers—and Nimby. She could almost have suspected that Nimby *was* the Good Magician, if she hadn't seen them together. Maybe they were related, and Nimby was performing a service for Humfrey, just as she was. For the good of Xanth.

The next note came. " 'The magic of Xanth has little effect in Mundania,' " she read, " 'and Magician Trent had been there twenty years. It took time for the Forget Spell to reassert itself with him. In due course he did forget it again.' "

QUESTION #4: WHEN BINK AND CHAMELEON, IN THE GUISE OF

SMART UGLY FANCHON, LEFT XANTH THAT SAME YEAR, THEY WERE
ABLE TO UNDERSTAND THE MUNDANES THEY ENCOUNTERED. HOW
COULD THIS BE, AS MUNDANIAN IS UNINTELLIGIBLE TO XANTHIANS?

She simply read Nimby's answer, because as usual, she had no
idea. " 'This is another trick question. Bink and Chameleon never
heard Mundanian; they remained in the fringe of Xanth magic, and
the Mundanes were automatically talking Xanthian.' "

So it continued. How could Girard Giant know of Magician Murphy, who had been banished over seven hundred years before Girard
was delivered by an exhausted stork? Because Girard did know some
history. Why did the Ghost Writer write, "Never (such) a cleavage"
when he saw luscious Nada Naga, when the Gorgon and Irene and
any number of buxom nymphs and centaur fillies had similar figures?
Because the Ghost Writer had not yet encountered those others, and
in any event he was speaking hyperbolically, as writers do. Why
didn't the centaurs teach Prince Dolph how to spell? Because they
had tried with his father, Dor, and failed spectacularly. There had to
be some learning ability in the student, or even a centaur couldn't
make much of an impression. Why did Prince Dolph sometimes
change form slowly, instead of instantly? For variety. Why did Magician Humfrey take Lethe elixir to forget Rose of Roogna for eighty
years, but forget everything else in that period too? Because there was
too much of her in their time together; to remember the rest without
her would have led to Lethe-nulling paradox.

Chlorine's head was reeling with all this arcane information. But
Nimby had all the answers, no matter how devious the questions, and
Sending's efforts were all blocked.

She read off the answers, hardly assimilating their details, until she
came to #19. It wasn't that it was any less devious or difficult, but
that she realized that they were reaching the end; this one, and one
more, and they would win! That gave her sudden shakes.

IN ONE OF THE MUSE CLIO'S VOLUMES OF THE HISTORY OF XANTH
WE ARE TOLD THAT THE NIGHT MARES ARE CONFINED TO THE LAND OF
XANTH. IN ANOTHER WE LEARN THAT NIGHT MARES ALSO SERVICE
MUNDANIA. HOW CAN THIS BE?

Chlorine dreaded that seemingly innocent query, knowing that it
wasn't innocent at all, it was a challenge. Had the malignant machine

caught the Muse herself in an error? Then how could the question be answered definitively? Her knees felt like noodles in heating water.

But Nimby never paused. He wrote his note and gave it to her. She read it and was delighted with the simplicity and clarity of the answer, so obvious in retrospect. " 'Mundania, like Xanth, changes over the years. Sometimes the borders are closed and the night mares are confined to Xanth; at other times the portal at No Name Key is opened and the mares go through unimpeded. The Muse notes the situation at the time of that particular volume. There is no inconsistency when time is taken into account.' "

The screen dimmed. The surly system had thought he had a winner, and had not. Only one more question, and it was bound to be the worst.

QUESTION #20: HUMAN COLONIZATION OF XANTH DATES FROM THE YEAR ZERO, DEFINED BY THE ARRIVAL OF THE FIRST WAVE, 1,096 YEARS AGO. YET THE SEA HAG IS KNOWN TO BE THOUSANDS OF YEARS OLD. HOW CAN THIS BE?

Now Chlorine's knees definitely softened. She knew of the wicked Sea Hag, who had indeed lived for thousands of years by taking over the bodies of young folk and using them until they were old and worn-out by her awful lifestyle and degraded attitudes. Where could she have come from, if she was older than human colonization of Xanth? She couldn't have been Mundane, for Mundanes had no magic; she had to have been delivered in magical Xanth. She was, despite her haggishness, definitely human. Could Nimby answer this one?

Nimby could. She cursed herself for falling into another neat little trap as she read his answer. Sullen Sending had played it sneaky right to the end. " 'The Sea Hag dates not from the First Wave, which signaled the beginning of continuous human occupation of Xanth, but from the first lost human colony of Xanth, circa minus 2200. That colony faded out three hundred years later, having been careless about love springs, and crossbred with other creatures, forming harpies, merfolk, naga, sphinxes, ogres, goblins, elves, fauns, nymphs, fairies, and other species. So the Sea Hag is approximately three thousand, two hundred and ninety-six years old, normally simplified as "thousands." ' "

The evil entity's screen turned furious red. Roils of smoke crossed it. Lightning jags flickered. Sending was not a good loser. But he *had* lost, and knew it. TAKE THE WINDBREAKER. A panel opened in the cave wall behind the screen, revealing a closet where a motley white jacket hung.

"Thank you ever so much," Chlorine said supersweetly. "You have been excruciatingly nice." And of course, the conflagration on the screen just got worse, as she had hoped.

She stepped up to the closet and took the windbreaker. It seemed entirely ordinary. But she knew it wasn't. It was the key to the solution to Xanth's current crisis.

MAY I ASK ONE QUESTION OF A PERSONAL NATURE? the screen inquired over its burning background.

Chlorine glanced at Nimby, who shook his head. "No," she answered with deep satisfaction, and walked out of the chamber. She knew the destructive device wanted to know how Nimby knew so many answers, so Sending could nullify that ability if they ever met again.

The cave exit became a blank stone wall. Sending was changing reality. "Nu-*uh*," Chlorine said, lifting the reverse wood ball she still held in her other hand. She could drop it and nullify the mangy machine at any time. And would do so the moment any untoward print or picture started to form on the screen.

The exit reappeared. They used it, and emerged into the night of Xanth proper. Chlorine was about to set down the ball, but Nimby shook his head, so she put it in her purse. Then she donned the windbreaker. It was very comfortable.

So their part of the mission had been successful. She wondered how the Mundane family was doing.

10
PRINCESSES

Trenita Imp sat beside Karen, because it had turned out that she couldn't see anything from in front, and Karen was thrilled. David was asleep, but she was wide-awake and bored. Now that the accommodation spell no longer affected them, she could appreciate just how small the imps were. Trenita was thirty-seven years old—the same age as Mom—but only nine inches tall. The seat belt looked monstrous on her, and was surely a heavy weight, but she didn't complain.

As the RV moved down the trollway, right through the increasingly realistic phantasms formed by the thickening madness brought by the ill wind, Karen questioned her companion. "Do you travel often?"

"No, this is my first time away from my community."

"But then how do you know the way to Castle Boogie?"

"Castle Roogna," Trenita said patiently, just like Mom. "Everyone in Xanth knows where that is. I have studied centaur maps, and of course, I know the way of enchanted paths."

"You mean like nobody can attack us on one?"

"Yes, of course. But also where they go and where they stop."

"They stop?"

Trenita smiled. "When you get where you are going. In this case, Castle Roogna."

"Is that a nice place?"

"I am sure you will love it. It has an orchard where all manner of things grow, such as pie trees."

"Gee—even chocolate pies?"

"Especially those. The royal children have insisted on them, and on bubblegum trees."

"There are children there?"

"Yes. Princess Ivy and Prince Dolph grew up there. Of course, they're grown now, and married, and Prince Dolph and Princess Electra have their twins, Dawn and Eve. They are now five years old."

"Do they have magic talents?"

"Of course," the imp woman replied. "Every descendent of Magician Bink has Magician-level magic. Dawn can tell anything about any living thing, while Eve can tell anything about any inanimate thing."

"Gee—I wish I had a magic talent, even a little one."

Trenita shook her head. "Mundanes lack magic. You have to be delivered in Xanth to have it."

"Delivered?"

"By the stork, of course."

"You mean it's literal here? Babies aren't born?"

"Born?"

"You know. From their mothers."

"Oh, borne. The storks deliver them to their proper mothers, of course, after they have been ordered."

"Ordered? You mean like from a novelty catalog?"

"From a cat? A log? No, a message is sent to the stork."

"Gee, things really are different in Xanth! How do they send the orders?"

"I must not tell you that; the Adult Conspiracy absolutely forbids it."

So things *weren't* so different. This woman was the size of a doll, but she was a typical adult. "Same as the bleep, huh? But why aren't children supposed to know?"

"Because then they might summon storks themselves, and not take care of their babies."

Karen considered that. She knew of cases in Mundania where exactly that had happened. "But the words—why forbid them? They aren't babies. They won't suffer if children say them, will they?"

"But others would suffer. Have you seen the burned foliage where harpies roost? Would you want human children to do that?"

"Gee—I could burn things with words, if I knew the words? I'd love that."

Trenita sighed. "Well, the full name is the Adult Conspiracy to Keep Interesting Things from Children."

"That's more like it," Karen agreed, vindicated.

"Oh, I must direct your mother to the bridge over the Gap Chasm," Trenita said. "Before she misses the turn."

"I'll do it," Karen said eagerly. "Mom! Mom! Turn coming up."

"But we're approaching the ferry station," Mom called back.

"The ferry will be closed, because of the high winds," Trenita said. "We must use the bridge."

"Makes sense, Mom," Sean said, coming to life. He had been pretty quiet recently, maybe because now there was no sexy Chlorine to gawk at. "Wind blows clouds."

"Very well. I see a diverging lane ahead. But will it take us off the enchanted path?"

"No, the paths to Castle Roogna are all enchanted," Trenita said reassuringly.

Mom made the turn. Karen returned her attention to Trenita. "What's it like, being an imp?"

"Much like being human, I suspect. Did you find our hotel strange, when you used the accommodation spell?"

"No, it was great. Especially that magic mirror with the historical pictures."

"It was showing you the Magic Tapestry of Castle Roogna. You will be able to see the original there."

"Gee! That and a chocolate pie tree will be about as good as candy and TV at home. Did you eat fun stuff when you were a kid?"

Trenita smiled. "Of course. And my mother, Quieta, disapproved."

"Did you have lots of pretty gems to play with?"

"No just the sparkles of morning dew that my mother made. It was only more recently that my father became mayor and had to supervise the making of more permanent kinds of gems."

"How did Ortant get to be mayor?"

Trenita smiled reminiscently. "My grandfather had once been ambitious. Then my grandmother died, and he lost his ambition. He got caught by an alligator clamp, which was slowly chewing off his leg, until a big ugly ogre named Smash roared it off. It occurred to my grandfather that if a creature that horrendous could do such a favor for one so small, the least he could do in return was to become worthwhile. So he resumed his ambition, and worked hard, and lived up to his name."

"And became Important," Karen said, liking it. "That's nice."

The RV slowed. "That bridge is too small," Mom said.

"No, it is the right size for whatever uses it," Trenita said. "Unlike the invisible bridge or the one-way bridge. Just go on it."

"Maybe I'd better hold you up so you can see forward," Karen said. "This is getting scary."

"Yes. Let me stand on your shoulder."

Karen lifted the imp carefully, until she stood on her right shoulder, holding on to a hank of her hair. "What pretty red," Trenita remarked, and Karen felt unreasonably pleased.

Dad had been snoring in the back, with the three pets. Now he woke. "Hey, don't drive into the chasm!" he exclaimed, alarmed.

"Go back to sleep," Mom retorted.

As the RV nudged cautiously toward the footpath-sized bridge, the perspective changed, and it became apparent that the structure was wider than it had seemed. In fact, it was also more solid. By the time they drove onto it, it seemed quite sufficient.

"Magic is weird," Sean muttered.

The Gap Chasm had been impressive by day on a cloud. It was awesome by night on a bridge just wide enough for the vehicle. There was a faint glow below, hinting at its depth, and darkness around the edges that seemed to loom twice as close the moment her eyes turned elsewhere.

Then the glow and the darkness clarified. Ahead was a dead end, with nowhere to go but into the dark depths.

The RV squealed to a stop. "The bridge is out," Mom said, her voice deceptively calm.

"No it isn't," Trenita said. "That's illusion. The bridge is enchanted, and will not harm you as long as you stay on it. Just drive on."

Mom hesitated, understandably. Karen sympathized; that was one frighteningly realistic drop-off. "Remember the fake goblin roadblock," she called.

"True," Mom agreed. The vehicle nudged forward.

As the front wheels crossed the brink, the illusion disappeared. The bridge was back. But it curved to the side.

"There's no curve!" Trenita cried. "The bridge is straight."

"Thank you," Mom said grimly, driving straight.

"Illusions can kill you," Sean said, shaken.

"If you heed them," Trenita agreed.

Now a huge dragon face formed ahead. Its mouth opened, showing gleaming glistening glittering teeth. The most noxious possible smoke surged out to encompass the RV. It coalesced around the vehicle, becoming blood-streaked slime.

"I wish the enchantment was effective against illusion," Trenita said.

"Oh, I don't know," Karen demurred mischievously. "We can have some fun with this. Sean?"

"Gotcha," Sean agreed, catching on. He came to join her.

They faced out the window. "Hey, slimeball!" Karen called. "Whatcha eating tonight?"

"How about fried worms and day-old squished caterpillars?" Sean inquired.

The slime quivered. It might be illusion, but it heard them. That was the great thing about Xanth: even the inanimate had feelings. Even things that didn't exist could hear and react. Karen had sort of figured it would be that way, and it was good to be back in form with Sean.

"I should have known you were a dragon without guts," Karen said. "Just slimy smoke."

"Pretty puny effort, if you ask me," Sean agreed loudly. "I thought at least we'd see a decent show."

The slime became guts. They were gruesomely realistic, oozing juices and slip-sliding over each other. Karen was on the verge of nauseated, but she controlled her reaction. "I've seen better guts on a drunk," she declared.

"On a drunk pig," Sean agreed. "This sure is a boring place. Maybe the next illusion will have some oomph to it."

The guts became a roaring furnace. This illusion was angry now. Good. Karen faked a yawn. "Booring," she said.

"For sure," Sean agreed. "Let's make faces at each other, Karen; that'll be scarier."

"*Anything* would be scarier," she agreed. She put her fingers in her mouth and pulled it wide as she stuck out her tongue.

Sean pretended to gouge out his own eyes and hand her an eyeball. Karen accepted it and popped it in her mouth. She made a burpy swallowing sound. "Yuck! It's *raw!*" Neither of them looked again at the illusion outside.

"It's gone," Trenita murmured.

"Right," Sean agreed. "Our act is so bad there's nothing that can stand it." He smiled at Karen. "Nice going, twerp."

"Thanks, bleephead," she replied as he returned to his seat.

"That was interesting," Trenita remarked. "I never saw anyone drive away an illusion before."

"It's Mundane talent," Sean said. "Nobody can stand us, in our normal state."

Trenita laughed. "You nevertheless have your appeal."

The RV reached the end of the bridge and pulled back onto solid land. Trenita returned to her side of the seat. Karen felt something relax; she had been really tight, knowing that if the illusion had succeeded in scaring or confusing Mom, they could have plunged into the dreadful abyss. But they had driven it away.

But she was not yet relaxed enough to sleep, despite the lateness of the hour. So she asked the imp something that was bound to be boring. "Why is it that all the men imps have punny names, like Ortant or Atient, while the girl imps don't?"

"Because the men are the ones who need the reassurance of meaningful names," Trenita replied. "We women already know our worth, so choose pretty names instead."

"It works for me," Karen said, and snoozed off.

*   *   *

When she woke, dawn was threatening, and the RV was approaching a thick forest. Sean was asleep in the backseat, while Dad was up front with Mom. Tweeter was perched in her hair, and Woofer was on the floor by Sean. So the night was done, and Mom must be good and tired, but they had to be close to where they were going.

She looked out the window. Massive tree branches swung down to block the way. Karen blinked and rubbed her eyes. Had she really seen that?

"Tell them you have come to save Xanth from the ill wind," Trenita called.

Mom rolled down her window and spoke those words. The branches swung out of the way, and the RV drove on.

"The guardian trees are very protective of the castle," Trenita remarked. "But they feel the effects of the magic dust."

Now they came into a lovely orchard—and sure enough, there were pie trees galore. "Castle Roogna!" Karen cried. "We'll have chocolate pie for breakfast!"

That woke David. "Wow," he said, gazing out.

The castle came into sight. It was just about the most beautiful building Karen had ever seen, framed by the morning sunlight so that it glowed, with sparkles radiating out. It had a moat and wall and turrets and cupolas and pennants and just everything a castle should have. "Ooooo," she breathed appreciatively.

"Ooooo," David mimicked her mockingly, but his heart wasn't in it, because he, too, was impressed. They had seen so much of the jungle and illusion of Xanth that this was a wonderful change.

The drawbridge was up, but now it lowered, and a girl in blue jeans ran out. She was slender and pigtailed, maybe about sixteen years old. Obviously a serving girl.

"Hi!" she cried as she reached the RV. "You must be the Mundanes. Welcome to Castle Roogna. I'm Electra."

"Yes, we are the Mundane family," Mom said. "We understand that we can help save Xanth from the ill wind, if someone in the castle can tell us where to go and how to do it."

"Sure. Come on in," Electra said. "You must be tired after being in that moving house so long."

"We are," Mom agreed. "But we're in no shape to enter a royal castle. If someone can come out and give us directions, we'll be on our way."

"Oh, no, you must come in," the girl cried. "King Dor insists."

"But we're grimy and rumpled and dirty," Mom protested.

"And hungry," David called. He would.

"Sure," Electra agreed brightly. "We'll get you nice and clean and fed."

"And we have three animals with us," Mom said.

"They are welcome too," the girl said enthusiastically. She looked back to where a nondescript young man was approaching. "There's Dolph now; he'll tell you."

"If you're sure . . ." Mom said doubtfully.

Trenita spoke up. "She's sure. That's Princess Electra. And Prince Dolph."

"*Princess?*" Karen squeaked.

"Certainly. I should have recognized her by her description. She's very informal. And that's her husband, Prince Dolph. I made the connection when I heard his name."

Mom had evidently heard and adjusted in the smooth way of her kind. "We shall be glad to come in, Electra. But we do have important business, so can't stay long."

"Yes, the Good Magician sent Grey Murphy to attend to it," Electra said. "He will talk with you as soon as you're ready. Come on; I'll show you where."

They piled out of the RV. Karen lifted Trenita carefully down to the floor, and then to ground outside; the imp lady had made it clear she appreciated such no-fuss assistance in the giant human realm.

"Oh, an imp lady!" Electra exclaimed happily.

"I am Trenita Imp of Erial Village," the woman said formally. "I guided the Mundane family here. I will not be able to return immediately, so I hope it is not an imposition if I remain for a few days."

"Oh, no, it's great having you," Electra said. "We have lots of space, and you won't take up much of it." She turned to the prince. "Dolph, why don't you give Trenita Imp a ride to the magic mirror, so she can tell her village she's safe?"

The young man became an imp-sized centaur. "Get on my back, and I'll carry you there," he said.

"Thank you so much," Trenita said. Karen lifted her to the creature's back, where she got a good handful of mane to steady herself.

"But don't get fresh with me, because my wife would screech," Dolph said, smiling.

"I will not!" Electra screeched after them. Then she broke out laughing, and the rest of them joined in. Princess she might be, but she was obviously a fun person.

"If you don't mind my saying, you are the happiest Princess I have met," Mom remarked.

"Thank you," Electra said happily.

They followed her to the castle. Karen looked longingly back at the pie trees, but realized that they would have to wait, though she was suddenly ferociously hungry.

As they approached the moat, a horrendous green head rose out of the water. Karen screamed, and the others stepped back. "Oh, that's just Soufflé," Electra said. "Castle Roogna's moat monster and babysitter; he loves children." She raised her voice. "It's okay, Soufflé; the Good Magician knows about these Mundanes." The monster nodded and disappeared back under the water.

They crossed the drawbridge and entered the castle. It was huge, with stone passages leading in assorted directions. There were tapestries on the walls and thick rugs on the floors. Karen loved it at first sight.

"Right this way," Electra said, stepping into a side passage. In a moment they were in a nice bathroom, with sinks and mirrors and all.

"We really should change our clothes," Mom fussed, "if we are to meet royalty."

"We already met it," Karen reminded her.

"Wash your face and get your hair done," Mom snapped. But her tone had no edge.

Soon they were reasonably ready. They returned to the main hall, where Electra waited. "The King and Queen will see you now," she said. "Then you can have breakfast."

Karen was glad of that, and knew the others were too.

They entered a spacious hall. There were a number of people there. "How are we supposed to address them?" Dad whispered urgently. "We don't wish to give offense, but—"

"Just speak when spoken to," a voice said beside them, startling them. Karen looked, but there was only a vase.

There turned out to be no difficulty. The King was striding toward them, with Trenita Imp on his shoulder. "Hello, Mister Baldwin," the King said, extending his right hand. "I am King Dor. We are very glad to see you."

"You can say that again," the voice said. This time Karen was sure it was the vase. There must be something in it.

Dad shook hands with the King. "Thank you, your majesty," he said. "We—"

"Oh, just call him Dor," the vase said. "Everybody does."

The King smiled. "I should explain that my magic talent is speaking to the inanimate, and having it answer. At times it gets rather impertinent. But the vase is correct; we prefer informality, especially since our business is urgent and vital to the welfare of Xanth. Standing on ceremony takes too much time."

"Thank you—Dor," Dad said.

"This is my wife, the Sorceress Irene," the King said. A rather pretty woman of about Quieta Imp's age stepped forward. Her hair was distinctly green, much more so than Chlorine's yellow-green, but less luxuriant.

Dad introduced the members of the family, but it appeared that the King already knew them, or at least Trenita was whispering them in his ear. Even the pets.

Then the King got to business. "The Good Magician informs us that you and a woman called Chlorine are able to help Xanth in a way that no others can, but that you need a guide to Mount Rushmost, where the winged monsters congregate."

"Winged monsters!" Mom exclaimed.

Queen Irene touched her arm reassuringly. "They are not our enemies, in this crisis; they wish to save Xanth as much as we do. Indeed, Roxanne Roc herself is now fetching your friends to that place."

"A rock?" Mom asked.

Karen nudged her. "The big birds."

"But the winds are now so high, and the magic dust so pervasive, that it isn't safe to let the rest of you travel that way," King Dor said. "So we are arranging for you to use one of the demon tunnels. However, not all demons can be trusted, especially in heightened madness, so we are trying to locate one who can."

"I can do it," a handsome man said, stepping forward.

The King shook his head. "We must keep you here at Castle Roogna, Prince Vore, as liaison with the demons. We can trust no one else in this particular crisis."

The man nodded and stepped back. "He's a demon," the vase murmured. "Wait till you see his wife, Princess Nada Naga."

"So we shall now adjourn to the dining room, while we wait for the demoness to arrive," the King said. "We realize that all this may be somewhat confusing to you, especially the children, so Jenny Elf will assist you."

A girl no taller than Karen stepped forward. Her ears were pointed and her hands had only four fingers, including the thumb, but apart from that, she seemed normal. She even had freckles, like Electra's. "I was new to Xanth too," she said. "I'm Jenny, from the World of Two Moons."

Karen seized her opportunity. "Can you find us chocolate pies to eat, instead of healthy adult stuff?"

Jenny glanced conspiratorially around. "Sure. I'll tell the kitchen." She slipped out.

They took places at a huge table. Dad, Mom, and Sean were absorbed in deep discussion with the King and Queen, not paying attention to anything else, which was a good sign. They didn't notice when a maid brought chocolate pies and chocolate milk for Karen and David, and dishes of dog, cat, and bird treats for the pets. Jenny Elf joined them, having some pie herself. And her cat, Sammy, joined the pets, seeming to get along well enough with Midrange.

Soon they were full to bursting with pie. Boredom was hovering like a specter. The adults remained oblivious. "What's there to do around this joint?" David asked in his crude boyish way.

"Joint?" Jenny Elf asked, perplexed. "Joy'nt Bones is not here."

"A Mundane term for a lovely castle," Karen said quickly, shoot-ing a dark look at her half brother. Sometimes she wished he were a quarter brother, or eighth brother.

"Would you like to meet the children?" Jenny asked.

"No!" David said. He was Being Difficult.

"No, he would rather see the Magic Tapestry," Karen clarified. "But *I* would love to meet the children."

"Right this way," Jenny said. She set off across the hall, and they followed her, and the four animals followed them, and the adults never noticed their departure.

Jenny showed them upstairs to a pleasant room. There on the wall was a huge Tapestry, depicting endless scenes of Xanth. "It will show anything you want," she explained. "Just concentrate."

David concentrated. Suddenly the entire Tapestry went dark and stormy, with angry flickers of lightning. There was the odor of burn-ing hemp, and a faint fuzzy image of a pair of scorched panties.

"Except Adult Conspiracy stuff," Jenny added.

"Oh." David did not look pleased. It was all Karen could do to keep from giggling. Served him right!

Midrange looked at the Tapestry. It clarified into a picture of the cat-a-pult, a monstrous cat with a basket on its tail. Then Woofer looked at it, and a pack of wolves appeared, turning human as they came upon a human village. Then Tweeter looked, and the Tapestry sky filled with great birds, orienting on some hapless land-bound crea-ture below.

Jenny drew Karen away. "That will amuse them for some time," she whispered. "Sammy will find more interesting things for them, if they don't. He can find anything but home."

But Tweeter saw them going, and flew to rejoin Karen. That pleased her.

They went to another room, and received a cheery "Come in!" in response. They went in, and there was Princess Electra braiding the hair of two sweet little girls not a whole lot younger than Karen herself. One had golden light hair, and the other had shadowy dark hair.

"These are Electra's children, Dawn and Eve," Jenny said. "Dawn can tell anything about any living thing, and Eve can tell anything about any inanimate thing. They are both Sorceresses.''

"Hi Dawn; Hi Eve,'' Karen said. She was amazed that they could be Electra's, because Electra seemed so young and carefree.

The two little girls turned suddenly shy, letting half a titter escape. Electra smiled. "They don't see many little girls here. Ask them to tell you about something animate or inanimate.''

"What about my bird?'' Karen asked.

Dawn smiled and lifted her hand. Tweeter flew to it. "Oh! You are from beyond Xanth,'' the girl said. "You were hatched from the third egg in your mother's nest and taken to a nasty cage, where Karen rescued you, two years ago.'' It was clear by the bird's reaction that this was accurate. "Since then you have been happy, except that she goes away every day and leaves you in a cage.''

"I have to go to school,'' Karen protested. "I'd rather take Tweeter with me, but the school won't let me.''

Tweeter nodded, forgiving her, and flew back to her hair. Now Karen dug into her pocket and brought out her nylon comb. She passed it to Eve.

The girl focused on the comb. "You are strange,'' she said. "You started as a blob of goo buried deep in the ground, until a big pipe sucked you up, and you got run through something like a dragon's gut and then got squeezed out into the form you have now. Karen found you in a drawer with many other combs just like you, but now you are the only one for her. Once she lost you under the—under a moving house—but found you the next morning. You have combed out forty-one snarls, a hundred and forty-two tangles, and several thousand curls, but are ready for more. None of them lived, for some reason.''

Karen was impressed. She hadn't counted the snarls and tangles, but the numbers sounded right. And she had indeed once lost the comb under the RV, and found it by chance in the morning. Eve had gotten all that just from holding the comb for a moment. "The snarls and tangles didn't live because they weren't in Xanth,'' she explained. "In Mundania, they are just pulled hair.''

"Oooo,'' both twins said with big-eyed horror.

"Why don't you girls go see the triplets?" Electra suggested. "I have to get princessly."

"Sure!" the twins said together, and dashed for the door. All their shyness had vanished after they demonstrated their talents. Jenny and Karen followed.

They went to another room. There was a big basket swinging gently from a tripod. In it were three little babies. "These are Melody, Harmony, and Rhythm," Jenny said. "They are too young to show their talents, but we found out anyway. Whatever they sing and play together will become real. When they are separate, their individual talents will be less. But since they'll mostly be together, it's a very strong talent. The centaur tutors will have a time making them behave!"

"That's a lot of magic," Karen said, impressed.

"Hello." It was an adult woman whose waist-length hair was light and very faintly green.

"Oh, hi, Princess Ivy," Jenny said. "We were just admiring the triplets the stork brought you. This is Karen Mundane."

"So I gathered," Ivy said. "With a bird."

"He's Tweeter," Karen explained shyly. "My brothers have a dog named Woofer and a cat named Midrange, so—" But she saw that the woman didn't understand. "They're Mundane words."

"I can see why the dog and cat would be named as you have them," Ivy said. "But shouldn't the cat be Meower?"

Karen tried again. "In Mundania, a speaker system—that is, something that makes sounds—has a big cone called a woofer, and a small cone called a tweeter, and a middle cone called a midrange. So—"

"Oh, I see!" Ivy exclaimed. "Midrange. How clever." But she seemed a bit uncertain.

"Let's go see Demonica," Dawn said brightly.

"Yes, she's more fun," Eve said darkly.

They headed for another room. Karen paused. " 'Bye, Mrs. Ivy," she said politely.

"You're welcome," the Princess said with an obscure smile as they left.

"When it's the wrong time of the month, we call her Poison Ivy," Jenny confided in a whisper. Karen would have laughed, but she wasn't sure it was funny. What did the time of the month have to do with anything, unless it meant a holiday?

Demonica turned out to be the half-demon daughter of Prince Demon Vore, whom they had seen downstairs, and Princess Nada Naga, a woman who would have popped Sean's eyes right out of their smoking sockets. She was rocking her baby as they entered, but was willing to let Karen hold her. "But aren't you afraid I'll drop her?" Karen asked.

"No, she would just bounce back up," Nada said.

Karen was set back. "Is that a joke?"

Nada smiled. "No. Demonica's demon heritage prevents her from being physically harmed by such things. She can become tenuous or solid, as she chooses. She can't do it as rapidly as her father can, of course, but it does protect her. However, I agree; it is better not to drop her."

"She's cute," Karen said, taking the baby. Already Demonica was changing shape, in the way Karen was coming to understand. Her face was growing larger and her body smaller, until finally she was nothing but a head. Then she became light, and floated out of Karen's arms.

Dawn caught her. "I told you she was fun," she said. "I could tell you everything about her, but everyone already knows. She'll be even more fun when she's old enough to play." She rocked the baby in her arms.

"I don't want to ask something stupid," Karen said. "But—"

"Stupid things are the most fun," Eve said.

That emboldened her. "There seem to be a lot of Princes and Princesses and little girls here. Is it always this way?"

"That is not a stupid question," Nada said, laughing. "No, it is unusual. When we received news of the developing storm, we all felt that the children and babies should be brought to the safest place in Xanth. So we all came to Castle Roogna, which is enchanted to protect its occupants, especially royal ones. So Grey and Ivy came from the Good Magician's castle, and Vore and I came from my father, Nabob's, cave, and of course, Electra and the twins were here to begin with. This is really our first reunion since the deliveries. Ivy, Electra, and I have been great friends since we were girls."

"Oh. I should have realized."

"You had no way to know, dear. Now, as to why all our offspring are female—that does seem curious. We think it is just coincidence, and that there will be males in due course. But we're happy with what we have."

"So are we," Dawn said. "Boys are a pain."

Karen laughed, agreeing. "I should know. I have two brothers."

There was a swirl of smoke. Two eyes appeared in it. "I resent that," the smoke said.

"Hi, Mentia," one of the twins said. "You came in too late. We weren't calling you a pain."

"We were calling boys a pain," the other said.

"That's what I heard," the smoke said, forming into a beautiful woman with her dress on sideways. Karen wasn't sure how that was possible, but it was the case. "Seeing as how the stork brought my better half a boy."

"A boy?" Karen asked.

The women looked at her. "You're new here, aren't you? So you don't know how my better half, Metria, moved half of Xanth to get the attention of the stork last year, and finally served it with a magic summons, so it *had* to deliver. So now she has Ted, on whom she dotes. He will grow up to love children too. Disgusting."

Karen managed to put it together. Demon Mentia—dementia. She was a bit crazy, as her clothing indicated. Demon Ted—demented. Demon Vore—devour. She laughed. These demons had a certain sense of word, just as the imps did.

"What brings you here, Mentia?" Nada inquired. "Were you curious about how the other half-demon baby was doing?"

"That, too," Mentia said. "They should be great playmates. Maybe they'll grow up and marry one day. But I came here because I was summoned. It seems Xanth needs me."

"Xanth certainly needs something," Nada agreed. "But I'm not sure it's a crazy demoness. We already have too much madness stirring up."

"Madness? That's it, then. The madder the environment, the saner I get."

Nada nodded. "So that's it. Then you had better go see the King; they've been waiting for you."

"Pronto," the demoness agreed, vanishing in another puff of smoke.

"We had better go down too," Jenny said. "That means the journey to Mount Rushmost is about to start."

They left the children and hurried into the hall. A regal young woman was approaching from the stairway. She was just about perfect in every way, but there was something odd about her. "Oh, hi, Princess Ida!" Jenny said. "This is Karen Mundane."

"Yes, I just met her family," Ida said. "I was coming to fetch you down, Karen."

"But I don't need a Princess to guide me," Karen protested, embarrassed. The oddness was related to the woman's head.

Ida smiled. "Think nothing of it. Right now there are so many Princesses in the castle that we are having to find ways to make ourselves useful."

Karen finally identified the oddness. There was something moving around the Princess's head. It looked like a Ping-Pong ball. "Princess, if you don't mind my asking—"

"You are curious about my moon," Ida said, not at all offended. "It arrived last year, and I didn't have the heart to send it away. It's really no trouble, and it reflects my moods. You may look at it if you wish, but don't try to touch it, for it will avoid you." She angled her head so that the plane of the moon's orbit swung down, and Karen got a good look. The surface was sunny, with little seas and land masses showing. There were islands and continents, and ice caps at the poles. A little cloud bank came into view as the moon turned, and there was a rainstorm over one section. It was a complete world in itself.

"Oh, how cute!" Karen exclaimed—and the moon brightened. "What's it called?"

"Why, we don't have a name for it," Ida said, surprised. "What do you think it should be called?"

"Gee, I don't know," Karen said, pondering. Then she had such a bright idea that a bulb flashed over her head, brightening the moon further. ''Back in Mundania there's an asteroid called Ida, and it has a little moon, and I learned in school how they named it Dactyl, which means something or other. But since this isn't that, it needs another name. So let's call it Ptero.''

''Terra?'' Jenny asked. ''What a funny name!''

''No, its got a funny spelling. Pee-tee-ee-rr-o. That's why I like it. You see, there's this sort of dragonlike flying reptile that used to exist, called a pterodactyl, and this is a flying moon, so—''

''That's a wonderful idea,'' Ida said. ''Moon, do you like that name?''

The moon did a little dance of pleasure. Karen hoped it didn't shake its raincloud off.

''So Ptero it is,'' Ida said. ''Thank you for the idea, Karen. I would not have been able to think of it myself.''

''Oh, I'm sure you—'' Karen started to protest. But Jenny jogged her elbow.

''We must go on downstairs,'' Jenny explained. ''Before they miss us.''

Oh. Of course. Karen had been so intrigued by Ida's moon that she had forgotten that they were supposed to be going somewhere. They started walking.

''You have a difficult mission ahead,'' Jenny said. ''Do you think you will be able to reach the top of Mount Rushmost and convince Fracto to help fight the ill wind?''

''Oh, sure,'' Karen said confidently. ''Dad can do anything he puts his mind to. He's a physics Professor.''

''I'm sure he can,'' Ida agreed. ''I'm sure he will be able to convince Fracto.''

Jenny seemed quite pleased about something, and so did Ptero Moon, though Karen couldn't see what. They stepped downstairs. Sure enough, everyone was gathering there. Even David had been dragged from the Tapestry.

''The demon guide has arrived,'' King Dor announced.

''Hear, hear!'' a chair said.

''The mission will be successful!'' Jenny exclaimed. ''Fracto will help.''

''That is good to know,'' the King said.

"And Ida's moon is called Ter—Pfter—"

"Ptero," Ida said firmly. "Karen named it."

"Ptero—as in feather or wing?" Dad asked.

"No, as in Dactyl," Karen said.

He laughed. "Surely so. I see you hit it off well with the Princess."

"For sure!" a rug said.

"That's good," the King agreed, nodding in a significant manner.

"Yes," Karen said, getting shy again. Had she been too familiar with Princess Ida?

"Everything's fine," Ida said. "I'm so glad to have a name for my moon."

Karen was relieved that she had committed no offense. But she suspected that there was something important she was missing.

Jim Baldwin saw his daughter's cute confusion, and wished he could ease it, but this was not the occasion. She had done far better work than she knew.

"I think we must be on our way," he said. "We thank you, King Dor, for your assistance."

"It is we who thank you for yours," the King replied graciously, and his buxom green-haired wife smiled agreement. "You did not need to risk your family to help Xanth."

Jim glanced at Trenita Imp, who now sat on Queen Irene's shoulder. "I think we did, after the hospitality of the imps, which presaged yours." Trenita smiled.

"It still will not be easy," the King said. "Our best hopes go with you."

"Yeah, we don't want to get blown away," the King's crown remarked.

"Let's go," D. Mentia said, floating toward the exit. She had finally managed to get her clothing on straight, which was just as well; a demoness might not mind what she showed, as long as it wasn't her underwear, but it could be distracting.

They followed her out. The madness had intensified; Jim could feel its oppressive effect despite the protective ambiance of the castle. Indeed, this was unlikely to be easy, despite their seeming assurance that they would succeed. The King had made that plain. Ordinarily such a trip, with a demon guide, would be routine, but with the stirred-up magic dust changing things, nothing was certain.

That applied to Ida's reassurance, too. Princess Ida's Sorceress-class talent was the Idea; whatever she believed was true. But the Idea had to come from elsewhere—from someone who didn't know Ida's magic. That was what limited it. The elf girl Jenny had cleverly solicited Karen's innocent endorsement of their mission, and Ida had agreed, which meant that they would indeed succeed—if the rising madness didn't interfere. No one knew exactly how the madness might affect Ida's talent. So the outcome was not, after all, sure. But he did not care to tell the children that. Mary and Sean knew, but they would keep silent too.

They got into the RV, with the demoness taking the front passenger seat so she could show him the way, as Nimby had before. The sultry creature was now in a tight clingy sweater and a too short skirt. He wasn't sure whether she was trying to flirt with him, or provoke Mary, or if this was her natural manner of appearance among humans. "South along the main enchanted path," she said. "And move rapidly, because the dust is getting worse."

"How can you tell?" he asked her. "Not that I doubt you, but with the effects of the dust, could that lead you astray?"

"No. This is why they summoned me. You see, I am only half a demoness. I am Metria's worser half, and normally I am slightly crazy, as you may have noted. But I have been in madness before, and found that it reverses my nature, making me increasingly sane. I feel that sanity closing in now. You are Mundanes, so aren't much affected by it, but the surrounding effects will bring mischief. It is best to avoid as much of it as you can."

Half a demoness, who got sane while others got mad. This land never ceased to produce novelties. "How did you come to separate from your better half?"

"Metria was always a mischievous creature. Then she got married to a mortal, inherited half his soul, and fell in love, in that order. I, her soulless crazy aspect, couldn't stand it, so I fissioned off and had my own adventure. Unfortunately it led me into madness, and I suffered sanity. I came to accept Metria's situation, and must confess her half-demon baby son is cute. So we two halves have reconciled.

But because I alone among regular Xanthly creatures can handle the madness, the King asked me to help, and because the rising dust makes me unconscionably sensible, I agreed. You will be able to trust my judgment, when you can't trust your own.''

"Well, I am becoming accustomed to trusting the judgment of inscrutable creatures, after Nimby.''

"Who?''

"Nimby is a striped dragon with the head of a donkey who knows what is going on. He assumes human form and travels with Chlorine, a beautiful young woman who was sent to guide us by the Good Magician.''

"I don't know her either. What's her talent?''

"Poisoning water.''

"Garden variety. But that dragon you describe—there must be some mistake. He might be able to turn human, or to know things, but not both. There's a pretty strict limit of one talent per person.''

"I think he said that one was a talent and the other was inherent.''

"Maybe. But I'm pretty sane now, and that sounds wrong. There is something strange about Nimby.''

Jim laughed. "There is something strange about this whole land!''

"Better than the excruciating dullness of Mundania.''

To that he had no answer.

They made good time, and in due course Mentia indicated the turnoff road. "Now we're leaving the enchanted path,'' she reminded him. "It may get nasty.''

"I know.'' There had been a time, two days or two millennia ago, when he would have laughed at magic. Now he felt a dread respect for it.

But instead of turning ugly, the scenery turned beautiful. "Hey, look at the flowers!'' Karen cried, peering out her window.

"Those look like carnations,'' Mary said. "A whole field of them.''

Mentia looked. "Uh-oh. Those look like re-in-carnations. Growing wild and strong in the madness.''

Jim experienced a chill. "What magic will they do?''

"Regular ones aren't too bad,'' the demoness said seriously. "Folk sniff one, and have a strong memory of a loved one. If they sniff several together, they may actually see and hear the loved one. But this is a whole broad expanse, strengthened by the magic dust. I think you should try to avoid smelling them.''

''Close the windows!'' he called back to the others. But he was too late; David had opened his. The thick perfume of the flowers was circulating in the vehicle.

Suddenly Jim saw his father standing by the road, waving. He slowed to pick him up; he hadn't seen his father since five years ago, when—

''Keep moving!'' Mentia said. ''Don't stop. Get on out of here.''

''But that's my father,'' Jim protested.

''Drive on—or I'll drive for you.''

That jolted him out of it for a moment. ''A demoness can drive an RV?''

''Metria learned how, last year, so I know it too. This thing is similar to a pickup truck. Keep moving.''

His father had disappeared, and he realized that it had indeed been an illusion. His father was dead.

''You didn't stop for Grandpa,'' Sean said. ''Go back, Dad!''

''He's dead!'' Jim said.

Sean was set back. ''I forgot. That's weird.''

''Oh, like a wraith,'' Karen said. ''Don't believe them.''

A woman appeared on the road. ''Oh, there's my godmother,'' Mary said. ''I must talk to her.''

Woofer growled.

''No,'' Jim said grimly.

''But we can't leave her here!'' she said, releasing her seat belt and getting up.

''She's not real,'' he said, accelerating.

''Jim! I'm surprised at you. How can you say such a thing?''

''He's right, Mom,'' Karen said. ''It's the magic. Don't be fooled.''

Then they drove beyond the field of flowers, and the fragrance faded. Mary returned to her seat. ''Of course that couldn't have been her,'' she said. ''But she seemed so real.''

''They do,'' Mentia said. ''But if you stop for them, at this strength of fragrance, you might never get away again. As soon as you escaped the ambiance of one flower, another would get you. Probably they would have gotten you anyway, had you been afoot; but in your rapidly moving truck you were too fast for them. That's why I said not to stop.''

"You were indeed the sensible one,'' Jim agreed. Mary nodded, appreciating the ability of the demoness. Sense was likely to be what they needed most in the next few hours.

A mountain loomed before them. "That's it,'' Mentia said.

"We can't drive up that!'' Jim protested, glancing at her, and catching a considerable eyeful of her burgeoning cleavage. Where had her sweater gone? Apparently she had changed into something more comfortable, in her magic fashion. "This is a recreational vehicle, not a tank!''

"The demon path is inside. I will guide you to it. That is why I am here.''

"Sorry, I forgot.'' Was that another effect of the dust of madness? No, probably merely the distraction of her changingly provocative form. "Where's the entrance?''

"Follow me.'' She floated from her seat, through the windshield, and ahead of the RV.

"Keen creature,'' Sean remarked, peering ahead.

"Not your type,'' Mary said, a bit sharply.

Sean did not argue, but it was clear that he believed that anything that looked like that was his type. Jim couldn't blame him; the demoness was about as well endowed a creature as was possible without stretching the masculine imagination beyond repair. Those entities who could choose their appearance usually seemed to choose impressively. Chlorine's appearance was chosen, after all.

Actually, he was glad to have Sean's reaction, because the boy had been unnaturally quiet since his close call with the goblin dam, not evincing much interest in anything. Jim was afraid he had suffered a concussion or some other hidden injury when the water swept him away. Now he was reverting to normal, an excellent sign.

Mentia led them to a large old tree. She pointed to its trunk. Jim, now having had some experience with such things, drew the RV slowly up to that trunk, which seemed to expand, and into it. Sure enough, it was an illusion-covered aperture. An entry into the mountain.

They entered a dark tunnel. Jim turned on the headlights. They speared through Mentia's clothing, silhouetting her shapely body. Then the clothing thickened, and the effect was lost. The demoness floated back through the windshield and into her seat. "This spirals up inside the mountain. Just keep going." She paused. "Those bright lights caught me by surprise. Did you see—?"

"Outline, no panties," Jim said quickly.

She relaxed. "We do try to honor the conventions. We don't show panties to anyone we aren't prepared to seduce."

"It's nice to have standards," Jim agreed. She didn't show panties—but she did show everything else. It seemed that in Xanth the underclothing counted for more than what it covered. "How is it that the demons maintain this tunnel, when you can float wherever you wish to go?"

"Actually it's an old vole burrow," she confided. "But we find it handy when we want to spy on the ceremonies of the winged monsters. They can see us in the outer air, but not in here."

"There must be mighty big voles in Xanth."

"As big as this truck, in the old days," she agreed. "Today only the diggle is this big, and it normally doesn't make tunnels; it simply phases through the rock without disturbing it."

The passage ahead came to a halt in a pile of rubble. So did Jim, perforce. "There must have been a cave-in," he said regretfully.

"Let me check." She floated out again. She phased through the rock. Then her arm came back, beckoning him forward. So it was more illusion.

He nudged forward, and passed through the seeming pile of stones. Beyond, the tunnel opened up again, curving up and out of sight. The long climb was upon them.

Mentia floated back. This time she didn't pass through the windshield, but came to the far door. She gestured to come in. Her cleavage was so full it threatened to burst its boundaries.

"I'll get that," Sean said, coming forward. He opened the door, and the demoness started to enter.

Then a second demoness appeared. This one shot through the windshield. "Close that door!" she cried.

Startled, Sean paused, looking from one to the other. Both looked the same, except for the lower décolletage of the one at the door. "Two of you?" he asked.

Then fangs sprouted in the mouth of the one at the door. She hissed and her head dived for Sean's arm.

The one inside extended one arm to twice its natural human length. The hand intercepted the fanged face and shoved it back out the door. "Close it!" she repeated. "That's a hostile phantasm."

"But it looked just like you," Sean said, shaken, closing the door. "Except—"

"No need to explain," Mary said tersely.

"It can be dangerous to judge by appearances." Mentia drew her body up to her arm, so that all of her was by the seat, and sat down.

"Yeah," Karen said from behind.

Jim realized that the demoness had inadvertently taught Sean a good lesson. He hoped the boy would heed it in more normal circumstances.

"What's the difference between a wraith and a phantasm?" Karen asked. She was the one who had been led astray by wraiths, so naturally she was concerned.

"They are similar, but phantasms are more versatile—and malignant," Mentia said. "And they have some substance."

"How come the spook had to come in the door, while you go through the window?" David asked.

"King Dor arranged to have a protective spell put on this vehicle," the demoness said. "I'm on your side, or on Xanth's side, so it lets me pass, but the phantasms are enemies of the natural order, so they are barred. But if you let them in—"

"Why not simply lock the doors and ignore all creatures outside the RV?" Mary asked.

"Because you might want to let in a friend, and the spell has no way to tell friend from enemy, being unintelligent, so has to go by your judgment. If you decide to let something in, then you overrule the spell. Sean was letting in that phantasm." She glanced back at the young man. "Don't let anything in unless your father or mother tell you to. Especially if it has unusual sex appeal, or anything else that's evocative. Your lives may be at stake." Her sculptured décolletage had been replaced by a conservative but still quite attractive blouse.

"Got it," Sean agreed, shaken.

"But we were fooled too," Mary said.

"The first time."

Good point. Adults learned well from experience. But Jim had a concern of his own. "When you go out, we can't tell you from the imitations. How will we know it's really you signaling us ahead, and not a phantasm? They could hurt us by misdirecting us and causing the RV to wreck."

"Um. Let me ponder." The demoness became thoughtful, her head swelling to twice its normal size. Then she returned to regular beauty. "I think you will have to come out with me, next time. Then you will know it's me."

"But then I'll be at risk, outside the enchantment."

"I will try to protect you. A demon has more power here than the phantasms do, because they are intruders."

"Perhaps in normal times," Jim said. "But these are not normal times. The dust is strengthening aberrant elements."

She glanced sidelong at him. "You may be Mundane, but you are catching on well."

He realized that this was a compliment, and he was unwisely flattered. Of course, appearances were not to be trusted, but she looked just like a supremely beautiful young woman, and her favor sidestepped his rational mind to register on a deeper level. "Mundane physics can develop some strange aspects, particularly at the quantum level," he said. "I am accustomed to thinking rationally in seemingly irrational settings."

"In my normal state I would not admire that," she murmured.

Implying that in her present artificially sane state she did. If Mary had been concerned about Sean's fascination with Chlorine, now she would have a similar concern about her husband's reaction to Mentia. With perhaps some reason. He had learned to tune out the occasional wiles of lovely coeds who tended to admire intelligent men, or who merely wanted higher grades, but the magic ambiance was laying siege to his judgment, and his fancy was testing its limits. The phantasms were not the only threat this mission posed.

The endless turn of the upward spiral brought them suddenly to a division in the tunnel. One fork curved away left, the other right. "Which one?" he asked.

"I've got to check," Mentia said, floating out of her seat.

"And a phantasm will imitate you and signal wrong," he said. "Even if I see you, I won't know which one is the real you."

"Oh. Right. You will have to come out with me. And we shall have to maintain contact."

"Contact?"

She smiled, evidently well aware of his concerns. "We'll hold hands." She extended her left hand to take his right. Then she floated through the windshield, with only her forearm and hand remaining inside.

Jim knew Mary was watching but holding her peace. There was, after all, good reason to hold Mentia's hand, however incidentally suggestive it might be. He opened the door and slid out, and her arm slid with him, through glass and metal without impediment. Yet her hand remained solid and warm. It was amazing how she could do that; he would have thought that a solid hand could not be supported by an insubstantial wrist or arm. Curious, he paused to pass his other hand through her seeming arm flesh, verifying that it was insubstantial. Indeed, the laws of magic were not those of regular physics.

Then the arm abruptly firmed. "Is there more of me you wish to touch?" she inquired dulcetly, her blouse becoming translucent.

"Ah, no," he said quickly, embarrassed. He closed the door and stepped out into the glare of the headlights, still holding her hand. He knew she was smirking. She might be increasingly sane, but her basic mischievous nature remained.

They advanced to the fork. He expected the left one to be the one, because the spiral had been counterclockwise. But there was solid rock there; the passage was illusion. He stroked his left hand across the cold hard surface, amazed; it still looked open. It was as if a perfectly clean glass wall barred them from a real tunnel. "I would have driven into this one," he said, chagrined.

"Never take illusions on faith," she said.

They walked to the other side, and Mentia put out her free hand. "That's what I thought," she said.

Jim reached for it—and encountered another glass pane. "But—"

"They are both illusion," she said. "Now we check outside their range."

"Outside?"

She led him on beyond the right fork. "Aha." She squeezed his hand. "It's here."

He felt the streaked stone—and there was nothing. "Illusion stone!" he exclaimed.

"Illusions come in all types," she said. "It can be as dangerous to mistake a passage for a wall, as a wall for a passage. But this is unusually sophisticated deception for phantasms."

"Suggesting that the dust has considerably enhanced them," he said, "or that some more sapient entity is involved."

"Exactly. So we had better explore a bit more before trusting the truck to this passage." She drew him through the seeming rock face and into the tunnel beyond.

This was completely dark. "I can't see," he said.

"Sorry. I'll illuminate." She began to glow. The soft light seemed to emanate from her person rather than her clothing, which made for some interesting effects. Since her clothing was demon stuff as well as her body, he presumed the effects were intentional.

They walked on through the tunnel. Then Jim's foot landed on nothing, and he plunged down through the supposedly solid floor. But the demoness's hand held his with surprising strength, preventing him from falling all the way into the void. The hand expanded to grasp his whole arm, and she hauled him back up. He scrambled to set foot back on the real, as opposed to the apparent, surface, missed, and found himself caught in her embrace. Her body was exceedingly sexy against his. "Well, now," she murmured.

She moved back, carrying him, and his feet found the rock. He stepped into her and through her, emerging behind her. All of her body was exactly as solid or permeable as she chose it to be.

"Thank you," he said as he recovered his balance and mental equilibrium. For it was clear that however seductive she chose to be, she had in this instance elected to put him safely onto land. She could have embarrassed him in the process far more than she had.

"There is a time for games, and a time for business," she said.

"We can afford no distractions until this mission is done. Thereafter—" She shrugged, turning to face him. She still glowed, but now her clothing was opaque. She had not let go of his right hand; her left had passed through herself in the same fashion as he had.

"This is evidently not the correct route either," he said.

"There are occasional side passages," she said. "We aren't sure what the voles used them for, but assume it was to allow them to pass one another. Presumably they had no problem with falling, being natural earth-boring creatures. The main passage is sure to be somewhere."

"I hope so," he said, still shaken from the narrowness of his escape.

They walked back toward the illusion barrier. From this side it looked like dirty glass; it was evidently a one-way illusion. The RV was visible, but its lights were muted, as if filtered through thick curtains.

Mentia paused. "Before we step back into sight of the others," she said, extending her right hand toward him. "If I may."

"May what?" he asked uncertainly.

"Straighten you up somewhat." Her hand became a small mirror, in which his hair and clothing showed tousled and mussed. Then her hand became a large comb, which she ran through his hair. Then it became a hand again, as she straightened his collar. She was prettily businesslike, reminding him oddly of Mary. "Your wife might otherwise misunderstand."

"Oh. Thank you." He waited while she put him in order. They still held hands; after what he had seen of the phantasms, he was not about to let go of her. "How is it that you have such sensitivity for family relations?"

"For two years I have been the third member of a two-person couple," she said, smiling darkly. "That has been instructive in several ways. Third parties are not necessarily welcome."

"For sure." He was embarrassed, and in a moment realized why. "I apologize for wronging you in my thoughts, Mentia."

"Oh, you thought I might do this?" she asked innocently, and suddenly stepped in close, pressed her provocative breasts and hips firmly against him, and kissed him. "For shame."

"For shame," he echoed weakly. Though fleeting, it had been a kiss of such competence that it left him light-headed.

"Naturally I wouldn't do a thing like that," she said, drawing back and disengaging a thigh that had somehow gotten wedged between his legs. "What do you think I am—a demoness?"

"I'm afraid I did think something like that," he agreed. This creature was no one to play games with!

"But if I chose to, I believe I could make an impression," she murmured.

"I apologize for my apology."

She laughed. "You have a certain poise. Don't be embarrassed. I—that is, Metria—have in my day seduced a married King. I am satisfied to have you know what I could do, and am not doing, in the interest of Xanth's welfare. Rationality can be such a curse."

"A curse," he agreed.

They stepped on through the veil of illusion, and into the glare of the headlights. Jim shaded his eyes from the bightness, and was able to make out the faces of his family peering through the windshield. He waved. Several hands waved back. They must have been concerned when he disappeared.

They walked across to the other side of the tunnel. And there they found another hidden passage. They explored it far enough to know that it was the real one, then returned to the RV. Jim opened the door and climbed in, the demoness floating around and through him, to the adjacent seat. He pulled the door closed.

"We're sure glad you're back, Dad," Sean said. "You wouldn't believe what the phantasms were pretending."

"Try me," Jim said as he eased the vehicle forward, and to the left, into the illusion rock wall.

"They pretended they were you and her, kissing," David said eagerly. "But we knew it wasn't so, 'cause there were five or six couples, and we'd seen you go through the wall."

"And we knew you wouldn't do anything like that anyway," Karen chimed in.

"Thanks for your confidence," Jim said, shaken in a new manner. The phantasms had tried to tell on him! They were getting more clever by the hour, trying psychological tricks when the physical illusions didn't work. The success of this mission was by no means assured. In fact, their family's survival was not assured. This sometimes pleasant land of magic was becoming steadily more deadly.

After that the trip became less eventful; apparently the phantasms had tried their best, but failed, so gone in search of easier prey. The motor heated with the continued strain of the climb, but didn't reach the point of quitting, to his relief. At length they emerged on a moderately sized plain and came to a stop. It was early afternoon.

The wind was fierce. There was a reddish haze. The sky itself seemed to bend and sway as if painted on a somewhat flexible dome, and the sun wavered in place. The magic dust was kicking up worse. And the plain was a mesa, with a frighteningly abrupt and deep drop-off.

"Now we have to gather wood, straw, dried animal dung, anything that will burn," Jim said. "We are going to make a big fire."

"Great!" David cried. He loved fires, the bigger the better.

"Don't go near the edge!" Mary called as the boy dashed off.

"Awwww!" David and Karen cried together. But they heeded the warning, because the drop was awesome.

"Is there going to be enough to burn?" Sean asked. "This place seems pretty barren." He seemed to be getting subdued again; he tended to look around, as if searching for something indefinite.

"King Dor said we'd get some help," Jim reminded him. He hoped the King was right.

"Something's coming!" Mary said. "But I fear not good."

Jim looked. "I fear you are right. I think those are harpies."

The awful creatures were battered by the winds, but compensating, heading for the plateau from the south. Jim looked around for sticks that could be used as clubs or staffs. They were going to need defensive weapons, unless they retreated to the RV—in which case they wouldn't get their job done.

"I'll check," Mentia said. She assumed the form of a huge harpy and flew out to meet the dirty birds.

"Something else," Mary said.

This was from the north, and it was huge. In fact, it looked very much like a roc. No sticks would beat off that monster! Even the sanctity of the RV might not suffice against a creature that size.

"Look at that!" Sean exclaimed. "A basket!"

"It must be Chlorine and Nimby," Mary said, relieved. "They are supposed to rejoin us here."

"Carried by a roc," Jim agreed, remembering. "With all the other distractions, it slipped my mind."

"The dust does that," she agreed. He wasn't quite certain what she might mean by it, and didn't care to inquire.

The monstrous bird glided to a landing on the middle of the mesa, carefully setting the basket down. From it three emerged: Chlorine, Nimby, and a splendidly sparkling huge chick. The roc folded her wings and settled down like a huge hen. But her eyes were watchful. They were the eyes of a mother, or a guardian. Jim had seen that look on Mary, on occasion.

The family convened and approached the new arrivals as a group. "Remember," Jim warned the children, "that bird is sapient. She understands everything we say, and she is a figure of considerable importance in Xanth. Treat her like royalty." For this was one of the things that King Dor had explained. There would be no threats to their mission, as long as Roxanne Roc was present. It wasn't just the power of the roc, which was formidable; it was that it was backed by all the other winged monsters of Xanth—and indeed, most other creatures, including humans.

Chlorine greeted them with hugs that even the children didn't seem to mind. She wore an incongruously Mundane windbreaker jacket that did not succeed in making her less attractive. Then she made introductions. "This is Roxanne Roc, the third most important bird in Xanth." She made a little bow to the roc, who nodded her head affirmatively. "And this is Sim, short for the Simurgh Junior, the second most important bird in Xanth. Roxanne is minding him for his mother, the most important bird, the Simurgh. We all will protect Sim with our lives, if necessary."

"Yes," Jim agreed for the family.

Chlorine turned to face the roc. "And this is the Mundane family Baldwin: Jim, Mary, Sean, David, Karen, Woofer, Midrange, and Tweeter. May the animals play with Sim?"

The huge head nodded. Jim was surprised by the trust shown, but realized that Roxanne, too, had been briefed. The three pets were now intelligent and disciplined, and they also understood.

The lustrous chick stepped forward. He was about Woofer's size, and his every baby feather gleamed iridescently in the sunlight as he moved. "Cheep!"

"Woof."

"Meow."

"Peep."

Then all four fell over laughing. It seemed that either they had shared some animal joke, or were all in excellent humor.

Now Mentia appeared, coalescing from a swirl of smoke. "Oh, hello, Roxanne," she said. "I'm Mentia, Metria's worser half. We met during your trial."

The huge head nodded again, remembering.

The demoness turned to Jim. "The harpies aren't here to fight; they're bringing wood for the fire. Word has really gotten around. Nobody wants Xanth to be blown away."

Indeed, Jim saw that the dirty birds were swooping over the edge of the mesa and dropping sticks of wood. That would be a great help. "Thank them for us," he said.

"I did. They say that more winged monsters will be coming with more fuel. This is their sacred meeting place, and it's under chronic truce; no quarreling here unless someone really asks for it. So you won't have to fear the monsters, but don't push your luck."

"That's a relief," Mary murmured. She had been watching the children and pets somewhat warily, exactly as the roc was. They were playing a game of lines and boxes in the sand, taking turns drawing the lines and scratching in the X's, and all were similarly intent.

"If you will excuse me, I have a job to do," Jim said.

Mary looked doubtful. "I should help you," she said. But she was evidently reluctant to leave the children and pets unattended.

"I'll help you," Mentia said.

"So will I," Chlorine said.

Then, of course, Sean was interested, and Nimby. But Mary did not look reassured.

Mentia floated over to her. "This is the safest place in Xanth for children," she said. "Roxanne guards Sim, and anyone Sim associates with, and all other winged monsters and most of the rest of Xanth supports her in this."

"We know," Jim said.

But Mary wanted more specific reassurance. She looked at Nimby, who nodded. "Then I will join you," she said, clearly relieved.

So was Jim. It was not that he minded the proximity of lovely creatures like Mentia and Chlorine, but he felt easier if Mary was also close. And he shared Mary's concern about Sean, who was too obviously intrigued by those same creatures, neither of whom was exactly shy with men.

They went to the growing pile of wood. The harpies had gone, but other winged monsters were bringing more: dragons, griffins, and some he couldn't exactly classify. Some were of considerable size, but they were all business; they dropped their loads and flew on.

But the wind was still rising, and the haze of magic dust was thickening. He saw how it affected the flying creatures, who were becoming increasingly unsteady, as if on mind-altering drugs. He felt just enough of the effect to appreciate its likely potency on the magical creatures. A significant part of the reason this mission had been given to a Mundane family was its lack of magic: not only could Jim and the others not do any magic, they were resistant to its effects. So, like the sane demoness, they could carry through while others were going crazy.

Many hands did make light work. Soon they had a fine bonfire going, sending up an enormous plume of roiling smoke. Now the winged monsters brought buckets of water, which they dumped at Jim's directive. This made a huge hissing, and added swirling steam to the mix. The result was a burgeoning cloud that loomed over the plateau and extended beyond it as the wind tugged at its fringes.

Magic dust infused the cloud, animating it. A gaseous face formed, glaring around. Jim would have thought he was imagining it, but the others saw it too. "Make a noise!" he yelled at it. "Show us what you're made of, fogface!" For even the inanimate, even illusions, had feelings in this magical realm. He had come to appreciate that when he had seen Sean and Karen employ mockery to drive off ugly illusions.

The cloud obliged by rumbling.

"You can do better than that!" he told it. "What kind of a wisp of vapor are you?"

This time the roar of sound was explosive. It could surely be heard for many miles. Which was the point.

Then there was a sound behind him, of a different nature. He looked, and saw Roxanne Roc taking off. "Where's she going?" he asked, alarmed.

Nimby wrote a note. *Che and Cynthia Centaur are getting blown away by the ill wind, so Roxanne is rescuing them. Che is Sim's tutor.*

Oh. Of course the sparkling chick would need competent education, so had a centaur tutor. And the wind was now so fierce and dusty that even the dragons had sought refuge on the mesa. They had done their part; the smoke/steam/dust cloud was now a hovering monster.

"Who is watching the children?" Mary asked sharply.

Who, indeed? They hurried across to where the children and animals were still engrossed in their game. There was a huge dragon matron watching them, wisps of fire showing as she breathed. It seemed that the roc had arranged for a substitute.

Jim and Mary turned back to the bonfire. Only in Xanth would parents see a dragon looming over their children, and depart with confidence!

Then a speck appeared on the horizon. It grew rapidly. It was the roc, clutching a tiny creature in each great set of talons. As she came closer, they saw that each creature was a young winged centaur, one male, the other female. Each would have been about eleven years old, in human terms.

"We had better meet them," Mary said. Jim agreed, and they turned back.

Roxanne landed, simultaneously depositing the two centaurs safely on the ground. Demoness Mentia appeared. "Che and Cynthia Centaur," she said, introducing them. "Jim and Mary Mundane."

"We heard how you turned back to help Xanth," Cynthia said.

She was a pretty thing, whose brown tresses matched her equine hide. She was bare-chested, but not (quite) yet developed.

Che looked at the child and pet game. "This may be an opportune time for a math lesson," he remarked.

"You're teaching that chick math already?" Jim asked, surprised.

"He is a very bright bird, and he has a great deal to learn," Che said.

"He has to know everything in the universe by the time he's mature," Cynthia added.

Jim nodded. "Agreed. That is a great deal. But can you teach math when your judgment is being distorted by the growing madness?"

"Quantum math," Che said. "Insanity is an asset to that study."

Startled, Jim had to agree. Centaurs were indeed extremely intelligent.

"Say, where's Gwenny Goblin?" Mentia inquired. "Don't you have to be her Companion?"

"She released me from that obligation," Che said. "She is grown-up now, with good vision and posture, and she governs Goblin Mountain, so is in no further danger of awkward questioning. But we shall always remain close friends, and I expect to visit her often. Sim should like to meet her, too, in due course."

"It works for me," the demoness agreed.

The centaurs went to join the young folk, and Jim and Mary returned to the bonfire. "Do you think this is going to work?" she asked worriedly.

"If it doesn't, we'll be left stranded on a mesa with no safe way down," he said evasively.

She did not challenge that. They came to the fire, which was still burning smokily, but now the wind was so strong that the cloud was being blown away as fast as it formed. Had it been enough? There would be no more wood; the winged monsters could no longer dare fly, and were now too crazy anyway. The madness had them writhing on the ground and growling at nothing.

Actually, Chlorine was looking somewhat distorted, though Nimby seemed unaffected. Jim kept seeing fantastic things with his peripheral vision, which faded when he looked directly at them. The madness was laying siege to them all.

"Look!" Chlorine cried. "Fracto!"

And there, on the horizon to the north, was the edge of a looming black cloud. Fracto was coming! The manifestation of a rival cloud had gotten the mean mist's attention.

The magic dust enhanced Fracto, too. In two and a half moments the baleful cloud expanded to ugly proportions. Purple blisters swelled and burst. Gray-green depths turned brown-black. They became malignant eyes. A cruel mouth formed. There was a whistle of wind as it inhaled, getting ready to blow out an icy blast.

It was time to act. "Fracto!" Jim called. "Cumulo Fracto Nimbus, King of clouds. Listen to me! I have a deal for you."

The cloud hesitated, surprised. The blast did not come.

"Xanth is in trouble," Jim called. "Xanth needs your help."

The mouth resumed inhaling. Fracto did not care about Xanth's welfare.

"We can offer you something really nice," Jim called.

The cloud paused again. The eyes narrowed. A curl of mist formed in the shape of a question mark.

"Romance! Another storm, only female." This sounded crazy, but it was a crazy situation. King Dor had reviewed it carefully with him, and now he retained sufficient sanity to carry it through. "Not this smoke cloud. That was only to get your attention. A real storm, the strongest Xanth has seen. Ideal for you."

The spongy face showed definite interest. Fracto seldom had any prospect for compatible companionship. He must be really hungry for it. The mouth formed a perfect O and a gust of wind emerged. He was asking WHO?

"Her name is Happy Bottom," Jim called. "She's from Mundania."

The cloud face recoiled.

"No, wait! She is no longer Mundane. She has swept up a lot of magic dust and become magic. But she doesn't understand it, doesn't know how to use her new power. She is wasting it with random blowing, not realizing her potential. She's becoming so strong she's going to blow Xanth away. Then she'll fade, of course. But with proper instruction she could learn to be the kind of magic storm she could be, with all that magic dust, and turn Xanthian. But she will need a teacher—and only you have the capacity to teach her this. Only you can tame this shrew. Only you can calm yon ill wind. If you do, you will have a wonderful female of your kind. I leave the rest to your imagination.'' He wasn't sure just how much imagination a cloud could have, but it was clear that this cloud was conscious.

Fracto considered. Then the mouth formed another shape, more like OW. That would be HOW?

"We must work together," Jim said, relieved that the dialogue was going well. "We must push Happy Bottom away from the concentration of magic dust, but we can't make her go in any particular direction. You must do that, by luring her into the Region of Air. Once she is there she will not know how to escape, until you teach her how. She will be yours to seduce."

The cloud considered. Fracto was definitely interested. But obviously uncertain about trusting a mortal creature. The mouth formed a windy OO. That would mean TRUE?

How could he prove he was speaking the truth? He couldn't blame the cloud for being suspicious. Fracto had no friends, and a Mundane mortal was the least likely person to believe. Fortunately, King Dor had prepared him with this answer too. "Here is a contract," he called, unrolling a large poster. "Signed by the Good Magician himself."

A gust of wind swept the paper out of his hand. It fluttered through the air toward the cloud. But wasn't being lost. Fracto was reading it.

Then the face changed. It became less threatening, more agreeable. The mouth opened. ESSSS, it blew.

Fracto had agreed to the deal! Now all they had to do was work out the details.

Jim settled down to those, explaining how they would take Chlorine behind Happy Bottom and use the windbreaker to drive her forward. Fracto would beckon her toward the Region of Air in north central Xanth. It would be a job, but they should be able to herd and lure her there, if they made no mistakes. He was buoyed by the progress already made. Soon enough they would complete this mission, and then be able to go home to Florida. He looked forward to the return of familiarity.

12
WILLOW

S ean stamped out the last of the fire in his section, near the edge of the plateau, and turned to look after the dissipating trail of smoke. They had done it; they had made the signal and summoned the cloud and done the deal. Of course, there would still be some work for someone before the ill wind was contained, but the corner had been turned. Xanth would be saved, and they would go home. It had been interesting and even fun, but he was ready to return to dull Mundania.

Yet there was something lacking. Why should he be ready to go home, when lovely Chlorine was here? And that supersexy demoness, Mentia? He should want to see as much of both of them as possible, though he knew that neither was for him. They were just dream material, pinup fancies—but when had unavailability ever stopped him before? He should want to catch every last glimpse he possibly could. Yet he didn't; somehow he had lost interest. Oh, he was showing some interest, but that was because the other members of the family had begun to glance at him strangely, and he realized that they would figure he was sick if he didn't strive for every last glimpse of hidden female flesh. But his heart was no longer in it.

Was it the rising madness in the air? It didn't affect Mundanes much, because of their determined unmagicality, but it did have some effect. He was feeling light-headed, and some things he knew were straight, like the surface of the ground, seemed wavy or insubstantial.

But that was perception; it shouldn't deplete his normal young-man interest in beautiful women. Neither should it give him an inexplicable sense of loss.

He walked to the far side of a lingering smudge of smoke and used its cover to answer a brief call of nature. In a moment he faced back toward the RV and the others. He stepped around a deep hole in the ground that might or might not be illusion. His job here was done; it was time to rejoin the family.

Then something appeared at the brink of the drop-off, catching the corner of his eye. He looked, realizing that one of the monsters might be returning from a scouting flight. For an instant he thought it was a harpy, for it was a winged female, but then he realized that its body was fully human, and clothed. It was a winged girl!

She rose above the plateau level and moved forward. Now he saw that she was terminally tired; her wings were fluttering weakly, and her head was lolling. She had exhausted her strength, flying up to the mesa in this stiffening wind.

Her dainty feet touched the ground. Her wings folded and she fell to her knees.

Sean went to help her. She was so delicate, so vulnerable, that he had to do something. "Are you all right?" he asked, extending one hand.

Her weary head turned. She looked into his face. "Sean!" she cried, and collapsed. Into the hole he had just avoided.

Sean's whole world changed in that instant. "Willow!" he cried, and leaped in after her. He caught her as they landed on a pile of soft debris that glowed slightly. His mind was reeling.

"Oh, Sean, you remember," she breathed. "I feared you would not."

"You called my name," he said. "Everything came back. But how could I ever have forgotten?"

"You walked through a Forget Whorl," she said. "I followed you here—"

"Now I know what I was missing," he said. "It was you, Willow. I love you." He kissed her, and savored the overwhelming sweetness of the returning memory.

*   *   *

They had stopped where the water flooded the trollway. The goblins had dammed the Crimea River, causing it to back up and drown out the bridge and road so that the RV couldn't safely pass. Dad had taken the branch of super cherry bombs down toward the dam, then left them with Sean and Mom while he went ahead to explore the dam for the best place to put the charge. But he had gotten caught by the goblins. They had been going to float the bombs down to the right spot, so as to be well clear of the explosion, but when Dad got caught, Sean knew he couldn't wait for that. David made a distraction so that Sean could do what he had to do. So he grabbed the whole branch of cherries and made for the dam, and just tossed them on it, and dived for cover.

The blast had thrown him away, stunning him. But he must have landed in the water, because suddenly he was choking and floundering. Fortunately he was a good swimmer, so after a moment of disorientation he managed to stroke strongly for the shore.

But he didn't know exactly where the shore was. Rushing dirty water was everywhere, carrying him along. There were branches in it, from the blown dam, jostling and getting in the way. Weakened by the shock of the close explosion, he was tiring. Where was the shore?

A figure flew above him. It was a large bird—no, a girl! A winged girl. "Here!" she cried, pointing ahead.

She must know. So he followed her, and soon threaded his way through the maze of debris to the shore. But in the process he wore himself out. The adrenaline that had kept him going drained away, and he sank down in the muck at the edge.

The girl flew down to help him. "You must get clear, because more is coming," she said. She put her little hands under his shoulders and tried to lift him up. But instead her feet slipped in the mud, and she landed beside him, thoroughly grimed.

"Your wings!" he exclaimed, appalled. The nice whiteness was hopelessly soiled.

"I can wash them. Come on." She tried again to lift him up, putting her arm around his waist. "Hurry."

Now he heard a change in the background noise of the flowing water. Indeed, the channel was shifting; it was probably cutting a more direct course through the terrain, and would catch him again. He hauled himself up with her help and staggered on. Her body was quite slender, and her support was more moral than physical, but he did appreciate it.

They reached a steep bank and used saplings to haul themselves up just as the water surged through behind them. They were safe for the moment. "Thanks," he said. "I probably would have drowned."

"Yes. I didn't know who you were, but it didn't seem right to let you drown, when I could help." She paused, cocking her head. "Who are you?"

"I am Sean Baldwin."

"Sean from where?"

He smiled. "That's my surname."

"Your sir-name? Are you royal?"

He laughed. "Far from it! I'm Mundane."

She shrank away. "Mundane!"

"Well, that doesn't mean I'm a bad person," he said.

"It doesn't?"

"You must have heard some bad stories about Mundanes. We aren't all like whatever you've heard."

"I hope not," she said.

He looked at her. Under the gobs of mud she was a pretty young woman, with fair hair to her waist, tiny hands and feet, and rather well proportioned in between. Her face was elfin, with enormous green eyes. "Please, I hope to persuade you that you haven't done wrong to rescue me from the torrent. Will you tell me who you are?"

"Oh, of course," she said, flushing. "I am Willow Elf."

"You're an elf? Like Jenny?"

"Jenny? Where is her elm?"

"Elm?"

"Her elf elm. All elves associate with particular elms. That's how we are identified."

"I don't think she has an elm," he said. "She's from the World of Two Moons."

"No elm? She must be strange indeed."

"Well, she does have pointed ears and four fingers."

Willow held up one hand, which definitely had five digits, then touched an ear, which was round. "It must be a very odd world. All Xanth elves are like me, except for some things."

"Oh? What things?"

"Well, my tree is a winged elm. So we have wings, unlike other elves. My tree is very large, so we are very large."

"Large? You seem beautifully petite to me."

"Large for an elf. Most are far smaller than we are. They are also bound much more closely to their trees."

"Bound to their trees?"

"You don't know?"

"Remember, I'm Mundane. I am supremely ignorant."

"Oh, of course," she agreed seriously. "All elves are bound to their elms. Close in, they are very strong, but they weaken as they go away from their trees, until they are too weak even to live. So they have no territorial ambitions, but even an ogre would hesitate to try to abuse an elf elm, because the elves there would be stronger than he was."

"You are weak away from your tree?"

"Yes. But it's not nearly so pronounced for flying elves, so we can go quite far. I think it's because our tall tree presents a direct line of sight far afield, with no interference by mountains, houses, or vegetation. Nevertheless, we are subject to the constraints of distance. At the edge of Xanth I would hardly be able to stand, while beside my elm I could carry you in the air with one hand. The variation is much less extreme than for other elf species, and it enables us to fly freely. My elm is in east central Xanth, so I'm in-between here, neither strong nor weak. Otherwise I might have been able to help you more."

"You helped me enough," he said. "I really appreciate it. I used cherry bombs to destroy the goblin dam, but got caught by the rush of water."

"We don't like goblins very well," she said.

"We don't like them at all." He looked around. The rushing water was subsiding. "I had better get back to my family."

"And I had better get back to my elm," she said.

"Thank you again for helping me. I don't know how to repay you."

"Oh, I do not seek repayment," she said, flushing again. "It was a thing of the moment. Normally we don't interact with humans at all; we're very shy. But I couldn't let you drown."

"I understand. I would have done the same for you, had you been the one in trouble, and not just because you're a pretty girl."

"Oh!" she cried, flushing much worse.

"I'm sorry," he said quickly. "I didn't mean to be offensive."

"Nobody ever called me pretty before. I'm a quite ordinary female of my kind, and I'm covered with mud."

Oh. He realized that she had not been joking about being shy. "Maybe you just look better to me because you helped me. And the mud is my fault. Is there a pool or something nearby where we could wash up? Before going our separate ways, I mean?" He was concerned about returning to his family as dirty as he was, because Mom would throw a fit about the upholstery in the RV, but he also found himself not too eager to leave this interesting creature immediately. It was a long shot, but he might get to see more of her, if they washed up together.

"I did see a pool close by," she said. "If you don't mind the delay—"

"I don't mind."

So she led the way to the pool she had spied. It was small but attractive, with sparkling clear water.

Willow began to remove her dress, then hesitated. "I have heard that Mundanes are very—I don't mean to be offensive, but—do you object if I strip?"

"Not at all," he said gallantly. He remembered the time he had skinny-dipped with friends. Was he going to get to do it with this lovely little lady? "Do you object if I also—?"

"Of course not. How else can you get clean?"

He laughed, relieved. "No way else. But I warn you, I won't be able to help looking at your body."

She smiled, and pulled her dress off. He wondered about her lack of reticence about her panties, but in a moment understood: she wore none. In Xanth, it seemed, nakedness was no problem, just underclothing. Her nudity was not only natural, but exquisite; it was the way he imagined Chlorine would look, only Willow was more, well, willowy. Suddenly he liked slenderness very well.

So he pulled off his clothing, and joined her in the pool quickly, because he did not want to stand exposed and maybe embarrass himself with a male reaction. The water was just right, neither hot nor cold. It caressed his bare skin in a special manner, making it feel wonderfully good.

Willow turned to face him, sweeping her hair behind so that her small but perfect breasts were clear. "Shall I wash your back?" she asked innocently, meeting his gaze for the first time since entering the water. Then she froze.

Sean froze too. He had been admiring Willow's body and face; now that admiration exploded into an overwhelming emotion. Beautiful? She was ravishing! It was as if she were framed in glorious light, with the sweetest possible music playing in the background.

"Oh, no!" she cried. "It's a love spring!"

A love spring. He had heard those mentioned. "You mean we're—?" But there was no need to say more, for he already knew it was true. He loved her.

"I never thought—" she said, chagrined.

"Do—do you feel the same way I do?" he asked.

"Yes," she said, moving toward him. "I love you. But—this—we can't—"

"And I love you," he said, meeting her halfway. "Though we are of two different worlds."

"We shouldn't do this," she said, putting her arms around him. His own arms circled her, passing beneath the feathery softness of her wings.

"I know." He kissed her. Half the dreams he might ever have had were realized in that moment.

After an eternity, she drew her face away just enough to speak. "You are Mundane. I am magical. We can not be together."

"How can we be apart?" He kissed her again, and she met him avidly.

"In time the spell will fade," she said as they broke for breath.

"How much time?"

She considered. "About four years, I think. But often the magic love is replaced by natural love in that time, so there may be no escape other than separation.''

"I couldn't stand that.'' He was about to kiss her again, but this time she beat him to it.

"Neither could I,'' she said after another precious pause.

"Oh, Willow, I know this is all magic, but I—don't even want to say what I want to do with you.'' That was the other half of his dreams, not yet realized.

"I want to do it too,'' she said. "The storks get a lot of business from love springs. But I beg you to wait while we consider alternatives.''

"Anything you ask of me, I want to do,'' he said. He made a supreme effort and withdrew from her. "But I can't stop loving you.''

"I am making the greatest effort of my life to be objective,'' she said. "I—I believe I would die in your realm. You—would not be comfortable in mine. Your people and my people would oppose our union. We would be pariahs. Our love can't be.''

"Yet it is,'' he said.

"So we must end it. I think there is a way.''

"Oh, Willow—''

"We know it is not natural,'' she said. "We know it can't work. So we must be sensible. If there is a way to get us out of love, that is best.''

"That is best,'' he echoed. "But I hate the very notion.''

"So do I. But we are not brainless or soulless creatures. We know what is right, and we have the will to do right. So we must do it.''

He didn't want to, but he forced out the words. "How can we cancel our love?''

"I saw an old Forget Whorl nearby.''

"A what?''

"A fragment of the original Forget Spell on the Gap Chasm. It broke up at the Time of No Magic, but some Whorls remain. They are invisible, but I could tell, because I saw insects fly though it and lose their bearings.''

"It—makes you forget?''

"Yes. They used to make any creature who passed through them forget everything, but now they are good for only half an hour or so.

That is, the creature forgets the last half hour he has lived. And that amount of time—''

"Would make us forget our love!'' he exclaimed.

"Would make us forget our love,'' she agreed sadly. "Please understand, this is not a thing I want to do, but I think it is best, for us both. My rational mind is at war with my emotion, and I have always prided myself on being sensible.''

"So have I,'' he said. "So I guess we shouldn't do anything that we might regret when we are out of love.''

"Yes. I'm glad you understand.''

"I understand that I don't want to mess up your life, and if loving you will do that, I should try to stop loving you.'' He smiled grimly. "But it gripes me that maybe the hardest, noblest thing I will ever do in my life—I won't remember.''

She nodded, agreeing about the irony, for them both. "Let's get clean,'' she said. "The spring can not do anything more to us. Then we can go to that whorl.''

"Yes.'' He was clamping down as hard as he could on his emotion. "But you know, I think if I had gotten to know you without the love spring, I could have loved you anyway, because you are a remarkably smart and sensible woman, as well as being lovely.''

"Thank you,'' she said as she scrubbed his back with her gentle hands. "Observing your restraint, when I know the desire you feel, I suspect I could have loved you, too, despite your origin. And you are not unhandsome.''

"Thank you.'' He turned, and she turned, and he did her back, working carefully around her lovely wings, and splashed water on the feathers until they were clean too. Then they both ducked under the surface to get their hair clean. Finally they hauled their clothing into the water and rinsed it, and donned it wet.

They waded out of the spring, and Willow led the way to the Forget Whorl. It was, as she had said, invisible, but he believed she knew whereof she spoke. "Who goes first?'' he asked, half hoping she would change her mind.

"I can readily fly home, now that my wings are clean. But you are in a strange land. I would prefer to watch, and make sure you are safely reunited with your family, before I go through that Whorl. Then I will be able to be in peace, I think.''

''So be it.'' He looked at her. ''But can we—one last time?''

She flung herself into his arms and kissed him several times. Then she hauled herself away. ''Now go, quickly, before I shame myself and do what I must not,'' she said, tears streaming down her cheeks.

He nerved himself, turned away from her, and strode toward the Forget Whorl. Part of him hoped it wouldn't work.

''But it did work,'' he said, concluding his intense memory. ''I found my way back to the RV, and never thought of you again.''

''I know,'' she said. ''I watched you.'' The tears he remembered were still on her face.

''But why are you here?'' he asked.

''When I returned to the Forget Whorl, it was gone,'' she said. ''I think it was in its last stage, very faint, and you used it up. So I could not forget.''

''Oh, no,'' he groaned. ''I should have let you go first.''

''No, my love. I would not have you suffer so.''

They kissed again. ''But how is it that I remember, now? And why did you follow me?''

''Once you complimented me on my sensibleness, but perhaps it was unwarranted. I was able to rein my emotions for the time we were first together, but not thereafter. I wanted you so much—'' She shrugged. ''I did try. I flew home and talked to my family, and to the elders of our tree. They knew of no other Forget Whorl I could use. And they pointed out something I had not thought of: that if the Whorl was so close to extinction when you used it, it might not have done the full job. You might come to remember, after some time had passed. Then I would have done you no favor. So they suggested that I do two things. First, that I meet you again, to see whether the forgetting held. If the sight of me made you remember, then you would have remembered later on your own. But if you did not remember, then the spell was holding, and you would be safe.''

''It did not hold,'' Sean said. ''It was weakening before I saw you; I know that now.''

"Yes. For your sake I hoped it would hold, but for my sake I hoped it would not. I was shamefully selfish."

"Shamefully," he agreed, kissing her again. "But what now? We still are not right for each other."

"We still are not right," she agreed. "I think we shall have to go to the Good Magician for the Answer. He surely has potions—"

"Damn it!" he swore, noting peripherally that he had managed to override the Adult Conspiracy on that one. Maybe it was because love was adult business. "We tried to do the right thing. Why must we try again? Is our love really so wrong?"

"Not wrong—unworkable," she clarified. "You must return to your realm, and I must remain in mine."

"But hasn't this sort of thing ever happened before? How do other forbidden couples work it out?"

She smiled wanly. "When animals meet at a love spring, they simply summon the stork and go their ways. When human variants do, they try to make the best of it. But I'm not sure that those unions work out as well as normal love does. Sometimes there are unfortunate repercussions. But none of them have had the problem we do: a Xanth/Mundane liaison."

"I would be willing to stay in Xanth, to be with you."

"But you have no wings. You can't fly. You can't go where I go."

"If you want to fly away from me, I can't stop you," he said. "And wouldn't if I could. I would never want you to be tied down."

"But I *would* be tied down—by love," she pointed out. "So I think the Good Magician is our alternative, though he does charge horrendously for his information."

"I suppose you're right. But we can't do that until the present crisis is over. First Xanth has to be saved; then our incidental problem can be dealt with."

"Are you being ironic?"

"You bet I am! What do we do in the interim?"

"Not what we would like to do. The constraints are still upon us."

"I wish we could just forget those!"

She gazed levelly at him. "If it is your choice, I will not deny you, Sean."

"I know you won't." He understood all too perfectly. She could stop herself from thowing herself at him, but would lack the will to resist his approach. Just as he could restrain himself, but could never actually push her away, if she—"But I think I must deny myself. Let's get out of here; at least I can introduce you to my folks."

"But how could they approve of me?"

"How could they not? We'll just have to explain the situation."

"Yes, as I did to my people," she said sadly. "They were horrified. They understood getting caught in a love spring, but not with a Mundane. They chided me for my carelessness."

Sean laughed. "They were right. You should have flown right past, when you first saw me."

"And let you drown? How could I?"

He shook his head. "You know, you're not doing anything to discourage my love. You're a lovely person."

She flushed in that fetching way he remembered. "Neither are you discouraging me."

They embraced and kissed again. But then he forced himself to pull partway away. "If we don't get out of here soon, all our noble resolutions will count for nothing."

"Yes." She grimaced cutely and pulled the rest of the way away.

He looked around the cave, then up at the hole in the sky that was the cave entrance. It was too high, and the walls were too steep, for them to reach. He considered lifting her up on his shoulders, but even so it was too high. The cave was too narrow for her to spread her wings, so she couldn't fly out, either. They were definitely stuck. "We've been here for maybe half an hour," he said. "I wonder why my folks haven't come to check on me."

"That's true," she agreed, surprised. She glanced at the eye on her wrist. "In fact, an hour. I was so glad to be with you again that I lost all track of time. Surely they would not depart without you."

"Surely they would not," he agreed. "It should have taken them maybe five minutes to realize I was gone, and five more to check."

"It is almost as if—yes! There it is!"

"There what is?"

"A thyme bomb. See, there's the sprig of thyme." She pointed to a dried-up leaf lying on the cave floor.

"Let me guess," Sean said. "In Xanth, thyme plants affect time, so when you get close to one—"

"Yes. Usually the living plants slow things down, and their seeds speed them up. But when leaves get separated and dry out, their effect reverses, and they stretch time out, in the manner of the seeds. So time expands explosively in their vicinity, and we call them thyme bombs. Usually they are harmless, because all folk have to do is walk away from them. But—"

"But we can't," he finished. "So we're stuck in the fast lane."

"In a cave," she corrected him gently.

He didn't bother to clarify his reference. "So how do we get away from it, so we don't die of hunger before anyone finds us?"

"Oh, I can nullify it," she said brightly. "I have a napsack in my purse." She produced a small purse and rummaged in it, pulling out all manner of things: clothing, slippers, fruits, a mirror, a fancy hat, a bedroll, and a collection of pretty stones. "Ah, there it is," she said, drawing out a strapped pack.

Sean was amazed. "How can all that fit in that little purse?"

"It's magic, of course. Don't Mundane women have purses?"

Sean remembered how much Mom could carry in hers. "Yes. But if you have a complete change of clothing in there, why didn't you use it when we came out of the pool, instead of putting your wet things back on?"

"I knew you lacked a change of clothing, so I did not wish to embarrass you."

"How do I love thee," he murmured. "Let me count the ways."

"I tried to count, but there were too many ways," she said. "Even though I know it's all just because of the love spring." She opened the napsack and put the sprig of thyme in. Then she rolled up the napsack and put it back in her purse. "That should take care of it."

"I don't understand," he said. "Why does putting it in there change anything?"

"Because anything in a napsack sleeps," she explained. "In fact, I seldom put it on, because then it makes me take a nap too. But it is useful for storing perishable food, as it won't spoil while sleeping, and the thyme bomb has little effect while napping."

Sean shook his head. "Knapsack—napsack. I keep forgetting how things work in Xanth. But if our time is now normal, how come I don't feel any different?''

"We didn't change,'' she explained patiently. "The time around us did. Now we are aligned with the time outside. Thyme bombs normally speed time up tenfold, so perhaps six minutes passed during our hour. If it requires ten minutes for your family to find you—''

"Got it. Let's make our remaining three or four minutes count.'' He held her and kissed her.

"Hey, whatcha doing down there?'' David called from above.

"Trust my little half brother to arrive at the least opportune time,'' Sean muttered, turning her loose. But he was glad to have been found. "I'm kissing my girlfriend, punk!'' he called up. "What's it look like?''

"Like making time with a strange woman,'' David called. "But it's too dark down there to see any detail. Do you have your clothes on?''

"Yes, we have our clothes on,'' Sean called. "Now, go fetch some rope or something to haul us out of here.''

"Okay.'' The head disappeared.

He turned back to her. "Quick, let's finish our kiss.''

Willow laughed and obliged.

Then the other members of the family were there at the cave entrance. "What happened?'' Dad called.

"I fell in a hole with a girl,'' Sean called back.

"Gee,'' Karen called. "Is she pretty?''

"Yes.''

Willow blushed.

Then Dad was letting down a knotted rope. "We've got it anchored. Can you climb?''

"Can you climb?'' Sean asked Willow.

"Yes. I have recovered from my fatigue, and this is closer to my elm than we were before.''

"Then you go up first. I'll wait till you're clear.''

"Thank you.'' She kissed him again, quickly, and put her hands on the rope. He put his hands on her petite waist and helped her up. He let go when she climbed beyond his reach. He looked up to be sure she was all right, but realized that it was now possible to see under her skirt, and hastily averted his gaze. In Xanth it just wasn't done, and he would never embarrass her in any way he could avoid. Even though he had seen the whole of her before, and knew she didn't wear those forbidden panties. He would look at her only when she wished him to. Because he loved her.

"Your turn," Dad called down.

Sean grasped the rope and hauled himself up. It was hard work, and he realized that Willow had climbed faster than he was. She had not been fooling about the way her strength increased near her tree; she was probably stronger than he was, now, despite her delicate physique.

He heaved himself up through the hole, panting, and Dad caught him. The whole family was there, as well as Chlorine and Nimby, the pets, and Sim. And Willow.

"What happened?" Dad asked.

"I love her," Sean said before he thought. "We washed in a love spring, back near the goblin dam."

"A love spring!" Chlorine said. She was wearing what looked like a Mundane windbreaker jacket. "But didn't you know—"

"We thought it was a regular pool. Willow helped me out of the rushing water. She maybe saved my life. But we both got all muddy, so—"

"But you returned alone," Mom said.

"I went through a Forget Whorl. But she couldn't. And when I saw her again—it all came back. It would have come back anyway, before long. I still love her."

"We had better get back to the RV," Dad said. "I presume Willow will join us."

"Yes she will," Sean said, going to her. "We can't separate again."

The others hesitated, but Chlorine clarified the matter. "When two people meet at a love spring, they are in love. Nothing else matters much. Not even species. It is useless to object. They must marry."

"No," Willow said.

Chlorine glanced at her. "You were not in the love spring?"

"I was in it. I love him. But I am a winged monster. He is Mundane. We can not marry."

"Monster!" David cried, laughing.

"That's what they call themselves, dolt," Karen said in superior fashion. "All the winged creatures. It doesn't mean they are ugly."

"Then why did you follow him here?" Chlorine asked Willow.

"I could not help it. But if we go to the Good Magician, we can get a potion to nullify the love."

"We can't go anywhere until Xanth is saved," Dad said.

"After that, of course," Willow said.

"And he charges a year's Service, or the equivalent," Chlorine pointed out. "I'm on Service for him now. How could Sean do that, when he has to return to Mundania with his family?"

"I will serve his time too," Willow said.

"No you won't!" Sean protested. "You would never have gotten into this trouble if you hadn't stopped to help me."

"I'm not sorry. The memory will be worth it."

"The memory of the love you will no longer have?" Chlorine asked.

"Yes. The love spring did it, but I know he is worthy of it."

"Sean?" David asked incredulously.

"I'll serve my own time," Sean said.

"But then you would have to stay in Xanth," Chlorine pointed out.

He glanced at her. She was still absolutely lovely and sexy, but he no longer cared. "So?"

"So if you have to stay anyway, why not stay in love with her?"

Sean was astonished. She was right. "Maybe take the potion after the Service is done," he said, looking at Willow.

But she demurred. "If we are not to marry, it would only be torture," she said. "And I know you have business in your own world. I am native; I will serve the time for us both. This is the practical thing."

She was right, too. Yet it wasn't fair.

They were now at the RV. "I think Willow will be with us for a while," Mom said briskly. "The rest of you show her the RV, while Jim and I discuss something outside."

Sean was not sure that was good news, but there was nothing to do but go along with it. "Come, Willow—we'll show you our magic moving house."

"I have seen it from afar," Willow said. "I do not mind where I am, as long as I am with you."

Chlorine shook her head. "If this is what a love spring offers, I'm going to find one when I'm ready to marry."

"You should," Sean agreed. "It's total." That was the understatement of the day.

13
COMPLICATIONS

Mary got Jim safely out of earshot of those in the RV. "That girl," she said.

"With wings," he agreed, as if he didn't know her concern.

"They can't be together."

"Mary, they can't be apart, either. They're in love."

"You know what I mean. He's going to want to sleep with her—and she'll let him."

He nodded. "This is the nature of young love."

"You're not taking this seriously!"

He looked at her. "On the contrary, I'm being realistic. I have heard about those love springs. They will not be denied. When animals get into them—"

"Jim, we're not animals!"

"In certain respects, we are. When it comes to—"

"Don't be impossible. What are we going to do?"

"Mary, he's seventeen, and she's about the same. That's old enough."

"It's *not* old enough!"

"How old were we when—"

"Thirty-one and twenty-nine."

"Our second marriages," he reminded her. "How old were you the first time you had sex?"

"Don't be uncouth."

"Sorry. The first time you tried to signal the stork?"

"That has no relevance."

"Doesn't it? I was seventeen—Sean's age. How about you?"

"Fifteen," she answered reluctantly. "But I didn't enjoy it."

"It's all right only if you don't enjoy it?"

"That's not what I mean. That girl would love to—" But she had to stop, because he had already shot down that approach. "Anyway, it was different in our day."

"Yes, we were teens. Now we're mature fogies whose sexual energies are diminished, so we can safely condemn contemporary teens for having our past urges."

"I didn't say that." Then she made a counter sally. "Did you bring the girl into your house and tell your parents?"

He laughed. "Think I was suicidal? They were just like us—as we are now."

That stung, but she plowed on. "Are we to give them space in the RV to—to share a bed? With David and Karen knowing?"

That concept finally set him back. "Point made. But let me play devil's advocate a moment. There is no passion quite so strong as unrequited or unconsummated love. Isn't it possible that if we provide them with Mundane antistork devices and let them indulge their passions, they would get over that aspect and be able to make a more rational decision when the time comes to separate?"

"Did our indulgence cause us to reconsider marriage?" she asked evenly.

He raised his hands in a surrender gesture. "No, I liked you even better after than before." He pondered a moment. "We have not had long to observe them, but it is my impression that they have not yet indulged—"

"They were alone less than ten minutes."

"Plus their bath in the love spring. They resisted temptation because they knew the relationship had no future. I think that must have been mostly Willow's doing, because Sean never showed all that much maturity in decisions before. She strikes me as—well, as a woman who would be worthy of him, in other circumstances, wings or not."

"No question," Mary agreed, surprisingly. "She's a sensible and generous person. What little I have seen of her so far, I like very well. But the fact is that they are *not* for each other, being of different realms and different species, and Xanth is stricter about babies out of wedlock than the real world is. But as you say, young passions are strong. How long could they hold out, if we put them constantly together?"

"Fifteen minutes?"

"So what do we do?"

He sighed. "We move Willow in with Karen or Chlorine, and Sean with David. We keep company with them—constantly. But I'm going to feel like a jailer."

"It is necessary." Then, satisfied with her victory, she kissed him.

"I'll take that as a promise for the time *we* get alone," he said.

"To be sure."

They returned to the RV. It was crowded, because there were now nine people in it, counting the demoness, plus the pets. At least the big chick had returned to his governess; they and the dragons would remain on the mesa until the winds abated. This had been the most remarkable menagerie she had encountered, even in imagination. She was privately amazed at herself for taking it all in stride. But what else was she to do? She was a long way from her specialty of archaic Mundane languages.

Jim took the wheel, and she the front passenger seat. The others were arranged all around the main section of the vehicle. Sean and Willow were holding hands, while David and Karen were eagerly questioning them about everything, especially love springs. "If David and I fell in a love spring, would we fall in love?" Karen asked.

"Yuckk!" David cried.

But Willow had an answer. "I think not, because you are not party to the Adult Conspiracy. But you might quarrel less."

"Were you nekked together in that pool?" David asked.

"Yuck!" Karen said, for nuisance value.

"Yes, naked," Sean answered. "We washed each other's backs. And that's all we did."

That last was for Mary's benefit, she knew. She appreciated it.

"Except for kissing," Willow said.

Jim nudged the RV forward. He circled toward the demon tunnel. The passengers opened the windows and waved to the roc and dragons, who flapped a wing and snorted smoke or fire into the air, respectively, in response. It had indeed been a good joint effort, and successful. But there was more to do.

Mentia floated out through the metal in the unnerving way she had and stretched her arms impossibly wide to indicate the outline of the tunnel entrance, which was otherwise invisible. Jim steered for it, and the vehicle seemed to sink into the solid-looking rock. Then the surface of the ground closed overhead, and Jim turned on the headlights to illuminate the curving tunnel. The demoness, caught by surprise again (really?), was shown in phenomenally full-breasted nudity, sans panties, of course, but recovered after too long a moment and formed a tight dress around her voluptuous torso.

"A man could get to like Xanth," Jim murmured in a tone just loud enough for her to hear.

"Oh?" Mary said in a tone just loud enough for the demoness to overhear. "Suppose she became a raving monster?"

Mentia obligingly became a raving monster, with spikes at every joint and enormous dripping fangs.

"I've been set up," Jim muttered, as Mary and Mentia laughed.

The drive down was slow but uneventful; the phantasms did not reappear. When they emerged from the base it was evening. "Do we have time to camp for the night?" Jim called to Chlorine in back.

She checked with Nimby. "Yes, if we don't mind the madness."

"We'll stay in the RV," he said. "But we'll forage outside for food, et cetera."

"Cetera?" Willow asked.

"He means natural functions," Sean said.

"Isn't everything natural?"

"Poop," David said, then paused in surprise. "Hey, I got the bad word out! No bleep."

"The madness is overriding the Adult Conspiracy," Mentia explained.

"But don't let it go to your head," Mary called severely.

"Well, I wouldn't want it to go *there,*" the boy retorted.

"What a mess," Karen agreed. "But are you sure your face isn't made of it?"

"What's on my face?"

"Nothing. That's the way you look all the time."

Things were getting back to normal. Mary was pleased to note in the rearview mirror that Willow was blushing. Definitely a refined creature. If only Sean could meet someone like her in Miami!

Nimby directed them to a reasonable place, and Jim parked the RV. "Pee break!" David cried, reveling in the newfound freedom from bleeping.

They got out and spread out, accomplishing their various purposes, and Mentia found a good pie tree. Mary would have preferred something more nutritious, but had pretty much given up on that particular fight in this realm. Pies were simply too abundant and convenient and popular.

Then they set up the RV for the night, and neither Sean nor Willow made any objection to Mary's bedding assignments. They did indeed comprehend the risks of doing otherwise. They settled down for sleep.

Which wasn't ideal. Because of the presence of Chlorine, Nimby, and Willow, their beds were all full, so that she and Jim had to sleep in the front seats. Jim simply slumped down with his pillow against the door and zonked out, but it took her longer to settle down. And naturally she heard something.

Someone was stirring in the RV. The sound was slight, suggesting that whoever it was didn't want to disturb anyone else. Was it a toilet call? The children had been cautioned not to go out alone, because Xanth really was dangerous, especially at night. The spell on the RV provided considerable security, but that was no good outside.

Mary was about to inquire, but decided to keep quiet. It wasn't that she was a snoop, but she did want to know exactly what was going on. There was too much about this magic land that was disturbing in the best of times, and the dust of madness made it worse, and night made it worse yet, and the addition of that winged girl, however nice a person she undoubtedly was, made it even more so. She loved Sean, without doubt; the human signs were all over her. But that was its own complication. Was she getting up, to go out for a solitary flying session, or to be alone with Sean? There was little doubt what the two would do, if they got alone together. So maybe Mary should follow them out, just making her presence known, and scotch that at the start.

The side door opened, amazingly quietly, and closed. Someone had exited the RV. Who? She thought by the sounds that it was just one; there had been no whispered dialogue. That argued against Sean and Willow. Then who was it? And why?

There was a light tap at her window. She jumped, caught by surprise. The person, far from hiding, was signaling her!

She looked. It was Nimby. Oh. He followed his own rules, and certainly wasn't bound by theirs. But what then of Chlorine? If Nimby and Chlorine wanted to indulge themselves together, it certainly wasn't Mary's place to oppose it, as long as it wasn't in sight of the children. But Chlorine hadn't left her bed; Mary could recognize her particular pattern of breathing.

Nimby beckoned. What could he want? Well, she would find out. He was a strange one, and she knew he was really a dragon, but she had no fear of him. Had he wished to do them any ill, he had had countless opportunities. Certainly he wouldn't find *her* a romantic object—not with Chlorine there. So it was something else.

She opened the door carefully and got out, closing it as carefully behind her. Then she turned to face Nimby. "Yes?" she inquired in a low whisper.

For answer, he became the donkey-headed diagonally striped dragon. This time she noticed two things she hadn't noticed before; either she had been unobservant, or he had changed. She suspected the latter. One change was that his scales were glowing, outlining him in the darkness so that she had no trouble seeing him. The other was that the scales in his center portion were formed into the shape of a saddle.

"You want me to ride you?" she asked.

The equine head nodded.

He surely had a reason. He seemed to know everything that went on in the vicinity. So he must know something now.

The head nodded again.

"Why, you can read my thoughts!" she exclaimed.

Another nod.

So he had known she was awake and listening, and had come for her. But why? Was there some danger?

One more nod.

And they could alleviate it? By taking action now?

Nod.

Then they had better get busy. She approached him and climbed into the saddle. It was surprisingly comfortable. There were projecting scales in front that served as perfect handholds, surely by no coincidence. Even some below for her feet to rest on. Nimby was the perfect mount.

The pastel pink stripes turned red. "Why, Nimby, you're blushing!" she murmured. "Because I complimented your status as a mount."

Embarrassed nod.

Then Nimby moved. Mary had had her youthful fling with horses, so had a fair amount of experience riding. Nothing fancy, but she was competent. Nimby's gait was odd—then less odd—and finally exactly like that of a good horse. He was accommodating her memory of riding. He was certainly easy to get along with.

They got up speed. Mary strained to see where they were going in the darkness—and then Nimby's eyes glowed brightly, sending out beams of light as if they were headlights, showing her everything ahead. "Thank you," she murmured, patting a scale. No wonder Chlorine kept company with this versatile creature. And he had made Chlorine look the way she did. He was really a remarkable entity. Just how powerful was his magic?

For a moment the dragon seemed nervous about something. Mary looked around, but saw nothing dangerous, and knew that Nimby wouldn't let anything bad approach. She returned to her chain of thought. No, potent magic wasn't necessary to explain Nimby. He was making the most of his shape-changing and mind-reading abilities, so seemed much more talented than he perhaps was. Possibly he drew on the mental powers of the person he was with, thus enhancing his abilities. That would explain a good deal. He was probably a very specially talented animal, who became more than that when associated with a human being.

Nimby seemed to relax. And now he reached his destination. There was a big old dead tree with a splintered trunk. The wood looked firm and dry, not rotten despite its evident age. In fact, it looked a bit like those two pieces of reverse wood that Chlorine had reported using to nullify that nuisance machine that had captured Woofer and Tweeter.

Nimby nodded.

"Reverse wood?" she asked, startled. "You brought me here to fetch reverse wood?"

Nod.

Mentia appeared. "What are you two up to, in the dead of night?" she asked. Then she spied the tree. "Oops—I can't touch that!" She vanished.

"And as a Mundane, I can handle it without suffering reversal of my magic," Mary said. "While you might be in trouble. Very well; how much do you need?"

It turned out that he needed a bundle. She pulled fragments from the tree and bound them together with a vine, then held the bundle in her arms as Nimby carried her back toward the RV. Then she laid pieces of wood in a large circle around the RV, spaced only a few feet apart. That should be one insidiously effective defense perimeter, she thought.

Nimby nodded.

Mentia reappeared. "Deadly," she remarked.

They finished the job and returned to the RV. Before she climbed back in, Mary kissed one donkey ear. "It's nice to have you looking out for us," she said. "Even if it is just to help Chlorine complete her assignment." The ear blushed.

Mary settled back in her seat, and Nimby resumed his human form and rejoined Chlorine in back. No one had missed them. This time Mary went right to sleep.

At dawn the others didn't even notice the circle of wood, but Mary saw that enormous tracks came directly toward the RV, touched the circle, and became hopelessly confused. Probably a hungry land dragon had sniffed them out, but been balked by the reversal of its nature or magic. Nimby must have seen it coming, and quietly taken the measure required to abate the menace. To protect Chlorine—and her mission. It was really Nimby the Good Magician had sent them, in the guise of sending Chlorine.

Mary gathered up the wood and tied it back into its bundle. Now it neutralized itself, as it did when in its original tree trunk, but its potential remained. She stacked it in the RV for future use.

Now Chlorine consulted with Nimby to see what route they should take where, to get the windbreaker where it would be most effective. To their surprise, he did not recommend the trollway. Instead it turned out that they would have to seek the help of a number of individuals scattered across the area. The first was Modem.

"That looks a lot like a Mundane term," Jim remarked. "Surely coincidence."

They found a gas guzzler and refueled, then set off on a tortuous trip through the forest until they came to an isolated shack. The windows were boarded over, but not because it was deserted; the family was battening down for the terrible storm that was building. The RV stopped beside it.

Chlorine was about to get out, but Nimby restrained her and indicated Mary. Oh? Well, there had to be a reason. Mary had a good deal of respect for Nimby's awareness of things. She got out and knocked on the shack's door.

"Go away, spook!" a voice called from inside.

"I'm not a spook," Mary protested, though she had a notion what kind of apparitions had been bothering this house. "I'm a dull Mundane woman looking for Modem."

The door opened a crack, held closely by a glittery hand. A gnarly eye peered out. "And I'm the hag of this hut. What do you know of Modem?"

"Only that we need him to help save Xanth from the ill wind."

The door cracked wider. "Let me get a look at you," the hag said. "Why, you're someone's mother."

"Yes."

"Then it must be all right. See that he doesn't get into mischief. He's got weird magic." She called back into the hut. "Modem lad, go with this mother."

"Yes, Haggi Ma." A boy about David's age appeared, tousled of hair and ragged of garb.

Now it was clear why Mary had had to be the one. Nimby had known. "Thank you," she said to Haggi. She took the boy by his grubby hand and led him to the RV. "We'll try to bring him back safely," she called. Then to the boy: "We have a magic moving house. You may look out the window, after you wash your hands. You will sit with my son David. You may call me Mom for now."

"Yes, Mom," he replied dutifully.

Chlorine came out to meet them. "This is Modem," Mary told her in a motherly manner. "Clean him up and find out the nature of his magic. Give him the window seat beside David." She really meant for Chlorine to find out from Nimby. Also, the boy would more likely hold still if Chlorine washed his face and hands. Chlorine had a certain effect on males of any age; might as well make positive use of it.

"Hello, Modem," Chlorine said. "I am Chlorine." She smiled.

"Chee." The boy looked stunned. That meant he was socially normal.

They resumed driving, looking for the next name on Nimby's list. This was Keaira, off in another direction. While Jim navigated the twisty turns of the almost trackless jungle, Chlorine washed the stunned Modem's face and hands and dulcetly questioned him.

It turned out that Modem's magic was indeed related to the Mundane term. It was what he called a magic mirror, only it was inside him. He could communicate with Com Pewter.

"With who?" Willow asked.

"Com Pewter," Chlorine explained. "The evil machine turned good. The one who first sent Sending. He changes reality in his vicinity."

"Yes," Modem agreed. "When I connect with him, I can do it too, but only because I'm a wo—wor—"

"Work station," Jim called back.

"Yes. That's what he calls it."

"That's nice," Chlorine said. "Can you show us?"

At that point the RV reached a dead-end trail. A huge tangly tree with dangling tentacular vines barred their way.

"Watch it," Mentia said. "That's a tangle tree."

Karen giggled. "Like my hair?"

"Not exactly. Watch." The demoness floated out and assumed the form of a little girl. She walked up to the tree.

Suddenly the vines writhed. They wrapped around her and hauled her into the tree. A big wooden mouth opened in the trunk. The tentacles stuffed the girl into that orifice. Wooden teeth clamped down.

Then the mouth opened and spat out the girl. The trunk turned green. The tentacles wilted.

Mentia resumed luscious woman form and floated back into the RV. "Any questions?"

"Yuck, no," Karen said, looking a bit green herself.

"Yeah," David said. "What made it spit you back out?"

The demoness smiled in a female dog way. "I gave it a whiff of stink horn."

"Of what?"

Mentia made a foul-smelling noise. The most ghastly imaginable stench filled the vehicle. "Like that," she said. "Only stronger."

"Ghaa!" Karen cried, rushing to open a window. Mary quietly did the same. That was nose-numbingly dreadful. Only Nimby wasn't choking.

"Great!" David cried. "And that's what that dumb tangle tree bit into?"

"I'm afraid so," the demoness said with mock regret.

Then they were all laughing, even Modem, despite the awful odor.

"I can change it," Modem said. "When I connect."

"Then please connect with Com Pewter," Chlorine told him. "And change it to roses."

Modem closed his eyes, concentrating. Suddenly a beautiful rose scent permeated the RV. Reality had changed.

"Do you know, I begin to see why this talent may be useful," Jim remarked. "Can he get us past that tangle tree?"

Chlorine spoke to the boy. The tangle tree became a pie tree. Mentia went out and harvested the best pies and brought them in for consumption as they drove on. Chlorine returned to her seat beside Nimby, and brought out a greenish bug. She passed this across her mouth.

"What's that?" Karen asked.

"A lips tic, of course. It colors my lips." Indeed, they were now a much firmer green.

What else? Mary thought.

They entered a windswept plain. The power of the storm continued to rise, and the flying dust made visibility short. Blasts of it struck the RV, pushing it around, and scattered phantasms flew by. Sword blades seemed to rise out of the ground, threatening the tires, but Nimby indicated and Mentia verified that they were mostly illusory. Still, Mary would not care to plow through much more of this.

Keaira's residence was an oasis amidst the barrens. Pretty flowering softwoods surrounded a larger dust-colored tree with a fancy tree house. "Oh, a cottage in dust tree," Chlorine said, pleased.

"Since when do pine trees flower?" Jim muttered.

"Since we came to Xanth," Mary replied.

They pulled up near the dust tree. Despite its name, there was no dust flying here; the air was calm and sweet. This seemed to be an enchanted spot—which was surely why Keaira had chosen to live here.

The door of the tree house opened, and a young woman with brown braids emerged. "A traveling house?" she asked, surprised.

Mary approached her. "Yes, and we would like you to join us, if you are Keaira. We are on a mission to save Xanth from the terrible storm, and we need your help."

"But my power over weather is very small," Keaira protested. "I can affect it only quite near me. I couldn't do anything about a giant magical storm like this."

"Your talent is weather control!" Mary exclaimed, catching on. "That's why your house suffers no bad weather!"

"Yes, of course," Keaira agreed. "But only as far out as you see. That's not very much."

"It should be enough to enable us to get through the increasingly bad weather we face," Mary said. "Will you come with us?"

"Of course, if it will help Xanth. Will it take long?"

"We hope not. But it could be several days. We have to travel behind the storm and herd it north."

Keaira looked wistfully at her house. "But if I am away too long, the ill wind will blow my house and trees away, and it has taken so long to cultivate them."

Mary appreciated her reluctance. But she had a notion. "Maybe we can do something about that." She turned to Modem. "Can you change her reality so that her oasis won't suffer?"

The boy considered. "Would a dome over it help?"

"Not if it got suffocatingly hot under it," Mary said.

"Maybe a thyme plant, to keep it unchanging," Sean suggested.

"But we don't have a thyme plant," Chlorine protested.

"Yes we do," Sean said. "Willow has a spring of thyme in her napsack."

"What knapsack?" Mary asked, for the girl had no more than her little purse with her.

"It wouldn't help," Willow said. "It would speed things up, when they need to be slowed down."

"How about with reverse wood?" Sean asked. "Mom's got some stashed with the luggage."

"Yes, that should do it," Willow agreed, surprised.

So Sean got out two pieces of reverse wood, and Willow pulled a knapsack out of her purse, and a sprig of thyme from that. They set the thyme in Keaira's tree house.

"But nothing has changed," Mary said.

Sean smiled. "Yes it has, Mom. Look beyond the oasis."

She looked. The dust was still flying out there, but very slowly, as if embedded in syrup. "I don't understand."

"We're living ten times as fast as usual," he explained. "Outside is normal. The thyme has speeded us up. But the moment we put the reverse wood with it, it will have the opposite effect, and the oasis will be a tenth as fast as the outside."

Now it was coming clear. Except for one detail. "How will you get out of there, once the reverse wood reverses the thyme?"

"I won't. I'll simply throw in the two sticks, and when they land, they'll separate and take effect. That's how Chlorine nulled Sending, way back when. She told me."

Mary looked at Nimby. He nodded. It seemed that it would work as specified. "Then it seems you can safely come with us, if your oasis will last for a day or so of its time."

"Yes, that should be all right," the young woman agreed.

They cleared the oasis, and Sean hurled the two sticks of wood in. They landed beside the dust tree and bounced apart. And the scene seemed to freeze. The magic had taken effect.

The RV was yet more crowded, but that couldn't be helped. Or could it? Mary had a notion. "Modem, do you know what an accommodation spell is?"

"A com a days in?" he repeated blankly.

"The imps use it to make their tiny house seem big enough for full-sized folk. It isn't really, but—well, maybe it is. I was wondering whether you could make this moving house seem larger inside, without being larger outside."

"Mom, you're a genius!" Sean exclaimed.

"Yes, I guess," the boy agreed doubtfully, "if Pewter knows it." He concentrated.

Suddenly the RV was twice its former size. There was room for everyone. Mary was seated on a seat big enough for two. The roof was twice as high. Jim was manhandling a monstrous steering wheel. But when she looked out the window, she saw that the RV was taking up no more road space than before. It was big only inside.

"Isn't magic wonderful," she breathed.

"For sure," Jim said, shifting to get to the edge of his seat so that his feet could reach the pedals.

But outside the weather still buffeted the vehicle. The gusts of wind were becoming frighteningly powerful, and visibility was diminishing alarmingly. Something had to be done, or they would be blown into disaster.

Mary had an idea. "Keaira—can you give us calm weather, in the vicinity of our moving house?"

"Certainly," the girl said. And suddenly they were in an aisle of calm. Beyond it the ferocity of the storm was undiminished, but no gust touched the RV, and the air surrounding it was clear.

"Thank you," Mary said, much relieved. Then she set about finding some blocks of wood or something else to enable her husband to reach the pedals more comfortably. She didn't want him to lose control of the vehicle.

The next name on Nimby's list was Chena Centaur. "I recognize that one," Mary said, sifting through her memory. "Carleton Centaur's little sister. He asked us to relay his greeting to her, if we saw her."

"You're right," Jim agreed, surprised.

"But I'm not sure how a centaur will fit in here, even with our increased interior space."

Nimby wrote a note. " 'Chena won't come inside,' " Chlorine read. " 'She's a winged centaur.' "

"Winged?" Mary asked. "I'm sure Carleton didn't say anything like that. She must be a regular centaur."

But Nimby, as always, turned out to be right. They came up to two somewhat bedraggled winged centaurs taking shelter in the lee of a large chest nut and bolt tree. Chests of nuts and bolts were scattered everywhere, harvested prematurely by the wind.

Mentia went out to talk with the fillies, who were somewhat taken aback by the RV. Then the two stepped into the calm surrounding the vehicle, evidently relieved, shaking out their wings. The folk inside stepped out to make introductions. The two were indeed Chena and her friend Crystal.

"But how is it that you are winged?" Mary asked. "Your brother Carleton sends his greetings and goodwill, but he said nothing about wings."

"I wasn't winged then," Chena explained. "I was a normal centaur. But then I met Che Centaur, and, well, I had a wishing stone, and it made me winged. Crystal was a human girl, whom I talked into converting. You see, we need more flying centaurs, of different derivations, if we are to have a viable species. So now I'm out recruiting. Crystal here agreed that her prospects would be better as a centaur. I have been showing her the centaur ways as we look for more recruits."

"But won't you need male flying centaurs too?" Mary asked.

Crystal flushed. "Yes," Chena said. "We are looking for suitable males of any species to recruit."

Mary studied them. Both were healthy fillies in the equine portions, and slender girls in the human portions, with the rather full breasts that the centaur species tended to have. "I suspect you will succeed. But I can provide an expert opinion, if you wish."

"You can?" Crystal asked, speaking for the first time.

Mary glanced to the side. "Sean, if you were not otherwise attached, would you consider becoming a winged centaur in order to be with one of these fillies?"

"You bet!" Sean agreed. Then he had another notion, and Mary could have bit her tongue for not anticipating it. "Say, I could be transformed to a winged elf to be with Willow!"

But Willow herself countered that, to Mary's great relief. "No, my love. Magician Trent can transform anyone to any form, but you are Mundane. He could give you the form of a winged elf male, but not the magic. Only if you already had magic could it change with your form. You would not be able to fly. Your wings would be useless. And . . ." She paused delicately. "I love you as you are. I would not have you change."

"We just can't make it in each other's worlds," he said, disheartened.

"Not very well," she agreed.

"That's sad," Chena said. "You fell in a love spring?"

They nodded together.

Chena exchanged a glance with Crystal, then looked back to Sean. "I don't mean to be crude, but if we find males to recruit—do you mind telling us exactly where that love spring is?"

Sean and Willow laughed together, ruefully. "I will show you, when this crisis is over. But I hope you will tell your stallions of its nature, before—"

"Oh, of course!" Chena said. "We wouldn't cheat! That leads to mischief."

"We know," Sean agreed, and Willow nodded.

Mary did not comment, but it struck her that for a random coupling of dissimilar species, the two were remarkably well matched. Sean had a wild side that needed taming, while Willow was quite realistic and sensible, yet they laughed at the same things. Sean could do a good deal worse in Mundania. In fact, some of the girls he had been interested in had had only one thing going for them, youth. That asset was all too fleeting, as Mary knew so well from her own experience.

But all that was beside the point. She had to explain things to the centaur fillies. "We were looking for you, Chena," she said. "And perhaps for Crystal too. Because we need help to deal with this storm, before it blows Xanth away. Will you come with us?"

"What kind of help?" Chena asked. "We can't safely fly in this fierce wind."

"I'm not sure," Mary confessed. "But I *am* sure that we need you, and that the manner of it will become apparent in due course. As for flying—you should be able to do that in the ambiance of our traveling house, because Keaira is keeping the weather calm here." She glanced at Keaira, who nodded shyly.

"Why, certainly, then," Chena agreed. "We can fly above it, or to the side. As long as the terrible wind is kept away. It isn't just the force of it, but the magic dust it carries. It makes us dizzy, and weird things attack."

"Like phantasms," Mary agreed. "Even when they are illusions, they are mischief enough. Very well, then, let's get moving again."

But Nimby was writing a note. Chlorine took it and read it aloud. "Why—why he says the house can fly! The fillies can make it fly."

Chena looked at the RV. "Well, we can make it light enough to float, but that's not the same as—"

"But then we could haul it along by ropes," Crystal said. "It could move through the air. It might be clumsy, but it could be done, in calm weather."

"Is this safe?" Mary asked, surprised.

Nimby nodded.

"And we can travel *over* the jungle, instead of through it?" The notion had definite appeal.

Nod.

This was evidently the way to go. "How do you make it light?" she asked the centaurs.

"We simply flick things with our tails," Chena said. "That's really our magic. To make things light enough to float or fly. When we flick bothersome flies, they become too light to sit, so must fly away. When we flick ourselves, we become similarly light.'' She looked at the RV. ''However, that's pretty big. It would take a number of flicks to lighten it enough, and we'd have to flick each of you who go inside it, too.''

''And the effect fades with time,'' Crystal said. ''With each passing moment, you lose lightness.''

''You lose moments of effect,'' Jim said. He was speaking technically, because this was in his specialty of physics, but it didn't matter here.

''Yes. So you have to get flicked again. I think you would have to settle to the ground every half hour or so to get renewed.''

''I wonder,'' Mary said thoughtfully. ''Modem, could you change that reality to make it last longer? Like maybe a day instead of half an hour.''

''I guess so,'' Modem said.

''Then let's try it,'' Mary said.

First the two centaurs worked on the RV. They were right: they were making it lighten, but only at the rate of a hundred pounds or so per flick. Mary could see the tires getting less flattened. But it would take about twenty flicks apiece to complete that job, and they had to pause briefly to recharge between doses.

''Say, can you split into your halves?'' David asked as they worked. Mary didn't like the way he was staring at their breasts, but the centaurs seemed oblivious. Obviously they wouldn't go bare if they felt there was any shame in it.

''Halves?'' Crystal asked.

''You know. Horse and person.''

''No,'' Chena said between tail flicks. Those breasts quivered with the effort of every flick, and so did David's eyeballs. But Mary was determined to give no sign of her distress. The centaurs simply didn't know how things were in Mundania. ''We are complete creatures, crossbreeds who have become our own species.''

''Anyway, it wouldn't be halves, it would be thirds,'' Crystal said. ''Equine, human, and avian.''

''Well, can you maybe turn all human, or all bird?'' the boy persisted. ''Back and forth.''

''No, that's not our magic. You are thinking of the merfolk, some of whom can make legs and become fully human and walk on land, or perhaps make a fish's head and swim underwater. Or the naga folk, who can assume human or serpent form, with their natural form being between. Others, like the harpies, are fixed in their merged forms."

"Well, could they maybe get together and teach each other?" David persisted. "So the centaurs could change form, and the naga could have magic talents, like flying?"

Chena laughed heartily, and Mary struggled not to wince. "Maybe so. But Crystal and I have been working so hard to master our present forms that we are not much interested in experimenting with any other type of magic. We are satisfied with the magic we have, which enables us to fly, and don't crave any other type."

Then one end of the RV lifted off the ground. It was just about light enough to float away. It was time to do the people.

"One person should be ready to hold each one as we lighten them," Chena said. "We wouldn't want anyone to float away." She smiled, but the warning was serious.

Jim took a stance by the RV. "I'll go last," he said.

They started in on the people. Karen went first, and of course, the moment she was flicked and lightened by Chena's tail, she leaped into the air to see how far she would go. As it happened, she leaped away from Jim, who reached for her but missed. But Mary had been alert for something like this, and snagged the flying girl. She was prepared, yet even so, was surprised; Karen really was featherlight, as if she were no more than an inflated balloon in girl form. Obviously centaur magic did work on Mundanes.

She passed the girl to Jim, who popped her into the open side door of the RV. "Hey, it's small again!" she cried. "How are we all going to fit?"

Mary looked at Modem. "That magic was temporary?"

The boy fidgeted. "No. But I can change only one reality at a time. You said to make the lightness last."

Oops. They needed two aspects of magic now. This was getting complicated. But maybe there was an answer. "Jim?"

Her husband rose to the occasion. "Modem, reality is mostly the way we see it. Agreed?"

"Yes," the boy said. "Only—"

"So what we need is a special kind of reality for this moving house. Suppose we think of it as having several properties: it moves, it is larger inside than outside, and it holds a given spell for a day or more. These are not different realities, but aspects of this particular structure. One reality covers all its qualities. Does this make sense?"

"I guess," Modem agreed. He concentrated. And suddenly the interior was twice its natural size.

Crystal flicked David, and Jim passed him inside. Then Chena did the next, and so on, until only Nimby and Jim were left outside. Mary suspected that Nimby didn't really need the centaur magic to make him light, but he accepted the flick and went in. Finally Jim closed the side door, opened the driver's seat door, and accepted his own lightening. All ten of them were inside, with the two winged centaurs outside, taking the ropes now attached.

The centaurs flicked the vehicle twice more, and the rear end lifted. They were floating!

"Where to?" Jim asked Nimby.

Nimby pointed south. But he wrote another note.

"South," Jim called out the window.

"One more to pick up," Chlorine read. "Adam. About an hour, as the house flies."

"An hour," Jim called out the window as the ropes lost their slack. Just as if this were routine. Chena looked back and nodded.

They were hauled smoothly up until the trees were below. Mary saw their branches being furiously whipped by the wind as the calm-weather patch left them behind. The storm was still intensifying, and it was not hard to appreciate how in time it could start blowing trees down. Happy Bottom was increasing to hurricane strength.

Now they bore south. The children peered out and down, fascinated, and so did Jim and Mary. It was as if they were in the cab of a blimp, floating silently across the terrain. The landscape spread out below, varied and variegated. The outline of Xanth, Mary knew, resembled that of Mundane Florida, but within that outline the detail could differ considerably. Here there were mountains and chasms and endless types of magic. She looked at the two flying centaurs, who made a pretty pair as their great wings rose and fell together. They were nice girls, she knew. In fact, most of the folk of Xanth were nice. Parents were trusting, because the average stranger deserved trust. The bad creatures, like dragons, were obvious—and even they weren't always bad. The winged monsters had pitched in to help save Xanth, even the filthy harpies, and none had broken the truce.

There were things she was coming to like about this land. She would be sorry to leave it. And she did want to save it. She felt somewhat responsible for the storm, because it had entered Xanth through the same aperture as their family had. She realized that that wasn't completely reasonable, but neither was it completely unreasonable. The storm was Mundane in origin; let the Mundanes defuse it.

The flight continued with no sign of weight gain. Jim's rationale for double reality shifting had worked. For someone who, until this adventure, had had zero tolerance for fantasy, he had made a remarkable accommodation. As had she herself. There was just something about Xanth, magic aside.

Nimby pointed down. Already? How the hour had flown—no pun. Now they had to fetch in Adam. What would his magic talent be? How would it integrate with those of the others? Only Nimby knew. Nimby, she realized, was the true leader of this expedition. A mute donkey-headed dragon!

"Below!" Jim called out the window.

The centaurs angled down. There was a squat stone house. At least that would be secure against the wind, for a while. They landed before it, but the RV tended to float up again when the rope went slack. The centaurs picked up rocks and brought them to the RV as ballast. Jim and Sean took the stones and piled them in the center of the floor in back. Then the vehicle stayed put.

"But watch it," Jim warned. "*We* still float."

Then the centaurs brought smaller stones, which Mary and Willow put in their purses as personal ballast, following Nimby's indication. It seemed that they were the proper ones to make the appeal to Adam.

They disembarked and approached the house. A face appeared in a window. "Are you real or spooks?" it demanded.

"We are real," Mary answered. "I am somebody's mother."

"I am somebody's love," Willow added.

"Then come in before the wind starts again." The door opened.

They entered. A rather stout young man stood there. "You must be Adam," Mary said. "I am Mary Mundane."

"I am Willow Elf."

"Yes, I am Adam. What do you folk want with me?"

"We are on a mission to save Xanth from the terrible storm," Mary said. "We need your help. Will you come with us?"

He looked astonished. "You want me to go with you?"

"Yes, if you will. We need you."

"But nobody needs me," he protested. "Nobody even likes me."

"Perhaps because nobody knows you," Willow said sympathetically. "Are you mean-spirited?"

"No. I am whatever I choose to partake of."

"Is that your magic?" Mary asked.

"Yes. If I see a rock, I can take its essence and become rock-hard. If I see water, I can become liquid. If I see a cloud, I can become light and fluffy. But that doesn't help anyone else, and I still look plain and stuffy."

Willow shrugged. "So do I, among my own kind. But I met a young man who thinks I'm beautiful, thanks to a love spring. Maybe there will be something for you."

"A love spring," he breathed. "What I wouldn't give to get dunked in one of those with a lovely girl!"

"Maybe it will happen," Mary said, realizing that this was why Willow had been the one for this. Her experience signaled what Adam's might be. "Please come with us, in our floating house, and help us save Xanth."

"Sure," he said.

So they brought him out, and it turned out that there was no need to make him light, because he simply looked at a cloud and became foggy light. He entered the RV and took a seat where one was available, beside Keaira.

"Any more people to pick up?" Mary asked Nimby.

Nimby shook his head.

"So our complement is complete at last!" Mary said, relieved. "Now we can head straight on south and save Xanth from Happy Bottom."

Nimby nodded.

"All the way south," Jim called out the window. "Are you fillies holding up okay?"

"We are getting hungry," Chena said.

"Do you like pies? We have a treeful."

"Yes, those will be fine."

So they passed out the pies remaining from the changed tangle tree, and the centaurs ate them as they flew. The speed picked up. They were on their way to their destiny.

14

ILL WIND

D avid woke as the RV slid down toward the ground. Was this boring flight finally over? It had been interesting for a while when they picked up Willow, who was sort of pretty, and Modem was his own age, twelve, so had some common interests. Modem had enjoyed the big stink the demoness made as much as David had, even if he had had to change it to roses to pacify the womenfolk. He sneaked just as many peeks at Chlorine and the topless flying centaur fillies. Oh, to be a few years older! But Keaira was an adult young woman, well covered, and no raving beauty either, while Adam was not only adult, he was fat. So once the novelty of flying in the RV faded, nothing much was left.

But now they were landing, and there might be some action. After all, they still had to drive Happy Bottom to where she couldn't do any more harm, and she wasn't going to want to go. He pitied the poor person who would have to wear the windbreaker jacket and try to herd her north.

Nimby, sitting beside Chlorine, turned his head to look at David. Oh, no! Did that mean David was the one?

Nimby nodded.

Nimby was eerie, but always right. So David would have to do it. But he wouldn't like it.

Nimby shook his head.

He *would* like it? Why? But Nimby merely smiled inscrutably. He could be sort of frustrating that way. Yet it did give David something to be interested in. How could he like wearing the stupid jacket and trying to herd the stupid wind anywhere? There must be something fun about it.

The RV touched down right beside the big pillow where Chlorine and Nimby had landed, at the beginning of the trollway. They had come full circle, or whatever, and seen a whole lot on the way. But what now?

Nimby had written some notes for Chlorine. Now she read them off. " 'Keaira and David will have to herd Happy Bottom north,' " she read. " 'He'll wear the windbreaker, and she'll keep the weather calm so they won't get blown out of the sky.' "

"Out of the sky?" Mom asked, her tone echoing the furrow David knew was in her forehead.

" 'They will be riding the winged centaurs,' " Chlorine read. " 'And Willow will show the way, flying with them.' "

Suddenly it dawned. He'd ride a bare-busted filly! Up in the sky by himself, like a flying cowboy, and he could sneak all the peeks he wanted. That would indeed be fun.

"But David can't go all alone out there!" Mom protested, as, of course, she would. "Suppose he fell?"

Um; good point. In the RV there was no chance of falling, because it was closed in. But though he liked the idea of riding a bare-chested winged filly, his actual horse-riding experience was small. He might indeed fall, and if they were high in the sky at the time, that would be the end of him.

" 'No, he will remain light,' " Chlorine read. It seemed that Nimby had anticipated all the questions. " 'Should he fall from his steed, he would merely float gently down. The centaur would have ample time to catch him before he reached the ground.' "

Oho! And how would she catch him? By flinging her arms about him and clasping him to her bosom? That was a risk he was prepared to take. And Nimby was right about the floating; he had forgotten how light they all were. So it was safe after all.

Dad had a more sensible objection: "If Keaira goes with them, what of the weather here? We'll be blown away the moment we lose her calm-weather protection."

"I can change local reality to revert the moving house to normal," Modem said. "Then it might not blow away." But he didn't look certain, because they could see the ferocious dusty wind beyond the oasis of calm. There were even phantasms forming around the edges of the calm region, making grotesque gestures to signal what they'd like to do to the folk in the RV if they could just get close. Of course, it would just be illusion, mostly, as long as they kept the doors and windows closed, but even illusions could be pretty bad.

But Nimby had an answer for Chlorine to read: " 'The present local reality must remain as it is, because soon the house will need to travel again, and no one must leave it. The centaurs will not be here to make it light again. Modem's local reality is the main force holding back the magic dust.' "

David could see that Chlorine was startled as she heard herself read that. "You mean Modem's doing more than just keeping the lightness lasting and the inside big?" Then she read the next answer, already in her hand. " 'Yes. His magic reality preempts the malicious magic fostered by the dust.' "

"It does?" Modem asked, surprised.

"I guess your magic is more potent than you know," Dad said, with a typical Dad smile.

" 'It is,' " Chlorine read. " 'Because the magic dust is enhancing it. Thus the dust of madness has the ironic effect of canceling itself, in this limited instance.' "

"Gee," Modem said, pleased.

David was, of course, too good a person to be jealous of the importance of anybody else's role, but he did experience a certain discomfort that an ignorant person might choose to interpret as jealousy. So he mentioned a legitimate concern. "If the RV, uh, house stays light, won't it just blow away, like Dad says?"

"*As* Dad says," Mom said in her obnoxious English-teacher way. He had tried to break her of that, but without much success. Parents were slow learners.

But this time fat Adam had an answer. "I can assume the properties of Xanth's heaviest rock, and be ballast."

"You can?" Keaira asked, evidently impressed.

"Oh, sure," Adam said. "When I'm cloud-light, I'm like a fat balloon. When I'm fruity, I'm like a fat apple. When I'm solid, I'm like a fat boulder. That's why folk don't like me.''

"I think it's a great talent," Keaira said.

"You do? I think your talent is the greatest. You can be always in sunshine, or have it rain when you want it to."

Keaira blushed. "Thank you."

"You mean you care what I think, even though I'm fat as a pumpkin?"

"Fat pumpkins are the handsomest," she said, still blushing.

This was getting disgusting. Time to break it up before they actually got mushy. "Well, let's get busy," David said. "Who rides who?"

"Who rides *whom,*" Mom said.

David ignored it, as he would any other crude remark. "Which bare-boobed filly is mine?"

"David!" Mom exclaimed, as Karen stifled a titter.

"Sorry," he said. "Which bare-boobed *centaur?*"

Mom looked as if she has swallowed a poop-flavored prune, but this time she held her tongue. Good. Maybe he had made his point. Of course, there'd be bleep to pay when she finally got him alone at home, but maybe she'd forget by then.

Chlorine read her next note. " 'Chena. She thinks you're cute.' "

David was flabbergasted. "She does?"

Nimby nodded. He should know, since he could read minds. No wonder he knew David would enjoy the ride!

Meanwhile Mom looked as if her prune had turned into a stink horn, but again she stifled her comment.

"And take some reverse wood," Chlorine read. So they made two small bundles of two sticks each, and David took one while Keaira took the other. They were bound together by duct tape so they wouldn't come apart accidentally, but of course, they could be ripped apart if they were needed. Then whatever threat they encountered would be reversed. " 'But use the wood only in an emergency,' " Chlorine read, " 'because it will nullify the centaurs too, reversing their magic lightness.' "

For sure! If David had to use his wood, he'd strip the tape to prime it, then hurl it like a grenade. Then it would affect only what he threw it at. He could make like Superman, nulling enemies galore. *Pow! You're reversed!* He tucked the bound sticks into his belt.

They got out of the RV. All except Adam, who looked out just long enough to spy a solid metallic rock. Then he assumed the qualities of that rock, and became hard and heavy. Keaira tapped her knuckle against his shoulder, verifying it, almost skinned a joint, and smiled with acknowledgment. Adam looked as it he were about to float away despite being boulder-solid.

With Adam's change, the RV was firmly planted, and the two centaurs no longer had to hang tightly on to the ropes. Chlorine gave the jacket she had been wearing to David, and explained to them what Nimby had written.

"Fine," Chena said, smiling. "Get on my back, David." There was something perky in her attitude, as if she really did find him cute.

He adjusted that jacket, which remained pleasantly warm from its contact with the beautiful woman, and smelled faintly of—of what? Of a commercial swimming pool. Of course—chlorine! The chemical used to purify the water. Only now it was like perfume.

Dad lifted him up and set him behind Chena's lovely white wings, which were folded but remained a bit out from her body. Then Dad did the same for Keaira, putting her on Crystal.

"Remember, you are very light," Chena told him, turning her head and the upper part of her torso so she could look him in the eye. That meant, unfortunately, that he had to meet her gaze, because he didn't want to give away what he really wanted to peek at. It was frustrating. "So you must hold firmly on to my mane."

"Mane," he repeated dumbly. Her hair flowed down from her head, and somewhere became the mane, but he wasn't sure where.

"In front of you. And try to wrap your legs around my barrel, if they will reach."

"Barrel." When she turned back to face the front, he could look—but now nothing was in sight. That was doubly frustrating.

"Take hold," she said, as she spread her wings.

Then, finally, he did. His hands found grips in the shorter hair of her mane at the base of her human portion.

She pumped her wings, and leaped, and sailed into the air. It seemed remarkably easy, until he remembered that she had made herself almost as light as he was, so that she weighed almost nothing. The motion of her wings was mainly to move her, rather than to lift her.

But though he could see the full beautiful sweep of those wings, he couldn't see the front of her torso. Here he thought he would have his best chance yet to peek without obstruction or discovery, and instead it was no chance. "Bleep!" he muttered.

"You might consider looking across at Crystal," Chena murmured.

She knew! Boys were not supposed to blush, but he was afraid he was doing so. But it was a good suggestion. "Thanks," he said, and looked.

He was rewarded by a splendid view. Crystal's wings were pumping gracefully, and her front was completely open to view. She was also slightly better endowed than Chena. In fact—

Then Crystal looked their way, and he had to wrench his gaze away. He couldn't peek if someone was watching him peek!

So, frustrated anew, he looked around elsewhere. To the other side was Willow, who flew readily in her dress because it was cut to leave holes for her wings.

Now that they were all airborne, Willow flew close. Crystal approached from the other side, so that they could talk to each other. "Nimby wrote me a note explaining how to do it," Willow said. "Happy Bottom is like a giant puzzle, with alternating bands of wind and cloud around her center. We have to find our way to the center, where her eye is, so David can use his jacket to push it. Wherever the eye goes, Happy Bottom goes; she can't help it. So we'll just keep pushing her north to the Region of Air, where Fracto will try to tame her. The problem will be finding her eye, and staying with it. She may try some tricks to hide it or move it away from us. David has to push in the right place, or it won't work, and Keaira has to stay near him so he has calm weather. I'm the only one who is free to explore. But if I go outside the fair-weather zone, I'll be in trouble, so you need to stay reasonably close to me while I search."

"Gotcha," David said.

"We shall do our best," Keaira agreed.

Willow flew on ahead. There was a solid-looking vertical wall of cloud, moving rapidly from west to east. It reached down almost to the ground, and up almost to the top of the sky. "Boy, she's a big b—bleep," David said, awed. He knew Happy bottom was a hurricane now, even if she had been a mere tropical storm when she entered Xanth; she had intensified. "Can one little jacket move all that?"

"The center is much smaller," Chena said. "And calmer, Nimby says."

"Oh. That should make it easier." But he wasn't quite sure it was so.

Willow flew back. "There's a hole in the wall!" she cried, excited. "Maybe we can get through it."

"Can't Keaira make it calm wherever we go?" David asked. "So we don't need to look for holes?"

"Perhaps," Willow said. "But it's better to go in without disturbing the ill wind's cloud banks, so she doesn't notice us. The moment she becomes aware of us, she could start fighting us."

"But she's just a storm!" he protested.

"So is Fracto," Chena reminded him.

"Oh, yeah." Here in Xanth even inanimate things had awareness. It was certainly better not to make Happy Bottom aware of them.

So the two centaurs followed Willow through the fleeting gap in the clouds. It closed in after them; they had made it just in time. Now they were between two walls of cloud, and the one ahead was moving faster than the one behind.

David remembered something about hurricanes, because he had seen their patterns shown on Miami radar. They alternated cloud bands with air bands, and most of the action was in the cloud bands. They got smaller toward the center, but also fiercer. "If we just keep going straight through them," he said, "we'll find the center. We can't help it. There's nowhere else it can be."

"I hope so," Chena said doubtfully. "It can be hard to tell direction, in the middle of fog and rain."

For sure! But soon another gap opened up ahead. They plunged through it. But this one closed up before they completed their passage, and suddenly they were caught in grayness. Keaira's controlled weather kept the winds from them, but rain sluiced down from above, drenching them. He heard the rain pelting the centaur's wings, and

Chena dipped until she flicked herself and resumed level flight. Happy Bottom was simply too big; Keaira couldn't clear a passage to the sunlight.

"Uh-oh," Chena said. "I think she's on to us."

David thought the same. Maybe the storm couldn't touch them directly, but she sure could cloud things up. Suppose they couldn't find their way out of this cloud bank?

Then they emerged, and it was clear. They had made it through, this time. "Let's pick a bigger gap, next time," David said.

"If Willow can find one," Chena agreed.

Willow searched diligently, almost getting caught at the edge of the calm section. David saw her do a flip in the air as one wing caught the edge. Yes, there was power in the storm, and it would blow them right out of Xanth if they got caught in it.

"Maybe I could help some," David said. "With the jacket. I think all I have to do is open it." There had been one of Nimby's notes about that, somewhere along the way. When closed, the windbreaker was passive, but when opened, its magic took effect.

"I think it's better to wait until we reach the eye," Chena said. "Happy Bottom may know of our presence, but not of our power. So she may consider us a nuisance, not a threat. Best to keep it that way."

She was making sense. So they hunted along the cloud wall, searching for that brief avenue through. While Happy Bottom's winds seemed to get stronger.

In due course another avenue appeared. But this time they were cautious; it could be a trap. So Willow made a feint at it, with the two centaurs following closely behind. Sure enough, it closed up, the fog imploding from every side. But they had sheered off just before it, skirting the fringe of the cloud wall. There was no doubt now: Happy Bottom was trying to get them. But her ploy had been simple, so she probably underestimated them.

They flew along the side, and found a thinning of the wall, where fog had been borrowed to make the implosion. They plunged into this. The storm had to know of their passage, but couldn't react fast enough to catch them, having been caught off-guard. By the time the wind and fog closed in, they were through.

They were in the next clear band. Apparently the hurricane's power was limited mostly to the cloud bands, where the magic dust swirled thickest. But they would be unlikely to catch her napping again.

They flew up to the next band, but it was solid fog. They couldn't get through. They didn't dare risk another bold charge into the fog.

"Maybe we can sneak below it," Willow suggested. "The hills and trees must interfere with the wind bands, so there should be gaps she can't help."

They flew down. Sure enough, there was a clear region in the lee of a mountain. They zoomed through that, just below the bottom of a cloud wall, skimming the terrain, and flew up into the next clear region.

"Look!" Chena cried. "That must be the eye!"

It surely was. It looked like a monstrous eyeball, turning in the center of the huge ring of clouds that was the innermost cloud wall. This was what they had to move north.

They came up behind the orb and hovered in the calm air. Then they oriented north, and David unzipped and opened his jacket. "Go!" he cried.

Nothing happened.

The two centaur fillies looked at him. Willow flew close. "Is there an invocation you have to use?"

"Nimby didn't say so," David said, disgruntled. What was wrong? Far from blowing anything, the jacket was completely calm.

Then David's ears popped. "Ouch! Feels like descending in an airplane," he said, shaking his head.

"I think the local pressure is rising," Keaira said. "That's odd, because I'm not doing it."

"There's a waft of breeze coming toward us," Crystal said. "I feel it in my mane."

"But none going away from us," Willow said. "And what we need is a strong outward blast."

Then Chena caught on. "It's breaking the wind! Air is coming in, but not going away. It's pooling around the jacket, building up pressure."

"And high pressure will push the low-pressure eye away," Crystal

added. "That must be how it works. All we have to do is let it build up enough."

"It's building, for sure," David said. "My eardrums are getting bonged." He held his nose and blew hard until he felt another pop in his head.

"Look!" Chena cried again. "The eye is moving!"

And it was. There was no actual wind, but the high-pressure zone around them was shoving the eye away.

The eye felt it, too. It spun around to fix its stormy gray iris on them. It blinked. The pupil widened. It saw them!

"Keep pushing it!" Willow said.

David tried, but the eye slid around to the side, instead of moving north. Chena flew to get directly south of it again, but it slid farther to the side. It was just plain hard to push in the direction they wanted.

"Maybe if we all try to channel the air flow," Willow suggested. "To surround the eye."

They tried it. Willow hovered to David's left, and Crystal to his right, and all three winged monsters did their best to push the dense air forward, surrounding the eye.

"It's working!" David cried.

But then the eye, irritated, reddened and expanded. It grew to twice its former size, then ten times as big. Now it was impossible to push the whole thing.

"Maybe if I used my reverse wood to mess it up," David said, tugging at the two sticks in his belt.

"Careful with that," Keaira said, touching her own bound sticks. "This wood is dangerous, if—"

Too late. David had grabbed just one stick. The other snagged in his belt. The tape let go, and the two sticks separated.

"Eeeeee!" Chena screamed, putting a good six *E*'s into it. She dropped out from under him like a rock.

He had separated the reverse wood, and one stick had landed on Chena, and it had reversed the centaur's magic lightness, making her magically heavy. He himself was falling too, but not as fast, because as a Mundane, he was more resistive both to magic and reversed magic. But even the limited effect on him was too much; he was falling toward the ground at normal falling velocity, and that would be enough to pulp him when he struck the ground.

So he did the sensible thing: he threw away the stick.

His plummet became a slow descent, as most of the lightness returned to his body. But he was still going down. Already he saw the trees below.

But that wasn't all. Happy Bottom's malignant eye reappeared, casting about, looking for him. She must have pretty will figured out the nature of the windbreaker.

The windbreaker! It was still open, still generating a high-pressure zone around him. That was what was enabling the eye to orient on him; it could probably see the crowded air. So he closed the jacket and zipped it up.

But there was still too much pressure in his vicinity. Happy Bottom's eye continued to cast about, looking to one side and the other, finding the pressure gradients. She would soon locate him, and then— she would probably blow him headfirst into a cliff. Jacket and all. He had fallen out of Keaira's calm-weather zone, so Happy Bottom could get at him now.

He looked desperately for some escape, but there seemed to be none. He no longer had the reverse wood, thanks to his idiocy, and he had no wings to fly with. All he could do was float gently down, while the hurricane worked up her strength for a doomsday strike.

Then a bit of fog formed below him. But it didn't look like Happy Bottom's fog; the color and texture differed. What could it be?

The fog thickened into a low-lying cloud. The convolutions of the cloud formed a fuzzy face. He knew that face from somewhere.

A cloud eye winked.

"Fracto!" he cried. How had he gotten here? He must have sneaked in, camouflaging himself as a section of Happy Bottom. Like most clouds, Fracto could be large or small, noisy or quiet, depending on his mood. Right now he was being as quiet as mist.

Happy Bottom didn't realize. David hoped his exclamation hadn't given Fracto away. But just what could the enemy-turned-friend do? The hurricane was about to blow him away regardless. Fracto, in his present form, had only a tiny fraction of the hurricane's strength, so couldn't counter that ill wind.

Then David fell into the cloud. The fog of its substance surrounded him, so that he couldn't see anything beyond it.

Which meant that no one could see him, either. Happy Bottom would not know where to blow, and he was such a small target that she'd never get anywhere blowing blindly.

His feet touched ground. David tumbled, but wasn't hurt, being still quite light. He was alone in the magic jungle of Xanth.

The fog lifted just enough to let him see around if he kept his head low. Fracto was still shielding him from the ill wind's view, giving him a chance to find his way back into action. But to do that, he had to find Chena Centaur. Or rather, she had to find him. He hoped she was all right. She should be, once she got away from that reverse wood stick. But if he was hidden from Happy Bottom, he was hidden from Chena too. But maybe she would know to look for him under Fracto.

So what should he do? Stand here and wait, or try to find a better rendezvous point? It might be dangerous to blunder around an alien jungle, but it might also be dangerous to sit and wait for whatever came to find him.

So he would at least try to find a less exposed region, a safer place. Then if he saw a flying centaur, he could hail her, and all would be reasonably well.

He started walking—and his right toe kicked something. Pain shot up his leg, and he fell to the ground. What had he stubbed his toe on?

There was nothing there but a regular pinecone. That couldn't be it. He reached for it—but when his fingers touched it, another jolt of pain encompassed them and shot up his arm. That *was* it!

He got up, staying clear of the cone. What kind of tree had produced that? To look so ordinary, yet bring so much hurt to anyone who touched it.

In a moment it came to him. That wasn't a pinecone, it was a pain cone. No wonder it had made him hurt.

He looked down at the turf by his feet, in case there should be anything else to avoid. And shuddered. There was somebody's severed finger! No, maybe not severed, as it wasn't bleeding. It was curved into the form of a circle.

Then he laughed. He knew what that was: a ring finger. A finger circled into a ring. Maybe ogres wore it.

He walked carefully around the ring. Ahead was a sign. It said TWIN CITY. A city? Maybe that would be a good, safe place to go. So he followed the path that led away from the sign.

He came across two girls of about his own age, playing by the side of the path. If there was anything he wasn't interested in, especially at this time, it was girls his own age. So he tried to pass them by.

But they didn't let him do that. "Hi, boy—who are you?" one called.

"And what's your business?" the other added.

Should he make up something to try to get rid of them? No, maybe they wouldn't believe the truth, so that was best. "I'm David Mundane, and I'm trying to save Xanth from being blown away."

Sure enough, they tuned it out. "I'm Mariana," the first girl said. "And this is my twin sister Anairam. Come see what we do."

He was stuck for it, because he didn't want to make a scene and maybe get tangled up worse. He went to see what they were doing. To his surprise, it turned out to be interesting.

"I do rock shaping," Mariana explained. She lifted a stone, and ran her hands across it, and it changed shape as if it were clay.

In fact, maybe it was clay. "Let me see that," David said.

Mariana handed it to him. He ran fingers over it. It was definitely rock. Yet he had just seen her mold it. He handed it back, and it changed again as she pressed her fingers into it, forming a crude doll figure. Then she gave it to her sister.

"And I animate it," Anairam said. Suddenly the doll came to life. It sat up in her hands. She set it down, and it ran off into the forest.

David couldn't help himself. "Those are pretty good talents," he admitted grudgingly.

"Thank you," Mariana said. "Want to play house?"

Naturally they wanted to get into girl-games. "Some other time," he said. Like maybe in three years. "I gotta go." He walked on. He hoped Chena would find him soon.

Soon he came to two girls, a little younger than he was. Was this going to be another dull session? He tried to walk on by.

It didn't work. "Hello," one girl called. "I'm Amanda, and this is my twin sister Adnama. We change hair color."

"Great for you," he called back. "I'm David, and I'm walking right on by."

"But you must see," Amanda protested.

"Yes, we have nice talents," Adnama added.

"And that's not all," Amanda concluded.

He was stuck for it again. Where was Chena?

"See my hair," Amanda said. Her hair was brown, but as he watched, it changed to yellow, and then to red. "I can change my hair color," she said proudly.

"And I can change the hair color of others," Adnama said, as her sister's hair changed again, to green.

"So?" David asked impatiently.

"So now I'll change yours," Adnama said.

David felt nothing, so figured she was bluffing. But then Mariana held up a mirror, and he saw his face—framed by blue hair.

"Change it back!" he demanded angrily.

"After you kiss us," Adnama said.

He was really stuck for it! So he kissed them each in turn, and Adnama restored his hair to its natural color. Then he got the bleep out of there, before they thought of any other games to play with him.

But farther down the path he came to two more girls. These seemed to be about two years older than he was. Each had long purple hair and green eyes. He was catching on to the nature of Twin City: it was filled with twins. But why was it all female?

This time he tackled them directly, knowing that they wouldn't just let him pass. "I'm David Mundane, on a mission to save Xanth," he said. "Who are you?"

"I am Leai," one said sadly. "I am suicidal, but I can't die."

"I am Adiana," the other said, as sadly. "I want to live, but I am dying."

Suddenly this was heavy stuff. "You can't just switch places?"

"We haven't found the magic for that," Leai said.

"Too bad." He wondered whether they were teasing him. If so, it wasn't the kind of joke he liked.

"Do you think I could die in Mundania?" Leai asked.

"I guess so. If it's magic that keeps you alive."

"It's magic," she said. "See." She brought out a wicked-looking knife and tried to stab herself with it.

"Hey!" David leaped to grab her hand before the knife could reach her flesh. He succeeded in turning it aside. "What are you trying to do?"

"I am trying to kill myself," she said. "But I can't, because something always stops me. Just as you did."

"That wasn't magic! I just couldn't let you do it,"

She looked squarely at him. She was rather pretty, for a girl. "Why not? What do you care about girls?"

"Nothing," he said. "But—"

"You'll make up some reason, but you'll always stop me. Or someone else will. I've tried to kill myself a hundred times, and I just can't do it. If there's no magic in Mundania, maybe I could go there with you and—"

"I'm not going to help you get there so you can kill yourself," he said.

She nodded. "I'm not surprised. But maybe if my sister went with you, she could live."

"But I couldn't leave you, Leai," Adiana protested. She was sort of pretty too.

"I don't think I can help you girls," David said. "Though I'd like to. I'd like to make you both willing and able to live." Then an idea struck him. "I had two sticks of reverse wood. I lost them, but they must have fallen somewhere around here. Maybe if you found them, they would reverse your magics, and—"

Both girls screamed with delight. "Ah, thank you!" Leai exclaimed, and kissed him on the right ear. "So very very much," Adiana said, and kissed him on the left ear. Then both ran off on a search for the reverse wood.

David would never have admitted it, but he really hadn't minded getting kissed. He walked on down the path.

Soon he came to two more young folk, but this time they were male and female. "I was afraid all the twins were girls," he remarked, relieved.

"They are, in that section," the boy said. "In the next section they are all boys. We're on the border between sections."

"Oh. Well, hi. I'm David Mundane. I'm—"

"You're on a mission to save Xanth from Hurricane Happy Bottom," the girl said.

"And you will succeed, in due course," the boy said.

David had intended to say something intelligent like, "How can you possibly know things like that, when you have just met me!" But as usual his mouth got into gear before his brain, so all he said was a stupid "Huh?"

Both boy and girl smiled. "We apologize," the boy said. "We sometimes forget that strangers don't know us as we know them. I am Déjà, and this is my twin sister, Vu. My talent is to see the future, and hers is to see the past. So when we saw you, our talents came into play, and we knew your past and future business."

Oh. "So can you tell me where to find Chena Centaur?"

"Unfortunately, we can't," Vu said. "We can't see the present. But I can tell you that your friend was most concerned when she lost you."

"And I can tell you that she will find you in about fifteen and one half minutes," Déjà said. "Thereafter your mission will be routine."

"If the thickening magic hasn't distorted his perception," Vu said. "We are somewhat protected from it, here in this valley, so things are almost normal here, but that may change. We are therefore very glad to learn of your mission."

"Uh, thanks," David said. "I gotta get on to meet Chena, then."

"To be sure," Déjà agreed. "We wish you the very best."

David went on down the path. There was a sign saying TRI CITY. At least now he was out of the twins section. He felt better.

Until he encountered three girls, evidently triplets. Oh, no! He knew he hadn't a chance of getting through unscathed, but he made the effort. He maintained his pace and tried to march on by them.

"Why, look—a singleton boy," one said. "Let's have some fun with him."

"I'm no fun," he said quickly as they converged. They were big girls, of the kind he would ordinarily like to sneak peeks at, considering their short skirts, but he didn't trust what they might think was fun. "I'm just David, a dull Mundane."

"A Mundane!" another exclaimed. "We must see how our magic works on him."

"Not very well," David said desperately as he came to a stop. He had to stop, because otherwise he would have walked right into the one who was blocking the path ahead.

"We shall soon see," the third said. "Hello, David Mundane. I am Sherry. My talent is to shrink things." She reached forth and touched him—and suddenly he was half his normal size. "You're right—my magic doesn't work well on you. I meant to make you much smaller."

"Please let me go," he cried, getting really worried. Déjà had said Chena would find him soon, but he hadn't said in what state.

"But we haven't finished playing with you," the second woman said. "I am Terry. My talent is to enlarge things." She reached down to touch him, and suddenly he was twice his normal size. "Oh, my, it is true; I tried to make you invisible giant size, not baby ogre size."

David realized that in his present condition he could bowl them over and escape. But he didn't want to stay this way, either. "I just want to save Xanth," he pleaded.

"In that case, we had better restore you," the first woman said. "I am Merry, and that's my talent." She touched his leg, and suddenly he was back to normal.

Vastly relieved, he pushed on by them and fled down the path. "Come play with us again," Sherry called after him. "We know other games too."

"Fascinating ones," Terry added.

"For a man and three women," Merry finished.

"Not without violating the Adult Conspiracy!" he called back, and had the satisfaction of seeing them gaze at each other in wild surmise. "I guess that pooped your panties," he muttered, pleased.

It must be close to the time for Chena to find him. David hurried on along the path, hoping he wouldn't encounter any more mischievous girls.

He was startled by a loud howl. It sounded halfway like the world's least-oiled door hinge, and halfway like the world's hungriest hound. What could it be?

It turned out to be a huge canine creature. But it wasn't flesh and blood. It was made out of wood. Its legs were like uprooted saplings, its body was like a section of a tree trunk, and its teeth were sharpened wooden pegs glistening with sap. It was a timber wolf!

David wasn't sure whether to freeze in the hope that it wouldn't see him, or speak soothingly to it in the hope that he could befriend it. So he took the compromise course: he ran like all bleep.

He heard the timber wolf bounding after him. He was going as fast as he could, which was pretty fast, because he remained pretty light, but he heard the bounding footfalls coming closer behind him.

"Heellpp!" he screamed.

A winged form swooped down on him. "Ah, there you are!" Chena exclaimed. She caught him in her arms and hauled him up as she pumped her wings. The timber wolf leaped and snapped, but they were just out of his reach. Phew!

"Now get on my back," the centaur said, wrestling him around behind her. He obliged, and soon was properly seated.

They rose up into the protective shroud of fog. Only then did he realize that one of his fancies had just been realized—and he hadn't even noticed. She had clasped him to her bare front when she lifted him from the ground, and he had been so distracted by the timber wolf that he had paid no attention to what else was happening. What an idiot he had been!

He covered his chagrin as well as he could. "How did you find me?" he asked.

"Fracto provided cover, and knew where you were. Once we learned how to communicate with him, we went right to you."

"We?"

"Crystal is flying right above us, but Keaira isn't using her power now, so we can hide from Happy Bottom. Fracto is being really helpful; we wouldn't be able to do this without him."

"Yeah, he hid me from Happy Bottom," David agreed. "But how did you talk with him?"

"We devised a fog-ball code. One ball for yes, two for no, and a fog arrow to show where to find you. He said you were all right, but that a tree dog was closing in on you, so we had to hurry.''

"That was a timber wolf!" David said, laughing.

Chena laughed too. "Timber wolf! Of course! We zeroed in from forest to tree, and from animal to dog, but couldn't make better sense of it in the time we had. Anyway, Fracto will lead us back to the eye, but after that it will be up to us, because he'll have to get in front of Happy Bottom and lure her into the Region of Air.''

"How is he leading us? All I see is fog.''

She pointed ahead. "See that flicker of lightning ahead? I have to keep flying toward that. He will lead me under or around or through the storm bands until we reach the eye. Then he'll fade away.''

"But how will we herd her, if she just explodes her eyeball like she did before?''

"*As* she did before," Chena murmured, but somehow it wasn't as offensive as when Mom corrected him. "I must confess that I am not sure about that. Now Happy Bottom knows what she's up against, so she'll fight us every breath of the way. We'll have to do it just right.''

"I hope somebody knows what she's doing, like maybe Keaira," David said, "because I sure don't.''

"I'm sure there was excellent reason for Nimby to designate you to wear the jacket," Chena said diplomatically.

"I dunno. Nimby reads minds, and knows what's going on, but he can't see the future. So he might be wrong.''

"He reads minds?" she asked, seeming modestly alarmed.

David realized that she didn't know that Nimby had told him she thought he was cute. Better that she not know. "Well, maybe he just knows what's all around, so it seems like mind reading sometimes. I guess if he'd looked in mine, he'd have known I wasn't the best one for this job.''

"No, I'm sure there was reason," she said. "As with the Good Magician's decisions. We merely have to fathom it.''

"Lotsa luck.''

"Yes, good fortune would definitely be an asset," she agreed, mistaking his irony. "Perhaps your mishap with the reverse wood sticks was not a true accident, but part of your qualification.''

"Yeah, sure, assign a foul-up kid to drive a fouled-up hurricane," he said, not thrilled with the analogy.

"Perhaps in Mundania, it is different," she said delicately. "But in Xanth, seemingly inconsequential things may have significance. Did you encounter anything on the ground that might relate?"

"Just a bunch of girls," he said disdainfully. Then, belatedly, "No offense intended."

She laughed. "None taken. I am a filly, not a girl. What kind of girls were they?"

"That was the funny thing. They were all twins. It was called Twin City, though it didn't look much like a city. They had sort of complementary talents, like rock shaping and rock animation, or changing her own hair color, or somebody else's hair color, or being unable to die or unable to live." He paused, because that last pair had touched his emotion, and not just because they were pretty. "Maybe I managed to help them, because of the dropped sticks of reverse wood. If they find those, maybe one can live, and the other can want to live."

"They were surely glad to learn of those," Chena agreed.

"Yeah, they kissed me. Of course, I hated that."

"Of course." She knew he didn't mean it.

"Then I met twins who were only half girl, Déjà and Vu. He saw the future, she the past. He said I would succeed. But I don't see how." His voice had continued on, but his mind lagged at Leai and Adiana, with the long purple hair and green eyes and the awful predicaments. He hoped they did find the sticks.

"The sticks!" he exclaimed, rudely interrupting himself. "That's how!"

"Beg pardon?" Chena asked politely.

"The reverse wood sticks! I think I got it! Together they are inert, but separate they mess up magic. I messed you up before, but now we can mess up Happy Bottom."

"I recovered as soon as I fell away from the wood," Chena said. "No real harm was done. But how can the wood enable us to accomplish our mission?"

"I lost my sticks, but maybe that was just as well. But Keaira still has hers, doesn't she?"

"Yes."

"Well, she should tie them to two separate ropes, so she can trail them together or pull them apart from a distance when she needs to," he said, working it out as he talked. "The range is limited, isn't it? So that way it doesn't affect us, but it should reverse whatever the eye is doing."

"Yes, certainly. But how can trailing the sticks at a distance enable us to accomplish our mission?"

"We can drag them by the eye, when it tries to escape by exploding," he explained. "So then its magic will be reversed, and the eye will implode, and we can keep on herding it. It won't be able to get away."

"Why, David, that's brilliant!" she exclaimed.

"Gee," he said, pleased to have his mess-up with the sticks turn good. Because he would never have thought of it, if it hadn't been for his misadventure.

Suddenly the fog ended. There was Crystal Centaur flying above them, with Keaira. There was Willow, flying to the side. And there was the glowering eye, directly ahead.

"Thank you, anonymous benefactor," Chena called as the fog faded. David knew why: she couldn't speak Fracto's name now, lest Happy Bottom overhear and catch on to his role in this. Fracto still had a job to do, once she was in the Region of Air. She wouldn't speak to him, if she knew his role too soon.

The three winged monsters rendezvoused, and David explained his idea. The centaurs had ropes; it was one of the things they routinely carried, and Willow had cord in her surprisingly capacious purse, too. They tied two ropes to the two sticks of reverse wood, keeping them carefully together. Because they didn't want those sticks to separate too soon.

Meanwhile the eye was staring at them, and the cloud wall behind them was intensifying. Happy Bottom was priming for action. She knew they were up to something, but she wasn't sure exactly what.

They oriented on the eye. David unzipped the windbreaker. The air pressure began to rise.

Happy Bottom didn't wait for the push. The eye expanded explosively.

Keaira tossed the two reverse wood sticks toward the eye. They were light as air, having been treated by a flick of Crystal's tail. When they floated to the end of their tether, actually inside the fringe of the expanding eye, Keaira jerked on one rope, and the sticks separated.

Suddenly the eye was shrinking implosively. The iris looked surprised. In a moment it was so tight and small that it was hardly bigger than a baseball. One stick of reverse wood floated near it. Stunned, the eye spun rapidly in place, a glazed look on its pupil.

Then Keaira reeled in the stick, until it lined up with the other. She had to do this because otherwise the wood would reverse their own magic, like it—*as* it had before.

Yuck! Now he wasn't even waiting for Chena to correct him; he was doing it to himself. Disgusting.

Meanwhile the air pressure was building up. David held his breath and blew out his ear tubes, happy to suffer this inconvenience.

Keaira hauled in the two sticks and held them together. Then Chena stroked with her wings, and moved slowly forward toward the eye. Happy Bottom had not yet realized what they had done, and the eye was just staying there. As they advanced, it retreated, wafted along by the high pressure.

That was the way of it. Each time the eye expanded, the reverse wood contracted it again, so that it couldn't escape. They pushed it north to the Gap Chasm. By then night was falling; they could see the curtain of darkness dropping from the sky in the east. The sun, afraid of the dark, fled to the west. It would be too hard to herd Happy Bottom by night. She was unlikely to pursue them southward, if she ever realized they were withdrawing. So they flew rapidly south, following Willow, who best knew the terrain. They were hardly concerned about the bands of clouds, because those had been pretty much broken up with the focus on the eye.

Even so, it was after dark by the time they made it to the RV. Fortunately it had a light on, so they could spy it from afar, and they landed safely beside it.

Sean must have heard them coming, because he was standing out waiting. Willow flew down into his embrace. There followed a disgusting amount of hugging, kissing, and breathless endearments. David made a mental note: never stray near a love spring.

15
REVERSAL

T weeter rather liked this magic land of Xanth, where birds were so prominently represented. It had been fun meeting Roxanne Roc and playing with Sim Chick, and Tweeter had taught Sim some dirty bird jokes that no nonbird would understand. But now he was about ready to go home, where things were more settled. He really wasn't an adventurous bird; good seed, a daylong snooze in the cage, and some fun with Karen at the end of the day were all he really craved. Even this business of being intelligent was becoming wearing, in part because it made him so much more aware of things. How could a bird be happy and secure in his ignorance, when he was too smart? True, it had been nice getting to know Woofer and Midrange better, and they had proved to be loyal friends, but all of them now recognized that they were not looking for independent existence. Let the human folk suffer the stresses of intelligent life.

Now it was dawn, and time for the winged monsters—nice identification, that—to take David and Keaira out to finish herding Happy Bottom into the Region of Air. By nightfall the job would be done, and Xanth would be saved. Tomorrow they could go home.

The winged posse headed out. David was clearly feeling pretty important, because he had figured out how to use the reverse wood to stop Happy Bottom's eye from escaping them. Now the hurricane had no choice but to be pushed ever northward, until she got locked into the Region of Air, where Fracto would seduce her and tame her. Fracto was probably more interested in that aspect than in saving Xanth, but certainly Fracto was helping them to accomplish the mission. Give the ornery cloud his due.

The winds had died with the retreat of the storm, and the magic dust was settling out. It fertilized the landscape with another layer of magic, so that the plants were recovering vigorously and the animals were getting frisky. They knew that the terrible threat to Xanth was being abated, so their lives were reverting to normal.

Now it was time to move the RV north, to be closer to the scene of action. With the storm abated, they needed neither Keaira's patch of calm weather nor the winged centaurs. Adam looked at a cloud and became as tenuous as it was. Without his rock-solid ballast, the RV floated gently into the sky. The Demoness Mentia became a crazy inflated giant hand and pushed it north. Tweeter went out for a fly and watched. It was weird seeing the ungainly contraption floating like a huge loaf of bread, with that big hand grabbing it. It was weirder when Karen came out to join him; she had no wings, but remained air-light because of Modem's spell of changed reality, so she floated. She had a tether so she couldn't drift; her sensible mother had insisted on at least that much. This was the first, and probably the last, time they would fly together like this.

By midday they were nearing Castle Roogna. They went inside the RV to clean up so they would be presentable for the royalty there. Tweeter settled onto his perch and did a careful preening. The adventure was nearing its conclusion.

Suddenly Nimby the transformed dragon got nervous. "What is it?" Chlorine asked. She had been paying Nimby more attention, now that Sean was no longer interested in looking at her legs. What humans saw in human legs, Tweeter didn't understand; they were such fat fleshy things that couldn't even take hold of a branch, with laughably inadequate claws. For that matter, the rest of the featherless bodies of the humans weren't very aesthetic either, which was why they usually covered them up. But evidently they had learned to live with their liabilities.

Nimby wrote a note. Chlorine read it, and was alarmed. "Land immediately? But soon we'll be at Castle Roogna. It's just jungle below us here."

Dad came alert. "If Nimby says it, we had better do it. Adam, can you shift slowly to stone nature?"

Adam could; he had emulated a stone so long that he remembered it. The RV lost its buoyancy and began to descend.

Mentia popped in. "Hey, what gives? You're sinking!"

"We have to land now," Chlorine said. "Nimby says."

"When we're so close to the comforts of Castle Roogna? Ask him why."

Chlorine turned to the nondescript man. "Why?"

He handed her another note. She read it aloud. " 'Because the Law of Averages has been overturned on appeal.' "

All of the humans drew blanks. A question mark appeared over Chlorine's head. "What law?"

"That's not something that can be repealed," Dad said. "It's a law of nature."

"You forget where you are," Mom said grimly.

"Who appealed it?" Chlorine asked Nimby. "Who overturned it?"

It turned out that the junior computing program Sending was the culprit. He had not liked losing possession of Woofer and Tweeter, or getting disconnected by the reverse wood, or losing his windbreaker jacket. According to the Law of Averages, he was bound to win some and lose some, but he didn't like losing, so he had appealed to the Muses of Mount Parnassus. He had claimed that no ordinary person could have answered his twenty questions, so something extraordinary was afoot, messing up reality. He wanted that reality changed.

"But that's just your nature," Chlorine protested to Nimby. "You know everything around you."

Nimby shrugged. Evidently the Muses had seen merit in the challenge, so had granted the appeal. The Law of Averages had been reversed.

"That's liable to have one bleep of a consequence," Dad said grimly. "The fundamental order of the universe is governed by—"

He was interrupted by a sudden buffet of wind that shook the RV. He staggered, almost getting thrown into a wall.

"Get it down!" Sean said. "Happy Bottom's coming back!"

Adam increased his solidity, and the RV dropped. Even so, the wind tried to bash it. Mentia extended an eyeball from her face and peered outside. "Ground coming close; lighten up," she said.

Adam did, and the RV made a halfway soft landing in the jungle. Tweeter looked out, and saw that it hadn't missed a tree by much. The winds howled as if angry to have let the RV get away. As if? They *were* angry.

"David!" Mom cried, distraught. "Willow! The centaurs! Are they being blown away?"

"Willow!" Sean echoed, agonized.

"Keaira's with them," Dad reminded them. "She can keep their weather calm. But they may have trouble getting back here."

Sean looked at Nimby. "Sending got the Law of Averages revoked—and now everything's going haywire? All the unlikely wrong things are happening? And we're all in deep bleep? Just when we figured we'd won the game?"

Nimby nodded four times.

"Why didn't you warn us?" Mom demanded hysterically. "Before we sent them out into disaster? My poor child!"

"Nimby is omniscient, not prescient," Dad reminded her. "He can't see the future. And probably this appeal Sending made was done privately, with no obvious evidence until the decision was made, so it didn't attract Nimby's attention. Even if a person *can* see everything, he can't pay attention to it all; the volume is overwhelming."

"Spoken like a true physics professor," she retorted bitterly. "That's our son out there."

"And my love," Sean added.

Adam also looked pained; Keaira was out there too, and she had shown an interest in him, which he evidently returned.

Dad spread his hands. "I'm concerned too. But it isn't fair to blame Nimby. Without him we couldn't have gotten even this far."

Mom suffered a pang of reasonableness. "Yes, of course." She faced the dragon man. "I apologize, Nimby. I spoke intemperately."

Nimby looked embarrassed. Dragons surely did not receive many apologies from human women.

"You guys are missing the point," Karen said. She faced Nimby. "What can we do about it?"

Nimby wrote a long note and gave it to Chlorine. " 'The success of the mission now hangs by a thread that is rapidly unraveling. We must go to fetch a new thread, before the old one breaks. Then all can be salvaged.' "

"Who must fetch the thread?" Sean asked.

" 'Nimby, Chlorine, and Tweeter,' " Chlorine read from the next note.

Tweeter almost fell off his perch. "Meep?"

Sean smiled. "Yep, youp, birpbrain," he said. "Go fetch the thread."

"When?" Chlorine asked, almost as surprised.

Nimby walked toward the door.

"Now," Chlorine answered herself. She looked around. "I promise to do my very best. Come perch on me, Tweeter."

He looked uncertainly at Karen.

"Do it, Tweet," Karen said. "But take care of yourself. What would I do without you?" She looked as if she had more than one or two tears to stifle.

Tweeter flew over to perch on Chlorine's greenish hair. It didn't have the special familiarity of Karen's reddish hair, but it was very nice regardless.

"May you succeed soon," Mom breathed as they stepped out into the howling wind. "We'll wait here."

"Thank God for a good anchor," Sean said, as another gust of wind tried to get at the RV.

Outside, Nimby assumed his dragon form, and Chlorine mounted him. "Are we going far?" she asked through her windblown hair. Tweeter was scrambling to get a better grip, lest he be blown right out of it. That was one savage ill wind out here!

The dragon shrugged, unable to answer. But Tweeter knew it couldn't be too far, or they would not be able to get the thread in time.

A swirl of magic dust stirred up ahead of them. Nimby plunged into it. Tweeter experienced disorientation; this was awful stuff, which didn't merely coat the wings and beak; it affected a person's interior too.

"Where are we going?" Chlorine asked, evidently as uncomfortable as Tweeter was. But Nimby couldn't write a note, in his dragon form.

So as the swirl of dust settled out, Nimby assumed his human form and began writing a note. Meanwhile Chlorine saw a path leading to a pleasant-berry patch, so she walked toward it. The berries looked good to Tweeter too, so he stayed with her, riding on her head.

She picked the first pleasant-berry and put it in her mouth. Suddenly an unpleasant man appeared. "You have stolen my berry!" he cried. "Now I shall steal something of value to you." He advanced on her, looking as if he happened to be thinking of the roughest, ugliest stork.

"Stop, or I'll poison your water," she warned him.

"You can't poison anything after eating a pleasant-berry," he retorted as he grabbed for her, and evidently it was true, because he did not double over in pain.

Chlorine tried to escape, but the path behind her had abruptly overgrown with horrendous brambles. So she screamed instead. Even that had a pleasant sound, as if she didn't really mean it.

"That won't save you, you luscious creature," the man said. "You are trapped. Nothing less than a dragon could rescue you—and what dragon would bother? Dragons don't like being pleasant." He reached for her.

Then there was a thud and crash, and Nimby came charging across. He did not look at all pleasant. Comical, maybe, but not pleasant. The man took half a look at the huge dragon body and fled. Tweeter was glad the man hadn't gotten a good look at Nimby's innocuous head; he would have realized that this dragon wasn't much of a threat even away from a pleasant-berry patch.

Nimby paused just long enough for Chlorine to get on him, then moved on. "You saved me, Nimby!" she cried, relieved. "This damsel needed a dragon, and you're my dragon." She paused. "But I guess you lost the note you were writing."

Nimby nodded, looking embarrassed.

"Well, I wouldn't have gotten in trouble if I hadn't asked you a stupid question and made you change to man-form, and then wandered away from you, like the shallow creature I am," she said. "So you just stay the way you are, Nimby; I'm sure you know where you are going, and will get us safely there."

But Nimby's donkey snoot looked doubtful, and that alarmed Tweeter. Suddenly he suspected that this mission might not be as simple or safe as they had assumed.

"No offense, Nimby, but I think I could use a weapon, just in case," Chlorine said. Tweeter agreed; Nimby wouldn't be able to bluff too many more hostile creatures. "So you won't have to rescue me from any more berry patches. Ah—there's a gourdless phone; let me make a call on that." And she swept up a small gourd that had no vine. "Hey, do you have any ribbons or bows in stock?" she said into it.

The dust cleared farther, and the forest seemed to be returning to a reasonable semblance of normal. Tweeter had a dropping to drop, so he flew to a tree ahead to take care of it. It wouldn't be proper to drop it in Chlorine's beautiful silken hair, after all.

He landed on a branch and took care of his business. But then a larger bird appeared. "Haa!" he cried in bird talk. "You have besmirched my tree, and now I shall besmirch you, you tasty morsel of a mouthful." He looked as if he were thinking of savory fresh gizzards garlanded with hot drops of blood.

Tweeter tried to flee, but the predator took off too, and he had more powerful wings. "I am rapt with the rapture of wrapping your ragamuffin remains with my ravenous rapier," the raptor rapped.

Tweeter flew desperately toward Nimby, but knew he wouldn't get there in time, and anyway, what could a donkey head do to stop a swift predatory bird?

Then a shaft flew by him, so close it ruffled his tail feathers. It was an arrow, and it passed close to the pursuing raptor too.

"The next one won't miss, hawk-eye," Chlorine said. "This bow is cross, if not actually angry, and it is eager to score." Indeed she held a crossbow.

The raptor considered, then veered off. It knew that irate bow wouldn't fire another mere warning shot; it would go for the kill. Chlorine had saved Tweeter from a fate worse than life. He landed in her hair, thankful for her help.

They moved on through the forest. Later they paused by another berry patch to eat. There was a man there, but he did not look hostile. "Do you mind if we eat some of these berries?" Chlorine inquired, smiling nicely. But Tweeter knew she was braced for possible trouble, with her crossbow near at hand.

"Not at all," he replied. "I'm just passing through. They are good berries."

"I'm Chlorine, and these are Nimby and Tweeter. We're looking for a new story thread. Have you seen any?"

"I'm Ray. All I have seen are worn old story threads, I'm sorry to say. They don't make them the way they used to. The person you want to ask is the Pawpaw Wizard."

"The who?"

"He's a storyteller," Ray explained. "He surely knows where all the best story threads are."

"Then we must go to him," Chlorine said. Tweeter saw Nimby nod; this was evidently where the dragon had been taking them anyway. "Could you tell us where to find him?"

"I'll do better than that," Ray said. "I'll show you where he is. It's not far from here."

Tweeter realized that the man was probably being so nice because Chlorine looked so nice, for her species. Still, they could use the help. Nimby had no objection, which was a good sign.

"Where are you going?" Chlorine inquired as they ate.

"I am looking for a money tree I was told grows in this vicinity," Ray said. "I've been looking all day, but I just can't find it."

"But money isn't any use," Chlorine said. "It just gets dirty."

"I know. But I have a pet money spider, and all it will eat is money, so I need some more."

Tweeter finished his berry and flew up to get a look at the lay of the land. In a hollow just out of sight of the berry patch he spied a tree whose leaves had green backs. That could be it. So he swooped down and plucked a leaf with his beak, then flew back to drop it by the man.

"That's it!" Ray exclaimed. "That's money! You found it! Where is it?"

Tweeter flew back toward the money tree, leading the man. Ray was delighted. "This will feed Spider Mon for a year!" he exclaimed, stuffing a pocket full of the leaves. "How can I repay you?"

Tweeter shrugged. He didn't need any repayment for such a favor; it was just an incidental thing.

"Well, maybe something will turn up," Ray said.

They resumed their travel, with Ray walking ahead to show the way. "There is a bad dragon in these parts," he said. "I prefer to avoid him, but he lurks near the Pawpaw Wizard's home, hoping to catch a careless child. He looks like this." An image of a ravening fire-breathing dragon appeared before him.

"Oh!" Chlorine cried, for an instant mistaking it for the real thing.

The image vanished. "I'm sorry," Ray said. "I should have warned you. That's my talent—to cause a picture of what I see to appear, in any size. I've seen that awful dragon so many times I can show it from my head. Normally I must be looking at something to picture it. I should have shown it much smaller." The image reappeared, harmlessly tiny.

"I certainly hope we don't encounter that dragon," Chlorine said. "I much prefer the harmless mule-headed variety." She patted Nimby on the scales. The scales she touched brightened.

But they were not in luck. There was a bellowing roar, and the ground shook as something solid tramped toward them through the forest.

"Hide!" Chlorine cried, looking wildly around. But they happened to be in a broad glade; there was nowhere to hide.

"Maybe I can make a picture of a tree or something," Ray said uncertainly. "To hide us."

But Tweeter had a better idea. He flew to the man and peeped imperatively.

"Maybe so," Ray agreed. "I'll try it." He fixed his eyes on Tweeter.

The dragon burst from the forest, trailing a plume of smoky fire. There was no doubt it had wind of them. But as its burning snoot oriented, a monstrous image of Tweeter appeared before them. As tall as the trees, Picture Tweeter peered down at the much smaller dragon.

The reptile hesitated, eyeing the big bird. It was clear it hadn't seen anything quite like this before: a parakeet as big as a roc. But it could smell Tweeter's bird odor, so knew there was a bird there. Tweeter hoped it wouldn't be smart enough to realize that the real bird wasn't as big as the apparent bird.

Tweeter took a giant step toward the dragon—and Nimby lifted a front foot and slammed it into the ground, making a dull thud. Tweeter took another step, with another thud. Tweeter opened his beak, and the giant mirrored him exactly. That beak was big enough to take in the whole dragon head.

The dragon had had enough. It turned tail and fled.

"Oh, glorious!" Chlorine exclaimed, delighted. "You saved us, Tweeter!"

Tweeter shook his head, and the giant bird did too. He hadn't done it; Ray's huge image had. Ray had more than repaid the favor he thought he owed. Yet Tweeter did feel a certain foolish pride; never before, and probably never again, would he back off a fire-dragon! It had been a great experience.

They walked on, and came to another glade. There sat a short fat man with short stocky legs, a bald pate surrounded by a fringe of gray hair, and an infamously huge stomach. Mundane-style spectacles perched on his nose.

He spied the party and smiled. "Hello, Ray. Who are your friends? They don't look much like children. Of course, few children dare venture out, with this remarkable recent weather we've been having."

Ray smiled. "They found the money tree for me! Now Spider Mon will be happy. They need to find a fresh story thread, and I told them you were the one to see." He turned halfway to face the group. "The damsel is Chlorine, the dragon is Nimby, and the bird is Tweeter. I hope you can help them. Now I must go home with my money, before the storm gets worse." He departed.

"I am Gerald Towne, once from Mundania," the Pawpaw Wizard said. "I believe I recognize a fellow Mundanian." He looked at Tweeter. "A parakeet."

Tweeter chirped agreement.

"So, of course, I'm not really a wizard in the proper sense, because only natives have magic, but the children do like my tales," the Wizard said. "I have many fine story threads. And I know where others are. What kind do you need?"

Nimby assumed man-form and wrote a note. "I think you folk must have quite a story of your own," the Wizard remarked, observing the change of form. "Perhaps someday you will share it with me."

"Maybe when the crisis is over," Chlorine agreed. Then she took the note. "We need a strong original reverse story thread."

The Wizard whistled. "You must be on serious business indeed! Then I won't delay." He gestured to a table beside him. "Have some peanut butter, jelly, and cheese sandwiches while I explain."

They settled down to share the sandwiches. Chlorine put some peanut butter on her finger for Tweeter to eat, and it was good, because there were some peanut chunks in it.

The Pawpaw Wizard began his story. "There was once, about two hundred years ago, a very unpopular Magician named Joshua. His talent was to reverse magical properties, whether these were talents or charms. Because most folk did not like to have their talents reversed, especially when they were nice ones, they stayed away from Joshua in droves. For example, there was one young woman whose talent was to smell of perfume; when Joshua touched her, she smelled of stink horn. There was a young man whose talent was to scale walls by sticking to them with his hands and feet; when he brushed by Joshua, he became slippery instead, so that he couldn't even stick to the ground without slipping. Another man could always find the right spot for something, whether for an excellent snooze or for a dog to mark territory. After he met Joshua, he always found the wrong spot, leading to considerable embarrassment. So Joshua was not welcome in his home village, or anywhere else, once the people had experience with him, though he was a perfectly decent and well-intentioned man. Fortunately his reversals were not permanent, unless done intentionally; they would slowly fade in the course of a few weeks or months, and the normal talents would reassert themselves. So people wanted Joshua to go away and stay away. And so Joshua traveled a lot.

"One day he happened to come upon a fine grove of Xanthorrhoed trees. They were unfamiliar to him, and grew so thickly they barred his passage, so he invoked his talent to reverse their magic. He did not realize that they belonged to a powerful witch, who had imbued them with special magic to enhance the magic of others. When he reversed them, they in turn reversed the magic of others, and were unusable for the witch's purposes. She, in a fury, set her pet griffins on Joshua, and they tore him to pieces before he could reverse them. Thus he died, and no one mourned him. The witch, still furious, then chopped up the trees and scattered them all around Xanth. She thought that would denature them, but instead the wood maintained its strength, and remains potent today. Thus the origin of reverse wood, the source of a great deal of mischief and some benefit throughout Xanth.

"But in the course of his career, Joshua once encountered a fine thread of a story. Again not realizing its nature—he was by no means the brightest of Magicians—he reversed it, ruining the story it was supposed to support. Disgusted, the tale teller of the time threw it away, and it was lost. Thus that reverse story thread remains somewhere, we know not where, if it has not been destroyed. That is the thread you require. But I have no idea how you can get it."

The Pawpaw Wizard sat back. Tweeter sagged. How could they get a thread, if it had been destroyed two centuries ago? Their mission was surely doomed.

But Nimby was writing another note. Chlorine took it and read it. " 'How do the forces of nature feel about traveling in time?' "

The Wizard whistled again. "They don't like it, because they regard it as being against nature. But they do have the power to give a person a pass to travel in time, if they can be persuaded that this is necessary. I suppose you could ask them, if you think your reason is persuasive."

"Well, it's to save Xanth from being blown away," Chlorine said.

The Wizard nodded. "That does seem persuasive. I wish you well." He hesitated, then remarked, "I don't mean to pry, but if you really have a way to go back then, I may have some additional information."

Chlorine looked at Nimby. "I think we do intend to go there."

"Then I must warn you of another person who lived in that time." And he plunged into his story.

*   *   *

He was Xanth's very worst vampire, a mean creature who really
sucked. His very name would strike fear into the bravest of the brave,
so I won't mention it here. Most people simply called him Fang Face.
It was thought that he could be killed only by a reverse wood stake
through the heart, but since reverse wood didn't exist quite then, it
seemed he was invulnerable. A few people knew that he disliked
garlic and feared sunlight, but it wouldn't be easy to kill him in those
ways. You couldn't just take a bloodthirsty vampire for a stroll in the
sun, or invite him to share a slice of garlic bread with you. No, it
was going to take more than that to dispatch old Fang Face!

But after the vampire sucked a woman so dry that she had to be
dunked immediately in a healing spring, and still looked rather des-
iccated, her husband decided it was time to get rid of him. "I'm going
to get that sucker," he swore.

Unfortunately his talent was just of the spot-on-the-wall variety,
not worth mentioning. When it came to matching anyone's magic, he
felt quite inferior. He knew that if he challenged the vampire directly,
he would merely become another blood donor. But he was a strong
man, and an intelligent one, so he concluded that he could probably
do it if he just used his head. His name was, uh, well, forgettable. He
wasn't a very memorable person anyway. All that matters is what he
did this one time.

He fashioned a dummy out of various objects, such as a milk pod
for a head and lady fingers for hands, and a pair of jugs for the upper
torso. But he turned out to be pretty good at dummying, and the result
had considerable stork appeal. It looked just like a very sanguine
young woman—that is, filled with tasty blood. He propped her up
atop a pile of dry wood. Then he covered her with supersticky sap,
and arrow grass, and tangled tree tentacles. The tentacles looked like
a skirt that covered not quite enough of her plump legs, and the sap
looked like a clinging blouse over her ample bosom. But anything
that touched that lush body would be stuck to it for some time.

He hauled the entire assemblage—body and woodpile—to a path
near the vampire's crypt and set it up in a marvelously appealing
fashion. The trap was set.

Now to bait it. "Help!" the man screamed in a falsetto voice from behind the dummy. "I'm an innocent lovely sweet juicy damsel in deep distress! I'm all tied up, and can hardly even kick my tender feet, let alone escape. Won't someone please rescue me before I catch a sniffle from all this exposure?"

Soon a man came along the path. He was a cool character, which was obvious because he wore snowshoes. But the snow almost melted when he spied the lovely dummy. "Well, now," he said, and took a step toward her. "The storks will get no rest today."

But this was the wrong man. He wasn't the vampire. He was just a typical sexist lunkhead whose elimination wouldn't make any difference to anyone. It was necessary to make him go away in a hurry.

"Oh, thank you, kind sir!" the husband cried in his cracked falsetto voice. "I never thought a man as handsome as you would take an interest in me. I'm just one of several aides to the cruel vampire."

The lunk paused. "You're a what?"

"One of the aides," the husband cried. "Aides! AIDES!"

"That's what I thought you said! I'm not touching any aides. I'm outta here!" And the lunk took off, leaving behind chunks of snow from his cold feet.

The husband sighed a breath of relief. Only his quick and dirty wit had saved his trap that time. He hoped the vampire would be the next one to pass by.

This time his fortune was good. The vampire arrived. "Methinks I see a luscious creature," he opined. "Sanguine and helpless—exactly the way I prefer." He marched up and plunged his fangs into the temptingly exposed flesh of the dummy.

Then he recoiled. "This isn't blood!" he cried in outrage. "This is milk! What are you doing with milk in your body?"

"Exactly where did you bite me?" the husband asked in his falsetto. "You should know better than to bite a milkmaid in the heaving bosom."

"I didn't bite your bosom, I bit your neck!" the vampire screamed. "Do you think I don't know where to bite a helpless damsel? Anyway, it wasn't heaving." Then he realized the significance of that. "Hey! This isn't a real woman—it's a stupid dummy!"

"Fancy that," the husband said, abandoning the falsetto, which was becoming a strain anyway. "I guess it takes one to bite one."

The vampire tried to pull away, but the arrow-grass hair had caught his head, and the tentacle skirt had grabbed his legs. In addition, the sticky sap had glued his face to the dummy's neck. "Help!" he cried. "All I wanted to do was have a nice snack of blood, and now I'm stuck."

"And in a moment you'll be a roast, you sap," the husband said gleefully. "Just as soon as I light a fire under you." And he proceeded to do just that.

"You fool!" the vampire cried out of the side of his stuck face. "You can't kill me! I'm immortal!"

"Oh, I'm sure that's an exaggeration," the husband said, warming his hands as the fire blazed up.

"Not much of one," the vampire clarified. "You'll see, you fool. I'll be back to taste your blood yet."

"If so, you'll have to do it as ashes, because that's what you'll soon be. Maybe you'll find a nice piece of ash to bite. Maybe I'll bury your ashes in a hole, making you an ash hole." The man laughed at his wit, which was just as well, because the vampire didn't find it very funny.

However, the husband should have taken the threat more seriously, because the vampire really was immortal in his fashion. As he burned to ashes, each ash became a mosquito. The mosquito knew only one thing, and that was to suck blood. Like cri-tics, they swarmed all over anything that lived, and sucked. The husband was their very first victim, but for some reason he didn't feel honored. He fled, swatting himself unmercifully.

"And ever since then, the vampire mosquitoes have plagued Xanth," the Pawpaw Wizard concluded. "And Mundania too, where it seems as if they have been forever, but that's only because of the itching. But that is of little concern to you. The point is that the vampire didn't die until shortly before the Reverse Magician did, and he lived in the same general region. In fact, they were friends of a sort. The one did not try to suck the blood of the other, and the other did not reverse the one into a blood-spitting image. So if you go there and then, you are bound to encounter him. And you probably wouldn't care to."

Chlorine shuddered. "Thank you for the warning. We shall do our best to avoid the vampire. At least we won't have to worry about mosquitoes."

"And some believe that the story thread Joshua lost may be in the possession of the vampire."

Chlorine looked at Nimby, evidently hoping for a negation, but Nimby nodded. "Oh, no," she groaned.

Now Tweeter understood why Nimby had not felt this would be an easy mission. But they had no choice; they had to go after that thread.

So they moved on, after thanking the Pawpaw Wizard for the information and the sandwiches. Nimby knew where to find the forces of nature, who, as fortune would have it, were not far distant.

They came to a region of ashes. Chlorine looked around in alarm, but Nimby was unconcerned, so she relaxed. In its center was a burning circle, and in the circle stood an attractive young or seemingly young woman whose long hair was the color of flame and whose short skirt was the color of smoke. She was evidently enjoying herself, doing a dance, her bare feet unhurt by the hot coals.

Chlorine read Nimby's note. " 'Fira, force of fire, we are on a mission to save Xanth from destruction. Will you give us a pass to travel two hundred years into the past?' "

Fira paused, and her fire and smoke paused with her. She eyed Chlorine as if resenting her beauty. "What's in it for me?" she demanded.

"If Xanth gets blown away, there will be nothing left to burn," Chlorine explained. "Your flames will expire for lack of fuel."

"Um," Fira said, impressed. "Very well, I will give you a quarter pass. But you may not find my sisters so amendable." She extended a flaming fragment of paper. Chlorine hesitated to take it, as did Tweeter, but Nimby took it in his hand. The fire died down, though the paper continued to glow.

"Thank you," Chlorine said. "We are burning with gratitude."

They hurried on. Soon they came to a small lake. In the center of it stood a woman whose gown and headdress flowed liquidly across her frame, which seemed to be as completely supple as water.

Chlorine read another note. " 'Mareen, lady of water, will you help us to save Xanth from dehydration?' "

It was clear that a key word had been uttered. "Please don't utter blasphemy in my presence," Mareen said.

"I apologize," Chlorine said quickly. "I meant that Xanth faces a severe loss of water, and will be all washed up, if we don't go to the past to—"

"Of course I'll help you," Mareen said. "Here is a quarter pass." She produced a blue square of water, which turned out to be an aqua-colored card when Chlorine took it.

"Thank you so much. We are overflowing with gratitude."

They went on until they came to a gray rock statue of a woman in a plant green robe decorated with red strawberries. She carried a cornucopia from which a wheat-shrouded pumpkin was about to emerge, and her other hand was extended with a handful of seeds.

" 'Alanda, lady of land, will you help us to save the Land of Xanth from being utterly despoiled?' " Chlorine read from Nimby's note. Tweeter was coming to appreciate the finesse of language employed.

The statue came to life. "How's that again?" Alanda asked sharply.

"Xanth will be blown into nothing but windblown mounds of garbage, hardly better than the spoils of war that harpies so love, if we don't travel to the past to—"

"Here is a quarter pass," Alanda said, presenting a cob of corn she culled from the cornucopia. The cob became yellow paper as Chlorine accepted it.

"Thank you most copiously," Chlorine said.

They continued, until they came to a windy glade. Here there floated a woman with waist-length windblown hair and a long windblown cape, and a big hawk on her arm. Tweeter was somewhat wary of the hawk, but Nimby did not seem concerned. Indeed, Nimby indicated that Tweeter should address the bird.

Tweeter gulped and made his best effort. "Oh mighty hawk," he said in bird talk, "will your companion Windona hear our plea?"

"Get to the point, hummingbird," the hawk snapped.

Tweeter decided to ignore the slight, as it was probably deliberate.

"Hurricane Happy Bottom is going to blow Xanth away, if we don't stop her by fetching a story thread from the past. So we need a pass to—"

"Why should we care about that?" the hawk asked. "We are creatures of wind."

Tweeter thought fast. "If the storm blows away all the trees, there will be no place for nests, and no prey species left. And Happy Bottom will be the most powerful entity of air, blowing Windona into has-been status. She—"

"Here is your pass," Windona said abruptly. Tweeter was startled; he hadn't realized that she understood bird talk.

"Thank you most breezily," Tweeter said, taking the pass in his beak. It resembled a feather, becoming feathery paper.

They continued on until they came to a private glade. There was a table in the center. It turned out to be made entirely of salt. "Table salt," Chlorine said, pleased. "Just what we need." She spread out the cards they had received from the four forces of nature.

Then they assembled the four passes. One was a quarter pass one, and the next was a quarter pass two, and quarter pass three, and quarter pass four. Together they formed a complete license to go against nature one time.

Chlorine filled in the time Nimby indicated: Apull 19, 900. Then she sat on Nimby dragon, and Tweeter perched on her hair, and she invoked the crime against nature. "Let us pass to the past," she said.

Suddenly they were in a different glade, or maybe the same one a hundred and ninety-six years before, clothed by different trees. They would have four quarters of an hour to complete their mission before the past passed and they reverted to the present, ready or not.

"And I hope we don't encounter the vampire," Chlorine said with another shudder. Tweeter agreed. "Maybe we can find the thread in his lair while he's out sucking up elsewhere."

Nimby wrote a note. Chlorine read it, and paled. "He wears the thread," she said. "He has a balky button on his cape, and the thread reverses the button's nature and makes it amenable. So it's always with him. How can we possibly get that thread without getting sucked?"

Nimby looked at Tweeter. Oh, no! Tweeter felt his stiff little legs turn to jelly. He should have known that he hadn't been invited along just for the ride.

But there was more. Nimby was writing again. Chlorine read the new note. " 'I can take you to the Vampire Gestalt. But it will not be easy to take the thread, because he values it.' " Chlorine looked up, causing Tweeter to adjust his perch on her hair. "I can fix that, I think; I can stand before the vampire, and stun him by showing him my panties—" She paused, seeing Nimby's head shake. She looked back down at the note she hadn't finished reading. Tweeter readjusted. "Oh. 'Panties don't freak out vampires. Only lush, pulsing, sanguine necks.' " She looked up again, and Tweeter rode with it. "Well, then, I'll bare my lush pulsing sanguine neck, and—" Another shake made her look back at the note. "Oh. 'We're not allowed to hurt the vampire, because that would change Xanth history in unpredictable ways. He must meet his destined fate as described.' " She looked up, and Tweeter shifted again. "But that means that Xanth will be plagued by hungry mosquitoes! Can't we eliminate them?" Another shake sent her back to the note. " 'A number of special creatures came to prey on those mosquitoes, such as a fine type of netting, and several repellents—' " She looked up. "I met a repellent once. It was a disgusting creature. But I suppose nets are useful." She resumed reading. " 'And their elimination would mess up Xanth in other unpredictable ways. It might even interfere with the story line we are in, eliminating us as characters.' " She gulped and looked up again. Tweeter was beginning to feel motion sick. "Suddenly I see the point! This is all in the past, so any change can affect us. And we don't want that, because we might cause ourselves never to exist, and our great adventure would be erased before it started. So what must we do?" She looked back at the note. " 'We must try to get the thread without Gestalt noticing.' " She looked up once more. Tweeter hoped that was the last one. "And that's it. We can't hurt him, or make too much of a fuss, lest we imperil our own very existence. This scares me."

Tweeter agreed emphatically. He wasn't a creature of Xanth, but he was affected by Xanth, because what would happen if the Baldwin

family blundered into it, and there was no Chlorine to help them get through it? No Nimby to know the spot answers? They could be in much worse trouble, and Xanth itself might be doomed without their help. He had never seen Nimby nervous before; now he understood how justified the dragon's attitude was.

And he, Tweeter, had somehow to get that thread. Without doing any harm. Or getting caught. So he could help save Xanth from the resurgent ill wind. It seemed to be altogether too tall an order for one little bird.

He realized that Chlorine and Nimby were looking at him. Well, Nimby was; the woman's eyes were trying to see him, but he remained perched on top of her head, so her gaze was missing him by about a wingspan. But she was trying. They wanted to know his reaction.

What else was there to do? ''Cheep!'' he said boldly.

''Well, I'm glad you have confidence,'' Chlorine said. ''You're the one who needs it most.''

For sure. Tweeter tried to control his unconfident shivering.

''But I'll help all I can,'' she continued. ''Maybe I *will* show him my panties, because that should distract him somewhat without actually freaking him out—which is what we want. But I'm not going to let him near my tender neck.''

Tweeter appreciated that.

''So I guess we'd better go find the vampire,'' Chlorine said halfway briskly. ''And I guess we'd better play damsel and dragon, so as to be as distracting as possible. While Tweeter goes after the thread.''

Nimby assumed his dragon form, and Chlorine got on him. Nimby knew exactly where to go, as always, so in only a moment and an instant, or perhaps two instants and a trace, they arrived at the lair of the dread vampire.

Tweeter was halfway disappointed. It wasn't a big spooky old ancient castle, but merely a hut formed of bloodroot roots, all tangly and red, with a thatch of bloodroot leaves. The sagging door was closed. The hut was in deep shade, because vampires weren't especially keen on sunshine.

"He must be asleep," Chlorine said. "I understand they sleep a lot in the daytime." Nimby nodded his donkey head. "So I'll just call him out," she decided.

She paused, as if hoping someone would tell her no, but no one did. So she adjusted her blouse and skirt to show just so much and no more, while Tweeter flew to a nearby tree, hoping to be able to approach the vampire from behind.

"But I wonder whether you couldn't just fly in and get it while he's asleep," she said, suffering a moderate afterthought.

But Nimby shook his head no.

So Chlorine completed her adjustments, which really weren't necessary, as she was equally lovely regardless, and lifted her chin and her voice. "Oo-oo, Vampire Gestalt," she called without a lot of volume. "Are you in there?"

In a moment the door opened, and a dark figure appeared. "Who calls me?" it inquired in a sinister tone or two.

Now Tweeter saw why the sleep approach wouldn't have worked: the cloak was just unkinking from a tight wrap, and the button on the side was just coming into sight. It would have been inaccessible while the vampire slept. Probably he slept in a closed coffin box anyway, making the chore even more difficult. So it had to be while he was up, and preferably outside, for a more ready escape.

"I called you," Chlorine said in a somewhat quavery voice. "I understand you—you like succulent young maidens."

The dark vampire brightened. "Indeed I do. Come into my den, succulent damsel, and we shall share a rare delight."

Tweeter moved closer. The button was now fully exposed, and he could see a strand of thread behind it. There was his target!

"But I don't like dingy interiors," Chlorine said. "I prefer the bright outdoors." She moved in her saddle, so that her skirt sort of accidentally fell askew, revealing a well-fleshed thigh.

"But the delights I offer are best savored in shadow," the vampire said. His eyes seemed to play about her neckline more than her skirt-line.

"Well, maybe if we meet halfway," she suggested, adjusting herself again. This time her blouse got accidentally disarrayed, so that some of her fair white column of a neck showed.

"Maybe so," the vampire said, licking his thin lips thirstily. He walked out toward them—and coincidentally past Tweeter's hiding place.

Tweeter nerved himself with what little nerve he had—he was a small bird, so it wasn't much—and flew around and behind the figure, coming in on the button. He landed on it, snatching for the thread with his beak.

Unfortunately, the thread did not give way. The vampire felt the tug. "What's this?" he demanded, glancing down.

"This is a tender panty!" Chlorine cried, snatching up her skirt to show it. Then, remembering, she reversed course and snatched open the front of her blouse to reveal her pulsing neck, and somewhat more. "I mean a silken bos—uh, neck!" Old habits died hard.

But she was too late. The flash of silken panty hadn't stunned the vampire, just as Nimby had warned it wouldn't, and by the time her tender neck showed, the vampire's gaze had departed her body.

His hand was no slower. It dropped down and closed about Tweeter. "We have an avian creature," he exclaimed, surprised. "Someone is giving me the bird."

"Pay no attention to that bird," Chlorine cried desperately. "He doesn't have more than a drop of blood, while I have half a slew, uh, wash, uh, jug!" She ripped open the rest of her blouse, showing her entire delectable front, which indeed had not one but two ample jugs.

But the Vampire Gestalt, canny in his fashion, would not be distracted. "All in good time," he told Chlorine without looking. "What were you after, bird? My button? Are you a button hooker?" He held Tweeter up before his face, helpless.

"No he's not!" Chlorine screamed. "He's just a stupid little bird, while I'm a delectable heaving-bosomed maiden girl damsel with a stunning pair of pan—uh, breas—uh, I mean, soft tender neck!"

But all her valiant efforts were for naught. "I think you are up to something, bird," the vampire said. "Things always occur as aspects of wholes, and I don't understand your part or your whole."

"Stop talking dirty!" Chlorine cried. But it was a fading ploy. The vampire ignored her, turned around, and swept back into his hut.

Inside, he closed the dismal door, checked the dirty windows, and let Tweeter go. "You can't escape this horrendous hovel, bird, so you might as well confess,'' Gestalt said. "What were you really after, and why?''

Tweeter thought fast. Maybe he had half a chance, if he used his little noggin well. Should he tell the truth? No, because the vampire wouldn't believe it. Nobody would believe that a stupid little bird came from the future, on a mission to save Xanth from destruction. But what else was there?

"Did someone send you?'' Gestalt demanded. "Understand, bird, I really don't care much about you; as the damsel says, you have only a drop of blood in you, while she is relatively luscious. But I like to understand the big picture. Tell me, and I'll let you go.''

Tell him what? That they had to have his reverse thread, to fashion a new story line before the old one broke? He wouldn't believe that either. None of this was really believable.

"Come, come, bird,'' Gestalt said impatiently. "I don't have all day. My last several victims have escaped, and I'm really pretty hungry. If that luscious damsel is gone by the time I settle with you, I shall be most displeased.'' He stretched his mouth, showing his fangs.

Then a little light flashed over Tweeter's little head. It was only a faint light, not at all matching the lights that flashed over Chlorine's head when she got good ideas, but it did illuminate his little mind. Suddenly he knew what to tell Gestalt.

"Ah, I see you have decided to cooperate,'' the vampire said. "Then let's get on with it. One nod for yes, two for no, three for further definition. Agreed?''

Tweeter nodded once. Gestalt did seem to grasp the whole of things readily.

"You came for something?''

Nod: yes.

"The button?''

Nod nod: no.

"Surely not my cloak!''

Yes—no.

Gestalt understood. "Bad phrasing. But what else could—the thread?''

Yes.

"But this is a very special thread. It reverses—"

Yes.

"Ah, so you know its qualities. I need this thread to hold my recalcitrant button."

Nod nod nod.

"There's more? How could you persuade me to part with this magic thread?"

Nod nod nod.

Gestalt smiled. "True. I need to get specific. Can you honestly say I would benefit from—"

Yes.

"Yes? Parting with this thread would do me good?"

Yes.

Gestalt stroked a fang. "This intrigues me. It would do me good with my cloak?" He saw Tweeter's negation. "My house? No. My sleep? No. My food? Yes." Then the vampire did a double take, or at least a one and a half take. "Are you telling me that this thread interferes with my feeding?"

Yes.

Gestalt stroked his other fang. "Let me see whether I can figure your rationale. This thread was made by Joshua, the famed Reverse Magician, with whom I share a reasonable portion of a friendship. It reverses things. It reverses the contrary nature of my button. Are you saying it does not stop there?"

Yes.

"So what else would it reverse? My fortunes? My—" Then a big bulb flashed over his head. "My prey! When I get close, it reverses the nature of my victims, and they become unamenable. Instead of being lulled by my aura, so that I can sip of their blood without their resistance, they become alarmed, and flee. Since all they have to do is step into the sunshine, I am unable to pursue them far. And so my fortune is changed—by the presence of this reverse thread."

Yes. He had fathomed it with marvelous precision, once given the clue. That was exactly the thought that Tweeter's little bulb had illuminated.

The Vampire Gestalt smiled. "We made a deal, and you have delivered. You have shown me why I do not want to retain this thread. You need it, I do not. Accordingly I will give it to you and let you go, on one condition.''

Nod nod nod?

''That you take it so far away that it will never be near me again. Agreed?''

Yes!

The vampire unwound the thread, releasing the button, which promptly became balky again. He extended the thread to Tweeter. Tweeter took it in his beak. It gave him a funny feeling. He spread his wings and tried to fly, but just sank down against the table.

''It is reversing you, now,'' Gestalt said. ''I think you will have to walk out of here, rather than fly.'' He opened the door. ''I trust you can make it on the ground.''

Tweeter tried to nod, but shook his head instead. He walked unsteadily out the door.

Nimby was there, with Chlorine. The dragon extended the tip of his tail, and Tweeter climbed up on it. Then without giving him a chance to scramble up to Chlorine, Nimby trundled rapidly away from the hut.

''Wait!'' the vampire cried. ''I have business with the succulent damsel!''

''Not anymore,'' Chlorine cried back. ''I showed you my almost everything, but you spurned me. I'll take my pan—bos—jug—my whatever elsewhere, thank you all the same.''

''Ah, well,'' Gestalt said philosophically. ''I should have no trouble, now, finding a replacement.'' He headed purposefully in the other direction.

Another little bulb flashed over Tweeter's head. He realized why Nimby was not letting him approach Chlorine. He had the reverse thread, and it was reversing him to a degree; if he took it to Chlorine, it would mess her up too. So he had to stay here far from the main action, to carry the thread without doing any damage to the others. Well, that was what he would do. He had succeeded in his mission. Now all Nimby had to do was get them back in time. Or forward in time, before their time ran out.

16
DEMON

T he Demon X(A/N)th was half-satisfied. He had enabled Chlorine and Tweeter to fetch back the reverse story thread, which had taken effect the moment it reached the present time. Now Sending's ploy had been reversed, and the story was back to normal. Happy Bottom was confined in the Region of Air, and Hurricane Fracto was romancing her, or taming the shrew, as Jim Baldwin put it in his Mundanish way. Xanth had been saved from one threat.

But the other threat remained. If Chlorine did not shed one tear of love or grief for Nimby, the bet would be lost, and then X(A/N)th would be demoted to the least of Demons, and the Land of Xanth would be forfeited. That meant it would probably be destroyed. That would be too bad, because X(A/N)th had recently come to know this land well, and it had grown on him. He had largely ignored it for millennia, but he would do so no longer. Becoming a character within it had entirely changed his outlook.

"What are you thinking of, Nimby?" Chlorine inquired brightly, interrupting his reverie. What a delight she had turned out to be! But she would not shed her last tear for him, because then she would be blind. That was the ultimate cost of his inattention that had allowed him to choose the wrong companion: defeat.

Of course, he couldn't answer her, but he twitched an ear in acknowledgement. That satisfied her; she patted his hide and rode on.

He liked it when she did that, which was a signal of how his attitude had modified.

Now they were nearing Castle Roogna for the big celebration of victory over the Ill Wind. Everyone was to be there—everyone who cared to be. Including Chlorine and her silent companion Nimby.

They came to the Mundane RV, or moving house. The child Karen spied them first and dashed out. "Hi, Chlorine! Hi, Nimby!" She threw her arms around his donkey head and kissed him on the striped pink and green snout. He liked that, too. "Glad you could make it!" She dashed back in to notify the others.

"That little girl belongs in Xanth," Chlorine remarked, dismounting. "With her own dragon."

True. Karen had not yet properly learned the arts of dissembling; her actions mirrored her thoughts. She liked Xanth, and she liked Nimby, not caring half a whit how odd he looked. Her greeting had been sincere. Which was why he appreciated it.

The others came out. "Glad to see you again, Nimby," Jim Baldwin said. "We'll be going tomorrow, but we wanted you to know that we couldn't have done it without you." Of course, he knew that Nimby already knew that, but his Mundane protocol required him to make a formal statement. That, too, he liked.

Mary approached. "But perhaps it would be better if you attended the festivities in your human form," she murmured.

"Yes," Chlorine agreed immediately. "In formal clothing, too. And I hope you know how to dance."

Of course he could dance; he had learned that in the course of his survey of the land and people and things of Xanth. So he changed to human form, in a royal robe.

Sean and Willow emerged. They were somber; they had not resolved their impasse. They were in love, and could not bear to be separated, but they were of different realms, neither suited for the other realm. In Sean's mind was a notion of separating from his family to remain in Xanth, but he was held back by the knowledge that this would so greatly hurt the other members of the family as to mire him in perpetual guilt. In Willow's mind was the thought of going with him to Mundania, where she thought she would die, but at least she would have a little more time with him. But she realized that this would be worse for Sean than separation. So she would bravely bid him farewell, and when he was gone she would do what she should have done at the outset, and fly to Mount Rushmost were they had reunited, tie her wings together so she could not fly, and throw herself off the precipice. Then she would be at peace, and Sean would never know, so would suffer no additional grief.

Nimby knew these things, but could not speak them and did not care to write them. He also knew that good news was on the way for them. So that affair would have a happy ending, and perhaps that was best. Just as it was best that all the folk of Xanth be happy this day, not knowing . . .

"Very well," Chlorine said, not knowing the nature or velocity of his thoughts. "Put me in a lovely party gown and hairdo for the party."

"Gee, are you going to change right out here?" David asked, his twelve-year-old pupils dilating. The presence of Chlorine accelerated his race toward maturity, especially since Big Brother Sean had lost interest.

"Right out here," Chlorine agreed, smiling. Suddenly her complete outfit shifted, as Nimby changed her according to her wish, in somewhat less than an eye-blink. Naturally David had blinked in that moment, so saw none of what he had hoped to.

"Aww," the boy said, disappointed.

Chlorine turned to Nimby. "You know, he's Mundane," she murmured low. "Would it be too great a violation if he caught half a glimpse, considering the spirit of the occasion?" Her mind made clear the nature of her request. She knew that she would not have this beautiful body much longer, because the adventure was almost over, and she wanted to leave a lasting impression on someone without actually being tried for Violation of the Adult Conspiracy. She also wanted to give the boy a treat, and she did not hold the Conspiracy in as much awe as was proper, because of her background as a woman nobody much looked at anyway.

So Nimby removed her dress for one full blink, at a time when only David happened to be looking, so that she stood in eyeball-numbing yellow-green bra and panties. Then he restored the outfit, as if it had never lapsed; there was no evidence and no other witness, so there would be no case even if someone suspected.

David's brown eyes turned yellow-green and his jaw dropped. Brief as it was, it had still been too much of a dose; he was stunned, and about to fall. But Nimby caught one arm, and Chlorine the other. "Promise not to tell," she whispered in the boy's ear.

David nodded numbly. He would recover, because he was Mundane and not quite of age for the full effect to register. But it was a close call. Mundanes, it turned out, weren't all that different from Xanthians. As it was, the boy would start pursuing girls a full year earlier than he would have otherwise; the secret glimpse had advanced his thyme-table that far.

"David! Are you all right?" Mary inquired, with a mother's instant awareness of any passing indisposition in her child.

David's mouth worked. "Jus—just great," he said, awed.

Mary glanced somewhat suspiciously at Chlorine's low and curvaceous décolletage. "Go with your sister," she said. She suspected that the boy had seen a bit too much, so was moving him away from it. Fortunately she suspected only about a quarter of the reality.

They walked as a group toward Castle Roogna. But David, still glazed, stumbled. Mary caught him and looked in his face. "Your eyes!" she exclaimed. "They're green!" Now she suspected half the reality. But being Mundane, she had an abiding disbelief of magic, so couldn't bring herself to suspect the whole of it. That was just as well. The boy's eyes had been stained permanently green by what he had seen.

Castle Roogna came into view, gloriously magical. And there, coming out to greet them, was a lovely princess they didn't recognize. "Who is that creature?" Jim inquired.

Then Karen spied a freckle. "That's Princess Electra!" she squealed. "Looking princessly!"

She was correct. Nimby had known, of course, but hadn't been asked. Normally Electra ran around in blue jeans, but on formal occasions she suppressed her nature and played her royal role. Clothes made all the difference.

Karen ran up to the princess. "How can you stand being so regal?" she demanded.

Electra made a careful royal moue. "It isn't easy," she confessed. "But somebody has to do it. After the official greetings are over, let's get together with Jenny Elf and sneak away to pig out on chocolate pie. We can wear—" she glanced around to be sure no one else was in earshot "—shorts and tank tops."

"Ooooo!" Karen squealed, delighted. "It's a date."

Then Electra put her royal face back on and turned to the others. "So nice to meet you again, good people. But I believe I have not met one of your number before."

"This is Willow Elf," Sean said quickly. "Her winged elm tree is very large."

"So I see," Electra said. "So nice to meet you, Willow Elf." She extended her hand in princessly manner.

Willow bowed, and her wings quivered. "Thank you, Princess."

"And how did you come to join this party?" Electra inquired. "I had understood that the winged elves seldom associate with ground-bound folk."

"Sean and I washed in a love spring, before we realized," Willow explained.

"Oh, I understand!" Electra said with instant sympathy. "When Prince Dolph kissed me awake, after my several centuries of sleep, the magic made me love him instantly. But he didn't love me. At least you were together."

"But didn't he marry you?" Willow asked.

"Oh yes, eventually. But at first he was more interested in Princess Nada Naga."

"How could any man not be most interested in you?" Willow asked, amazed.

"When you see Nada, you will understand." Electra paused. "Oh, there are the winged centaurs arriving. Come, Willow, I must introduce you to them; I'm sure you'll like them." Then, remembering her royal duties, she paused again. "But first I must conduct all of you to the castle in style." Yet it was evident that she wanted to greet the centaurs first.

Mary was the one to find a way to alleviate the problem. "We'll be glad to wait until the centaurs can join us, Princess. Then we can all enter together."

"Oh, thank you! Come, Willow!" The princess hurried toward the field where the centaurs were landing, and Willow went with her.

Sean remained behind. "I think they have girl things to discuss," he said. He was right; Electra wanted to compare notes on magic love, having met another woman who had encountered it.

The Baldwins and Chlorine waited while Electra and Willow met the centaurs and exchanged more introductions. Then that group returned to join the family. There were four centaurs: Che, Cynthia, Chena, and Crystal. The family had met them before, of course; indeed, Chena and Crystal had helped significantly in the effort to herd Happy Bottom north. It was a nice reunion.

But there was a nicer one coming. As the princess was about to conduct them all to the castle, Nimby nudged Chorine and gave her a note. Her eyes widened. Then she spoke. "Princess, could we wait just a bit more? Nimby says other centaurs are coming."

Electra looked blank. "More centaurs?"

"The Good Magician invited them."

The princess nodded. "Then we had better wait for them. But I hadn't realized that any more centaurs had participated in the Ill Wind venture."

Now they heard the beat of galloping hooves. "Two ground-bound centaurs," Che said. He could tell by the sound. "They don't normally care to associate with our kind."

"They certainly don't," Chena agreed. "Are you sure—?"

Then the two came into view: a male and a female.

Chena screamed. "Carleton!" She galloped out to meet them.

"Her brother," Jim said, remembering. "We promised to relay his greeting to her, and we did."

"And Sheila," Sean said. "I'd recognize that bosom anywhere." Then, conscious of Willow beside him, he added: "Not that I care."

"I'm not jealous," Willow said. "I could show you something similar, if I dared." She meant that it was not safe to risk an exposure that might cause them both to forget the danger of summoning a stork, since they could not be a family. Her words were also an invitation

of a sort, because she expected to be dead long before any stork found
her, so she might as well do it—if he agreed.

"You already did, in the love spring," he reminded her. "I almost wish we had—" Then he remembered that they were in the
company of his family, and stifled it. But Jim and Mary were already exchanging a knowing glance. They well understood the invitation and the tentative acceptance. Indeed, Jim was inclined to give
them leave, and Mary was weakening. It was evident that the love
of the two young folk was complete, but that they would have to
separate soon.

Meanwhile Chena Centaur collided with her brother, hugging him.
"I thought I'd never see you again!" she cried through her tears of
joy.

"I had a similar concern," he admitted. "I feared for your safety
on the brutish mainland." He drew back a little. "But you seem to
have changed."

"I have joined a new species," she said. "I am now a winged
monster." She spread her wings.

"So I see. I suppose it is for the best, if you are satisfied."

"Yes I am. Except for one thing. Two things."

"One? Two?"

"I miss my family. And I would like to find some winged stallions.
Do you suppose that any on Centaur Isle—?"

He smiled. "I suppose it is time to confess. I found myself dissat-
isfied with things on Centaur Isle, and thought that if you had found
a suitable situation, I might join your group. In fact, I know of some
others who also might wish to join, if it were clear that they would
be welcome."

"Ooooo!" Chena cried, just like a human maiden. She hugged him
again, then turned to Crystal. "Would you welcome a new stallion
from Centaur Isle, if he put on wings?"

"We are among human folk," Crystal said. "Therefore the Adult
Conspiracy prevents me from answering in detail. But I think a very
general affirmative would be in order."

Carleton glanced at her. "You have not been a centaur long, I
suspect," he remarked. "You are speaking as you think a centaur
would speak."

Crystal blushed. "Is it so obvious? I'm trying so hard."

"I think a centaur stallion would be glad to exchange elocution instruction for flying instruction."

While this dialogue was occurring, Sheila Centaur was renewing her acquaintance with the family and Chlorine, and David was staring at her front. "Why, David," Sheila remarked, "your eyes are green." Centaurs were observant, and had good memories as well as good mammaries.

"Yeah," he said. It didn't occur to him to wonder why a glimpse of a green bra should stain his eyes, while a complete look at a fine bare bosom merely made his eyes dilate. This was, of course, the magic of certain garments.

"How come you came here?" Karen asked. "I mean you helped us on our way, and we're glad, but do you really care about mainland Xanth?"

Sheila looked as if she was possibly pondering the merest hint of a blush, which would have been very unusual for a normal centaur. "It is true that my main interest is in Centaur Isle. But Carleton wished to see his sister again, and I was indisposed to allow him to travel that far alone."

"I get it!" Karen cried with juvenile lack of circumspection. "You're sweet on Carleton!"

"Karen!" Mary cautioned.

"While that is not the way I would have chosen to express it, the sentiment is accurate," Sheila confessed. "Where he goes, I go." There was a slight stress on the words, because she had a notion where Carleton was going.

They got organized and started for the castle again. But there was another arrival. It was a young woman with tangled hair, and a small dog.

Immediately Woofer and Midrange took note, and went out to meet the newcomers. Tweeter, perched on Karen's hair, chirped. That alerted the girl. "Snarl—and his lost mistress!" she cried, running after the pets.

So it was. Snarl had received an invitation to the party, because he had helped the Ill Wind effort, and he had brought Ursa along too, not wishing to separate from his mistress again. The girl seemed a bit baffled by it all, but Karen quickly filled her in while cuddling Snarl. There was another round of introductions.

They started in again—but were paused by still another arrival. No one recognized the four women striding purposefully toward them until Tweeter cheeped again. Then Chlorine, who had been talking with the centaurs, looked. "The four forces of nature!" she exclaimed. *"Everyone's* here!"

There were more introductions, this time made by Chlorine. "Fira—the force of fire," she said of the fiery woman. "Mareen—the force of water. Alanda—the force of land. And Windona—the force of air. They helped us go to find the reverse story thread." The four women nodded graciously. Fortunately Chlorine did not clarify that the women had enabled them to travel back in time.

Now at last they all went to the castle. Soufflé Serpent was in the moat, standing tall, with a little black bow tie on his neck to show that he was part of the resident staff.

They crossed the drawbridge, which was gaily decorated, and entered the castle proper. There, in a gown that made Mary wince, was Princess Nada Naga. And suddenly Willow understood why Prince Dolph had been distracted from Princess Electra, in the early days of their relationship.

But there were also the Demoness Mentia, and Trenita Imp, and Princess Ivy, and many others, and any concerns about who might catch on to what were lost in the welter of additional introductions and remembrances.

Then Jenny Elf and another woman approached Willow. "Hello, Sean," Jenny said. "This is Wira, the Good Magician's daughter-in-law. She must talk with Willow."

"Wira?" Sean asked. "But isn't she—" He caught himself.

"Blind," Wira finished for him. "That is why Jenny is guiding me, here in this less familiar castle."

"I am Willow," Willow said, approaching her.

Wira smiled. "Magician Humfrey asked me to give you this." She held out a card.

"Thank you," Willow said. "But what is it?"

"It is a pass to Xanth. Present it at the station on No Name Key in Mundania and you and your companions will be admitted."

"But I can't go to Mundania," Willow protested. "I would die!"

"The Good Magician says that isn't true. But you would lose your wings and become a human maiden while there. Your problem is not in leaving Xanth, but in returning. Keep this pass with you always."

Willow's eyes widened. "You mean I can go with Sean? And have my wings when I return? And he can come back with me?"

"Please don't speak so loudly," Wira cautioned. "The Good Magician would not like to have it widely known that he ever did a favor without charge. But considering your service in helping to save Xanth from the Ill Wind, he felt it was warranted."

"Oh!" Willow cried, on the verge of fainting from joy and relief. "Tell him thank you! Thank you! Thank—" But Wira was gone.

"We can be together," Sean breathed. "I'm sure Dad will let you travel to Miami with us."

"But what of your mother?"

"She will be silent. That's her way of agreeing without actually saying yes to an arrangement some might consider untoward."

"Untoward?"

"You and me sharing a room."

"Sharing—?"

"In my generation, it's acceptable for engaged couples to share residence."

"Engaged?" Willow was staring at the pass, still getting her new bearings.

"Willow, will you marry me?"

Suddenly her bearings were gotten. "Yes!" She hugged him and kissed him, and little hearts floated out.

"Oh, look!" Karen cried, spying a heart as it floated by her nose. "Little hearts! They're engaged!"

Then everyone looked, and there was applause.

Nimby was glad the Good Magician had not come in person, because he would have had some hard questions for Nimby. It was not easy to keep the truth from Humfrey, who was the Magician of Information. Obviously the Good Magician knew that Nimby had asked Willow to help herd Happy Bottom north. But, as obviously, he had not fathomed Nimby's full nature. Yet.

The party began, and everyone had an excellent time. Nimby

danced with Chlorine, and it was wonderful. She had not been an expert dancer, but he quietly made her so, knowing it was her wish. Then she danced with other males, dazzling them, and he danced with other females. Meanwhile Princess Electra, her royal duties done, reverted to blue jeans and then to (gasp!) shorts, and went out with Jenny and the children to pig out on pies. If anyone noticed, anyone had the sense to ignore this infraction of protocol.

Willow's winged parents arrived from their flying elm tree, and met Sean and his family. They did not seem completely thrilled about her betrothal to a land-bound Mundane, but quickly saw that the situation was hopeless, as Willow adamantly refused to take any love-nullifying potion. They also grudgingly appreciated the fact that Sean's family had helped save Xanth from destruction; that was worth something. So they would live with it.

Somewhere amidst it all King Dor formally presented Jim Baldwin with a Certificate of Thanks for the family's volunteer effort to save Xanth from yon Ill Wind, now confined to the Region of Air. "Without you and your traveling house, and the special effort of all of your family members and pets, we could not have done it," the King concluded. "We owe you an enormous debt of gratitude, and regret that we have no way to reward you that will be effective in your homeland. But be assured you will be welcome here at any time you choose to return."

"Return?" Jim asked blankly.

"When you use the pass Magician Humfrey gave Willow," the King explained. "Any of you will be able to accompany her and Sean when they visit. Your three pets are included, of course."

"Woof!" Woofer agreed.

"That's telling them, mutt!" the floor under him agreed.

Jim looked at his wife. "We might wish to visit," Mary said cautiously.

"Yea!" Karen exclaimed.

In time the festivities wore out, and folk retired to their rooms in the castle and temporary rooms set up around it. Folk pretended not to notice how Sean and Willow shared one of those rooms. "She's a good young woman," was all Mary would say.

"He's a good young man," Willow's mother said with similar

reservation. The two women, one Mundane, the other winged, exchanged a glance that transcended cultures. That was enough.

In the morning the family and Willow piled into the RV and headed
for the trollway, waved on their way by a King, a Queen, and a
number of Princesses. The Demoness Mentia went also, to make sure
that they found a suitable gas guzzler and suffered no other problems.
They also had the Mundane addresses of Dug and Kim, two others
who had visited Xanth and knew something about it. Some of them
would surely be visiting again.

Then Chlorine knew it was time for her to go home; her big adventure—bigger than she had really expected—was over. Her folks
might be wondering where she was. So, reluctantly, she bid farewell
to the royalty and set off for the backwoods, riding Nimby in dragon
form.

When they got close, Chlorine had a notion. "I know this is all
about to end, Nimby," she said. "You promised me one good adventure, and you certainly delivered it. You have things of your own
to do, and can't take forever catering to my whims. But at least I'd
like to show you to my family, before you go away forever. Will that
be all right?"

Nimby nodded. It was all right because anything she wanted was
all right, by the terms of his situation. But far more hung on her
decision than she realized—and he could not tell her that.

"So okay, I'm taking my medicine and declaring this wonderful
adventure over," she said, and at that point she reverted to her natural
appearance and nature. "You are free to do whatever you want, with
my thanks. But if you will be kind enough to wait here until I can
bring my family to see you, I'll really appreciate it. It's been great,
Nimby." Her reversion hadn't quite registered yet, so she was still
being nice. Then she turned and marched away from him, not looking
back because she was afraid she would break down and ask for what
she thought to be impossible: a permanent life as a lovely, smart,
healthy, and nice woman.

And Nimby lost his power of motion and magic. All that remained
was his awareness of all things in Xanth, but he could no longer affect
them in any way. He had been reduced to a donkey-headed hulk, and

would remain so until he rotted away, unless Chlorine should shed her tear for him. And why should she do that, knowing it would blind her?

The Demon X(AN)th was depressed because he was about to lose his wager, and with it his governance of the Land of Xanth. Some other Demon would take it over, and might change it or destroy it, because no other Demon cared about it the way X(AN)th did. For he had indeed come to care for it, very much. And therein lay another irony, for he had also fallen in love with Chlorine.

Of course, he knew that the beautiful, smart, healthy, nice edition was a creation of his magic. He had made her, literally. But he had done it by her request, to her specifications. She had become the woman she chose to be, when she had the option. Therefore the seeds of it had been within her; she had known her deficiencies, and acted to eliminate them. Chlorine, as she had been the past few days, was what she would be always, given the chance. And it was Chlorine Ideal that he loved. She was just the perfect woman. In all but one respect—the one she hadn't thought of. And that was the capacity to love. Her hard life had washed that out along with her tears, until only a vestige remained. And so she did not love him back. He knew it, because he knew her mind as no other did. And without that love, she would never shed a tear for anyone other than herself.

X(AN)th himself had not known the meaning of love, before this adventure. He had not cared about anyone or anything except himself and his competitive ranking among Demons. But in order to win Chlorine's love he had had to learn about love, and in the course of that he learned how.

It had not been easy or sudden, because Chlorine herself did not truly understand it. She thought that love came automatically with beauty and niceness. She was mistaken; such things merely facilitated it. So she had practiced her craft, impressing young males by displaying teasing portions of her healthy body and clothing. She had teased Nimby, too, and indeed she had been interesting, and he would have liked to summon the stork with her. But storks were not identical to love; they were more like fellow travelers. There could be storks without love, and love without storks. Chlorine had finally realized that distinction, and broken off the effort, and in that decision had sown the seed of what she lacked. She had realized that she was coming to care for him enough to make playing unkind, but she hadn't realized what she was actually searching for.

It was the Mundane family Baldwin that had begun to show him the immense potential depth and breadth of love. The children's love for their pets, and Mary's love for the children. Neither had anything to do with storks, but in their subtle ways they were as significant. Any member of that family was prepared to die to protect any other member. Not all of them realized it, such as David, but it was true. X(AN)th had studied that quiet underlying emotion, laboring to understand it, and gradually had succeeded. Mary had helped him most, by showing her concern for everyone, even for him, when he had come in soiled from the meatier shower. She had treated him like a son, and though he was infinitely older than she, he had appreciated it. She had cared for him, and thereby shown him how to care for her. It was a kind of commitment that required no magic; it was just there, like water seeping silently through ground. But it was the base on which the more dramatic forms of love were laid.

Such as that between Sean and Willow. True, it had been sponsored by a dip in a love spring. But neither would have been affected as they were, if they had not had solid family love first. They had understood the aspects of love, and were ready when suddenly it caught fire. Otherwise the water would merely have caused them to mate uncontrollably, summoning as many storks as they could in a short time, and then to separate, the mood expended, in the manner of animals. Instead they had resisted the mating urge for the sake of a larger commitment that they were, ironically, unable to make. For the love they wished to realize in its entirety.

It had taken X(AN)th some time to analyze that, and to emulate it to be sure that he *did* understand it. But that turned out to be a door that, once opened, could not be closed again. He loved Chlorine.

Now she had ended the adventure, without knowing its significance. Unable to love herself, she had not appreciated how a donkey-headed dragon could love her. It had all been for fun, as she saw it, a glorious adventure of the type Princesses were wont to have. Indeed, she had danced with a Prince, and conversed with a King, and not made a fool of herself. This was her notion of the ultimate. Now it was over, and she was going home. And Nimby was dying.

Perhaps it had been doomed from the start. From the time he had allowed his attention to wander, and had addressed the wrong young woman. The one without tears. But somehow he could not regret that now, because he could not have loved the other woman more than he loved Chlorine. Though he lost the bet, and his status, and the Land of Xanth, he had gained something infinitely precious in return: the knowledge and substance of love. Perhaps it was worth it.

Yet how different it might have been. Had Chlorine possessed just a smidgen more awareness of the true nature of love, she might then have asked for an enhanced capacity, and then she might have learned to love him. But as it was, she merely liked him. And so his mission here was doomed.

Had she been able to shed her last tear for him, he would have won, and then what a great and wonderful surprise he would have had for her! He would have made her all that she had wanted to be, and so much more, more than she had ever imagined. She could have become the Goddess of Xanth, below only himself, because he could not make her a Demon. All knowledge, all power, and all joy, too, could have been hers. He would have assumed any form she wanted, especially the handsome Nimby-man one, and obliged her in any way she wished. He could have given her any magic talent she wished, being no longer limited by fear of discovery of his nature. But perhaps most important of all, he would have given her his love, and enabled her to love him in return, in the manner of Sean and Willow. And in thanks for the way those two had showed him how gloriously complete true love could be, he would have given Sean the talent of flying without wings in Xanth, so he could share Willow's life completely. No one else could do such a thing, but the Demon X(A/N)th had all magic power in his own land, and he knew now that a favor done required a favor returned.

Everything, everything, could have been Chlorine's, for herself and her friends who had helped her battle the Ill Wind. Even those who had come in late, like Adam and Keaira, who were now discovering a romance of their own. He knew the parts all of them had played, and could reward them all.

All lost, for want of a tear.

He spread his awareness. Chlorine had arrived home, in her homely bad-natured form. She tried to tell her mother about her adventure.

"Where's that sprig of thyme you were supposed to fetch, you disreputable wench?" her shrewish mother demanded, slapping her. She did that often, because she knew the girl didn't dare hit back.

Chlorine had completely forgotten about that. In fact, she didn't even remember that she hadn't been the one sent for a sprig of thyme; that was Miss Fortune. Chlorine had gone for a bow from a bow-vine. But the two had collided, and gotten confused, and proceeded on each other's missions. "I—I got distracted," she said, realizing just how awful her family life had been. Why had she ever bothered to return to this?

"Distracted?" her brutish father asked. "Did you sneak out to see a stupid boy?"

A stupid boy. That was about as far from the truth as it was possible to get.

"Not exactly. You see I encountered a funny-looking dragon who changed into a handsome man, and made me beautiful, and we had the most wonderful adventure and helped save Xanth from the Ill Wind, and—"

"Shut up!" he shouted, lifting his hand to knock some respect into her. "Don't try to tell me any crazy fantastic story! Where's this oaf?"

Chlorine realized that they were not about to listen, so she tried another tack. "Out near the thyme plant. Do you want to meet him?"

"Sure I do," her father said, fetching his club from the wall. "I'll bash his head into pulp! You don't deserve any man."

Bash Nimby? Gross chance! She did not realize that Nimby was now immobile. So she led them back to where Nimby lay. "There he is," she said. "The dragon who made me beautiful and gave me the best adventure of my life. Now do you believe me?"

"A dragon ass!" the man exclaimed, recognizing the species immediately, because it was so close to his own type. "We don't want that kind here. Not in my back yard. We'll destroy it." He bashed Nimby on the head with his club, but it made no difference. Nimby could not move, but neither was he vulnerable to the weak strength of a dissipated mortal man. Only time would wipe him out, or a hot fire.

"It's already dead, you fool," Chlorine's mother said. "Soon it'll begin to stink."

"Then we'll burn it," the man decided. "Come on, pile up some brush round it." He and his wife got to work gathering dry brush.

Chlorine was stunned. "Nimby—what's the matter with you?" she cried. "Get up, get away from here! I'll go with you. Maybe we can have another adventure somewhere else."

But Nimby didn't move. He had lost that power.

"So you're slacking off, as usual, you slut," Chlorine's father said. "Just for that, you will have the privilege of doing the final honor." He brought out a torch, and lit it. "You will set fire to the pyre. Let that be a lesson to you." He shoved the blazing torch into Chlorine's somewhat flaccid hand.

"Nimby!" she cried, a strange emotion rising in her. "Get up! Get away! Don't let them kill you!"

But Nimby just lay there, unable to respond. If only she had been able to fathom the one thing she needed to!

"Do it, girl, or you'll get a beating the like of which you won't forget!" her father said grimly.

Chlorine realized that she had no choice. She was back in the real world of Xanth, no longer in the dreamworld of beauty and Princesses and great adventures. She was subject to the brutish whims of her family, and she herself was rather more like them than she liked. For a while she had been nice as well as beautiful, but now she was neither. She wished she could have loved and been loved while she was worthy of it, yet somehow she hadn't known how to make it happen. Why hadn't she thought to ask Nimby? So she had squandered her chance even for that. She was a loser. Her best bet was to burn up the dragon and be done with illusions of grandeur.

She lowered the torch. But as she gazed directly upon Nimby's ugly donkey head, a despairing realization came. "I'm not beautiful, I'm not nice, I'm no good, I'm poison, like my talent—but for a while you made me seem otherwise. I owe you that wonderful dream that never could be. I owe the Mundane family too, because they showed me how good a family could be. I think maybe I could learn to love like that, given half a chance. Oh, Nimby, I don't know what happened to you, but I fear it's my fault. Maybe I poisoned your water by accident when I reverted to my normal nature. It's too late now to make amends, and I'd mess it up if I tried. But now I know I love you in my worthless way, and if I can't gaze on you, I don't care if I never see anything again! In fact, I'll join you in this pyre, so maybe my third-rate spirit can be near yours. Nimby, I beg you, forgive me for messing you up.'' She touched the torch to the brush, and the pyre flamed high, heating her face, singeing her hair.

And the two halves of her only remaining tear flowed from her eyes, blinding them, and merged on her nose, and that tear fell.

Author's Note

I do a lot of writing—far more than ever sees print—because I'm a writaholic; I love writing. But my working schedule suffered a significant disruption. I was writing *Hope of Earth,* which is my third GEODYSSEY historical novel, and hoped to complete it in 1994. But I had a number of collaborations to do—no, don't all you readers write in asking to collaborate, because I hope to do no more of those—and those delayed *Hope.* Then I got to work on it, and was about 50,000 words along, when the last collaborative manuscript arrived, *Quest for the Fallen Star.* I read it, and had mixed emotions: it was a major fantasy that would surely put my collaborator on the map when published, but it needed the kind of editing and revamping I could do to give it full effect—and it was 240,000 words long. On each of the more recent collaborations my collaborator has written the novel, then I have gone over it to fix any problems that might make it unpublishable. So my part is fairly fast. But this one would take me two and a half months to revamp—as long as it takes me to write a typical Xanth novel. If I took that much time off, how could I finish *Hope* on schedule? So I discussed it with my researcher, Alan Riggs, and he suggested that he try going over it first. He could take care of the routine adjustments—the kind that can take a lot of time—and then I could go over it and polish it to my standard. That would reduce my time to about a month, with as good a result. I liken novel writing to building a highway: first you scout the territory, plot the route on the map, obtain the right to use the land, clear the site, bulldoze out hills, fill in ravines, bridge over bogs and rivers, level it—and then you are ready to start hauling in your supplies and actually constructing the road surface. My collaborator had done all that, but his surface was not quite of drivable level, so needed to be regraded and finished. Alan could do the regrading, and then I could come with my finishing tools and complete the job. So we consulted with the author, and he agreed, and Alan got to work on it. But that meant I had lost my researcher, and because Alan has not had my quarter century experience revising novels, it was much slower for him. So he was out for most of the rest of the year, and *Hope* ground to a halt anyway without him.

What to do? A dim bulb flashed: do the next Xanth novel. I had scheduled it for 1995, but my fan suggestion list was already overflowing despite using up about 150 on *Roc and a Hard Place*. Some were pretty substantial notions, too, such as having the Demon $X(AN)^{th}$ assume mortal form and have an adventure in Xanth, or having a Mundane family named Baldwin get blown in with a storm. Ah, I see you recognize those notions. So I filled in by writing this novel.

Then my father, eighty-five, fell and fractured his hip. There were endless complications as he wended his way through surgery and recovery, culminating in a trip to Pennsylvania my daughter Penny and I made, to make sure all was in order with him. I believe we did succeed in enhancing his lifestyle in a number of ways, as well as renewing family ties. So that was time off from this novel.

But not the main time off. That was the process of learning a new word processor. I had used Borland's Sprint for six years, and liked it well enough. But it never had an update, and the news was that the company was going to let it fade away. It required a special patch to run on a 486 system; what about the 586? So it seemed to be time to get with a word processor that would stay with the times. The winnowing out has occurred, and for my IBM clone system there were now two main choices: Word Perfect or Microsoft Word. Of those, only the latter would call up multiple files. Since I normally call up nine working files, for text, contents, characters, notes, and so on, that clarified my decision. (Later I learned that Word Perfect for

Windows now calls up nine files—but MS Word for Windows seems to have no limit.) So I tried Word for DOS, but after a week moved to Word for Windows, because that was about two upgrades more advanced, and had a number of features I wanted. I am one of those who don't much like Windows or the Mouse, but got around that by getting a trackball and then finding ways to avoid using it. Windows and Word and associated programs turned out to be monsters to learn, evidently crafted by programmers who had been too long away from the real world. I don't just accept the defaults offered, I want to make the machine serve me, rather than vice versa. Word did not want to yield mastery, but eventually I did get things mostly my way, and it is a powerful program, even if it hasn't yet caught up to Sprint in a number of features. So I started this novel on Sprint, and changed to Word for DOS early in Chapter Three, and to Word for Windows by the end of that chapter. So if you notice a change in the novel at that point, you know whom to blame: Microsoft. And yes, of course I wrote Microsoft a long letter detailing the ways Word was pointlessly User-Unfriendly, such as having an almost invisible vertical line in lieu of a cursor so you have to operate almost blind. Oh, what fun, deleting the wrong file because you thought you were *here* instead of *there!* The company could at one stroke greatly improve its product. But I received no response. Par for the course. After all, if they wanted it to be User-Friendly, they would have listened to users long ago. But I must say that once that pit bull is muzzled and trained, it does have a lot of authority.

Then Microsoft marketed a new "ergonomic" keyboard, which looks as if it was designed by Salvador Dali, he of the melted watches: take a regular keyboard, melt it halfway over a flame, stretch it so the keyboard separates in the center, push it together again so that the center humps without rejoining, and put a bar under it that lifts it in the front, rather than the back, so that the keys tilt slightly away from you, and you have it. The Microsoft Natural Keyboard. Only a crazy person would try to use that. Right: I bought it, and I love it. Because now my hands can address it halfway naturally, easing the pressure on my wrists, so that maybe my carpal tunnel syndrome will alleviate. I tried it for ten days, getting used to it, then tried my old keyboard again—and in one minute gave up; I can no longer stand the type of keyboard I used for ten years. I fancy myself as an ornery independent cuss, and I dislike Big Business on principle, but Microsoft got my number on this one. I changed to the new keyboard, with my Dvorak layout pasted on, in Chapter Nine, during Chlorine's seduction scene, right after the window fan and before the ogre eater. So, again, if you notice a change . . .

So my life shifted in the course of this novel, and not just because I turned (ugh!) sixty. Thanks so much to all of you readers who wrote to remind me of that milestone, in case I should overlook it.

Long-term readers will remember that Jenny Elf is based on a real girl, who got struck at age twelve by a drunk driver and was in a coma for almost three months before my first letter woke her. Then it turned out that she was almost completely paralyzed. That was several years ago, and as I write this she is eighteen, still mostly paralyzed, but doing better. She can use a powered wheelchair, and can walk a few steps using a walker, and can speak some words. Her computer helps a lot. She hopes to take college courses. At this time the collection of my first year's letters to her, titled *Letters to Jenny,* is being published in paperback. Jenny Elf was a major character in *Isle of View,* and has been around as an incidental Xanth character since, as in this novel.

Readers keep sending me puns, characters, and suggestions. This year I have written two Xanth novels, and used about 150 reader notions in the last, and close to 100 in this one, and there are still half a slew waiting in line, with more crowding in. The wait for admission to a Xanth novel is getting long. Apart from a number earmarked for the next novel, *Faun & Games,* I'm caught up through roughly JeJune 1994. There will be another year's worth by the time I write *F&G,* which will take place mostly in an unusual setting, even for Xanth: Ptero Moon. This is no ordinary site.

Here are the credits for reader contributions to this novel: Mundane hurricane and Baldwin family into Xanth, Willow Elf—Michael Weatherford. Hurricane Fracto—Tim Cumming. Demon X(A/N)th assumes mortal form for quest—Brian Laughman. Aqua duck, antacid—J. W. Manuel. Miss Fortune, "No thyme like the present," block parents, scents of humor flowers, ogre eater, junk male, spoils of war—Princess Mandy Owston. Bow-vine, punish-mint—Gershon

Allweiss. Toad stools—Isaac Hansen-Joseph. Wrist watch, ear drum, cow bell, ring finger—Daniel McBride. Speed demon, kinder/meaner garden—Aimee Caldwell. Fly-by-night, fly-fishing frogs—Brian Visel. Magic marker—Joel Hayhurst. Com-bat, re-in-carnations—Matt "Powerman" Powers. Dock spider, centaur/mermaid, naga/harpy crossbreeds—Kevan Gentle. Poul-tree—Nick Kiefel. Mean well—Stephanie Erb. Mean time—Bill Fields. Blobstacle course—Garrett Elliott. Meatier shower—Eric Sanford. Imp names—Leighton Paquette. Gem puns—Jew Leer. Car pool puns—John R. Short. B-puns—R. J. Frey. Fire ants, pain cone—Jake Watters, Chris Warren. Thim bull—Brock Moore. New, clear cherry bombs; thyme bomb—Daniel Serrano. Crimea River, whinery—Brandy Straus. Cat-ion—Damion D. Betts. Art-illery—Adam Ross. Glass jaw—Paul-Gabriel Wiener.

Centaur/night mare crossbreed—Emily Waddy. Tree-men-dous—Melanie Wahl. Snarl—Louis Kammerer. Upsy-daisy, talent of making pictures—Ray Koenig. Ursa (Snarl's girl)—Ursa Davis. Junk shun, Déjà and Vu, Law of Averages overturned on appeal—Richard Vallance. Trenita—Trenita Taylor. Window fan—Thomas-Dwight, Sawyer, Dorr. Twenty questions (and more) answered—David H Zaback. Melody, Rhythm, Harmony—Eric and Melody Moyer. Poison Ivy; Sherry, Terry, and Merry—Rachel Gutin. Demon Ted—Michelle Aakhus. Fracto's side—Sarah Gordon. Che's release from Companionship—Erin Kay Sharp. Napsack—Sara Rosehill. Modem—James Morrow. Keaira the weather girl—Eden Miller. Lips tic—Drew Beauler. Crystal Centaur—Crystal Centaur. Centaur magic conjecture—Brandee Irwin. Adam—Adam McDaniel. Fat character in Xanth—Jenna Grambort. Mariana—Bryan J. Moll. Twin girls who shape and animate rocks—Jenifer Trapp. Twins who change color of hair—Amanda Galli. Leai and Adiana—Michelle J. Siedlecki. Timber wolf—Brent Rowe. Gourdless phone, crossbow, money tree—Scott Thompson. The Pawpaw Wizard—Suzanne T. Persampieri. The origin of reverse wood—Joshua Breitzer. Talent of sticking to walls—Kevin Crisalli. The right spot—W. D. Bliss. The origin of mosquitoes—Jessica Grider. Snowshoes—Murray Sampson. Ash hole—Brian Bouchard. The four fair forces of nature—Amanda Dickason. Table salt—Andy Hartwell.

And one additional credit, of a different nature: as I edited this novel, I tired of the regular background radio music, so listened to an audiocassette tape sent to me by reader Judy Furgal: Loreena McKennitt's *Elemental*. I do like folk songs, and Irish music, and there are a number of such singers I can enjoy. But the one that caught my fancy this time, Loreena arranged but did not sing; it was sung by Cedric Smith: "Carrighfergus." It's the story of an alcoholic who longs to return there and die. I'm not alcoholic, but I do at times long for the old isles.

And so farewell, for another fantastic year. Dismember 3, 1994.